ALSO BY KELLY COLE

Supernaturals of New Brecken

The Maker

Blade of Traesha Trilogy

Daughter of War

Weapon of Rulers

Speaker of Fates

THE ALPHA'S DEN

SUPERNATURALS OF NEW BRECKEN
BOOK 2

KELLY COLE

ISBN 979-8-9853212-8-9

This one is also for Anna since I wrote her a book and she didn't like the main character.
Let's start Nora's redemption.

CHAPTER 1

Nora stood in the alley, breathing deeply and grateful the day was finally cooling. At least out here. Inside the restaurant was hot, loud, and humid with human essence. There was a dark stain of grease beneath Nora's black tennis shoes. The smell of grilling burgers and fry oil flattened the air around her.

Nora lowered her phone, blinking. It was still hard all these weeks later. Matt didn't answer, but he hadn't blocked her like everyone else. Well, she assumed everyone else. Nora never tried calling Gabriel. Matt's phone always rang to voicemail, but that only meant he knew she was calling and chose each time to ignore her. Nora tried to swallow the pain. Tried to talk herself through the sting in a voice that sounded a lot like Annaliese's. The problem with that was Annaliese always ended up asking why Nora kept calling in the first place. Nora didn't have an answer, which just left her hurting and confused to be hurting at all. A strange guilt that she'd done this to herself underlie it all, yet… she missed them.

To her right, two cooks complained about the kitchen manager while rhythmically lifting cigarettes to their lips. Nora fidgeted with her braid, wishing she smoked if only for something to do with her hands aside from using her disappointing phone.

The thought brought her back to an apartment across the city. A boy with sad eyes and an eerie stillness, the cigarettes he compulsively brought to his lips the only indication he was less than calm. Then, of course, thoughts of him brought thoughts of his sister. After a beat of hesitation, Nora pulled up a different contact. *Vampire Colbie.* She stared at the name and suppressed memories bubbled. Nora rolled her eyes at the shifting emotions in her chest, shoved her phone back in her pocket, and turned to go back inside five minutes before her break was supposed to be over. No one would notice she was early.

Nora tried to smile at the manager at the expo window, gratified when Jess only had time to nod before the clicking of another ticket printing pulled her attention. The rail had six yellow slips with faint black type hanging from it. They had gotten tables since Nora went out back. Hopefully, more people were on their way, bringing distraction and tips.

Annaliese hadn't believed serving burgers would suit Nora. Her frown had been telling when Nora came home after dropping off applications at the restaurants lining the street below their new apartment. "You sure you want to wait tables?"

The question had been hesitant. Nora hated this new aspect of their friendship. There had been weeks of Nora's quiet, of too many tears, and of aimless staring at the wall. Annaliese, who had never been careful with Nora like this, had learned this new tone, this soft voice that wouldn't startle Nora or set off another round of crying.

The push that broke Nora through her fog of misery came from the most unexpected person. After Nora lost her home, she'd been living with Annaliese in her family's basement for two weeks before Annaliese's stepfather came home during lunch and found them both in the kitchen. Tim was pale, tall, buttoned up in plaid, bald, and consistently blinking a touch too hard like his eyes hurt. It was only Nora's third conversation with the man. Her social anxiety at the time blurred the memory of him sitting down, clearing his throat, opening a website of apartment listings, and asking Annaliese if she was ready for her own place. Ultimately, they settled on a slightly higher-end apartment that was a popular building for students due to its location close to campus. Tim asked them both to find jobs and contribute a certain portion of their paychecks toward rent. Then, being a man in finance, he went above and beyond and came up with financial plans for both of them. How much to put toward rent, savings, everyday costs, and even retirement in Nora's case, since she wasn't sure she'd ever have a job with a 401K. He offered to invest a small percentage of their money but was gracious when they were both declined, already too overwhelmed by the spreadsheets he'd made in under fifteen minutes. Tim vacated the kitchen as quickly as he'd entered but left so much in his wake. Their lives had suddenly become far more settled.

Annaliese talked about the plan over dinner that night, and her mother had her heart in her eyes for the rest of the meal. Later, Annaliese joked that if she wasn't so excited to move out, she might have been hurt that Tim was going to get laid as a reward for getting rid of her.

When all was said and done, Nora had needed a job that hit the goal paycheck Tim set for her. She found this fast-paced burger joint between their apartment and campus. The restaurant menu was deliberate. Poppy Jennings, and therefore anyone else she was connected to, would never eat somewhere like this. The bean burger offered was bland and mushy, and the other vegetarian options even less exciting. Nora wasn't worried about any surprise visits from the people she'd met last winter.

Annaliese started tutoring and Tim paid for over half of the rent, but at least in this aspect of life, Nora had landed mostly on her feet. His interference had been helpful enough that Annaliese was finally warming up to her stepfather. She went home every Sunday night for dinner and returned to the apartment with stories about her little sister's antics, advice from Tim, and a story her mother had shared about her grandparents.

Nora's family was broken and scattered, but Annaliese flourished with the new space and freedom. The other day she'd even mentioned her biological dad. Just a brief comment in passing, but Annaliese had never brought him up before.

Annaliese was moving forward. The events of last March had left her shaken, but she had an entire life separate from the city's supernatural side. There was never a reason for her to go north of the river again. Secretly, or maybe not so secretly, Nora hoped this life would be enough for Annaliese. She hoped her best friend never got caught up in the supernatural again. Nora just needed to keep that portion of herself separate.

Moving, decorating, learning a new neighborhood, and then training for work had briefly pulled Nora from her slump. These positive changes made her a little less pessimistic. But at the end of the day or in the slow moments between tables, thinking of the future eventually reminded her of all she had lost. Nora would fall back into her haze of pain and quiet. She never stopped trying to reach Matt. She was torn in two, the ripping constantly a fresh hurt that robbed her of breath whenever she had time to think.

Keeping busy helped, but Nora feared it wouldn't last. What if she lost the motivation to even go to work? What if Annaliese stopped being careful and Nora couldn't handle blunt words? What if Annaliese never stopped being careful and their friendship suffered from the tiptoeing and half-truths? What if Annaliese left? What if this ache for a pack made it harder and harder for Nora to turn from wolf to human to wolf? What if she stopped being able to swallow thoughts of

Colbie and they started to overwhelm her as painfully as thoughts of her old pack?

The doorbell jingled as a group of white boys fresh out of their frat house sauntered in. Nora donned the customer service smile she'd perfected, welcoming any distraction—even the smell of cologne, the skin-crawling cadence of poor flirting, the discomfort of too purposeful eye contact, and jerky movements of men trying to be casual in front of their peers. Nora fought the urge to wrinkle her nose. Her favorite coworker, Ricky, muttered, "Better you than me." Nora rolled her eyes at him and crossed the stained black and white tile floor to greet them at their scratched red table.

They ordered beers, laughing at each other for getting carded even though they were twenty-two at the oldest. Nora brought them water; proud she could now carry four glasses without a tray and with minimal spilling. She went to the bar to wait for their beers, relaxing when Ricky came up next to her. She'd never met a human with a smell like his, but the strange scent had a way of soothing her nerves. Perpetually eager to please, Ricky was the most welcoming of the staff. He invited her out to drinks almost every night, never considering a no to be Nora's permanent answer.

Ricky was quiet for a minute, face contemplative. He kept his dark curly hair styled perfectly, long on top. His freckles splashed charmingly across his cheeks. He was the same height as Nora and his bulk betrayed the hours he spent at the gym. One of his best attributes was his ability to read Nora's mood almost as soon as she entered the restaurant. He could match her energy, making her laugh on lighter days but then giving her space on the more solemn. They both watched a cluster of college-age girls pass outside. Hair bright, smiles happy, steps purposeful. Nora's eyes lingered before she caught herself.

"Do you ever feel weird on this street? Just like you're watching a TV show or something? Because they probably have jobs and friends and go out same as us, but they all have this weird thing that's more important connecting them?" Ricky asked.

Sadie set down Nora's beers, out of Ricky's reach because he was on a streak of breaking glasses. She canted her head, blond ponytail swaying. The bartender was a part-time student, so Ricky wasn't asking her. They both looked to Nora. Once again, they were parsing her out, trying to pull her into the workplace friendship everyone else had cultivated.

"You have no idea," Nora said. She was apart from everyone her age in this section of the city because she didn't go to school. She was apart from her old pack. Her old friends. The humans around her. The supernaturals everywhere. Half Mexican, half white. Unsure of even her sexuality. Colbie had awoken something within her, but Nora still hadn't entered the LGBTQ+ community on any level that left her feeling she had the right to claim its culture.

Unsettled and looking in from the outside was Nora's natural state.

She scooped up the beers and went back to the frat boys. At least they flirted and treated her like she was no different from the next girl.

Moments later, Nora glanced up from the computer screen after putting in the surprising number of salads and gluten-free burgers her table had ordered. Her eyes went to the street outside. The sidewalk filled as the hour ended and classes released. Nora froze.

As if her thoughts from earlier had conjured the witch, Poppy and Oliver were walking by. Seeing them felt like an omen, the world narrowing into their sudden appearance after so many weeks. Oliver made broad gestures, and Poppy listened intently. The witch looked exhausted, Oliver as vibrant as ever. His smile wide and easy and unfamiliar. Nora had considered him a happy person before, but this version of him proved how difficult the winter had been. How much it had weighed on all of them. Nora's heart squeezed. She tried to ignore it. She swallowed the urge to burst outside and catch up with them. To demand they tell her how everyone was and what was happening in the supernatural community she hadn't heard from since the night at the warehouse.

Nora wanted to ask about her pack. And about Colbie. She wanted to be let back in.

But she stayed frozen, staring after them until they rounded the corner. She was startled from her thoughts when a crash of ice sounded and the frat guys broke into a round of laughter, clapping for Ricky as he blushed and began picking up the blue plastic cups he dropped. Nora grabbed a rag, shook her head, and focused on the mindless tasks ahead.

Her shift ended with the sunset. The full moon approached and the energy of it buzzed beneath Nora's skin. She had a choice to make now—the same choice at the end of each shift. Free time, when she found herself floating within it, was uncomfortably vast. Nora only allowed herself a few options. She could go home to the quiet apartment while Annaliese studied for her finals. She could go to the nearby national park. Run free, maybe search for her mother. Always avoiding the scent of any and all other wolves. Or she could go across the city, standing at the base of a certain apartment as she did in her lowest moments.

Nora did what was safest for her tightrope mood. As she walked home, she called Matt three more times. On the last attempt, she'd reached the apartment building where she and Annaliese lived. Nora paused at the door. The hair on the back of her neck stood on end. A growl built in her throat. Nora coughed, hoping to dislodge it, but her heightened senses now had a persistent way of making themselves heard. She squinted into the glass door, using the reflection to look behind her and across the street.

There was a woman there, platinum blond hair a bright blur, but when Nora whirled around, she was gone.

Nora checked the neighborhood twice before she assured herself it was clear. The spike in adrenaline the woman's reflection caused meant she couldn't find sleep when she finally put herself to bed. Maybe Nora had only imagined the woman's reflection. Lying in bed, she couldn't quite convince herself. Nora's hackles were at attention, and though she knew it was ridiculous, she got out of bed to sit in front of the apartment door.

With her body blocking the entrance, Nora was able to fade into a doze. She never found real sleep, so when Annaliese's bedroom door opened in the early hours of the morning and her friend let out a yelp, Nora only jumped a little.

"It's just me," she said into the tense darkness. She stood, stiff but already bouncing back. This new strength she carried had finally settled over her. Nora's body was no longer disjointed and clumsy. Annaliese was often startled by Nora's quick reflexes and her swift walk was a source of much laughter between them as Annaliese fell behind on her short legs without Nora realizing.

"I know! I thought you were dead or something!" Annaliese said, hand to her chest.

Nora winced. "Sorry. I just…"

"Were you protecting the apartment again? Nora, we agreed you'd talk to me about potential dangers."

"I thought I saw something last night. I couldn't sleep. I didn't want to wake you up."

"What did you see?"

"It was probably nothing."

"Then what did you think you saw?" Annaliese sounded at once encouraging, exasperated, and… hopeful?

Nora shrugged. Annaliese crossed her arms, waiting. Her look, one Nora could easily make out in the soft morning shadows, was pointed.

They had an agreement. One Annaliese insisted they stick to and that Nora reluctantly kept in order to live with her friend. Nora sucked in a deep breath and blew it out, forcing herself yet again to shift the mindset enforced her entire childhood. The one that said humans were meant to be protected. That they weren't to get involved in the supernatural. It was the werewolf's job to ensure the dangers of magic didn't bleed into humanity. Gabriel had allowed Annaliese to come over, but no one could talk pack business or even hold their wolf form in front of her. When Annaliese came over, she had been treated as human.

Annaliese made Nora swear to hold no more secrets. To treat her as an equal. Their home wouldn't be an echo of the pack Nora had been abandoned by. Communication kept them close; it kept them on one team. Secrets and protectiveness would be the one thing that drove Annaliese away. She'd promised Nora. It was at once comforting and terrifying to have this stated so clearly. Nora knew how to keep Annaliese happy with her and stay in her life, but she also knew there were things Nora could do to push her away.

This ate at Nora. She slowly realized that unconditional love promised to children didn't exist. At least, not for her. Her father died doing pack business. Her mother left her. Her pack turned their backs. Colbie was pushed away. Annaliese was all Nora had left. Annaliese with her firm boundaries, communication, demand for vulnerability, and steady reciprocation. Nora knew this had all been put in place because of Nora's attempt to push her friend away last winter, that she deserved these parameters and that they were healthy, but she also knew at any moment she was capable of messing up again. To trust Annaliese to stay meant trusting herself to deserve her.

Terrifying.

"I saw, *thought* I saw a reflection of a blond woman in the doors of the building. When I turned around, she was gone." Annaliese kept waiting. Now that Nora worked to be more open, her friend had gotten too good at being able to tell when Nora held back. She winced. "I think it was Lana."

Annaliese's eyebrows shot up. "What would *Lana* want with us?"

"I don't know. It can't be good, though. And I'm still not sure it was—"

"Don't doubt yourself. If it looked like her, it probably was her."

Nora blinked. This was another aspect of her living situation she was getting used to. Being believed. Being listened to. It was something Nora hadn't realized she was lacking before. At least, she hadn't realized the extent. "Right. I checked the neighborhood but didn't see anything else, but I was watching the door. Just in case."

Annaliese sighed. She was wearing the hoodie she slept in and stuck her hands in the pocket, thinking. Weighing her words. Had Nora taken it too far? Been too protective? She felt her body tightening. She swallowed words building to defend herself.

She braced herself for Annaliese to tell her it was over. That Nora had used her last chance.

Annaliese sighed, shoulders softening. "Can you wake me up next time? Just let me know what's happening. We could have slept on the couches. I know you weren't sure it was her, but I'd still like to know. Does that sound fair?"

Nora deflated, the relief making her head light. "Yeah." They both ignored how her voice cracked.

Annaliese offered a small smile. "He probably isn't up, but do you think we should call Topher? He'd know if it was Lana."

Nora was already shaking her head. "Please." She didn't expand, but Annaliese understood.

"We'll just keep an eye out then. I'm going to shower. If you're awake for the day, can you make some coffee? I'm going to study for my finals."

Clearing her throat, Nora nodded. "I can do that."

"Then you should go for a run or something. Let out some tension."

Nora wanted to protest. Tell Annaliese she couldn't leave her alone. The wolf instincts begged Nora to follow her friend around all day even though the vampires *were* probably all sleeping. But Annaliese lifted a brow in challenge, and Nora only hesitated one more beat before she agreed. "I'll go to the Park for awhile."

And she did as soon as the coffee was brewing. Nora took Annaliese's car and drove out of New Brecken, emotions warring as the relief of leaving the stifling city coupled with her worry at the distance from her friend. Nora passed the sign marking Golden Springs National Park. Past the first clearing with a half-full lot. The days were getting warmer, and hikers came out early to watch the sunrise. Nora continued until she found the tire tracks worn into the grass leading to another dirt lot with only one other car.

No one in her pack had warned her how much busier the park got in the warm season. Nora had hiked and camped here in previous summers but hadn't considered the challenge it would present when the desire struck to run as a wolf. She went deeper into the trees than most of the hiking trails ventured, but finding a spot hide her clothes and make the shift wasn't as easy as it had been even just two weeks ago when the peak of the rainy season kept people within city limits.

Nora hiked on her human feet, relishing the sense of anticipation that tingled over her skin and up her spine. Her wolf half was like an entirely other being in these moments. Almost as if looking in, Nora felt its pleasure and desire to move. To run. To sniff and howl. She could feel a separate fondness for it, like it was someone else. Someone carefree and restless and sometimes selfish. It was hard realizing that was *her* now. She was all those things *and* the Nora she'd always known.

She just had the ability to let go now and it was delicious. Freeing. No one could take this gift from her. Her wolf was her new constant.

Nose in the air, tasting the wind, and listening to the forest around her, Nora found the coast was clear. She pulled off her layers, blinking as the sky let loose yet more rain. Opening the world to a riot of new smells.

Grinning, she shifted. Howling, she started to run.

"How was the dog park?" Annaliese asked when Nora returned.

Nora smiled. "What I needed."

"And how badly does my car smell like wet fur?" Annaliese tilted her head toward the downpour streaking their window.

"I used the towel in the back to wipe the front seat but… badly."

Annaliese rolled her eyes, but not in a way that exhibited genuine annoyance. She sat on the floor in front of their coffee table. The wood was covered with notes and even the plush, cream-colored rug surrounding her was stacked with books. Her laptop precariously balanced on one of the piles.

Annaliese's decorating preferences had come as a surprise to Nora. They had settled on contrasting the dark woods with creams and pastels. The apartment was feminine, strewn with blankets and coffee mugs. Annaliese regularly put flowers on the kitchen island they used as their table. The place smelled like the coconut-scented hair products Annaliese favored and books.

Nora missed the Den with an ache that never eased, but she loved this apartment. It had become her comfort and home.

"And how is the studying going?"

Annaliese gave her a smile and thumbs up that were way too enthusiastic and out of character. This was another thing Nora loved. The lightness Annaliese adopted at times. A part of Nora suspected Annaliese acted in this new, silly manner to make Nora laugh. And it did. Nora hadn't smiled or laughed so often since her dad died. It was strange how the devastating circumstances that led to Nora and Annaliese living together mirrored how happy the situation made them both—Nora's life, filtered as ever in a binary.

"You'll do great."

Annaliese shrugged. "We'll see. Maybe we can celebrate when I'm done Tuesday night?"

Nora stiffened. She hadn't been social. Hadn't gone to a club that would remind her of last winter. Hadn't risked running into anyone they knew. Annaliese's dark eyes softened, seeing the no already. "It's okay. Molly and I can get drinks if you aren't up to it."

Swallowing the urge to protest Annaliese going out unprotected, Nora nodded. "I'll think about it, okay?"

"Sure. Go shower. You stink."

Nora snorted. "You know they say I'm an incredibly powerful alpha werewolf. You, puny human, need to stop ordering me around."

"But you love it."

"Shut up." Nora went to shower, smiling. She really would think about going out. Maybe even take Ricky up on his invitations with the rest of their coworkers. Maybe she would find more to life than her old pack.

Terrifying.

CHAPTER 2

"Penelope…"

Poppy refused to acknowledge the voice. Her final was approaching, the material she studied weighing on her almost as much as all her other concerns. The quiet apartment made her skin crawl. When she did look up from her textbook, it was to glance at Topher's shut door. Poppy hated summer. She hated how the sun became so powerful Topher couldn't fight it. His nights were so short, his sleep so deep, sometimes Poppy worried he wouldn't wake up.

There was a rustling of sheets from Colbie's room, at least. Someone else would be joining her soon.

"Penelope. Stop ignoring me."

Poppy didn't stop. She waited for Colbie and pretended to study. Her constant, haunting shadow disliked the vampires. He always settled into the background, nearly vanishing when Poppy's roommates were nearby. Especially Topher. The poltergeist was getting weaker. He resembled an average ghost most days without more blood or acknowledgment or life energy given to him.

Poppy had to believe that, or she'd burst with anxiety over her lack of knowledge on what to do about him.

Unfortunately, this was when her wards flexed and Ru entered the apartment. Poppy loved her sister dearly, but their shared blood and Ru's raw magic brought the poltergeist into a stronger form. He grinned in satisfaction, sweeping Poppy's notes off the table and into the air. He replaced them in front of Poppy on the coffee table, getting in her face. Poppy didn't let herself react as he shouted her name.

Poppy leaned around him and cut Ru a glare.

"Sorry!" With a frown, her little sister pulled in her strength and simultaneously worked to banish the unwanted presence from the room. With a dejected sigh, their grandfather faded until he was only an awareness that someone was watching. A form of blurred colors that kept shifting in the corner of her eye. Still annoying, but at least she couldn't hear him shouting.

"You're getting better at that," Poppy told Ru, an unspoken apology in the words for her glare.

Ru bent to help Poppy gather the scattered papers. "I've almost got it figured out. We might be able to banish him fully soon. The full moon could help."

If he had simply been a ghost, a shadow of an impression, they would already be done with him. Few witches were careless enough to give a ghost their blood. So few that Poppy had never heard of anyone else in her situation. Poppy didn't know how to get rid of a poltergeist, and Ru's education on witchcraft was even more lacking. In moments like these, Poppy wished she'd studied harder when she had access from within their coven.

A thump sounded behind Colbie's door. Her roommates didn't know Poppy was being haunted. She couldn't say why it was so important to her that they didn't find out, but she wanted to deal with this on her own. Mostly on her own. She couldn't avoid Ru's help because Ru was the real witch in their lives now. Her untamed, brimming magic meant she was capable of far stronger spells than Poppy without the crutch of herbs and drawing from the life around them. Ru had seen the poltergeist immediately, just like she saw most ghosts and shifts in the Veil. Ru was just so damn powerful.

And Poppy was doing her best to teach her little sister, picking up where their mother and Jane left off, but she didn't know enough. She'd spent too long studying potions and hardly any time on simple chants and casting. Poppy understood magical theory well enough to cast within her limits, but she knew more about supplementing magic than controlling it or reigning it in.

They had only just gotten to the point where Poppy trusted Ru to hold her personal wards strong (but not too strong) and avoid certain parts of the city, allowing Ru to go out on her own. Ru used this freedom to start dog walking. Her sister now added cash to the jar on the counter to help pay for rent. Without Topher's funds from the Maker, they were surviving off savings, but all of them were doing what they could to help out. Poppy had several brews tucked in the back of her and Ru's shared closet and was trying to gain the courage to return to the black market, a shifting scene in the city that ignored the laws set on supernatural citizens and constantly pushed the boundaries. They sold unregulated witch's brews and vials of vampire saliva containing unknown risks. With everyone so concerned about the unclaimed popping up, focus had turned away from the sellers. Topher told Poppy weeks ago to avoid the black market, but Topher was sleeping all the time now. Someone had to keep their little household afloat, and it wouldn't be Ru and her dogs.

"Has he been bad today?" Ru asked, glancing toward the flickering outline of the poltergeist.

Poppy shrugged, not willing to go into detail about his incessant pestering. The ideas he tried to put in her head. The havoc wrecked on their belongings when Poppy wasn't paying close enough attention. Poppy didn't know what he wanted, how much of him was still tied to her mother, or how to get rid of him. "He's bored, I think."

"What does he want to do?"

Poppy pulled in a deep breath. "He keeps telling me to go find Mom but doesn't say why."

"Should we make him? He's bond to you. You must have some control over him."

Poppy cringed. She knew she did. He'd told her as much. But it was one thing to consume the overflowing life force of those around her. One thing to grow plants to use their properties in her spell-making. It was another to force a conscious being to her will. The only thing she wanted to force the poltergeist to do was to leave her alone, but the magic binding them had overridden such commands.

Ru read most of this in Poppy's face. Her dark eyes softened further with sympathy. "What if he wants to help? What if you stopped ignoring him and listened to what he had to say? Maybe he'd be more useful willingly?"

"Ru, I really don't want to talk about this. I've gotten through this just fine by ignoring him. I think he's getting weaker."

"It hasn't been fine, though, has it? I hear him at night, waking you up. Even when I can't see him, you're always looking at him. He's *haunting* you. That's not fine for anyone. But maybe if you kept him busy, he would leave you alone more."

"I'll think about it. But right now, I need to study."

There was a beat while Ru considered dropping the topic. Finally, she shrugged. "Want help?"

When Poppy gave her a relieved smile, Ru plopped herself down on the couch. Living in this apartment had gradually drawn Ru from her shell. Poppy didn't know this version of her little sister, but she loved it. The now seventeen-year-old jumped less at small noises that reminded her of demons. She blushed less when Topher gave her his undivided attention. She disappeared into Colbie's room for hours, giggles filling the apartment long into the night as the smell of nail polish tainted the air. Ru's presence was what they all needed. A new member of their lives to focus on instead of the drama that went down last winter.

Poppy smiled, proud she had provided a safe place for her little sister to thrive. She knew nothing about parenting or getting Ru into school next fall like Ru wanted, but Poppy was doing a decent job with what she had.

Poppy handed Ru her out-of-order notes. "Read the descriptions for me and I'll try to name them."

They'd been going back and forth, Ru nodding in satisfaction or offering gentle corrections, for twenty minutes before Colbie stumbled out of her room.

"Morning, Pop Tart. Rueben."

Ru grinned. The West siblings were valiantly trying to devise as many nicknames for Ru as they had for Poppy, but the options were slim. Poppy loved it. She loved that neither of them had asked if Ru's staying in Poppy's room would be permanent, only made offers to help. She loved that Colbie went dog walking with Ru whenever she was awake for it. More rarely, Poppy found Topher and Ru lounging on the couch, yelling at whatever reality show was playing.

Poppy had never been closer to one of her sisters. No one had come to her for comfort or advice or even just to ask *why*. It did so much to heal the riffs their mother had stuck between them but also brought so much pain. Ru constantly badgered Poppy about searching their sisters. Trying to find those who were alive and figure out what happened to those they couldn't See. Ru wanted justice and to rebuild their coven, but Poppy was afraid. Seeing their mother again had left her more confused than ever. Having the consequence of a poltergeist made her think how much worse it could have been. Maybe it was Topher's cautions or Poppy's desire to protect her youngest sister, but Poppy was hesitant to let herself get wrapped up in the supernatural life of the city. Witches had always been targeted. Exposure only brought trouble.

Colbie made her way into the bathroom, keeping the door cracked so she could talk to Poppy and Ru while within. "Any thoughts on our discussion from this morning, Pop Rocks?"

Ru instantly turned, curiosity burning. Poppy rolled her eyes. "Colbie, you said it would be a secret."

That was the wrong thing to say. Ru only grew more intense. "What's a secret? What's going on?"

The vampire came out of the bathroom with a foamy toothbrush in hand. "Lana wants a meeting with Soda Pop. Of course, Topher told Lana no and kissed her ass until she dropped it, but it should be Poppy's choice. Lana has been surprisingly helpful lately. If Poppy wants more supernatural connections, Lana is the person to go through."

"Why would I want more supernatural connections?"

Colbie ducked into the bathroom to spit. When she came back, she had that same cautious approach Ru adopted when she brought up their mother or coven. "With everything that happened, you don't have questions? Poppy, the supernaturals are splitting off. No one trusts each group. Lana is the only one who seems to think banning together is a more helpful solution than cutting the other groups out. That's what Topher and I believe, too. How much would it help to have contact with other witches? How much would that help with Ru's lessons or finding your other sisters?"

Poppy resisted the urge to glare at her little sister. This conversation sounded like Ru's words on Colbie's lips. Is this what the two of them talked about when they holed up in Colbie's room?

Ru grabbed Poppy's hand. "Please, Poppy. You won't let me look, so can you at least find out witches are still dying? Can you just ask if anyone has heard from any of them or figured out what killed them? If they have any leads on the sorcerer?"

The thought made something nasty crawl up the back of Poppy's throat. To purposefully put herself in this situation went against every protective instinct she had cultivated since their mother dismantled their coven. But Ru had a different relationship with their sisters. She was the shining little prodigy. Not the dismissible middle child of failed expectations. Ru missed and mourned their sisters on a level Poppy barely understood. But she did understand. A bit. They were alone. The city looming over them. Why did witches always have to be such solitary creatures? Looking at Ru's pleading dark eyes, Poppy didn't want this to be her sister's whole life. Poppy was afraid, but she'd done scary things before. She'd picked up her life after her mother destroyed it. She'd sold potions in the black market and gotten accepted into UNB. She'd stood between warring werewolf packs and survived the city for this long. For Ru, Poppy could swallow her hesitations long enough to agree. "Okay. Fine. I'll find out what Lana knows."

Throwing the flashcards up and freezing them mid-air to avoid making another mess, Ru lunged forward to hug Poppy and she couldn't regret the words. It felt like a new beginning.

The meeting with Lana was scheduled for the following night. The maker wanted it sooner, but Poppy had to finish this final. Then she could let the supernatural world distract her. When Topher finally woke up, he only seemed resigned to Poppy's decision. "If it's what you want, we'll help you however we can."

The words replayed in Poppy's head as she and Ru settled into bed. Mouse cautiously curled up between them. With the poltergeist quiet, the cat would stay near. As soon as Ru submerged into a deep sleep, her wards would fall. Mouse would take off, and the poltergeist would be right back, whispering nonsense in Poppy's ears, ruffling the curtains, or threatening to knock over her plants if she didn't answer him. He'd yet to fulfill that promise, seeming more interested in how Poppy used the plants for her magic than destruction, but every time Poppy's heart dropped anyway.

She got maybe three hours of sleep in before Ru's ward faded. Mouse threw himself off the bed and ran into Topher's room, landing with a poof on Topher's thick, abandoned comforter.

Poppy longed to follow the cat's example and get away so easily. To hide in Topher's cozy, clean bed and be entirely alone. She was never alone anymore. The whispering started, and Poppy was too nervous about the poltergeist, her meeting with Lana, and her final to ignore the noise enough to sleep. Poppy slipped out of bed and into the quiet living room.

Neither of her roommates was in. Without the Maker, Poppy hated having little idea where they disappeared in the late hours. She knew they were working close with Lana on something, but Poppy's hatred of the maker meant they rarely mentioned her. Now, with her conversation with Lana looming, Poppy wished she had asked more questions.

Whatever Lana was doing, it had her lowers more animated. Topher's guilt over the events last winter ate at him, but Poppy had never been less worried for her roommates. Topher ate regularly. Colbie was actively dating, and though Topher and Poppy both hated it, her involvement in the supernatural world had given her more purpose. Colbie's shifted focus and work on self-fulfillment assured Poppy her roommate wouldn't fall into the same instant love as she had for Nora again. But Nora was a forbidden word in the apartment, so Poppy couldn't confidently say how well Colbie was truly recovering from their breakup.

The bar was low, but when she swayed toward worry for her friends, Poppy reminded herself that Topher was eating. Colbie was smiling. Zayn was more relaxed when he and Oliver came over.

Their little family would be fine. Maybe Poppy's involvement in Lana's business would help even more. Topher had assured her it wasn't bad, just something big. Something that would take a lot of commitment. A lot of exposure. Lana made him promise to say nothing more. Whatever it was, Poppy should be involved to watch their backs at the very least. But to do that, Poppy needed to be stronger. She needed to keep brewing.

She needed more knowledge and less fear.

Everyone was right. Poppy should talk to another witch. One that wasn't a teenager with an interrupted education. She needed to find out why the hollowness in Topher's eyes wasn't going away, and what Lana asked Colbie to do that gave her roommate such confidence in her vampire gifts. She needed to help Ru control her bursts of magic. She needed to contribute more than wards and cautions.

The remote slid off the coffee table and hit the ground with a clatter. "Penelope, we *need* to talk. You cannot do this thing with Lana. No one can be trusted."

Engaging only made him clearer, his voice louder. Poppy straightened her back and walked to the stove, ideas for a new brew swirling in her head.

She needed to get rid of this ghost so she could give all her attention to truly important matters.

CHAPTER 3

Topher sighed, checking the smartwatch on his wrist. He was fairly sure it was meant to be a gag gift from Colbie as it was constantly telling him his heart rate was dangerously low. But the constant tapping on his wrist made him think of his sister, so he kept it on.

Josh was late. Topher tried to reason his mind out of panic, but he knew how quickly someone could disappear in New Brecken. He resisted the urge to call, Josh wasn't that late yet, but the temptation was strong. Topher sniffed the air instead, and his stomach twisted further when he still didn't smell his friend's approach, only craft beer-drenched human blood. But maybe Josh was coming from downwind. Maybe he was fine.

Maybe he'd been grabbed off the streets. Locked in a basement. Maybe he—

"Sorry, I'm late!" Josh was too cheery for Topher's dark thoughts. It felt like being dowsed in a bucket of ice water.

Topher sucked in a breath and turned. He was sitting on the outside patio of a popular brewery on Twenty-Fifth so he didn't smile for fear of charming the susceptible around him, but Topher hoped his face conveyed he was glad to see his friend. The sky above was crisscrossed with twinkling lights and every few feet a propane fire warmed the night. The clientele here was older college kids or young professional locals grabbing a few beers while wearing their lightest flannels. As a human, Topher would never have come here. As a vampire, he loved the open atmosphere. The lack of questions. The easy jokes, vocal opinions on beer, and inclusivity. It was the New Breckeners like this that voted in favor of supernaturals, focusing on rights and potential revenue rather than horror stories.

This street was becoming the hub of progress in the city. The last five years had witnessed an enormous boom. Right along the river, between the warehouses and nicer neighborhoods like Annaliese's family's, this section of Twenty-Fifth Street was to the east. The warehouses tapered off a few buildings over, but they weren't a threat on the south side of the river anymore. Barely even on the north after last winter and Hunter's resulting quiet. It would seem the vampires had fully won the north, as Colbie loved to say after watching too many fantasy TV shows. The nearest warehouses had now been successfully converted into hip apartment complexes where many of the people who frequented these breweries, vegan restaurants, and cafes lived. They loved having a werewolf landlord, though Henry followed the vampire clubs' examples and didn't openly advertise this fact.

Twenty-Fifth was growing, a new business opening seeming every week. Buildings retained most of their historic facades, yet the insides were modern, open, and flourishing.

Lana had chosen the location well. Hopefully, they could get Henry on board. Topher found himself looking forward to spending more time here.

Josh fit in with the crowd perfectly. His blue and cream-colored flannel matched the person sitting at the table behind him. He scooted onto the bench seat, carefully holding his beer.

"You're not late. I was early," Topher said.

"Oh, well then, sorry you were early." Josh shrugged. "Either way, you had to wait."

Topher didn't give in to the desire to laugh, but it was on the surface. These dark lows and relief-filled highs were messing with his control.

Being with Josh was always nice. No matter the events of the winter, the wolf was entirely unfazed. He'd seen way worse fights between supernatural groups with the work his pack did. Multiple times, he'd told Topher he'd been lucky, all things considered, and that one of the things he liked most about New Brecken was the supernaturals' desire to cling to their humanity, though they often slipped. There were way worse monsters out there compared to Solas, Patter, Gabriel, and the unclaimed. Even the unclaimed were less of a problem these days. The tide had stemmed significantly with the packs helping Topher and Lana keep them contained.

Josh had seen way worse than what happened to Topher. Worse than what any of them could likely imagine. Topher was lucky. He was fine.

His grip tightened around his beer. Topher forced himself to release before he shattered the pint glass.

"How've you been?" Topher asked. Josh seemed the same as usual, constant and easy. The beginnings of summer weather had tanned his skin. He smelled only like his pack, so Topher assumed he'd been keeping out of other groups lately. His ready smile spoke of little drama. "Good, good. You?"

"I'm fine. How's the pack?"

"Oh, just packing around. Henry likes New Brecken a lot, save for Gabriel and his folks, but we've been able to keep out of each other's fur for the most part. Now that most of the remodeling is done, we've gotten the whole pack here and started searching for jobs and stuff."

"The *whole* pack?"

"Yeah," Josh said with a laugh. "We were just trying New Brecken on at first. Now that we think we're staying, Henry sent for the families to join us. Parents and kids in school still that we try not to move around more than necessary."

"Wow." The supernaturals in New Brecken had already been shocked by the size of Henry's pack. This was beyond the scope of what the city had yet to imagine. "Are you applying for any jobs?"

Josh shrugged again. "I'm more involved in the day-to-day of pack life and helping my uncle lead. Like, I'm unofficially the go-between for the younger pack members while Quinn speaks for the older. Lately, I've been dealing with Daniel. He wants to apply to UNB, but he insists on doing so as a werewolf, so we've been discussing that a lot with Henry. It's falling on me and Henry to figure out those risks and logistics while Quinn is ensuring the older pack members enjoy their jobs and navigating how much exposure we get on that end. Most of the older people don't want to advertise being supernatural, so don't tell her I said this, but she's definitely got it easier. Then, there's Yvonne, who thinks she can make it as a social media influencer *as* a werewolf, so we've been talking about that since I'm more familiar with social media platforms. If she did that and the pack went viral or something, we'd need some form of a PR person, which Daniel has offered to study alongside marketing if he can go to college… anyway, it's all a lot of talk about. Some of us still don't even like putting down roots and want to stick to the way of life that doesn't involve commitment like this. If Daniel goes to school, that's four years here. Then, the more progressive pack members feel New Brecken opens doors nowhere else does and by using our lives here, we could spread the change. Lots of debates that make my head swim."

The idea of Danial openly attending a university as a werewolf was as shocking as learning Henry's pack was even more extensive than they initially believed. Topher couldn't imagine the doors that would open up for the supernatural community. There would be pushback, there always was, but so far, the numbers are putting werewolves in the lead for the most accepted and liked supernatural group in the city. The unclaimed, despite not actually being unclaimed vampires, were chipping away at the approval ratings vampires had previously held.

"So… the pack is good," Topher said, fighting a smile as Josh caught his breath from the rant.

"Geez. Yeah. I didn't realize how long it's been since I've talked to anyone outside the pack about all this. That felt good."

"Good. Feel free to keep going if need be."

"No, no. I think that was about everything. How are things with you?"

It was Topher's turn to shrug. People said time healed all wounds, but the more time passed, the more real his situation became for him. The less he could hold onto who he was *before*. The less he liked who he'd been before. The less he knew who he was now. Things he could push to the back of his mind months ago were plaguing him, and on top of all that, the situation with Julia wasn't improving. Always Julia, gnawing at him. "What have you all seen of the unclaimed?"

Josh's eyes softened with sympathy at the deflection. After a beat, he allowed it. "It would seem the sunshine has been keeping them at bay. We found one last night and Gabriel's pack the night before, but the numbers are decreasing. And I still think we need to figure out something else to call them."

Topher made a noise of agreement to that. "And there are still no local humans reported missing?"

That was the mystery that was truly eating at Topher. Where were the unclaimed coming from? Out of all the wild lowers that had been found, only a few reported missing were New Brecken's citizens. Mostly only the murder victims left in the wake of the unclaimed were locals. Luckily, those deaths had grown less and less frequent as the packs and Topher tracked the brief, sulfuric flare of magic they were getting better at identifying.

"Right. We're expanding our search, but there are a lot of missing people to go through. Unfortunately."

Topher nodded, and the sad fact lingered between them for a beat. Josh sighed and glanced around the patio seating and the people walking by on the sidewalk. "I like this part of town," he said.

It was the opening Topher needed, but he still hesitated. "Good thing you live just down the street."

"Yeah. You should come by again. You won't even recognize the place from what you saw two weeks ago. It's so lively now with all the new tenants and the whole pack here. Henry talks like we might have to pack up and go again one day, but he's putting a lot into these apartments."

"I'll try to stop by soon."

Josh noticed Topher was hedging. Not getting to the meat of the conversation. "So, you said you had something Lana-related you wanted to talk about?"

Even though they were far from Fourth Street, Topher sniffed once more, checking the air. He only smelled humans. He dropped his voice so Josh's sharp hearing would catch his words and no one else. "Lana has been making big plans. Plans for this area. For obvious reasons, she wants Henry on board."

Josh tensed. "What kind of plans?"

"The decrease in unclaimed has freed up her time to focus on other things."

Again, Topher hesitated. Josh leaned forward, elbows on the table. Topher couldn't quite read his soft brown eyes. "Like what"

"What else? Herself. She's tired of being snubbed by the other vampires. Since they joined with Gabriel, she hasn't heard from Solas or Patter. Some of Grace's other seconds will meet with her, but they prefer a spot on Fourth Street over her alliance. She doesn't get invited to leader meetings and is ignored when she goes down to Fourth."

"So what's she planning?"

"To get power elsewhere if the vampires won't unite with her. Some of them still want to blame her for the murders and unclaimed. She's suspended from making lowers, so she can't expand our group. Lana wants alliances and is more willing to work with other supernaturals than the vampires on Fourth are, though she does think Solas and Patter will follow eventually for the same reasons they initially broke out from under Reelings. Lana wants to work with people like Henry and Poppy. I think she's hoping to get witches out of hiding and on her side. She also asked about Nora, but no one has seen her since, well…" Topher stumbled there.

"Last winter. Right. Do you think this could be a good thing? Everyone has been so split since Grace died. Even the reports we get about the vampire leader meetings sound tense."

Topher nodded. He'd heard the same from the lowers he had been able to keep contact with. Everyone is worried. They're afraid. The right to move freely as supernaturals was still so new that no one knew what to do for fear of rocking the boat. There were more human protests and questions being asked. The power was still mostly condensed on Fourth Street, but the tone of it shifted every day. "I know that at the core of this plan, it's about elevating Lana. But I think she's also capable of doing good to better her own position. At her heart, she's always had a love for supernaturals. Becoming a vampire was a very intentional move on her part. She doesn't want to lose this way of life. Either way, good or bad motives, I wanted to warn you all before she reaches out. If Henry decides to work with her, he needs to go in with open eyes."

"Right. Thanks. I'll make sure to tell him." Josh took a long drink from his beer, slipping into his thoughts momentarily. He shook himself out of it and focused on Topher again. "Really, though. How are you?"

Topher avoided Josh's eyes, watching people walk down the street. Laughing, touching, releasing puffs of whatever they were smoking or inhaling. Sunburnt and sun weary and sun drunk. Topher wished he could see what life they contained during the daytime.

He wished to be anyone else.

He wished he could answer that question honestly without bringing everyone else's mood down with him.

"I'm just waiting for things to settle more," Topher said. "Between the unclaimed and Lana's new plans, I don't have time to think." And that was true for the most part. It was also probably for the best.

"I'm here if you need anything." Josh reached across the table and squeezed Topher's arm, his palm warm. How could Topher's heart still skip from contact like this? Why wasn't this part of him dead alongside Dylan or starved with Julia? Why did his body crave contact and connection when it always went so, so badly?

"Thanks." Topher gently pulled his arm away. "You should go talk to Henry. Lana wants to meet with Poppy tomorrow night. Now that we have most things in place, she's moving quickly. I'm guessing she'll be calling Henry any moment now."

The building was almost ready. Raven said it would be done by the end of the week. Lana didn't want to give anyone time to think or back out if they agreed to her plans.

Josh seemed reluctant to go, but he was used to Topher's distance by now. They said their goodbyes and paid their tabs, Topher leaving his full, flattened beer on the wooden picnic table. On the sidewalk, Josh waved and walked off toward the right. He melded in effortlessly among the humans. They didn't even watch him as he passed, though some returned his smile. Envy curled Topher's stomach. Werewolves gave off nothing that attracted human attention or triggered their instincts to identify the uncanny. Josh had seen and done more in the world of the supernatural, but his daily life wasn't impacted negatively because of what he was. In fact, he was born into what he was. It was all Josh had ever known, and he was raised to understand his dual identity.

Topher did not have that. He wanted to pretend he was just another New Brecken citizen walking among the vibrant nightlife, but heads turned to watch his progress. People stepped closer to bare their necks or they shied away. Topher ducked his head, hiked up his shoulders, and walked faster.

Lana had assigned Topher two tasks to complete tonight. At least with her new goals at the forefront of her mind, she was more prone to giving out jobs than insisting Topher stay by her side, night after night, as they hunted the New Brecken streets. Now, she only insisted one of them remain with her at all times. Tonight, Colbie was with his maker. She never complained, but Topher knew his sister hated Lana. The two rarely spoke to each other about anything other than being vampires. Lana taught Colbie, and Colbie listened and practiced. It was nearly scary how quickly his sister's abilities had improved now that she was less ambivalent about them. She'd come far enough for Lana to trust Colbie with her own tasks.

As Topher walked to the first task, he texted to let Colbie know and she responded with what she was doing. Their group message with Zayn was full of similar messages. Their locations were on constantly, and they checked Lana's explanations, intentions, and instructions against what she told the others. Lana had been surprisingly less cagey and honest with them, but they kept her accountable. Colbie figured Lana was afraid of Topher after Grace's death. Topher chose not to speculate.

Topher knew he didn't have time to be dragging his feet like he was currently, but he hated this building. The small, rundown apartment complex. Despite its drooping and boarded exterior, the door had an electronic lock and a security camera blinking down at him. Topher lifted a hand in greeting to Lana. She would no doubt be informed he was entering. He punch in the code, his birthday, and slipped inside. There was moaning down the halls. The carpet smelled faintly like mildew from them coming in and out during this exceptionally rainy spring. Topher hated that Lana had been willing to invest so far as buying the building and fitting it with security but did nothing to make the inside more inhabitable.

This apartment building was only three floors. It consisted of one- and two-bedroom apartments, two on each half of the hall. Enough for eighteen occupants total. Topher made quick stops in each room, his charm flowing and words sharp. Then up the stairs. Another set of four apartments. Up the last set of stairs. He turned to the left, repeated the process, locked the door from the outside, and faced the door to the right.

He tried to float above it, but his body felt so much now. The guilt rose in the back of his throat and made his stomach heavy. His vision tunneled and breath grew so constricted that he just held it. He didn't know how long a vampire could go without breathing, but in this room, he tested himself.

As part of their deal with Lana, Topher had to stay well-fed, adding to the heaviness of his life and ensuring there was actually something in his stomach to turn. He used to fall to bouts of dry heaving almost as bad as when he'd saved Ru and drank both witch and demon blood in one night. That memory haunted him every visit when he felt this sick and nauseous.

He forced it down. Visualizing his stomach going still, freezing like ice, and it spreading throughout his body until he didn't feel anything else. He acknowledged each way his body was reacting, froze it, and imagined it traveled until it was only in his hands. The ice condensing in his fingers. He clenched his fists and shook them out, stepping forward.

Topher himself inside the last apartment, locking up behind himself and pocketing the key. He clenched his fists again when he heard the near-silent footsteps approaching. God, he hated this. Still facing the door, Topher summoned his charm. His head was already hurting from the other rooms, but he ignored that too.

"Stay by the window."

There was a hiss of protest, but the footsteps retreated. Topher turned.

Julia had changed drastically. Her skin was gray. Her movements anemic. Whatever force created monsters like her didn't allow them to consume life force properly. They had to drain it completely to get their energy back. Killing to replenish. They hadn't let Julia or any of the other unclaimed here do so in weeks.

"Sit down on the couch."

Julia curled her lip and tried to resist, but Topher used his charm more than ever. He'd been "flexing and working the muscle," as Lana would say. He ate regularly. Topher was stronger now than he had been even when he broke a werewolf's alliance with her pack, and that was a level of charm previously unimagined.

Topher was careful with it. He knew from more and more exposure to the unclaimed which questions made their minds snap. He knew how much force to apply. He hadn't broken anyone since Mary.

With his careful, forceful finesse, Julia didn't stand a chance. She slunk onto the couch, movements jerking and stiff. Like a zombie, Colbie said once. Topher had gotten so quiet after she said it that no one had repeated the comparison. But Topher saw it. He saw exactly what he had done when he brought Julia into this world. He should have ended things as soon as he became a vampire. Even before. Topher had been spiraling for years and pulling anyone he loved into the abyss with him.

He wished he knew how to stop.

Topher left his place against the door and sat across from Julia, perching on the edge of the coffee table. He looked into her eyes. Eyes that said so little compared to her old self. They were cloudy like cataracts, but a rotted black film rather than white. Her expression was wild, straining, jaw and head jerking as she fought against his unspoken commands for her to be still and calm.

Colbie and Lana had both told Topher to stop attempting what he did now. But he was the only one with this power. He couldn't just give up.

"Jules, listen to me. It's Topher," he said, charm desperate and firm in his voice. "Talk to me like you used to."

It always happened, but Topher couldn't stop the hope from rising every time. Julia sat straighter, blinked, and Topher imagined the black fog cleared for a moment. He pushed harder. "Tell me a memory of us."

Julia appeared to be thinking. The level of charm Topher emitted was making his head light. He held on, pushing it out to her, but keeping it from overwhelming. His hands clenched so tightly that his nails slipped into his palm. But he couldn't bleed, and the pain was distant, so he didn't loosen his grip.

She opened her mouth, and always, the hope was there. "You came and fed me."

Topher deflated. It wasn't even Julia's voice anymore. She sounded frail and sick and like she spent her hours here screaming. Lana assured him the cameras would pick up the sound if that were the case, but Topher didn't trust Lana.

"A memory from before, Jules. From when we were human." His head was truly pounding now. "We grew up together, remember?"

"Will you feed me again?" Julia asked, head cocking to the side too abruptly.

Topher wanted to sit and keep trying. He had passed hours in this manner. So long that Lana would send Zayn or Colbie to get him so he didn't attack the first human he came across to replenish his strength. Tonight, he couldn't do that. There was one more job, and Topher couldn't put anyone at risk. Standing, he went to the fridge. Raven, Lana's remaining human follower after the Maker burning and Grace's death, restocked the fridges with the freshest blood she could arrange every day. Topher hated the idea of a human in here alone, but Raven said the sunlight kept the unclaimed down as well as it did Topher. She hated the apartments as much as they all did but was never afraid. Lana assured them both Raven was always safe.

But Topher didn't trust Lana.

The fridge was kept locked, a heavy chain wrapping it and a padlock. The toothmarks marring the metal bit into Topher's hand when he grabbed it and opened it. He pulled out the single red pack the fridge contained. The blood had to be fresh, no more than a day old, and their efforts were still barely keeping the unclaimed alive.

Only Topher's charm kept Julia waiting on the couch. When Zayn, Lana, or Colbie was in charge of feeding, they usually had to keep the unclaimed shut in the bedroom, physically pushing them inside while they were weak with hunger and locking the door. They would place the bag on the floor in front of it, unlock it, and make a run for it while the unclaimed ate. A couple of times, the unclaimed had bypassed the food and chased them out of the apartment, but they couldn't get out the front door. Topher would come to subdue them, charming the unclaimed back into their designated apartment if they were too difficult to move physically.

He had it easy, Colbie joked once.

Topher went quiet and she didn't make the joke again.

Topher poked a hole in the top of the chilled bag with his nail and handed it to Julia. He turned away, ignoring the slurping noises she made as she feasted on the small offering. He left the apartment, locked the door behind him, and went down the stairs while ignoring the renewed energy with which the tenants pounded on their doors. Topher stepped back into the night, flipping off the security camera with both hands as he reached street level. Then he bent and dry heaved into the bushes until his stomach ached and his entire body trembled.

Standing, he shook out his hands and moved on. He fed on a group walking to Patty's from the direction of Fourth Street. Everyone he used to feed on had stopped calling, claiming full recoveries. Barely anyone came to him directly for a fix. Rebecca was on vacation with her kids. She'd emailed him a picture of them on the beach.

Lana thought he should be proud they were doing better, and he was on some level. He just hated finding new victims every night.

One last task. His time was almost up. The scant hours of night passing too quickly. Topher had no idea how long this would take. He eyed his watch and got out his phone to share his location with Poppy in case she would have to retrieve his sleeping body when she woke up.

CHAPTER 4

Nora couldn't get her head out of the Park. She returned for the third time in as many days. It was quiet once she cleared all the campsites, then the tents further in where teenagers loudly partied, thinking themselves untouchable. Hidden. The bravest people in the forest. Nora had once attended a party like that. She'd followed a boy into the shadows, and he kept teasing her for being afraid. She'd hated that he desired to see her as fearful and dependent on him so much that never bothered to see past the image he created of her. She'd let him kiss her anyway.

It hadn't been a pleasant kiss. His tongue had been too warm and tasted like beer sitting in the sun all day. His hands were soft, fumbling, and sweaty. Nora left him in the trees. Annaliese had laughed so hard when he stumbled back into the clearing, checking over his shoulder and frightened of the darkness behind him.

That was before Nora lost her parents. When a wolf howled, Nora had recognized the timber of her father's voice and knew exactly what had chased the boy. She'd smothered her laugh as her classmates fell silent to stare wide-eyed into the shadows. It was strange to think how easy life had been back then. She'd just *known* things: her father's voice, her friendship with Annaliese, her ability to kiss and feel nothing.

How simple things were when you didn't understand them or bother to think any deeper.

The forest was almost too quiet. It wasn't a full moon, but she still usually caught the scent of more werewolves. At least a couple from Henry or Gabriel's packs. It was only the natural animals that lived here tonight. Something must be happening within the city. Something Nora was yet again not a part of. Was her life simpler because she didn't understand what the supernaturals were up to? Was she thinking too hard? Should she just settle into this easy life built with Tim's help? Few people were as lucky as she and Annaliese were.

But… if it didn't last and Nora knew nothing of where the supernaturals stood, she hated the notion of diving back into that world blind.

A scent pricked Nora's nose. As always in wolf form, she couldn't keep a train of thought for long. She investigated, heart lifting in anticipation for what should be a brief chase. Only it wasn't. The owner of the scent was *fast*.

Nora put her head down and let her stride lengthen. She wove between the trees, running much faster than she had in days. Fighting the urge to howl at the joy of it, she focused on keeping the trail. Her prey swerved right, and Nora kicked up rocks and leaves as she pivoted. She could feel every branch and puff of wind along the fur of her body.

Trying to identify the scent, Nora caught a layer she hadn't noticed before. Immediately, she was swept into her childhood. The lap she crawled onto for comfort. Blond hair and blue eyes nothing like her own. Recipes that made the Mexican members of her family laugh for their bland flavor. The improvement as Nora's abuela taught her better. The comforting embrace when Abuela died.

The soft singing in the night. The quick hands braiding her hair. The musical laughter and softening in her father. Then, the strength. The way she proved herself. The way she rose in the pack and became everything Nora wanted to become herself.

Nora was chasing her mother. She was gaining on her, but suddenly, this wasn't a fun chase. Abruptly, Nora couldn't separate her human mind from the wolf. She made the change. It ripped through her so quickly that she stumbled on her two feet, hands and knees hitting the forest floor.

"*Mom!*"

Silence fell through the trees at her outburst. Nora tried to catch her breath, but the tears were too close. Her mother barely even smelled like a werewolf. There was so little human left. This was the closest Nora had come to finding her and now Nora knew why. A blondish-gray wolf appeared between the trees. Nora stopped breathing. Her heart raced at the possibilities. Did she recognize her daughter? Had it been too long? Tears were wet on Nora's face, and the wind pricked at her bare skin.

"Mom."

Blue eyes blinked. Before the change, Nora wouldn't have been able to tell their color in the darkness. It was painfully familiar.

This was all so painful.

"Mom?" It came out in a whisper.

The wolf's ears flattened, then she backed away. Before Nora could even think to make the change again to follow her, her mother was gone. Again.

Nora barely remembered leaving the trees by moonlight. Now she was home, showering in human form and wondering what her mother's life had become. Nora almost turned off the faucet to go back and search for her again. But she stayed, thinking about the quiet in the trees and knowing something was happening in New Brecken.

Annaliese needed her. Her mother left her. The choice should be simple.

Nora finished her shower right as Annaliese threw something at the wall between them. *Oops.*

Knowing Nora could hear her, Annaliese said, "For someone with superhuman hearing, you sure don't seem capable of considering just how loud you are. Drop another shampoo bottle, I dare you."

"I'm sorry!" Nora hadn't even noticed she dropped a bottle. She'd been too caught up in thoughts of her mother.

As she reached for a towel, three quick knocks struck the apartment door. Quiet but deafening in the stillness. Nora sniffed, trying to separate the scents floating in the bathroom steam. Nothing, yet she was fairly sure she should be capable of smelling their guest from this far.

Unless…

"I'm just going to check the peephole. Get dressed."

"Annaliese, don't—"

But the human was already leaving her room and moving toward the front door. Swearing, Nora hastily dried herself just enough to get her clothes on. She heard the knob on the door turn and ran toward Annaliese. "Don't op—"

"Topher?" Annaliese opened the damn door. Sure enough, Topher stood frozen just outside. His expression unreadable. An uncomfortably long moment drew out. Annaliese cleared her throat. "Do you need a special invitation to get inside?"

"Vampire jokes are beneath you," Topher said, coming back to life and sniffing in mock pretension as he stepped past her.

"You can't just let vampires in here!" Nora hissed at Annaliese, adrenaline pounding. Sure, it was Topher, whom Nora was mostly sure they trusted, but he worked for Lana.

Annaliese crossed her arms, tipping up her chin. It was only then Nora noticed the kitchen knife in her hand. The knife Topher hadn't even bothered to acknowledge. "Stop ordering me around, Nora."

The protest and protective instincts clawed in the back of Nora's throat. Topher waited, attention bouncing between them until Annaliese won their standoff and turned back to him, lowering the knife. Her best friend was alarmingly happy to see the vampire. Annaliese was never glad to see *anyone.*

Even Topher seemed wary of her smile. It was enough to make Annaliese remember herself and smother it into an unconvincing glower. "What the hell?" she said.

His eyes cut away. Hiding laughter? Hurt? "Nice to see you, too."

"We haven't heard from any of you in weeks."

Topher raised an eyebrow. "You do know Nora cheated on my sister, right? *Then* she tried to kill us? Then I… well. What part of all that was supposed to make us feel like keeping in touch?"

Annaliese crossed her arms again. Nora let out a soft growl. With the amount of attention Annaliese paid the blade in her hand, she was likely to cut off a nipple. And Topher was watching her just as carefully. Waiting for blood to spill? Had he eaten? He looked better than he used to, but Nora didn't know him well enough to know what that meant.

"And what does that have to do with me?" Annaliese asked. "I was there the whole time trying to save you. I thought we were friends."

Topher's eyes flew up from the knife, surprise breaking through his control. "We are?"

Nora couldn't say which of their faces was more heart-breaking then. Annaliese recovered first. With an eye roll, she moved to push Topher out the door. Of course, Topher was quick enough to dodge her shove, though he remained at a loss for words. They stood there for a beat, guardedly watching each other, until Topher's eyes dimmed again. His vampire control and stillness settled back into place. Annaliese sighed.

Nora didn't know what to feel about this interaction, only that it didn't seem like something she should witness. That rift between Topher and humans was again unbreachable. Nora wondered what it cost him.

"Sorry. I didn't realize. How are you?" he asked, emotionless.

"You don't care. Why are you here?"

Topher went to the kitchen, perching on a stool at the island. After a glance, Nora and Annaliese followed him into the apartment and stood on the opposite side of the counter-top. Annaliese set down her knife with a decisive click on the glossy stone while Nora tugged the towel off her hair. She was uncomfortably aware of how her leggings stuck to her wet legs.

"Lana sent me," Topher admitted. Nora and Annaliese stiffened.

"Why?" Nora asked.

Topher didn't comment or acknowledge her wet appearance, reminding Nora he lived with only girls and had probably seen worse. Which, of course, reminded Nora of his sister. She pushed the bubble of pain down. Topher rubbed at his neck and tried to fight a yawn. He lost the battle, and they waited for him to finish. "Sorry. It's been a long night. As you probably noticed, the unclaimed have been quiet."

Nora ignored Annaliese's questioning glance. Topher kept going. "Now that we aren't focused on hunting them, Lana wants us to meet about what's next for the city—or the people willing to hear her out to meet. She hoped that would include you. She knows better than to try Solas, Patter, or Gabriel."

Nora flinched at her former alpha's name and then flushed with guilt. They were still fighting off the unclaimed. So busy that no one had any time to think about what their presence meant for the city. So busy they had all forgotten about the new alpha in their midst until now. Nora hadn't even tried to find one, let alone join the battle to protect the humans of this city. Her old pack was likely still keeping the streets safe without her.

Matt again correct that Nora was too weak to make a difference in the fight. "Why would Lana want to talk to me? I don't
even have a pack."

Topher level Nora in an intense stare. The vampire's full
attention had always been difficult to handle. His gaze felt like
it was stripping her raw. His sister had been playful, usually,
with her attention. Clever and wanting to prove it in how she
read people.

Topher met your eyes like he was deciding if escaping to
your mind was worth leaving his body behind. Nora had no
way of knowing what he saw in her, but the scrutiny made her
feel smaller in that moment. She used to dream of power, yet
here she was. Hiding. All he knew since he'd been changed was
power and look what *he* was doing with it. Helping the
unclaimed. Working with the city leaders. Staying informed.

What did he see in her now? Colbie had claimed they all
knew Nora was an alpha as soon as it happened. Nora was
more settled in her body and new abilities, but she hadn't
noticed a fundamental shift in her personality aside from the
grief of losing her pack. What had alerted everyone of her
alpha status?

"Lana got Poppy to agree to meet by promising to get her
in touch with more witches and help figuring out who is
attacking them. She can probably make you a similar promise.
Put you in touch with others in your situation. You aren't the
only lone wolf in this world, maybe not even in this city. Have
you considered building yourself a pack or challenging Gabriel
for leadership?"

Nora's silence was answer enough.

Topher gave a curt nod. "Lana has studied supernatural
beings for years. As a human, she was an avid researcher. She
knows more than anyone about the different groups. Before we
were legal, she tracked down and interviewed werewolves,
witches, and vampires. Even spent time ghost hunting. She was
among the first to apply to make the change and go through

the process legally. None of the leaders like her, I don't even like her, but her love of power goes hand in hand with her love of the supernatural. She swears she wants to make the world better for us. Yes, that means bettering herself and her position in the city by organizing alliances, but she might be able to make a deal with you. She might have more connections than you can imagine."

"Lana is that new of a vampire?" Annaliese asked.

"Almost five years now, but like I said, she was—"

"You think I should make a *deal* with her?" Disbelief saturated Nora's voice.

Topher shrugged. "I'm not telling you to trust her. But I am doing what she asked and presenting you with reasons why you should meet with her. It's up to you." Topher pulled a business card out of his pocket. He picked up the pen Annaliese left beside her notes on the counter and scribbled something on the back. "We're all meeting at this location tomorrow night. Nine o'clock."

"All?" Nora asked carefully.

Topher met Nora's eyes yet again with too much intensity. She dropped her gaze as he answered, "Colbie will be there too."

Nora glanced at Annaliese but didn't even know what she wanted to see in her friend's face. Approval? Encouragement? A warning? Reluctance? Did Nora want her permission? Just some comfort?

Annaliese squared her shoulder. "Can I come?"

Topher frowned and shrugged like it hadn't crossed his mind that she wouldn't. As if it wasn't a big deal for a human to be involved. "Oliver will be there."

"Absolutely not!" Nora practically shouted. *That* was the last thing she wanted. Nora felt the shift in her tone that reminded her of Gabriel.

Annaliese rolled her eyes. "Don't try to alpha me. I want to go and I make my own choices, remember?" Annaliese shifted her attention back to Topher while Nora struggled against her dueling instincts. One to keep her friend happy and one to keep her protected. "I'll see you there, Topher."

Annaliese snatched up the business card and walked to her room. Just before she closed the door, Topher softly bid her goodnight. Nora glared at him for the gentle tone. He didn't need to be encouraging Annaliese. Didn't need to be making her friend pause before shutting her door a touch too hard.

Topher smiled, almost guiltily. Now that the door was closed, he could open his expression. "She'll be safe tomorrow night. It's no one she hasn't met before, and we can handle Lana. If Annaliese wants to know what you're up to, you shouldn't shut her out."

"I don't need you telling me how to protect her."

"But maybe you need someone telling you it's not necessary." He ignored Nora's scowl. "Will we see you tomorrow?"

Nora didn't want to see Lana. She didn't want to get involved if it meant involving Annaliese. But Annaliese would be going either way. And...

And she had to admit to herself she was desperate to see Colbie. To see if she was okay. If she was surviving all this bullshit better than Nora.

"I'll think about it."

Topher gave her a small smile that squeezed Nora's chest. God. She missed Colbie's smiles enough to see them on Topher's face. "That's all I ask. Goodnight, Nora."

"Goodnight."

Nora stood with water dripping from her hair. The longer she went without moving, the more she knew she was stuck. The more certain she was that she would be attending this mysterious meeting. She would hear Lana out if only for the chance to glimpse Colbie.

.   .   .

Poppy's brain felt like complete and literal mush. But she was done. Finally. She was so busy convincing herself not to stress or go over all the answers she'd chosen on her final that she didn't even pay attention to the poltergeist on her heels as she left the physical science building.

That also meant Poppy wasn't paying attention to the person waiting for her outside. She started when Annaliese stepped into her path. "Hi. Got a minute?"

"Sure." They had spoken occasionally since everything happened but mostly only asked about each other's respective roommates, talking with Oliver present, and going over homework assignments. They'd even studied with Molly on one tense occasion. She and Alex had broken up (a love potion only goes so far) and they'd mostly spent the time assuring Molly there was someone else out there for her.

She and Annaliese never went out of their way to hang out. They shied from certain topics. Colbie and Nora were never mentioned in the same sentence, but it was nice to hear the werewolf was landing on her feet without her pack. Annaliese had confessed it wasn't easy letting Nora back in, but she knew to blame the stress of Nora's first shift on many of her actions. Poppy wasn't as forgiving, but her anger and blame landed mostly on Gabriel. Poppy had never liked the pack dynamic as she had heard about it from Nora. Nora was far better off living under Annaliese's influence and figuring things out independently.

"What's up?" Poppy asked after they'd walked for a moment in silence. She was still trying to shake the lingering effects of the final and the way the poltergeist walked just ahead, blowing in the faces of students as they passed and making them blink in surprise.

"Topher said you were meeting with Lana tonight."

Poppy tore her gaze away from the poltergeist. "You talk to Topher?"

"Only last night when he came by. Lana sent him. She wants Nora there, too."

"Oh. I guess that makes sense. From what Colbie said, Lana is reaching for people on the outskirts. People in a similar position to her now."

"That fits Nora, I guess. I want to go tonight, too."

"Alright." Poppy expected as much. Oliver told her this morning he was coming and dropped hints that he knew more about Lana's plans than Topher had been allowed to tell her. Zayn was a horrible secret keeper where Oliver was concerned.

Poppy glanced around before pulling out a plastic bag with the protective dust she had used on Annaliese and Oliver to keep them safe all those weeks ago. "I gave Oliver some this morning."

Annaliese rolled her eyes at how secretively Poppy tried to pass the bag off to her. "Make this look more like a drug deal, would you?"

"You'd have to pay me for it to look like that."

Annaliese shoved the bag into her hoodie pocket. "Is it expensive?"

Poppy shrugged. "I could probably charge a lot for it."

"Why don't you?"

"I might just have to. Topher isn't making tips like he used to, but of course, he'd rather I not get involved with the type of people selling witch products. So far, Lana's been able to pay occasionally for Topher and Colbie's services, but I don't know how long that will last with the Maker gone."

Annaliese blinked. "Well. That was more than you've said to me in a week. Seriously, you look exhausted."

Poppy shrugged. "There's been a lot going on for everyone. I'm just glad school is over for the summer."

"You don't think whatever Lana has planned will be more consuming than school?"

And Poppy's shoulders dropped. She rubbed at her

temples. "You're right. She's probably going to want my whole summer."

They walked in silence. The grass was a riot of new green, the trees beginning to burst with leaves. Poppy absorbed the life released and sighed.

"Have you talked to Josh recently?" Annaliese broke the peace.

Poppy's expression shuttered. "I doubt he'll be there tonight."

"That isn't why I asked."

"No, I haven't talked to him. I've been busy. My little sister lives with us now, and this semester has been murder. How do you think your final went?"

Annaliese pointed in Poppy's face. "That's called deflecting. You really weren't into him?"

This section of campus was now a ghost town. Poppy's final was one of the last exams taking place. Freedom was laced like a high in the air. Summer vacation a sweet taste that made steps lighter and laughter easier. It should finally be Poppy's turn to feel that way. Instead, her shoulder's hitched. "It's just... I feel like I'm always giving myself away. And that isn't a bad thing. I love my roommates and my sister. I'd do anything for them. But... Josh wants something more from me, and I don't have the space to offer it. I don't want to hurt him more."

"Maybe you're hurting him more by ignoring him. Maybe he would just love to be friends."

"Did you know Topher and Colbie are my first friends? Like, literally my first." Poppy slowed. It felt yet again like giving away a piece of herself, but she wanted someone to understand and Annaliese seemed like a person who could shoulder a complaint. "Then, they introduced me to Zayn and Oliver, and I honestly thought I would burst with all the talking and feelings and acceptance and bickering. I'm still figuring it out. I can navigate the harder things with Topher because I have to. Proximity means it can't stay awkward between us, but the energy it takes to face him every night is still so much. I *am* exhausted. I just don't know if I have space for another friend."

"Friendship is usually easier than roommates. A good friendship eases burdens. Have you tried explaining any of this to Josh?"

"I don't know how." Her head pounded thinking about the confrontation.

"You just explained it to me. Listen, I think Josh is great and these things aren't black and white. It isn't nothing or best friends or romantic partners. There are so many shades in between that can be worth the awkwardness and possible hurts. That's what it means to be human."

Poppy snapped, blue sparks crackling between her fingers. "I'm not human."

"You all are where it counts."

And Poppy had to smile. Maybe Annaliese was right. After all, talking with her was easy. It made her shoulders feel lighter. Made her feel like she was doing something right. They parted ways soon after. There was much to prepare for tonight.

CHAPTER 5

Lana wanted to meet in a building on Twenty-Fifth Street. Warehouses up to the bridge had been demolished, and a riverwalk added. Lining the walk were new breweries, band posters, bookstores, spilling flowerpots, pride flags, and twinkling lights cutting the view of the night sky. This neighborhood almost exactly between downtown and Fourth Street wasn't somewhere Poppy had spent much time, though she immediately liked the open life energy flowing from the occupants. The plants, river, and conversations were enough to make Poppy put up her wards before she took in enough to start glowing.

There was sidewalk chalk scuffing under their shoes, pastel colors depicting more rainbows, flowers, enticements to enter businesses, and cartoonish characters. There was the distinct smell of vegetarian restaurants, a Thai food truck, the new vegan cafe that everyone was raving about, and a few doors over a stubborn burger joint that spilled the smell of grease into the streets.

Poppy smiled as Colbie's head tipped back to take in the lights. "Maybe we should move over here," Poppy said, glancing up the block at the apartments Henry had begun leasing. Just the idea of having a pack around instead of protection relying entirely on Poppy's wards made her shoulders relax.

Colbie flashed Poppy a grin, but it died too quickly. "I'd rather have some distance from Lana. She's going to be a lot."

Oliver leveled his hands up and down like he was weighing scales. "I love this block maybe more than I hate Lana. I'm trying to convince Zayn to move over here, but even Henry's apartments are almost as expensive as downtown, and it's not like the two of us have an in with him. Without the Maker, we can't afford it."

"I bet Josh would put in a good word for you," Colbie said. "Maybe get you a discount."

Oliver sighed. "Even if he could, Zayn's still nervous around wolves. He doesn't trust them, not even Henry. He said we trusted Nora too much, and look where—" He cut off abruptly, remembering who he was talking to and clearing his throat.

Poppy tried to think of a subject change to cover for his stumble, but Colbie responded first. "If the city is going to move forward, we can't just hate people because of whatever supernatural group they do or don't claim."

"*I* know that, but Zayn's been involved with vampires longer than me." Oliver shrugged. "I'll keep asking him. Usually, if I pester him long enough, I get my way. And maybe this will help, whatever it is Lana has planned." Oliver wiggled his eyebrows, though Poppy was beginning to suspect he was only pretending to know what the night had in store for them.

"Hmm," Colbie said, switching quickly to noncommittal. She knew what was happening but had remained as tightlipped as her brother. Earlier, she'd claimed the surprise would be worth it. Poppy already suspected what was going on. Vampires weren't nearly as unpredictable as they thought they were, and her tea leaves, though vague, had given her a sense of what to expect. But she didn't speculate out loud and let Colbie think the surprise was unspoiled.

Poppy watched her friend intently. Topher had confirmed Nora would to be there tonight. He'd tried to tell Colbie she didn't need to come, but she'd only rolled her eyes at the suggestion. For the first time in weeks, Colbie and Nora would be in the same room. Poppy still hadn't gotten Colbie to tell her what was said at Annaliese's house when she told Nora she was an alpha, but Colbie was in a dark mood for days after. Then, the shift when she began bringing girls home from random human clubs and working with Lana on her vampire abilities.

Poppy hoped seeing Nora again wouldn't be a step back in Colbie's healing. "Are you doing alright?" she asked.

"Yeah. I'll be fine. This is my turf now, right?"

"Right."

Poppy and Oliver shared a glance when Colbie turned toward the closed bookstore. They both wished Topher was with them, but Lana had wanted him and Zayn there early. Colbie had run some other errand before they all met up at the apartment and drove together.

Topher was better at reading Colbie. He'd know just how concerned to be about her too-light tone and too-dark expression.

"I need to wake up early tomorrow to get here and buy the new Ana Rosales book," Colbie said, pointing at a fantasy book on display.

"I can get it if you don't get up on time."

Colbie smiled, but it didn't reach her eyes. She threw an arm over Poppy's shoulders, and Poppy held her friend back. "Thanks, Popcorn. I do miss browsing around in bookstores, though. Why must they all close so early?"

Poppy didn't have a response to the longing in Colbie's tone. Oliver came around, wrapping Colbie up from the other side so the three of them walked obnoxiously linked on the narrow sidewalk.

They were nearing the address when the wind shifted.

Colbie stepped out from under their arms, eyebrows raised. "I didn't actually think she'd show," Colbie muttered.

Oliver raised an eyebrow. "Fill the human in?"

"I smell Nora."

Oliver and Poppy shared another glance. Do they try to lift Colbie's mood again? Offer encouragement? Just silent support?

Oliver wasn't one to keep his thoughts quiet. "What do you want us to do? Pretend she's invisible? Act like mean girls? Be normal?"

"Just… act like she cheated on me and tried to kill me, but my maker wants to do business."

"Not quite business casual, then," Oliver said, nodding as if his words made any kind of sense.

"We still have a couple minutes before we have to be inside," Poppy said. "Want me to go put a curse on their car? Make lights turn red or something?"

Colbie still couldn't muster a smile but pressed into Poppy's side. "I think I need a minute."

Poppy and Oliver watched helplessly as she pulled away and ran across the street. For a second, Poppy wondered if Colbie would keep going and skip the meeting entirely, but instead, Colbie tipped over the railing lining the boardwalk, looking down into the rushing water.

They watched Colbie's back rise and fall with her breaths. The tension in her posture belied the heartbreak. Yet Colbie had been insisting for weeks she was over Nora. That what happened was done and in the past.

Colbie straightened, and Poppy crossed the street to her. "Whatever you want to do, we're here for you."

"I just wish stuff would stop changing so quickly. I can't catch my fucking breath. Even over here, everything smells like her."

"Maybe you need closure?"

"Maybe." Colbie shook out her body like she sometimes

did before they started playing soccer. "I'm nervous to see her. But I don't want her to know."

"If anyone can hide it, you can."

Colbie nodded, confidence bolstered. She threw back her shoulders and winked at Oliver as they crossed the street again. She stepped up the curb and threw open the door. "Are you two coming?"

Zayn opened the back door for them so quickly after Nora's knock he must have been waiting. Lana had sent instructions to an alley on Twenty-Fifth where Annaliese could park. Nora hated that they had now exchanged phone numbers. It felt like she was already committing to this plan of Lana's, and she didn't even know what it was.

Eyes skipping right over Nora, Zayn warmly welcomed Annaliese and lead them down the hall. A darkened room to the right might have once been an office space. They neared the front and the room opened up. It was arranged like a small cocktail bar. Glittering back, shining shelves for bottles, four high-top tables with two to four stools.

"A big step down from the Maker," Annaliese said, noting the small space but similar themes between it and Lana's previous club.

Lana bared her teeth but kept her fangs hidden so the expression held little malice. She stood behind the bar in her customary red and black. Seeing her platinum bob, Nora was confident it had been Lana outside their apartment. She would need to have some words with the vampire after the meeting. Her and Annaliese's home was off limits if Lana wanted Nora involved in whatever scheme she was concocting.

Lana turned back to Topher, hand on his bicep as she murmured something. On Topher's other side, a human girl nodded along. She was familiar, likely one of the faces that had populated the Maker, but Nora didn't know her name.

Nora was slightly disappointed to note the loss of her status, club on Fourth, and maker had done nothing to humble Lana's composure or appearance.

While they waited for everyone else, Lana gave them a verbal tour of the room they stood in. Lana explained that it had been a deli in its past life. The building was tucked between a brewery and a thrift store, almost perfectly in the center of the riverwalk. Lana mainly spoke to Josh, who stood across the bar from her. He'd offered a smile to Annaliese and Nora but was clearly tense.

Lana explained how the space was perfect for this small bar up front with a quieter, more upscale atmosphere and patio in the back. The front door opened in the middle of Lana pitch, but Nora didn't move. She smelled Oliver and the tang of Poppy's magic, but a glance at Annaliese's face warned her that the two weren't alone. Strange how, after all this time, she still expected Colbie to have a scent. Something that was distinctly her own and flooded Nora with memories like everyone else's smell. But instead, it was just the shift in the air that brought it all back.

It was the way Topher's face loosened, his stance growing less rigid with his sister near. It was Zayn's wink as he lifted an arm for Oliver, tucking his boyfriend in close. It was Poppy's nervous shuffle to stand closer in solidarity with her friend. And it was Lana's smirk. "Nice of you to join us. How were our tenants tonight?"

Everyone was confused by Lana's question except her lowers. Colbie's voice was easy, no tension evident in her response. "They were fine. Missing you."

Lana snorted, coming around the bar. "I'm sure." The maker wore a loose black dress and velvet red boots that hit her mid-thigh. When she spun, the dress fanned out. The act was too young for her and her total lack of innocence. "That's everyone. Follow me. Maybe the next room will be more to your standards," she said, shooting a pointed glance at Annaliese.

Nora bristled and moved to stand in front of Annaliese, only for Annaliese to shove her out of the way as she followed directly behind Lana. Another reminder of how little she wanted Nora's protection. Nora hurried after, and the rest filed behind.

They went to the small hall behind the bar. To the right was a heavy door like the walk-in cooler at the burger joint. It was likely where the deli had kept meats and where the bar would now store things that needed to be kept cool. Except… Nora barely kept her mouth closed as Lana yanked the heavy door open, revealing a set of stairs and not refrigerated shelves.

"SPEAKEASY!" The word burst out of Oliver. There was a loud clap. Nora still refused to look behind her and accidentally make eye contact with Colbie, but she would guess it had been Oliver and Josh high-fiving.

Zayn let out a low, rumbling chuckle. Even Annaliese smiled back at Nora before she followed Lana down the stairs. Nora was still a little shocked that this was the entire group. Lana led a bunch of college-age kids into her next phase of life like everything was normal.

The hair on Nora's arms rose as they descended. Her breathing shortened. She couldn't help but wonder if she was alone in this. Stairs had been difficult for weeks now. Basements were haunted with the memory of her mind being consumed by the wolf and Gabriel's power smothering her. Were the flashbacks bad for only her, or were Poppy, Oliver, and Annaliese the only ones not remembering being led down another set of stairs? Being locked in the room at the base. Ahead of her, Lana seemed unaffected, but Colbie, Zayn, and Topher were silent.

Maybe it was even worse for the vampires. They'd been trapped in that basement for days. Nora continued to resist the urge to look back at Colbie. It was like ignoring an itch, believing it would go away if she waited, but the more she thought about it, the more its presence nagged at her. Nora wanted to see her. Had time eased the hard expression Colbie wore the last time they saw each other? The memories surrounding Nora's first change were hazy, but she remembered *that* conversation all too well.

"Nora, you're not unclaimed. You're an alpha."

Colbie had spoken those words and broken Nora's already crumbling world. Nora had just killed someone. She'd lost her pack and home for reasons she hadn't fully understood. She'd lost Colbie. Yet Colbie had spoken as if she were delivering good news. As if she were doing Nora a favor.

Nora was still trying to figure out if those words meant anything. If it was even true. She didn't feel like an alpha. Didn't know how to be an alpha. Either way, it was enough to get Lana's attention. It might be some time before Nora could tell if this was a good or bad thing. Again, that itch. Above all, she was here because she'd wanted to see Colbie, and now Nora was too much of a coward to meet her eye.

Nora wished she could reach for Annaliese's hand. One of the things she missed most of pack life was casual physical affection. She couldn't remember the last time she'd been hugged. She settled for wrapping her own arms around herself, squeezing like the pressure might calm her thoughts and overwhelming emotions.

The basement was in the stages of a deep remodel. The black, glimmering tile beneath their feet was covered in dust. Oliver sneezed from how much was in the air. A bar was in the process of being built against the far wall. They were surrounded by splashes of red fabric, gray bricks, dim lighting… it was the Maker remade. Only slightly smaller in scale, everything was the same—even the mirrors behind the empty shelves that would hold bottles of alcohol eventually.

Nora wasn't the only one to put it together. "Holy shit," Annaliese gasped.

"But…" Poppy shook her head, turning to Lana. "You can't have a vampire club south of the river."

Lana tilted her head. "Can't I? Show me the law. It wasn't written, only verbally agreed upon. Anyone coming here won't snitch. Plus, this is just a bar. A bar with a few vampire bartenders who might be nice enough to feed on a human if they ask nicely. Nothing more."

"Why would they come here when Fourth Street exists?" Annaliese asked. Nora nearly shook her head. The bravery Annaliese was capable of in front of supernaturals was astounding. It highlighted Nora's nerves and hesitations. The last thing Nora wanted to do right now was call more attention to herself, yet Annaliese's voice rang with confidence.

"Fourth Street is intimidating. And it doesn't have Topher. People beg for his bite." Lana smirked, winking at him. "I know I have."

Colbie gagged loudly, and Lana's face flickered with annoyance. Nora had many questions, but the ones at the forefront concerned the relationship between Colbie and the maker. Colbie was working with Lana now. How involved had she become in the supernatural side of New Brecken? Did she like it? Had she chosen it?

Zayn stepped out of the cluster at the base of the stairs and walked the space, towing Oliver by the hand. The human girl went to the center of the room and righted a step stool before taking a seat. She'd obviously been down here often and heard Lana's following speech enough to tune it out.

"Patter and Solas are too comfortable," Lana said. "They're enjoying watching my fellow seconds fight for Happenstance. They think that's the ultimate goal for a vampire within this city. They think a spot on Fourth Street is something I have lost and mourn. But I've never had a problem with stepping out of the shadows, and I believe that New Brecken can be more for us than a few streets in which humans can ogle while vampires play at control. I believe we can all mutually benefit each other if we only learn more about each group. I've been quiet lately, but we need to remind them I'm here. This club will be a safer place for humans than Fourth. We'll follow the laws and show the city how well they work. Any inspection will find too many overly blissed at places like Blank Space, but I can trust my lowers not to overindulge. People will come here. They'll begin to respect me. I'll make inroads where Patter and Solas and even Grace burned bridges. We'll push past the mess of last winter, solve the problem of the unclaimed, and find balance."

"I still think we need another name for the unclaimed," Josh said as if he hadn't heard anything else.

Nora found her voice. "Gabriel will hate this."

"Oh, well, we wouldn't want to upset Gabriel. Let's scrap the whole idea."

Nora's cheeks flooded with embarrassed heat at the sneer in Colbie's voice. Her body went rigid under the cascade of emotions. The sensation that stung the most was an emotion Nora didn't even have a name for, but it stemmed from how Colbie's words had made Nora feel small. Colbie had never done that before. The feeling was one Nora linked to Gabriel, Matt, and her old pack. She hated it linked to Colbie. The sting to it wasn't quite betrayal. It was sharper than the familiar heartbreak surrounding Colbie. It held a bit of loss. The force of its facets converged and made Nora's shoulders bow, her chin dip as she bit her bottom lip.

There was a step as Colbie came nearer. Her voice was softer but no less vehement. "Seriously. Fuck him."

Nora didn't know if she was meant to take this as an assurance that Colbie hadn't been mocking her, but she was able to draw in a breath again anyway. She fit in her body again, as easily as that.

Nora finally let herself make eye contact with Colbie. After weeks without her, Colbie was painful to behold. Sharp and soft and beautiful and strange. Nora blinked past this and tried to read Colbie's face. She couldn't, but Colbie raised an eyebrow at her. She was silently daring Nora. Daring her to do what?

Her voice wasn't quite right, but Nora made herself keep going. "I just mean, he might try to shut it down. The pack has leeway in the law to shut down activities they think will harm humans. The leaders listen to Gabriel."

"Why do you think I invited you, Alpha?" Lana asked.

And then, Nora firmly held the room's attention. She hated it. It made her skin crawl so physically that she thought she might be making the change. Lana was oblivious as she continued, "The only person who can combat Gabriel's reputation is the daughter of his former alpha. Gabriel's pack still invokes the Morales name. Gabriel can't use it if you start claiming your legacy." Lana speared Nora with one last look before speaking to the room at large once more. "Like I said, this will be a safe place. It will be protected, and so will the human patrons or any supernaturals visiting who want to discuss making actual progress in the city. I want you, Henry's pack, and the witch to keep this place safe when we, the vampires, can't. I'll allow you the power to check us and make sure our feedings don't get out of hand. But I will also expect your protection. I won't have another club burn. I won't lose any more of my people."

"You mean anymore of your power," Annaliese muttered, quiet enough that Nora hoped she was the only one who heard it.

"Why would we risk so much for this place?" Poppy asked. Nora couldn't say who needed the most convincing out of the group, but Poppy's expression held the highest level of skepticism.

Lana answered, "Because I know *you* in particular will do anything to watch my lowers's backs. Because you need connections in this city as badly as I do. We all do if we don't want to be run out. What do you all think happened to the other packs before Henry arrived? Why do you think the witches hide so well? Why do you think there aren't vampires that weren't claimed by the Big Three, or Two, now? Have any of you heard what is happening with the vampires? Because I haven't, and they were my closest friends as of a few months ago. I find it hard to believe the murders have just stopped. We won't only be a safe place for humans. We'll welcome anyone without somewhere to turn. That means I can help you build a new coven, and you," Lana turned back to Nora, "your own pack."

"And you more lowers?" Annaliese asked.

"Well, once I have some credit again, people will be welcome to apply for a position under me." A pause. "When Topher isn't there."

Another gag from Colbie. A glare from Zayn that wilted the smirk on Lana's face. Nora couldn't tell if Lana had been joking, and Topher's face was the only one that betrayed nothing. He observed his surroundings with blank indifference.

"You think Henry will be interested?" the human asked Josh. Her first words. The worry behind them showed how invested she was in Lana's vision.

Lana answered before Josh did. "I have a meeting with Henry tomorrow night, but he is gorgeously open-minded. I'm sure he won't have any issues, and his pack's proximity means he'll keep an eye on things while our resident alpha builds her pack, or should she come up short. I just wanted Josh here to tell Henry I was serious. We're nearly finished with the remodel."

Even though Nora hadn't agreed to be the resident alpha, her instincts bristled at the idea of working with Henry or any other wolf. Her human side swallowed it.

"You're serious about this," Annaliese said, not quite a question. "You think it'll work."

Lana nodded. "I'm pissed off. Whoever is out there attacking the city killed *my* people. All this mess led to my maker's death. I *know* that Gabriel and the other makers have something to do with this. I want them as pissed as I am. I want them to know they can't pull anything like they did last March again."

"You don't think that will lead to more attacks?"

"I want to see them try. The people in this room, this next generation, have a potential the leaders haven't imagined. We can take them. We'll get their attention and inform them of their place in this changing world. I won't make you decide tonight," Lana said to Poppy and Nora. Her lowers weren't being given an option. "But I need your answer soon. We're on schedule to open Saturday. Could you ward it in that time?"

Poppy started. "I, I think I should be able to. It will take a minute for the magic to sink into the building. How do you feel about plants?"

"Make it into a jungle for all I care, so long as it won't burn. And you? Can you be ready Saturday?" Lana asked Nora.

Nora felt herself nodding. She hated that this appealed to her. She loved the vision Lana created, even if it was deeply tainted by Lana herself. She liked the idea of connection and a means to protect the humans of this city.

She stupidly liked the thought of working so closely with Colbie. In this space, she would have time and opportunity to truly apologize for what happened.

When no one immediately protested, success brightened Lana's smile. She faced Nora again. "You'll make big changes, Alpha. We all felt your power when you changed. You'll show everyone who wronged you just how strong your family is." Lana spread her arms wide, hearing the rapid beat of Nora's heart. "This place won't just be mine. It won't just be another club on Fourth. It'll be yours too. Welcome to the Alpha's Den."

CHAPTER 6

There was a hush after Lana's practiced announcement of the club's name. Annaliese whispered something in Nora's ear. Josh shuffled a step closer to Topher. His attention was also on the alpha. Nora had changed in the last weeks. She stood straighter. Her dark brown eyes were wary, her movement quick and controlled. She listened to Annaliese like a lifeline.

"You think she'll go for it?" Josh whispered, voice barely above a breath.

Topher hadn't been sure until Lana had told them the club's name. Nora's eyes had sharpened with something wolflike. Something possessive and smug.

Colbie asked if the meeting was over and immediately left with Zayn, Oliver, and Poppy. Nora watched Colbie's retreating back in a way that removed any lingering doubts. She was all in.

Nora's eyes landed on Topher once Colbie had vanished up the stairs. She jolted as though caught doing something wrong. The gleam left her eyes and made her human yet again.

"Yeah. I think she will. What does she have to lose?"

"Annaliese?"

"Annaliese wants to be involved." This was easier to be sure of. Annaliese's curiosity had always been stark on her face. Now, it mingled with excitement. It made her heart race; that intoxicating cadence to her blood calling to Topher. The memory of its taste putting dark thoughts in his head. He shook them off quickly and swallowed the charm that tried to sing back to her. "If she's determined to interact with supernaturals, this club will be the safest place for that. At least, if you think Henry will agree?"

Topher looked at Josh, noting the new freckles across his cheeks. He also sported tired dark half-moons under his eyes. He had tensed nearly the entire tour. Topher assumed it was all about Lana and her scheme until Josh relaxed when Poppy left.

The itch to ask what was going on between them was even harder to suppress than his charm.

Josh tipped his head back, fully taking in the space and the hints at what was to come. Topher had been here nightly to see the progress the builders made during business hours under Raven's watchful eyes. At first, Lana had considered this building as another space to house unclaimed. When they saw how the block was flourishing, Colbie's suggestion to make it a speakeasy had lit a fire in Lana. It had been an offhand comment on Colbie's part, but Lana saw Colbie differently ever since. Watching her close as if waiting for another idea that could help Lana toward her goals.

"I think this is the type of thing Henry has been searching for," Josh said. "A place for all supernaturals to gather, none with the upper hand. It's named after wolves, owned by a vampire, protected by witches. It's a risk. A huge risk. If Gabriel, the Big Two, or any other covens decide they don't like this possibility for the future, they could easily overpower us together."

"That's just it, though. Lana doesn't think they'll come together. Not in a real way. Not like she believes we can."

"They've tried though. They've been trying to work together for years. All those leader meetings…"

"All those pissing contests? They keep each other in line by trying to prove they still hold power. But no one does right now. The humans don't support us as much now. The old gangs are quiet, the hole where their power used to be a new prize to fill. Gabriel worked with Solas and Patter, but none of them got what they wanted from it, and reports say their communications have been strained ever since. Not at any point have their attempts to align worked out. Not when Morales worked with —" Topher stopped, clearing his throat when he noticed Nora was listening in.

"Yes, but if this was a big enough threat, they still have the humans on their side. The humans with power."

Topher shrugged. "Maybe the ones who currently hold power aren't the ones we need to care about. If we get *this* block and people like Annaliese, the human city leaders will have to listen to us. Before the supernatural laws, UNB was the only thing keeping the city afloat. The university is more open to supernaturals, given how well we draw in students. Now take in people like Daniel wanting to openly go to school…"

Josh nodded, sighing. "People who like progress will like us. But there will always be those that resist, tooth and nail."

Topher rubbed at the rose bush tattooed on his arm. He knew exactly what kind of humans Josh worried about. The kind that had tried to kill Topher not once, but twice now. The ones who feel their power slipping were willing to go to desperate measures to keep it. "I know. We have to have faith. Or we go back to hiding. To tip-toeing. Lana wasn't meant for those things. I don't have a choice but to follow her lead. I hope Henry thinks this through and you come to a pack agreement. I hope we can work together, but I understand if you all find the risk is too great."

Josh shrugged. "Who knows? Talk to some people, and

you're the biggest threat in the city. Maybe the risk would be greater to get on your bad side."

Topher smirked and winked. "You can get on my bad side whenever you want."

He immediately felt smarmy, Lana's innuendos too fresh, but Josh let out a full laugh and whisked away the ick. Josh's laugh was worth any embarrassment that came from the poor flirting that had become a running joke between them. Topher had to remind himself he wasn't like Lana and would never treat Josh as she treated him. The blatant flirting had taken Josh a while to get used to it, but now that he'd spent more time with Colbie and her outrageous innuendos, he'd stopped being shocked by what came out of either of their mouths. When he finished laughing, Josh shook his head and squeezed Topher's arm, right where he'd just been rubbing his tattoo. It made Topher's heart skip. "I appreciate the deflection, but just know, Henry is eager to stay in contact with you. And I do mean you specifically."

Topher affected a pout. "Is that the only reason you hang out with me?"

"Yes." The twinkle in Josh's eye betrayed his lie. "I need to go update my uncle. You think she'll have this place ready by Saturday?"

Topher nodded. "We're getting the alcohol shipment at noon today, and Raven is doing the first round of interviews for bartenders. Then it's just final touches and Poppy's wards. Lana didn't want to advertise to humans until the place was protected, and she didn't want to give anyone supernatural enough time to change their minds about joining her. She's going to open with no fuss on Saturday. The humans we know will show, and she thinks between them and the club's name, we'll get enough of a crowd for word of mouth to keep us going for a while."

"Even if Henry doesn't want to get directly involved, I'll come by to check it out."

"I'm looking forward to it," Topher said with a wink. Josh smiled, waved at Annaliese and Nora, said a brief goodbye to Lana where she stood at the base of the stairs, and left.

Annaliese and Nora still stood by the bar talking, but Topher occasionally sensed the weight of Annaliese's eyes. Her attention was something difficult to keep. Topher was always far too aware when he held it.

Lana sidled up to Topher's side, slipping her arm in his and disrupting the warm echo of Josh's touch.

"Do you think she'll go for it?" she repeated Josh's question, thirsty gaze on Nora. Salivating at the power that emanated from the alpha. Since he'd been changed, Topher thought about magic in terms of potential. Power in terms of what someone could do rather than what they had done.

Potential rolled off Nora in heady waves.

"I hope so," Topher said, surprised how true the words were. It felt disloyal to Colbie to admit, but he'd never personally had a problem with Nora and his sister missed her. Colbie tried to deny it, but Topher saw how much. Maybe, now that Gabriel was out of the picture and her wolf had calmed, Nora might have the space to be a better partner. Time would tell.

"Me too. If she's half the wolf I hear her father was, she'll be quite the ally."

An ally. An equal. The respect in Lana's voice surprised Topher.

Nora had left their lives in ruin last March without even a phone call to Colbie to ease the hurt. Yet, Topher never stopped rooting for her. He wanted her to grow past what her old pack expected. He wanted her to find her way in the supernatural world.

Topher wanted Nora on his side, too. Hopefully, they'd be able to get her there without any more pain caused to Colbie. Either way, his sister had always been too eager to play with fire.

. . .

After locking the back door behind Nora and Annaliese, Topher and Raven shadowed Lana as she walked through the rest of the building. The maker inspected all the progress made in the last few days. She noted any final touches she wanted done to Raven, who looked nearly dead on her feet from staying up all night. The staircase led to a narrow hallway, the first door opened to a meeting room not unlike what Grace had installed at Happenstance. The size of the table and number of chairs seemed optimistic to Topher. Lana was prepared for meetings the same size as those formerly held by the Big Three. Her fingers trailed over the new table as she walked the length, smiling slightly at the possibilities.

Topher remained by the doors. The meeting room only contained the large oval table, chairs, and a projector setup at one end with a slim metal podium by the screen. Everything was startlingly white. Lana's deep red and black outfit was a vivid contrast. She would always stand out in this room. "I want to meet with Henry in here tomorrow night now it's finished."

"Do you need me to get anything for the meeting?" Raven asked.

"Just some snacks, maybe. Nothing too special, but werewolves are always hungry."

Raven nodded and wrote another note in her planner. Topher pushed off the wall and snatched the notebook from her hands, snorting at the extensive to-do list. He shook his head and took Raven's pen too. "You deserve a raise. Go to bed. I'll write down whatever else she wants done."

With a glance at Lana to make sure this was okay, Raven sighed. "You better not miss anything," she said, a threatening finger in his face. The relief in her eyes softened the effect considerably.

Topher nipped at the digit and knew Raven was truly exhausted when she barely reacted to the brush of teeth. "Go get your beauty sleep. You need it."

Once Raven left, Topher let his mask slip. Being around humans for so long was wearing. Raven could brush off most of his unintentional charm like Oliver did at this point, but Topher still had to be careful. Although Raven had few qualms against being charmed or bitten. She had worked at the Maker as the only human on the night staff. She was in the process of registering when the former club burned. Though Lana was suspended from changing humans, Raven kept working as Lana's daytime assistant in hopes the restriction would soon be lifted. She spoke with construction workers daily to make Lana's vision for the Alpha's Den came true. Raven was the one filing paperwork and calling loan offices and making sure the insurance from the Maker came through.

"You really should pay her more," Topher said.

Lana smiled. "She's been instrumental. I wish I could give her what she wants. That's why she does this, Topher—to be one of us, not for raises."

Topher's jaw clenched. Lana thought he should be grateful for his position and the deal he and Colbie had struck. Their cooperation in exchange for Julia's care and Lana's help uncovering the mystery behind what Julia was now and what changed her.

But there was no progress. They had more unclaimed and a safe space for Julia, but she was getting weaker. Losing her humanity daily. Nothing they tried had truly helped. They were always too late when they caught the scent of the dark magic that produced unclaimed. Never catching the culprit, only stumbling upon the aftermath.

Nothing they did helped Julia or the situation. Nothing Topher did changed the fact that he was a vampire against his will. That he couldn't see the daylight, and his actions ensured Colbie couldn't either. That Topher was here and Dylan wasn't.

It was impossible to be grateful. He could never be the

lower Lana wanted him to be. When would she content herself with his compliance?

Lana narrowed her eyes when he remained silent. "I still worry about you, darling. Maybe you eat now, but when I look in your eyes, and you're not even there. Things will keep getting harder. When we open and when we hold meetings, I expect you to be welcoming. To build connections. And when shit hits the fan like it always does, you need to be prepared to lose more. You can't keep letting it eat at you."

When Topher only glared at Lana in response, she sighed. "You'll see. One day. This will all be worth it, and you'll be too powerful by my side to have regrets."

Topher snorted, pressing his boundaries. Lana only handled so much disrespect before she lashed out. Luckily, she was in a good mood tonight and willing to brush him off.

"Come see the rest."

They left the conference room, moving down the hall and bypassing the apartments until they reached another set of stairs. At the top, the wallpaper was a near-dizzying pattern of red on white. The floor a black tile and a white plush rug cut through the center. Topher almost snorted again. It was completely ineffective. Ridiculous to have a white rug covering black floors.

"It's perfect," Lana muttered, touching the wall, idling tracing the swooping pattern.

There was a black door at the end of the hall. A crystal knob and a silver door knocker. Lana led them inside.

Lana's new apartment was more of the shocking array of white to contrast Lana's wardrobe. The kitchen area was to the right and had been broken down into the simplest setup possible to feed Raven. There were construction papers, contracts, blueprints, and two laptops open on the table to the left; further evidence of the impossible hours Raven was putting in to get this place ready to open.

Lana smiled, taking a chair at the small white marble table

with white flowers as a centerpiece. She gestured for Topher to take the other. Out of all the tasks and jobs she assigned him nightly, this was by far the most exhausting. He sighed, took a seat, and woke up a laptop.

Lana got to business. "Let's go over as much as we can. Raven can walk us through the rest tomorrow night. I want to ensure everything is set with the liquor license and employee paychecks. If Poppy is starting work tomorrow on the wards, I want a system in place for her to log her hours and expenses."

"Right." Topher couldn't argue with the importance of that. He found the correct file, and they began working with their new system to keep track of all the business profits and expenditures. Lana anticipated a hugely successful first week, but they had to budget as if this wouldn't be the case.

Topher hated that they were good at this. He barely scraped through high school and learned everything business-related from Lana when they were going through a similar process opening the Maker. He couldn't deny he knew what he was doing now. Lana was a great teacher and savvy busi-nessperson. When they bent their minds toward a task, their communication was superb and their ability to problem-solve together never ceased to amaze him. Topher had never met someone as smart as Lana. For all her egotism, she knew a little about everything, and running a business was simple when she explained it. She innately understood budgeting and had a keen sense of when to take risks. In her clubs, Lana was a good leader, ensuring everyone succeeded so the business would benefit.

Topher hated the thrill he got when they worked together. When the solutions came to them so quickly. Maybe it was because she made him. Maybe their give and take was perfectly balanced in business matters. Whatever reason, Topher knew this new club the potential. It had its own magic. Now, they just had to do everything in their power to keep it from meeting the same end as the Maker.

CHAPTER 7

P oppy woke to Mouse's whiskers in her face. Ru was in the other room, keeping the poltergeist at bay. When Poppy left her room with the cat circling her feet, Ru rolled her eyes. "I gave him breakfast so he wouldn't bother you."

They watched the cat scurry across the room to his food bowl and start eating now that Poppy was awake to witness. Poppy chuckled. "Maybe one day he'll let you feed him."

Colbie had given on getting the cat to eat the food she poured. It used to spread an intoxicating warmth in Poppy's chest to know she and Topher were the cat's chosen people. It seemed as good a sign as any that they were operating on the same wavelength. That they were meant to move in tandem. That they would work once they got together the way Poppy fantasized about. Now, Poppy knew Topher snuck treats into the bowl and always tucked Mouse carefully into his bed so the little guy was comfortable. He had spoiled Mouse into fondness, while the cat liked Poppy for no extra incentive. Poppy figured it was because she had spent the most time with Mouse as a kitten, being the only one awake during the day. Likely, nothing connected her and Topher except that they were staunch cat lovers.

The fact was getting easier to deal with. Only, why did he have to be so beautiful? Why did he have to make Poppy feel special when that was the specific ache she'd chased to have soothed since childhood? Why was he so giving? So good with Ru and protective and funny? So obviously in need of comfort?

When Poppy voiced the last thought to Oliver, he'd snorted and told her you couldn't date someone for the sake of being a shoulder to cry on. That wasn't entirely what she meant, but Oliver hadn't gotten it when she tried to explain, making Poppy doubt her feelings. Yet again, it had felt like the people around her continued to reduce her "crush." People understood Topher's appeal but didn't get the pain that came with it for Poppy.

She couldn't really understand it herself at this point.

Maybe this confusion was the first step to getting over her roommate. It was already easier to control her emotions whenever Topher was around. Not that he ever was. Poppy sighed at his open door. "Topher never came home last night?"

Ru shook her head, mouth full of bagel.

Heart dropping as it always did when Topher had to spend too much time around Lana, Poppy went to the bathroom to get ready for her day. She braided her hair and whispered into her charms. She dressed in a sports bra and her favorite patched overalls. Today, Poppy would start warding the Alpha's Den. Lana hadn't given her much time to complete this process, so Poppy dressed appropriately for the work she'd have to put in.

In her room, Poppy studied her leather-bound journal. It seemed old and worn and had a pentagram branded onto the front. Of course, it was a gift from Colbie. Who knew how she'd managed to make it appear so much like a movie prop? But Poppy had left her school backpack and notebooks in her car, so she used this to write her lists for the day.

There were two stops to make: the grocery store and Golden Springs Park. It was too early in the growing season to get the plants she would have liked fresh from the community garden plot she'd begun, but she had plenty growing on her herb shelf and in the small flower garden she kept on the fire escape accessible through her bedroom window. Ru joined Poppy, helping her tie bundles together and asking more questions than usual about herb magic.

The impromptu lesson meant that by the time they had all the plants she could fit packed in her car, Poppy was behind schedule. She carefully placed the propagations in their glass vials on the passenger seat last. Poppy closed the door as she answered Ru's most recent question. Her sister was excited about Poppy's new job, though she was disappointed to hear Poppy was the sole witch involved so far.

"I'm sure it's only a matter of time before I meet others," Poppy said.

"Or you find one of our sisters!"

Poppy's smile tightened. "Maybe."

Ru wrapped Poppy in a squeeze of a hug. "You sure you don't want me to come help?"

"No, Ru. I got this. You focus on your wards and school." The last thing Poppy wanted was for the city to discover Ru's power. Her magic was too easily traced when she didn't ward it properly, and Ru wasn't there yet. Also, Lana wanted this building marked. She wanted people to know she had a witch on her side, which meant Poppy couldn't hide her identity in her spell work. She had to claim the club as much as Nora and Lana and anyone else involved. Not that Poppy's signature would mean much.

Ru needed to focus on figuring out how to live a normal, safer life. She had recently decided a GED would be the easiest course of action. It was a lot of studying, but Ru was determined to take the test this summer and picked things up so quickly no one would guess she'd never had any schooling that didn't involve magic before. Ru wasn't sure what she wanted to do after. UNB was a possibility, but Poppy speculated Ru was waiting to see what happened within the supernatural community before deciding.

Ru loved all things magic. If Poppy told her it was safe to enter the world as a witch, Ru would jump at the chance. But for now, Ru understood the dangers as well as anyone. She would stay in the wards and learn under Poppy's protection while their city remained unstable.

With one last enthusiastic wave, Ru went back inside and Poppy started the car. She glanced at her phone and noticed a few unexpected notifications.

Annaliese: Hi. I'm joining you today. Need me to pick anything up?

Poppy: Actually, yes. I was about to go to the grocery but don't have room. Can you grab cinnamon sticks, garlic, ginger root, doormats that don't say welcome in any way, blueberries, anise seed, a coconut, cumin, dill (not dried), and blackberries

Annaliese: GARLIC?

Annaliese: You know it's Lana's club right? You shouldn't try to get rid of her or the other vampires

Poppy snorted. Since Annaliese hadn't said no, she figured it was a yes and checked the trip to the grocery store off her list. Biting her lip, she dealt with the other notifications—a text and voicemail from Josh.

The rush of butterflies she experienced seeing his name on her screen was as shocking as his message. They hadn't spoken in weeks. It was excruciatingly uncomfortable seeing him last night, but he and Topher stood together and talked with ease. Feeling too weak to call him back, let alone listen to his voice, Poppy opened their text thread and was painfully reminded why he'd stopped trying to reach out.

Josh: Hey P, what are you up to this weekend?

Poppy: Sorry, busy with school

Josh: That's alright, next time :)

. . .

Josh: Hey, do you have an opinion on demons in summertime? Should we expect less of them?
  Poppy: I don't know. I would think so.
  Josh: Want to grab a coffee and discuss theories?
  Poppy: I have a test tomorrow

Josh: Are you busy with school this week?
  Poppy: No, but Ru's been having a bad few days
  Josh: How's it going living with her?

Josh: Hey!

Josh: Can we talk? It's just about the club.

Poppy winced at the message before this most recent one. She'd never responded. She remembered intending to but hadn't been able to summon enthusiasm to match Josh's. She had eventually forgotten about it. Some weeks were better than others concerning her feelings for Topher and where her memories of last March took her. Josh was too neatly tied into all those things. Not that he cast any extra darkness on that time, only guilt. Feelings of inadequacy. Poppy could admit hearing from him made her squirm. She was supposed to back him and his pack after they'd risked themselves to get her roommates and Zayn back. Instead, she'd retreated into school, avoided all her feelings, and put in minimal effort to keep from insulting Henry.

Now, Poppy's evasions were coming back to bite her. Josh deserved more than a text. Steeling herself, she opened the phone app and played his voicemail. It began with the sound of Josh clearing his throat. She hated the false cheer. "Hey, Poppy. I actually need to talk to you. Call me back soon, or I'm going to try again in like five minutes. It's supernatural stuff, but not like... well, we want to ask some questions. We as in the pack. But not like witchy, invasive questions. Just stuff about, um, you know. Stuff. So just call me back. Please."

It shouldn't have made Poppy feel better that he was as uncomfortable reaching out as she was. It gave Poppy the courage to call back, holding her breath until he picked up.

"Hello?" Josh said, his best impression of himself sounding normal.

Poppy pressed her cheek with her free hand, realizing, despite all her nerves and guilt, she was smiling. He was so nice to hear from. She suddenly couldn't fathom why she'd waited so long. "Hey! Sorry, I was packing some things into my car. Didn't hear my phone. What's up?"

"Oh, that's fine. Um, do me a favor and delete that voicemail then, okay? And if you already listened to it, pretend you didn't so I don't feel so embarrassed."

"What voicemail?"

Josh let out a little laugh. Nothing like his normal one. The wave of pleasure from hearing his voice began to evaporate. "I was calling because Henry wants me to talk to you about that meeting last night."

"What about it?"

"Well, we still haven't contacted Nora. Mostly, we just want to know your thoughts as another non-vampire. Make sure we, uh, have each other's backs if Lana tries anything." His hesitation was evident. His wince audible. Josh didn't think she had his pack's back after what happened with the demons. She'd placed basic wards on their new apartment complexes, but Henry had mentioned other things he wanted to work together on. Poppy ignored his calls.

"Oh. I mean, yeah. I think that would be best."

"So, would you want to grab coffee today? Or are you busy with school?"

Poppy sank back into her seat, wanting to disappear. The joy had fully faded, leaving all the roiling emotions from before in its wake. The second call-out stung worse than the first. "I'm sorry, Josh. Everything has just been a lot. I didn't want you to get— Never mind. No, I'm not busy with school. I took my last final yesterday. I can do coffee. My only plan today was to start warding the club."

"Where do you want to go?"

"There's a place close to the Alpha's Den I wanted to check out. It's a vegan café and bakery. Would that work?"

"Yes. I'm at the park, I can start heading that way."

Poppy bit her lip. Fortune was either playing with her or trying to help. Asking Josh for a favor seemed wrong, but it would save her the drive... "Can you grab me a few things from there?"

He agreed and Poppy texted him the list of forest flora she needed. After, Poppy sat in the stillness of the car for a moment, feeling the thriving plants around her, the sun beginning to beat down on her windshield in earnest, and the faint echo of Josh's voice in her ear.

Poppy drove to the bookstore on Twenty-Fifth. She bought Colbie the new fantasy book and another one the store owner insisted she had to read if she liked Rosales's writing. Colbie deserved the pick-me-up after last night, and Poppy had some time to kill browsing while she waited for Josh. She smiled at the tarot decks on display, coming up short when she spotted a hand-painted one. It was Margot's artwork. Tiff Jennings wasn't supportive of Margot's painting and drawing until she'd put it toward tarot deck making. Her cards were beautiful and vibrant. Poppy's plant-themed deck was one of the few possessions she'd grabbed when the wards fell around their home. This deck was full of grayscale, slashes of red and angry violet. Poppy picked it up, showing it to the store owner. "Is this a local artist?" Her voice shook.

"Yes. We've only had them stocked for a week and nearly

sold out. That's our last deck until next Thursday when she's bringing more."

Poppy's hand trembled, setting the deck back on the shelf. She'd known Margot was alive from her and Ru's attempts to See her, but Poppy figured their sister left town after she'd visited Margot's abandoned shop last winter. But Margot was still in New Brecken. She was doing business on the same street as Poppy. After today, would she pass the Alpha's Den, feel the wards, and know Poppy was nearby? Would she care?

Josh texted to let Poppy know he was close, startling her from her thoughts. She went to pay as Annaliese texted that she was heading to the grocery store. Trying not to think of her sister, Poppy walked the short distance to stand in front of the café, Vegan Your Day. The poltergeist took advantage of Poppy's distraction. She nearly wasn't fast enough to halt the mischief he was intent on, already a challenging act without acknowledging him or drawing attention to herself. He opened and closed the door to the thrift shop to their right, making the bell tinkle and tinkle until Poppy used a gust of wind to hold it shut. She inadvertently locked someone inside. The poltergeist cackled when the woman finally got the door open, frowning with confusion. Only Poppy could hear him. She ignored his pleased smile and the flustered woman, shrugging when they made eye contact.

The poltergeist scurried around in front of Poppy. No Ru, no vampires, and he acted like a kid finally let out to recess. "That was funny. I should have thought to lock her in. Look how well we work together, Penelope. If you'd just listen, we could keep working on—"

Poppy focused as hard as she could to banish him. Her power like a sputtering flame. Her magic tied him to her, and it didn't like working against itself. He was still standing there, talking, though muted. Poppy closed her eyes and resisted the urge to cover her ears. She wanted to scream at him, beg him to leave her alone. She knew it was better when he focused on her, not the humans around, but she was exhausted. The constant chatter and attempts to banish him were wearing on her. If she were to scream or acknowledge him in any way, he would get stronger. It had taken her this long just to be able to mute him.

Poppy was losing her mind. "You're okay," she whispered to herself.

"What?"

Poppy jumped and whirled around. She hadn't heard Josh's approach, and the sight of him caught her off guard. She hadn't let herself stare last night. His cheeks were flushed. His hair windblown. His eyes so open and readable and kind. His life-giving, calm aura reached out to her, whisking away any effect trying to suppress the poltergeist had on her strength.

It was good. So good to see Josh again.

"Ohhh," the poltergeist said, eyes bouncing between them. "This will be fun," he sang.

Josh's energy fed her magic, giving life to the poltergeist like Ru often did. Poppy could see the splashes of color, like the red of his tie, deepening in the corner of her eye. It took so much for Poppy to quiet the poltergeist. Now, with this flush of energy, she couldn't do it at all. Panic clawed at Poppy's throat. She couldn't sit and have coffee with the poltergeist screaming in her ear or throwing things around. What would Josh think of her distraction?

"Nothing, sorry. Just talking to myself," Poppy said, hoping Josh didn't notice her blush or the quick glare she cut in the poltergeist's direction.

Josh accepted this with a stiff nod. He sniffed the air and tilted his head back take in the sea-foam green walls of the bakery. "Are you vegan now?"

"I'm trying it out. Becoming a vegetarian was surprisingly easy, but giving up cheese might be asking a lot of myself."

"Really? Was it easy? I can't even imagine. How long have you been vegetarian?"

Poppy felt herself relaxing. She'd forgotten how Josh did that. Made her feel interesting. Like he wanted to know her. Like he craved an understanding of Poppy to her core. It was something he had in common with Topher, yet the underlying motivation felt different. Topher's attention was less selective, he wanted to understand everyone. Josh fixated on Poppy in a way that didn't quite seem to be a personality trait. It wasn't something he offered just anyone.

And after weeks of not talking, the attention was working on Poppy in unexpected ways.

"Well, it was easy for me. I never liked a lot of heavy, meat-based meals. I can afford a lot of vegetables, and my green thumb means I can grow a lot of herbs and stuff myself."

Josh's smile was the sun coming out at the end of winter. Abrupt and bringing forgotten warmth and relief. "I missed you, Poppy. I'm glad you agreed to meet me."

Poppy had to drop her eyes. She brought her thumb up to her mouth and bit at her hangnail, jumping when Josh's hand darted out and pulled the affronted digit away. She looked at him in surprise at the casual touch.

"Sorry. My brother bites his nails, and I've gotten in the habit of stopping him."

"It's okay. I didn't realize I was doing it." Poppy tucked her hands behind her back. She'd been stressed and anxious about so many things that she made a habit of biting at her hang nails until she drew blood.

And, of course, Josh didn't let her hide it. He reached around her and gently tugged on her wrist. Poppy knew she could resist him. She could step back so he wasn't in her space. She could ask him to stop, and he would. But she was frayed at the edges, just like her nails. Too tired to summon the energy to resist. Poppy let him bring a hand into view.

"Poppy…" His voice was disproving.

Shoulders slumping, she dropped the glamor he could tell was there, clearing the image of healthy nails and showing the angry red and multiple scabs. He ran a thumb over the base of her cuticles. "What's been bothering you?"

Him. Money. School. Her future. Her questions. The poltergeist. Her mother. The demons. The unclaimed. The humans going missing. The healing powder that she couldn't get right. The fact that she missed cheese but wanted to be a better person in this dying world. The way she didn't like how her hair had been growing out but wasn't sure she wanted to cut it again. How Oliver wasn't getting enough sleep and having nightmares, and Zayn was worried about him when not even his saliva did enough to help. The way Topher wasn't letting himself grieve. How Colbie was dating as if she needed to fill a void and would probably hurt someone or herself. How Lana and everyone else depended on her to protect them so they could usher in a new future for the people of New Brecken. How Ru turned to Poppy for—

Josh squeezed Poppy's hand. "Take a breath, Poppy."

She pulled in a breath, drawing from Josh's ease. "Sorry. *Everything* is just a lot right now."

He laughed. "Are you sure coffee is a good idea on top of that?"

"I need the energy to cast, and that usually wears me out enough that I don't feel as anxious."

Josh didn't let go of Poppy's hand as he turned to go inside. He was loud in his admiration, loving the decor with its pastel walls and white seats and tables. The poltergeist was quiet, watching Josh with an interest that made Poppy's jaw clench. At the counter, Josh asked questions that made it obvious he didn't know what a vegan diet involved, or even baking for that matter, but Poppy loved how he laughed at his ignorance. Josh finally ordered himself a drink and a scone before pulling Poppy forward for her turn.

She tried to protest when he paid, but he insisted it was on the pack, making the barista's eyes widen.

Poppy was slightly stunned herself. Supernaturals avoided

declaring themselves. Even along the clubs at Fourth Street, the vampires' presence was an unspoken thing. But Josh didn't notice their expressions and tugged Poppy to a corner table. When his focus landed too heavy, Poppy dropped her eyes fielded Annaliese's text about whether or not frozen berries would work.

A beat of silence passed. Josh looked around. He sniffed like a dog, making the girl behind the counter's eyes widen. She pulled out her phone and tried to start texting discretely. Poppy hated the exposure, even if it was just in relation to the supernatural. But she took a deep breath and shook off the feeling. This was precisely what she was signing on for by joining Lana. She'd better get used to it.

Poppy tried to think how to break the silence. At the counter the girl gasped, and there was a clatter. The poltergeist grinned mischievously as the girl swooped to pick up her phone. She hastily pocketed it, cheeks red, and began making their drinks. Focusing, Poppy forced her magic to stop sampling Josh's energy and directed her will toward banishing the poltergeist. All she managed to do was make him leave the bakery. He stood directly outside the glass, staring down at Josh and Poppy's table in a way that he knew unnerved her.

Head already beginning to pound from the effort of keeping him at bay, Poppy turned back to Josh as he unwrapped his scone and took a bite.

Poppy spoke around her clawing guilt and addressed the elephant in the room. "I'm sorry I ghosted you, Josh." She ignored the urge to glance out the window with her poor word choice. "I… It was a lot. What happened with my mom and Topher and Ru. I wasn't, I mean, I probably am still not in a place to juggle more relationships, and I knew you wanted more from me than I had to offer."

Poppy couldn't meet his eyes. She started picking at her thumb cuticle. Josh covered her hands, and she stilled. "It's okay, Poppy. Sure, it would have been nice if you'd just told me you didn't have the space for more friends or whatever. I would have backed off without getting too hurt, and if you feel the need for distance again, I ask that you communicate that. But friendship shouldn't be a burden. Maybe I asked too much when I said you had to be there for the pack, but I meant it when I said we would be there for you. If you need help, I'm here. And I understand you have feelings for Topher. I'm serious about being friends. I like you a lot and want to get to know you, even aside from romance."

"Really?" Poppy asked. It felt like she was fishing, but she'd missed Josh's presence. Even his energy was addictive. The lightness she experienced every time she saw his face would be worth getting through this. If they could uncomplicate their time together, it would be amazing. For just a moment, she thought about how it might feel to unburden herself to him. Maybe in his travels, Josh had learned about ghosts. Maybe he knew more witches. Maybe he had talked to Topher enough to tell her how her roommate was doing when he wasn't forcing cheer into his face. Maybe Josh knew where he and Colbie vanished to at all hours of the night without telling her.

"Really, really."

For now, Poppy held back. She'd been dealing with all of this alone for so long that the potential to ask Josh for help again was enough. Poppy's fingers stilled, the urge to bite her nails lessening as their coffee was dropped off at the table. She sipped of the oat milk latte she had chosen. It was good. Exactly what she needed. Feeling centered, she set it down and looked back up in time to see Josh take a long drink of his iced hazelnut latte, eyes sliding shut in bliss.

"What's the pack business then?" she asked when the pleasure on his face made her cheeks too hot.

"Henry wants to know what you think of Lana's latest scheme."

"Wants to know what *I* think?"

"Yeah. So far, you're the only witch she's contacted."

Poppy let out a laugh. "Oh, I'm not qualified to speak on behalf of the witches. I can barely even cast."

Josh cocked his head. "You did a lot of really powerful casting right in front of us. Don't play that down."

Poppy waved a hand dismissively. "That was just potion work and blood magic. Crutches."

"After all these years, it takes a lot to impress Henry, and you did. That means something. Now, for obvious reasons, we don't like Lana. We don't trust her. Within the vampire makers of this city, she seems to be the lesser evil, but we have to tread carefully. We would love to trust you."

Poppy nodded. It was making more sense. "But I ditched and Henry doesn't think he can rely on me to take your side anymore."

"That isn't exactly—"

"It's fine. I get it. But I'm not influential enough for him to decide based on what I think anyway. He shouldn't go into this believing I'll have power to keep you all protected from Lana or whatever damage she causes. I can ward with the help of my potions and plants, but I can't do memory swiping or See or anything that would actually be useful."

Josh rubbed at his neck, frustration in the movement. "Poppy. Don't talk your magic down like that. Whatever another witch can do, I'm sure you know the potion equivalent or how to boost your magic to get there. Honestly, from a non-caster point of view, the potions seem more useful."

Shifting in her seat, Poppy shrugged. Maybe, but the magic was less precise and involved proximity. It wasn't real casting. "Either way, Lana told me she's going to put me in contact with other witches. I'm sure my presence is just to show Lana has a witch friend. She wants to make the powerful witches more comfortable until they agree to work with her. I can try to put Henry in contact with them when they come."

"Is that why you agreed to work with her? Because you didn't think you'd be playing a large role?"

"For now, it feels like a large role. Very few people know who I am, so just coming out of the shadows is terrifying. But I need information to help Ru. Her magic is stronger than mine, and I'm not qualified to help her master it. Between exposing myself and her, it's much less risky for me to ask the questions."

Josh frowned, tapping his fingertips against his coffee cup. "So far, we know the vampires are at risk because they're getting blamed for the unclaimed—which we need a better name for, by the way. Calling them unclaimed keeps them in the same category as the vampires when they aren't. Anyway, despite this, we know witches are the ones being actually hunted. Vampire killings have stopped since Grace died. It's not bad for wolves like it is for witches. I'm worried about you exposing yourself now of all times."

"It might be bad for wolves."

"What do you mean?"

"There used to be more packs here than Gabriel's. No one knows what happened to them. Most people figure Morales was territorial and chased them away, but why would one pack want to monitor the whole city? Especially right as they were debating the laws. Plus, even though Gabriel doesn't seem to want anything to do with you all, he hasn't tried to get rid of you, right?"

Josh froze. "No. I didn't know about the other packs. No one talks about them. Do you know any of their names? We could try to find them."

Poppy shrugged and lowered her voice as three high school kids took the table next to them. "My mom knew. I bet Lana does too and she's the better option to find out."

"And this is the kind of information you want from joining her?"

Poppy nodded. "I want to know what's killing witches. I want to know if the wolves were the first ones to hunt the unclaimed and if that was why they were chased from the city.

I want to know why they keep involving Topher. I want to know if I can play any role in making this city safe for Ru."

"I think Henry wants the same things."

"So I guess my answer is yes. For as little help as I might be, I'll work with you."

CHAPTER 8

Nora tried to get ready as quietly as possible. She'd barely slept after returning home from the meeting. Her head had spun for hours, wondering what Gabriel would think of her joining Lana. It seemed the final step she could make to break ties. Not that becoming an alpha wasn't, but sometimes Nora found herself reverting to her childhood mindset. Believing that if she just behaved in the way her father had taught her and followed the rules of his pack, they would accept her. She'd find herself making choices based on a flimsy, stupid hope that if she acted the right way, maybe Gabriel would take her back.

But the more she did that, the more she resented this conditioning. As Annaliese said repeatedly, Nora should never have had to earn her family.

So whenever her thoughts spiraled, imagining Gabriel's disproval or Adriana's mocking or Matt's told-you-so's or Heather's disappointment, she had to remind herself she shouldn't care. It was uncomfortable not having control of her own mind. This desperation to please Gabriel wasn't right. It didn't align with the morals Nora was only now understanding she possessed, yet it was still the first place her brain went and always where it ended up again.

It was getting easier to admit that her old pack wasn't in the right. And still, Nora tried to call Matt. Shame flooded her for hitting the button and waiting with bated breath until he failed to pick up again.

That was when Nora finally gave up on sleep. She didn't know what to think. She didn't trust the way her brain worked. Nora needed a distraction, and the only thing that had felt like freedom since she'd made the change was this opportunity Lana presented.

Nora texted Poppy. *Are you starting today? Did you decide if you're going to help Lana?*

Nora had finished dressing in jean shorts and a simple black t-shirt by the time Poppy responded. Nora was surprised she responded at all. Annaliese told her Poppy wasn't happy with Nora's actions last winter.

Poppy: *Yes. I'm getting coffee now. Will probably head over there in a little bit. Aren't you with Annaliese?*

Not currently. Can I join you? If we're protecting the club together, I should know what you have in place.

Holding her breath, Nora watched the dots showing Poppy typing. The witch was so secretive about her casting. Would she allow Nora into the process?

Finally, her phone buzzed. *That's fine. Talk to Annaliese first. Josh is here, too.*

And that was almost enough to send Nora back into bed. The idea of working with Henry, of going to him with her questions about being a werewolf, somehow felt like even more of a betrayal to her pack than aligning with Lana. Nora wavered, but her stomach rumbled. She would decide while she ate if she was going to go or not.

Opening her bedroom door, Nora saw Annaliese was already dressed and waiting. Nora had been so consumed by her thoughts that she hadn't heard her roommate get up. Nora's shoulders tensed. Every part of her still rebelled against involving Annaliese. Was there a way to leave without Annaliese tagging along?

The way Annaliese stood with her arms crossed and chin lifted said she knew exactly what Nora was thinking. "Heading to the Alpha's Den?"

Nora snorted at the name. "There's no way Lana's actually going to name it that."

"She will. She wants an alpha involved. She wants to brag about having an alpha involved."

"That's hardly me."

"*Yet.* You need to start acting like one so you stop directing all this overprotective bullshit at me. Once you have your own people to watch out for, maybe you'll loosen up."

"I haven't decided if I'm going over there," Nora said, trying to change the subject. She didn't know the first thing about building a pack, and she knew it was more of her conditioning that made her shy from asking questions. To start a pack was to publicly state she believed she was on the same level as Gabriel. It meant she was competition.

"Why not?"

Nora hesitated.

"No lying, Nor."

Nora deflated. "I asked Poppy if I could join her while she warded the place. She said yes, but that Josh would be there."

Annaliese nodded. While she was not against pushing for Nora to break out of her conditioned patterns, she understood what they were as well as anyone. She knew why this would sour Nora's plans. "Well, I'm going over there. I already ran to the grocery to buy witchy things for Poppy, I just came back to see if you were coming. Is she still getting coffee? We're out, and I forgot to get some."

"I think so?"

Annaliese wasn't content with her answer. She brought her phone out and put it to her ear. "Hi, P. What's your plan?…

Oh, perfect. We haven't eaten yet, and coffee sounds great. Are you okay with us all meeting there and then heading over?… Awesome. See you soon."

Annaliese hung up and raised her eyebrows at Nora. Pressing but not demanding. Nora grabbed the car keys and led the way out of the apartment building.

Nora could admit she was a little skeptical of a vegan bakery. Annaliese had no qualms against it being plant-based, but she did scoff at the bakery's name. Their issues brought them up short, looking at the scrawling text above the door from their diagonal parking spot. Neither of them reached to open their car door. "If we start regularly hanging out at a place called Vegan Your Day, we may have to officially cut ties with these people," Annaliese said.

And Nora had to laugh. She realized she hadn't in a few days when do so made her feel instantly lighter. She hadn't felt close to laughing since seeing her mother in the forest.

"It's more conveniently located," Nora said. Patty's was too close to Fourth Street for comfort. Nora missed their burgers dearly. "But the vampires would never be able to join us here, given the hours."

Annaliese raised an eyebrow. "Nora! You say that as if it's a bad thing. Are your feelings toward vampires more positive since seeing a certain someone last night?"

Nora didn't answer. She opened her door as Annaliese reminded her that the sun wouldn't rise as early in the winter. The vampires could end their nights at the bakery with them. "…or veg-end their nights," Annaliese finished as she followed Nora. For someone against puns, she came up with horrible ones often.

"I wish my hearing was worse so I wouldn't have been subjected to that," Nora said.

Annaliese pushed her, but Nora didn't budge, making

Annaliese roll her eyes as they crossed the sidewalk to the bakery doors. Nora spotted Poppy and Josh near the window. He was slanted toward the witch, entire body riveted by whatever Poppy was saying. When he laughed, he brushed Poppy's arm, and Poppy appeared to flash with blue.

"Oh, god. He's still into her," Annaliese muttered, pity in her voice.

Nora's sympathy wasn't the same as Annaliese's. Hers was marred too much by the memory of hearing Colbie's voice last night. Finally seeing her again after all these weeks. She knew exactly how Josh was feeling.

Hopefully, her pitiful state hadn't been as obvious.

They ordered their pastries and drinks to go. Poppy joining them to get herself another latte, earning a frown from Josh that she pointedly ignored.

"How have you two been?" Josh asked while they waited.

Annaliese and Josh took control of the conversation. Nora's wolf side still wouldn't allow her to loosen up around another wolf to think of small talk. Poppy stood off to the side on her phone, letting Josh be friendly and do the catching up for the both of them. She hadn't met Nora's eyes, but her jaw was set. The cold shoulder was noted. Nora didn't know how to thaw it, but she knew if they were going to get along, she would need to make the first moves. At least Poppy had let them join her today.

Brown paper bag of baked goods and drinks in hand, they left Vegan Your Day. They stopped at Annaliese's car for her groceries and went up the block toward the club, turning to go down the alley and into the lot in the back. Poppy's car was parked there already, filled to the brim with green plants that pressed against the glass as though begging to be let out.

"Should I let Raven know we're here?" Nora asked.

Poppy nodded. "We won't go inside. I'm placing the exterior wards today mostly and—"

"*Joshua!*" Annaliese's shout interrupted Poppy's planning. Nora spun, heart surging with fear.

Josh was only stripping, rolling his eyes at Annaliese. "I won't show you the important bits," he said, unzipping his pants. When her eyes widened, he winked and shimmied. Nora was surprised to find herself fighting a smile at his antics.

Annaliese threw her hands over her eyes. "I don't consent! I don't consent!"

In a practiced move, Josh shifted as he removed his underwear, somehow hiding the "important bits" without confining himself to clothes or ripping out of them. Then, free and in wolf form, he pranced around the area. Poppy picked up the pile of clothing and set them on the three concrete stairs leading to the back entrance so they wouldn't get stepped on. She turned to Annaliese, unfazed. "Do you have the doormats?"

Annaliese and Nora handed the mats and reusable bags over, letting Poppy sort their contents. Poppy dug around until she found the blueberries. She scattered them on the landing before settling the doormat on top. She spoke to Nora over her shoulder. "You should follow Josh's lead if you want people to know this place is under your protection."

Nerves crawled along Nora's skin. The last time she shifted in front of people was a terrifying memory. She'd only done it alone in the forest since. People saw more to Nora when she was in wolf form. Saw what made her alpha, something she herself hadn't glimpsed. Nora didn't want any more bombs dropped in her lap. Being packless and an alpha was bad enough. "And do what? Sniff around?" Nora asked. "Let people see me?"

Poppy dipped her chin in Josh's direction in time for Nora to see him lift his leg and pee on the corner of the building. "Do wolf things. I don't know."

Face burning, Nora went around Poppy's car and removed

her jacket. She was not nearly practiced enough to undress in front of everyone without flashing them.

Poppy trailed her hands over the doorframe, muttering under her breath as she did. To Nora's surprise, Josh came to sit at her side, watching the alley close as Poppy began casting, the air around them tinting blue.

Nora stopped to watch. Poppy took a potion from her bag and swallowed the contents. She began to radiate a more vivid hue. Josh pressed his nose into her side, and Poppy flushed darker. Nora stared as Poppy took out a knife and cut her palm, never once breaking the flow of words she muttered under her breath. Reaching up, Poppy pressed her bloody palm above the door. Her body swayed with the magic, her unin-jured hand reaching down and seeking Josh's fur. She grabbed a fistful, and he leaned into her touch. A pattern of blue light began flowing out from under Poppy's palm. What looked like narrow tree branches spread, twisting and forking until they had reached the roof or traveled around the corner of the building. The air smelled charged, like a thunderstorm and an overflowing greenhouse. It didn't match the sunny day in the middle of the city.

Poppy trembled as she lowered her hand. A small tree of blue remained where the bricks should be wet with blood. Poppy sat heavily on the steps, clutching her head as she caught her breath.

"What happened?" Annaliese asked. Staring at the building like nothing was amiss. Nora snapped her mouth shut. She'd been gaping at the show of magic, but Annaliese's inability to see it was enough to bring Nora back to earth.

"That's the first level of wards," Poppy said. As she spoke, the blue light faded until the small tree appeared to have been etched into the brick for years. "Now, we start with the plants. We'll be planting them around the base of the building. I'll tell you where. Some are better in certain lines of sunlight. Oliver is on his way to help, too. We need to start while the cast is still fresh. Nora, if you're going to mark the building, do it now. It'll infuse your energy with the wards."

Nora found the courage to join Josh in wolf form as Annaliese joined Poppy in breaking up the concrete and skeptically digging in the dry, crumbling dirt beneath. Nora's hackles went up as soon as she shifted. She wasn't used to sharing this changed space with other wolves. Josh came over, sniffing at her and making whining noises in the back of his throat. She bloomed with authority over his show of submission. His wolf recognized her wolf's power. It was enough to give her confidence and stop baring her teeth.

Nora felt the separation between her and Josh more now; a wall that was Henry's declaration that Josh was his, but there was still a connection she didn't expect. It left her dizzy with longing. If she had a pack, this bond would be less flimsy. She *knew* it would be so much stronger. More grounded. A steady connection that would allow her the ability to communicate. To share her fears and receive comfort as well as give it even without her human tongue. She could tell Josh was linked with his pack even now, a hint of the bond flickering at the edge of her wolf senses. Indescribable, but there. Out of Nora's reach.

Jealousy swirled in Nora's stomach.

Nora physically shook off the longing. Together, they sniffed around this hidden back half of the building, Nora adding her own urine and scent to claim the space. She felt the wall and something from Poppy reaching for her, but she continually blocked it, casting it off as she would charm.

Eventually, Josh let out a huff of frustration. He picked up his clothing with his mouth and went to Nora's spot behind the car to change. As soon as he was human, he said, "Nora, you have to let her pull from you."

Resistant to any order, Nora's wolf went all alpha. She bared her teeth and growled. Josh raised his hands, submitting. Even as a human, he gave off that yielding energy that assured her he knew his position, and she instantly calmed. "I only mean, if you want your essence to be part of the spell, you have to let it take from you, and if you want Poppy to cast as strong as possible, you have to let her draw from you."

Surprise flitted across Poppy's features. "You *let* me?"

Josh laughed. "Of course. It's not like we let any witch we come across use our strength." He turned back to Nora. "Poppy doesn't take too much. She's accustomed to casting with the energy of things around her, so she knows the boundaries. I barely feel what she takes. Let her in. You can trust her to borrow your power."

Poppy stared at Josh, touched. That was enough for Nora to understand Poppy deeply appreciated his help. She wouldn't flaunt Nora's. It felt unnatural to let that barrier down. The last time she had, Topher's charm had snapped something essential in her being. After a moment of concentration and fighting panic, Nora felt the building pull from her. The blue vines flashed to life again, and Poppy sparked with a blue that bordered on white. "Oh." Poppy's exclamation was hushed. She stared at her glowing arms.

"Way to show me up, Nor," Josh murmured, but he wasn't mad. He pressed his hand into her neck as he passed, scratching at the base of her ear. If Nora's form were more catlike, she would have purred at the contact made to her touch-starved being.

With Nora and Josh lending their strength, even Nora could feel how well the wards took hold. When Oliver arrived, Poppy had him and Annaliese digging and planting. The witch took the time to grind seeds and stalks in her mortar and pestle, sprinkling the dust around the building. She tied a bundle of flowers and herbs above the door, placed cloth-wrapped seeds at the building's corners, and deliberately set down aspen tree twigs, other sticks, leaves, and stones around the perimeter. At no point did Poppy stop murmuring words like protection, prosperity, luck, wards, positive energy, and so on.

Nora sensed the magic listening.

Eventually, Raven came out to help. She looked like she was running on zero sleep and was even less of a fan of small talk than Nora, but she and Oliver knew each other well. They chatted about Zayn and Topher and other small vampire dramas they'd heard recently. Josh and Nora shifted back to human form and helped with the planting, too. From that point, they made quick work around the side of the building and to the front. When the sun peaked in the sky, Poppy switched up the plants and spells, using the changing time to boost a whole different set of magic.

By mid-afternoon, Poppy had the wall covered in freshly grown vines. They inched up the building at startling speed. Huge, matte red flowerpots overflowed on either side of the front and back doors, and more colorful blooms spilled from boxes under the windows. The blossoms smelled stronger than regular flowers and radiated warmth. People walking by seemed tempted to stop and appreciate them, but Poppy had kept most bystanders away with a spell to redirect them until the wards were finished. The sidewalk in front of the building was chalked up with drawings of trees and ancient-looking symbols, many of which Annaliese admitted she couldn't see with a scowl.

The pizzas they'd eaten for lunch became a distant memory. Raven was inside arranging the alcohol they'd helped her unload an hour ago. Everyone was exhausted and hungry when Poppy sat back on her heels, swaying enough that Oliver reached to steady her. "I think that's all I can do today without really overextending myself."

The witch was pale, and her eyes squinted in pain. Josh held out his hand, helping Poppy up. Even he trembled from the amount of energy he shared. "I think it's food and nap time," he agreed.

Annaliese, who had just buried the last of the crystals, nodded. "Are we doing this again tomorrow?"

"I think I'll work on some more intricate spells on the inside of the building tomorrow."

"Meet at Vegan at the same time, then?" Annaliese asked, standing and wiping her hands on her pants.

Poppy nodded and looked at Nora. "If you could come, you're helping the spells a lot. I appreciate it."

Nora agreed to be there. The day's work had eased Poppy's cold shoulder enough that another day together didn't fill Nora with nerves.

"It's a date then," Josh said.

With her smell all over the building, a public declaration of her new alliance, Nora knew she was all in. Gabriel would know of this soon, and there would be no going back.

She felt oddly free as she and Annaliese walked to the car. This place was *hers*. She wouldn't let anyone take it from her. Now, all that was left was finding a pack of her own to fill it.

CHAPTER 9

Poppy didn't think she'd ever been more spent.

Ru looked up from her book as she stumbled inside, the wards sighing to let her pass as if they could tell how little she had to fight them. Poppy gave her sister a small smile and ruffled her hair as she passed.

"I should have been there to help," Ru said, as close to a pout as she got.

"We all left our marks on the place. Anyone who knew about magic would know what you can do if you had too. They would try to find you."

Ru rolled her eyes. Concern backed the attitude, though. "I just hated sitting around here alone all day."

"Colbie is here."

"You know what I meant." Ru returned to her book, mumbling, "There's food in the fridge."

In an effort not to concern her sister more, Poppy forced her tired body to the bathroom to rinse off the dirt. She threw on a sweatshirt Topher had left on the hook and a pair of sleep shorts. As she ate the leftover Thai food hunched over the counter, Poppy frowned at Topher's open door and checked her phone.

His location wasn't always sharing, but he'd left it on from last night. Poppy frowned, realizing they'd been at the same place all day. Topher was at the Alpha's Den. Sleeping. With Lana. But *with* Lana? Poppy hated not knowing. She hated that she hadn't realized they were so close all day. Her attention had been consumed by Josh and his easy trust. Simple affection she'd never expected to experience again. Topher and Josh were literal night and day. So why had Josh's smiles conjured thoughts of Topher? Why had his warm touch made her think of Topher's slim, cold fingers? Why couldn't she just turn everything off?

Poppy thought Topher stayed with Lana because his maker made him remain to protect her. But nothing about their relationship made sense, even when she was at her best. Wasn't Topher stronger than her? They didn't have the typical maker-lower bond, and with Colbie registered, Lana had nothing on him. Why did he act so subservient?

After a day of casting, a day in Josh's presence and her confusing emotions, picturing Topher and Lana together was too much. Poppy swallowed exhausted, rejected tears. She just needed to sleep. Ru left to walk dogs, the apartment still and quiet in her wake.

Head aching, Poppy went straight to bed, ignoring the poltergeist standing at the window, staring down at her as she settled. He reached and knocked a cactus off Poppy's dresser. She was too spell-spent to keep it from crashing to the ground. More tears threatened to well, but she just rolled away and fell asleep more quickly than she had in years.

To be almost immediately lurched awake.

"PENELOPE!"

She buried her head under her covers, frustration building in her throat. She felt practically ill after using so much magic, but the poltergeist siphoned off more. He bounced onto the bed, jostling her and feeling like he weighed as much as any corporal being. Poppy debated calling Ru to come home early.

She wished Topher was here. She glanced at the clock. It was only four. Maybe she could get in bed with Colbie and be left alone.

But Poppy was too tired. Sleep came again, pulling her down rapidly. She began dreaming, flashes of Topher, crouched and crying though he could no longer make tears. Colbie, knife in hand, fangs bared. Nora in danger, unable to shift. The plants surrounding Poppy wilting to brown, the vines above her turning to ash and raining down. She coughed, choking. Josh, stepping closer, grinning as he wiped the ash from Poppy's cheeks and—

"PENELOPE!"

Poppy sat up with a jolt, gasping at the cold wash of fear from being ripped from her dream. *"WHAT?"*

They blinked at each other. After weeks and weeks, Poppy acknowledged the poltergeist for the first time. Tears finally spilled over Poppy's cheeks when a smile spread across his face. "Oh, Mother." Poppy dropped her head in her hands, rubbing at the tears and drowning with regret. She didn't have the energy or will to deal with this.

"Finally. Dry your eyes. We have work to do, girl. You can't ignore me anymore. Not if you want to get tied up in that haunted space."

"*You* were the only one doing any haunting."

He was delighted by Poppy's engagement, but she didn't know what else to do. Nothing worked to get rid of him anyway. If she tried to go back to sleep now, he would only continue yelling with renewed volume and energy. She'd interacted with him. She had acknowledged him. There was so much power in that act.

"*That* is because your Sight is truly atrocious."

Poppy rolled her eyes, wiping her cheeks. She checked the clock. She'd only slept an hour. Shocking he'd allowed her that long. "You sound like my mother."

"I don't. Your mother would be far less kind."

Poppy didn't have a response to that. "What do you want?"

"To be entertained! To study magic! To figure out what makes this world turn and why it spins in different directions for different species."

"We aren't different species," Poppy muttered, throwing back her covers. She began to pace she was so full of jitters now. What would this mean? How much worse could the haunting get now that she was speaking with him?

Sleep wouldn't happen anytime soon. Deciding now was a good time for tea, Poppy went to the kitchen, shooting a longing look at Colbie's shut door. Poppy wished it was winter. The sun set later each day, and Poppy had no idea how late Colbie would sleep.

Poppy shook the tea leaves into her infuser. The poltergeist jerked her wrist upward. Poppy jumped back, watching the leaves scatter. He'd never touched her like that before. How was he *warm*?

"What is the *matter* with you?" she hissed.

"I can smell it now. Just a bit. You know your grandmother loved Earl Gray, too."

"I didn't know," Poppy said. She swept the dried leaves back into her palm, still too spell-spent to gather the light pieces with a simple cast.

"What did you mean, you aren't different species?" he asked.

Poppy frowned, biting her lower lip. Her mother hated Poppy's theories and studies. Her sisters sneered about how weird she was for questioning things. For not getting it like they did. Poppy learned early not to discuss magic as anything other than a divine power gifted by the Mother. A sacred right just for them, separate from the corrupt nature of vampires, werewolves, sorcerers, and whoever else was out there. Until she began studying demons, Tiff Jennings was as traditional a witch as they came. Poppy was more progressive. Where would a poltergeist fall?

Why did Poppy care? Reminding herself that she was proud of her new life and how she saw the world, Poppy briefly explained. "I learned from my classes in population ecology it is generally agreed that while most supernatural populations don't interact, it is believed we could. So, while behavior keeps us separate, we could still reproduce. Or, if not, because no one agrees on the working biology of vampires and they lean into the confusion so much that even my roommates won't give me a straight answer, likely a witch's child could become a vampire. Without the wards I have in place, it could be possible that *I* could be turned into a vampire, meaning I'm not so different from them or the humans they are capable of changing. Then, if I procreated with a werewolf, my children could potentially make the shift into wolves later. We don't know because there is no material to study, but if all that is possible, then we aren't different species."

"But, without proof, why wouldn't you go in the other direction?"

"Mostly, I like the idea that we aren't as different as our traditions make us out to be."

"So what *does* make you different? What is magic?"

"It's… well, I don't know exactly, but the patterns in which it spreads are more comparable to diseases or parasites than genetics. Likely, witches and wolves have a hereditary disease. Vampirism acts more like a parasite, but it could be spread similarly to STIs, too—"

"STIs?"

Poppy remembered suddenly she was talking to her grandfather. "Um, like, you know… fluids." She pushed on, cheeks hot. "And given *that* nature of magic, I think that means we're all the same species, just being influenced by magic, rather than all of us being inherently different because of the magic we wield."

The ghost blinked at Poppy like he'd never her before. "So, the different communities—"

"Populations."

"Is there a difference?"

"Well, communities, ecologically speaking, are made of multiple species."

"So the different populations—"

"Behaviorally isolated populations. Technically."

"Right… So the different *behaviorally isolated populations* are all just different strands of humans?"

"You can say it like that. That also allows for humans who possess some magic, mediums and "witchy" people, you know?"

"And ghosts are?"

Here, Poppy stumbled. She didn't think much about the forces behind the Sight because she lacked it. "Imprints? If magic is life and life is power, as is the belief in the witch community, then you must have had some magic or been influenced by it enough to copy you. Maybe seeing you is just a manifestation of my mother's magic or mine or my grandmother's. I can only think scientifically of how magic is spread and passed, but it leaves science when used. Like… AI. The implications of what computers can do following their initial coding are too many to guess."

"You've lost me."

"Well, get with the times."

"I would if you loosened your hold."

Poppy reared back. "I don't even want you here! What do you mean, my hold?"

"I mean, Penelope, that while you were so busy smothering me in any way you and your sister could, that also means you were keeping me *right here*."

"Then leave!"

"I can't just leave. I have to leave within the confines of your magic like an IA!"

Poppy blinked, confused before she realized he meant AI. "You can only go where I tell you?"

"Not really. More so, I can't go unless you loosen your grip."

"But I could tell you where to go?"

"Maybe. I can't guarantee I won't find loopholes and do my own thing." He looked proud of the fact.

"Then *why* would I let you go?"

"Because you aren't your mother. You are a free thinker. I admire that. Maybe you got that from me. You think men in my generation regularly sought out witches? You think many found one and married her? No. All I've ever wanted to do was taste magic. Learn it. Even now."

"Is that why you didn't pass on?"

He shrugged. "You think I know more than you do? Your grandmother kept me in the know just enough to intrigue me and keep making babies. Your mother was my only child who would preform magic for me, and soon, she used me in her own way, too. Neither explained what was happening or anything about the other… behavior populations."

"It's easier to call them supernaturals."

"Either way, I don't know anything about them. Just demons from watching your mother."

Poppy set her mug down hard on the counter. The biggest temptation when it had come to the poltergeist all these months was asking him about her mother's activities. She couldn't believe it had taken them this long to get on the topic. "How did she summon them?"

If possible, the poltergeist's cloudy white grew even whiter. He faded into his fear of the memories her question summoned. After a beat, he straightened. "I'll tell you if you loosen your hold."

Poppy raised an eyebrow. "Can I make you tell me?"

"I don't know, *can* you?" He wasn't correcting Poppy. He was testing her morals. He had heard more from her conversations with Ru than Poppy realized after her sister banished him.

"Where do you want to go? I can't let you go back to my mother. I don't trust her. Not after what she did to Topher."

"I won't. I just want out of your space. I want to breathe again. Why don't I figure out what Topher is doing? You keep staring at his room. I'll go find him."

Poppy blushed again. "What? Why would I want you to do that?"

The poltergeist shot her a knowing look. "You watch him. You ask him what he's up to. You don't like how your roommates leave you out of vampire business. You were happy to be in that basement last night. Happy to be included and leading today. Let me follow the boy for a night. I can tell you what he gets up to. Then you will know if they need your help."

"But…" How had he seen this secret desire? This desperation to keep her roommates safe and her frustration that they wouldn't let her. He knew just how to entice her.

To offer spying… It was wrong.

"They could be putting you and your sister at risk, Penelope. Do you truly trust them?"

"Of course I do!"

"Do you want to help them? Especially him. The poor boy acts like the world is crushing him."

Poppy sipped her tea, her hands unsteady. The thought was so *tempting.* She did want to help, but she couldn't as long as Topher kept her in the dark. She wanted to know how awful Lana was when no one else was around. She wanted to know what kept Topher so on edge. She wanted to know what people Colbie was dating. If the two of them were healing or giving into even less healthy habits. She wanted to know if Gabriel ever approached Topher anymore. That alpha had seemed too obsessed just to let things go like Topher claimed he had. Were Solas and Patter actually out of the picture, too?

If Poppy was going to risk going into business with Lana, she should know all the facts. Right?

Just then, Poppy felt Ru enter the wards she'd set around

the building. Her sister's aura brushing Poppy's was light and cheerful.

It was Poppy's job now to keep it that way.

"Fine. Tonight, follow Topher. Don't lie to me about what you find, and then, tomorrow, we'll talk about my mom."

The poltergeist clapped soundlessly, practically cackling with glee.

When Topher came home three hours later and wrapped Poppy in a tight hug, she almost called it off. But his expression darkened when he thought they weren't looking, and he only stayed long enough to ask Poppy for an update on the club wards as he readied for the night.

"What are your plans?" she asked him.

"Some Lana tasks. There's a lot to do to get ready for opening."

"Will you be more or less busy once the club is opened?" Ru asked.

"Unfortunately, Arugula, I have no idea."

Ru accepted the answer with a sad smile. All Poppy could see was the barrier in his expression, the secrets behind it. He was hiding things even after she'd put herself at risk and agreed to work with Lana. She deserved to know, to help, and to be a part of this supernatural nightlife.

When Topher left, Poppy nodded to the poltergeist looming in the corner. With a quirk of his lips, he slipped through the wall and followed Topher into the night unseen.

Topher's phone buzzed in his pocket. Zayn's name on the screen made his heart drop. Zayn should be off tonight. Colbie had lessons with Lana. Topher was in charge of the unclaimed and Lana's other tasks. Topher rarely heard from Zayn on nights like these, especially this early when Oliver was still awake.

"Hey," Topher attempted to keep his tone light, hoping it wasn't bad news.

"Hey, T." Zayn already sounded apologetic. Topher's heart dipped. "Sorry to do this to you, but Oliver and I were heading uptown to get drinks and I smelled some activity down east Thirty Sixth. Would you mind handling it?"

"Of course." Topher turned that way, picking up his speed. "Can't ruin date night."

"Thank you!" Oliver yelled into the phone.

"I owe you one," Zayn promised.

Topher snorted. They owed each other so much that it was useless to act like they were keeping track. "Have fun."

Topher hung up and focused on running, already working to separate himself from the business ahead. He reached the area Zayn described in ten minutes, knowing he was probably too late. Slowing, Topher tipped his head to smell, finding and following the sweet sulfuric tang that had alerted Zayn. It had been six days since Topher had caught the scent of one of these strange lowers, and Gabriel's pack reached the scene first that night, so Lana had them leave it alone. Tonight, Topher smelled no one else around. Zayn was the only one to pick up the trail.

Topher found the summoning circle quickly and bent to examine it. As usual, it was scorched into the concrete, nothing left but ash. He still ran his fingers through it and lifted them to his nose. Nothing but fire. Lana was convinced that one day, the sorcerer would leave behind something to identify them. Topher searched the area. In the last three findings, there had been no bodies around. They found that, on average, with every five unclaimed, a witch's corpse was also located nearby. That was typically how many times the sorcerer could pull from the witch's magic to create these monsters. Whatever they were.

There was nothing this time but the circle and the lingering chill surrounding it. Topher stood, rubbing his forearms. Now, he had to find the product of the summoning before it killed anyone. The change took about two hours to fully set in after the ceremony. They had yet to find a way to reverse the effects, but at least within this timeframe, they could be reasonably sure the unclaimed wouldn't kill. The sun had relinquished its hold an hour ago. Topher still had time to track the monster before humanity was replaced with hunger.

He took in his surroundings. He was near a hospital. The summoning circle at the base of a parking structure, tucked in the shadows. Visiting hours had just ended he assumed. There were too many people and cars moving on the floors of concrete above him. Hopefully, the monster was hunkered down, hiding and denying its thirst with the last of its humanity.

Topher paced along the side of the structure, inhaling repeatedly until he found where the lower had jumped the wall. He pulled himself over, startling a worker in scrubs. Topher flashed them a small, sheepish smile. Enough to charm the worker into a startled, unsuspicious laugh. "You scared me."

"Sorry."

They waved his apology away and continued to their car with little prodding. Topher hugged the line of bumpers, following the scent up and up and up. Hunger pulled at his stomach, reminding him he hadn't fed yet tonight. So, Topher switched gears, ignoring the dread that built in the back of his throat. These unclaimed were at their strongest after their first feed. If Topher was too late, he'd need strength to take it down.

It was even more complicated than usual, finding a victim to feed off of in a hospital parking garage. Everyone here either gave themselves entirely to helping the sick and injured, were the sick and injured, or were worried about their sick and injured loved one. In the end, Topher found a woman on the phone, claiming everything went well and a person named David would come home tomorrow. He still felt horrible choosing her, but better than the others.

As soon as she hung up, Topher gave her a look that made her head tilt. He grabbed her wrist instead and quickly swallowed a few gulps of hot, crisp blood. His stomach begged for more, but Topher stopped himself from drinking his fill.

When he straightened, she smiled at him. "I didn't even realize how tense I still was."

"Don't drive for awhile," he said.

"I'm going to nap in my car." She went that way, climbing into the backseat. With Topher's saliva in her system, she wouldn't even wake up sore from the cramped space. Topher turned once the door shut behind her. He was being watched.

The young man stood stiffly, shoulders hunched, arms hanging low. "You made that look so easy. I… I want—"

"No." Topher stepped forward. The man, the creature, shied back. Topher wasn't too late. He hadn't fed yet. "You don't get to kill. What happened to you?"

The man's head tilted, intrigued by the charm in Topher's voice. "What do you mean?"

"Who changed you?"

And there was that exhausting block that Topher couldn't break. Their minds broke before he ever got past it. The lower took another step back. As Topher watched him, his dark skin grew ashy. His lips already tugging back to bare his teeth. His movements more jerky. Within an hour, he would be twitching. His eyes would sink in and turn a cloudy black. This was the last real conversation the man would have, and Topher was already losing him.

Topher remembered Mary from last winter. At that time, these creatures still appeared human. It was subtle mannerisms that gave them away. A quick lunge. A strange head tilt. The burning hunger in their unfocused eyes. That was why Topher was briefly convinced he was one of them at the beginning. But whatever or whoever was changing these humans had learned to make this process stronger. More and more, they leached out all traces of humanity. Soon, Lana predicted they would start making immediate demons. She theorized that was the ultimate goal. No need to wait for ghosts to give in to their corrupt craving for life.

As always, Topher hesitated. He had to believe there was a way to reverse this. To save the human inside.

"Are you going to stop me?" the creature asked, stumbling.

Topher nodded, sighing as he sank into a fighting stance. "I don't want to hurt you. Come with me, and I'll take you somewhere you won't hurt anyone."

"I want… I need her blood. I need…"

The man lunged, and Topher met him midair, their bodies colliding. They rolled, thudding against the woman's car. She let out a sleepy protest within. The sound of her voice drew the unclaimed's scattered attention. It was quick work subduing him after that distraction. Topher pinned him to the concrete floor.

Here, Topher paused, ignoring the creature thrashing beneath him. Usually, they hunted in pairs or with a member of Henry's pack nearby. They'd been trying to find a new unclaimed without the pack's help recently. Lana wanted to study one to see how quickly they deteriorated compared to those made months ago. This was the first they had found in two weeks with no one else alerted. Now, Topher had to somehow get him to the apartment by himself.

There wasn't a ride share or taxi service that deserved to risk their life to solve this for him. Topher glanced at the parked cars surrounding him, remembering lessons from the past. His first forays into crime. At this point, he couldn't remember which of Hunter's men showed him how to hijack a car. The adrenaline it had offered a teenage Topher was what it took to hook him into that life. So far from his suburban house and disassociated parents and sister preparing to leave him for college or modeling or whatever fell into the lap of beautiful, open-minded, and hopeful people like herself.

Maneuvering the lower, Topher tried to figure out how exactly he would keep hold of him while getting the door open. Another car pulled onto Topher's level and he froze. Zayn's scent reached Topher before he could really panic.

It was truly incredible how the tension and worry immediately drained from his body. Topher turned with a wry smile as Zayn parked and got out to help. "Sorry it took a second to drop Oliver off."

"You didn't have to ruin date night."

"I just left him with Poppy. I'll pick him back up after we get this taken care of. A what, thirty-minute delay? Not a big deal, T."

Topher flooded with warm gratitude for his friend. For the reminder he didn't have to do everything on his own. "I appreciate it."

They loaded the unclaimed into the back of Zayn's red Jeep, wrapping him with the ropes Zayn had just for this purpose. In far less time than it would have taken Topher on his own, they were driving uptown toward the river, past the warehouses, and into the lower-income neighborhood beyond where the apartments waited.

Zayn glanced back at the unclaimed when they stopped a red light. "Damn. They keep getting worse."

"They are."

"I think Josh was right."

Topher took a second to figure out what Zayn meant. "About renaming them?"

Zayn made a noise of agreement. "But, if we don't think they're a breed of vampires, what are they?"

"Isn't that the question. Closer to demons, maybe? According to Lana."

"Maybe. Nothing was left behind to explain how they're being made?"

"Nope. Just the usual."

"Corrupt magic and possibly demons… I guess we could go with something like the corrupted? Or the drainers? More what they do since we have no idea what they are."

"That's accurate. Since they've shown up, they've definitely drained my free time and energy."

"Drainers it is, then," Zayn said with a tense laugh. The stress of monitoring, feeding, and catching these creatures was wearing on him, too. Topher took out his phone to text Josh the suggestion as they pulled to a stop.

"How are we doing this?" Zayn asked, eyeing the building. It was so deceptively vacant and peaceful from the street level.

"I was wondering the same thing. We've never put two in a room before."

They glanced back at the drainer attempting to tug out of the ropes. Topher sighed. "Why don't I move two weaker ones together and see how they do with that?"

Zayn might have argued, but his phone started ringing. "That's probably Oliver."

"Answer it. I'll clear a room and be right back."

Topher got out of the Jeep. He let himself into the apartment building, ignoring the camera. He went to the first room on the right. Aside from Julia, this occupant was their oldest captive. It should be quick work to charm him into moving next door.

As soon as Topher opened the door, something felt wrong. Freezing in place, Topher tried to place it. The smell was off—more the sweetness of rot than the cringe of sulfur. Not surprising as this shift had been happening gradually, but it was more noticeable today. With a gut roll of dread, Topher ventured deeper into the space, checking dark corners for the drainer to be crouched, ready to pounce.

Nothing.

Topher rounded the couch and stopped short. It was the stillness. That was what was off, even more than the smell. Staring at the unmoving drainer that looked more like a demon than ever, Topher couldn't breathe. Edging closer, he nudged it with his foot. Still no movement.

It was dead.

With a tug of horror so strong that Topher's vision swam, he ran out of the apartment and up the stairs to Julia's unit, scrambling to open the door. She turned with hungry anticipation at his arrival. Topher didn't think. He darted up to her and wrapped her in a hug. She felt feverishly hot. Papery skin and bones. Alive.

Julia hissed and clamped her teeth on his shoulder. Topher ripped her off. They stood staring at each other for a beat, her glancing past him to the open door. Fueled with adrenaline, Topher's charm snapped out like a whip. "Tell me how to help you. I need to save you, Jules."

Her response was screeched. "LET ME FEED!"

"I can't! I can't let you kill! Tell me how you were changed, and I'll—"

Julia dashed for the open door. The sound Topher let out could only be described as a sob. Tearless and hopeless, he caught her around the middle and threw her onto the couch. She sat, breathing hard and scowling. Her yellowed teeth bared, gums a blackish gray. She was dying, too. She was the oldest drainer they had.

Julia would be next.

And Topher slipped beyond feeling. He hadn't disappeared like this in weeks, not since he'd had to feed and become more open with Colbie. In the following hazy minutes, he fed Julia and the other drainers then went out to help Zayn move the new one in.

"You figure out how to make them all fit?" Zayn asked.

"Yes. We won't have a problem there."

Zayn looked at Topher sharply, catching the flat tone.

Topher only shook his head so Zayn ran inside and came out withdrawn. "We'll save her. We'll figure this out."

"You don't know that."

"Maybe if we…" Zayn fell quiet. He didn't have any more idea what to do than Topher. "We still have time, T."

"I don't think Julia does."

CHAPTER 10

It took Nora two hours to sleep off the effects of sharing her power. She woke more hopeful than she had been in weeks. As Nora stretched, the soft pleasure of accomplishment fizzed in her chest. She'd *done* something today. Nora had acted like a supernatural. Like an alpha. Like someone who wanted and made moves to get what they deserved.

Because of the strength Nora lent, when Annaliese was in the Alpha's Den, she would be protected. If Colbie ever chose to spend her days sleeping there, she would not burn like Lana's last lowers. Poppy said the building was probably as safe as her childhood coven, and their home wards had been woven with the power of eight witches.

Nora had done that. Broken tradition and boundaries and — "Shit!" The warm feelings vanished as Nora caught sight of the time. She had to be the restaurant in five minutes for her first bartending shift.

Annaliese watched Nora fly through the apartment, amused. Nora waved as she left, no words spoken between them. Not that they needed to say much this far into their friendship. Annaliese knew exactly what was happening.

Still blinking sleep from her eyes, Nora ran to work and, for the first time, really considered not showing up. Tim had pressed the importance of keeping a job for Nora's resume, and she still had her portion of the rent to cover, but after all the power she'd expelled today, the idea of serving humans greasy burgers sat like a rock in Nora's stomach.

Adriana's words from so long again ground in Nora's memory. *"Some like to keep wolves as pets. You a tame pet, Nor?"*

After today, she didn't feel content to blend in. After today, she felt her potential. Had tasted it and watched her strength flash with blue magic. She'd publicly declared her den. She should be there.

After feeling like an alpha today, she wanted to act like one.

The bell jangled when Nora entered the burger joint. The stink of fry oil was cloying. Her manager stood at the host stand, glare in place. Nora could smell the power trip. It made the back of her neck itch. It made her want to bare her teeth.

"You're late, Nora. I'll have to write you up."

"That's fine." Three write-ups and she wouldn't have to come back here. She'd have burnt a bridge and disappointed Tim, but those consequences felt small.

Ricky watched with wide eyes as Nora strode past their manager, her chin high. "You good?" he asked, concerned. "You've never been late before. I was worried you wouldn't show."

He was genuinely rattled. Adrenaline spiked in his strange scent as he stepped in close, his side warming hers while she walked toward the bar. Not knowing what to make of his behavior, Nora forced a smile. Maybe she *would* miss something about this place. "I'm fine. Just lost track of time."

His shoulders relaxed. "Some of us are grabbing drinks tomorrow night. Want to join?"

"Maybe. I've had something come up that will make me pretty busy."

"What is it? I could help," Ricky offered, bright smile faltering.

Nora sensed his anxiety again and slowed, ignoring her manager's glare. "Are you okay, Ricky?"

He nodded too quickly. Nora didn't have time to press. She was summoned behind the bar and thrown into training. That night, when Nora finished up far later than she would have as a server, the hesitation to quit she had felt when Ricky approached her was gone. Nora pulled out her phone.

Lana answered on the second ring. "Morales. I was just admiring your contributions to the ward. This place reeks like wolf." Her tone made it sound like a good thing.

Goosebumps spread up Nora's arms. Why did that make her flush with pride? "It is my place to mark, right?"

"As much as mine."

Nora chewed her lip, trying to make her territorial self right with that. "I have a question about that."

"What is it? I'm about to meet with Colbie for her lessons. I don't have long."

The question slipped from Nora's mind. "Her lessons?"

"Yes. I need her as strong as possible before we open. All my darlings need to be in peak condition. She's getting there, but her charm needs work. What was your question?"

"I…" It came back, though Nora had a hard time ignoring the thought of Colbie refining her charm to use against humans. "I was wondering when I could expect to get paid. If it's time for me to quit my current job."

"Topher and I worked on paychecks last night. I can get you one for your work today, then I'm thinking biweekly. Plus tip out nightly."

"Nightly?"

"Well, at least until you have a pack to help you take rotations guarding the door. This is your den to protect, Morales. I expect you to be as involved as I am."

"My den." The words tasted sweet but empty. Nora knew what they were missing, but the idea of building a pack was as heartbreaking as it was daunting. "I'll be over later."

"Looking forward to it, darling. There's Colbie. I need to go." Lana hung up before Nora could say more, but the conversation felt unfinished. Before she'd fully made up her mind, Nora's feet turned in the direction of the new club. She paused long enough to text her manager that she wouldn't be back. Nora's days of serving burgers were over.

Nora approached the block where Alpha's Den was located. The new club was about halfway down the length of the river-walk that distinguished this bustling street. It was amazing how Nora already felt at home here. Maybe it was the smiling people. The aroma of potential. The pride flags and people of all genders holding hands.

Maybe it was just knowing she'd been invited.

Nora strolled down the sidewalk, peeking into shop windows and bars. Across the street, she spotted Colbie and Lana at a slight overlook on the riverwalk. Colbie rested against the rail, breathing hard and shaking her head. Lana pointed to a woman walking by. After a brief argument that Nora crossed the street to hear, Colbie set her shoulders and called out to the stranger. Inching closer and staying down-wind, Nora listened.

"Where are you heading?" Colbie asked, the sweetness of charm in her voice. So unlike how she usually spoke.

The woman paused, hesitating, but the charm drew out an answer. "I'm meeting someone."

Lana said something in Colbie's ear. Nora swallowed her rising feelings at the intimate communication. "Who?" Colbie asked.

There was a beat, and then the woman frowned, visibly shaking Colbie's charm off. "I have to go."

She hurried away, and Colbie sagged, rubbing her forehead.

"Pathetic. Remember what you're doing here— picking up

on their underlying feelings, emotions, and desires. Twisting the easiest available to get them to listen to you, and once you have that, morphing it to compliance. That woman was upset at someone else, likely the person she was going to meet. Why didn't you expand that? Make her too angry to meet with them and, therefore, happy to listen to you instead?"

"I was trying to suppress! You said to suppress feelings that wouldn't benefit my—"

"It works both ways! You just have to figure out what will bend them to your advantage. What were you trying to suppress?"

"Her wariness of strangers. But—"

"No. Of course it's not easy to dismiss someone's instincts. Going for raw, fleeting emotions is much easier. We're heightening or suppressing *those*. Go again. That man. Make him forget his plans."

Colbie crossed her arms, angling away from Lana. "I need a break."

"You've had a break for over a year. It's time to get to work. Now."

Colbie took a breath. Nora heard it shutter, and suddenly, she wasn't standing still anymore. In the next breath, she pulled Lana out of Colbie's face. "What's going on?" Nora barely recognized her own voice. The authority dripping in it was something she'd rarely accessed.

"Vampire shit," Colbie said, a sneer on her lips. But it was forced. She was too tired to put real venom in her expression.

Lana laughed, feasting on the drama as always.

Nora knew there was no reasoning with the maker. She kept her attention on Colbie. "You can't just charm people like this. It's dangerous."

"So do something about it. Why don't you drag me to Gabriel for breaking your rules? Join his pack like you so desperately want to?"

Nora stepped back, stung. Colbie's glare settled, but there

was more behind her narrowed eyes. Hurt and wariness wrapped Colbie's anger. Fear backed the way she was pressing on the bruise she knew Nora carried. Nora straightened. "Just… keep Gabriel out of this."

"Because you kept him out of you so well?"

"Colbie. I…" Nora stopped, shaking her head. There was so much she wanted to say, but not here. Not now. But… would she ever get a moment like this again? If she did, would the words come any easier? Maybe she should just *try*. Nora opened her mouth to start over, but Lana stepped forward, breaking their eye contact.

"If you want to align yourself with powerful supernaturals, you'll have to allow us to practice our gifts, Morales."

"I don't have to *allow* you to do anything that puts humans at risk."

Lana quirked an eyebrow. "So, what will you do then?"

There was that looming quiet again as Nora's words fled. Growing, growing. Memories threatened to fill it. Nora's skin itched. She wanted to run. Wanted to lash out. Wanted to step in closer to Colbie's side. Wanted everything she couldn't have.

Desperate to keep her composure as the longings piled, Nora said the first thing that finally came to mind. "Practice on me."

Colbie blinked. "What?"

"If you want to test your charm, practice on me."

Lana laughed, delighted. "Did you enjoy it so much last time? I *thought* you would come around to being happy Christopher freed you."

Nora winced, pain striking deep. "No. I didn't… I just—" Nora stopped and took a deep breath. "I would rather she practice on me than the humans."

Lana considered, eyes bouncing between the two of them. With a jerk of her head, she nodded. "Fine. Good. I'm too busy for this anyway. Practice until she seems ready to attack the nearest human, let her feed, and then go again. Have fun!"

Colbie protested, but Lana walked away as if she heard nothing. Nora hadn't intended for her offer to end in being left alone with Colbie. She stood frozen and even more tongue-tied as Colbie groaned at the sky, whirling away from Nora and resting her elbows against the railing that lined the riverwalk. Colbie tipped forward, over the water. It was such a familiar position that Nora was transported back to the rooftop of the Maker and the intensity of her feelings then. The inability to look away, to resist Colbie's charms.

"Um, do you want to start?"

"I don't want to do anything with you."

Nora shuffled her feet, the last of her confidence dissipating. "We have to try a little so Lana doesn't make you charm humans."

"Why wouldn't I want to charm humans?" Colbie asked. She was being difficult, but Nora understood her well enough to know Colbie had hated what she and Lana were doing. Nora knew Colbie used her charm but never to hurt. She fed and danced and bewitched, but every human eye she caught had already been staring. If charm was enhancing human emotions, Colbie would never have struggled to find someone who wanted her attention. She probably didn't even need the charm that came out when she fed. It was just instinct.

"Just... C'mon. It's easier not to fight." Nora winced. When she talked like that, she felt the memory of Matt's words when he tore her down. That was exactly what he was talking about. Nora was meek, afraid of confrontation, not a true alpha—

Colbie glared at Nora. "Why would I want to make this easy on you?"

"Fine. Don't. Make it easy on yourself."

Colbie sighed. Nora debated leaving. If Colbie wanted to work with Lana, what could she do about it? If Colbie wanted to practice on humans... well, Nora didn't trust Lana, but maybe she could trust that Colbie wouldn't hurt anyone.

And yet Nora found herself stuck. The streetlamps illuminated Colbie, setting her loose curls to golden light. Nora was as trapped as always by the crystal shade of Colbie's eyes. The wry, intriguing twist of her lips. Colbie's arms were wrapped tight around her middle, the cool night air off the river hitting her. Pushing away the urge to offer her sweatshirt, Nora recognized she'd been staring for too long. Gaze always traveling back as if on its own accord. Starved for the sight of Colbie.

How had she stayed away so long?

Nora knew the answer. By swallowing all the feeling. By burying the way she missed Colbie under the pain of losing her pack. By calling Matt instead of her and letting that hurt consume instead.

"Stop looking at me like that," Colbie finally said.

Nora dropped her eyes. The submissive gesture felt far less familiar than it used to. "Do you want to practice, or do you want me to go?"

"You'd really let me use my nasty little vampire gift on you?"

"Nothing about you is nasty." The words came out before Nora could check them. She definitely couldn't meet Colbie's eyes now. Not with the memory of their first kiss swimming in her head. Pressing Colbie up against the stall. The first touch of her addicting saliva. The smell of cleaner and toilets. Colbie biting her neck, Nora finding the courage to bite Colbie's. Being wild and free and centered all at once. *"I hate that our first kiss was in a public bathroom."*

"We're nasty. I love it."

The silence between them lasted long enough for the entirety of the memory to replay and for Nora to linger over her favorite moments. The touches that came after. With the pack gone and the possibility of getting them back basically a whisper of a hope, Nora could think of that time with less fear. With less conflict. She wasn't torn in two.

She lost the pack either way. But Colbie was right here.

Colbie straightened, facing Nora abruptly. Her brow furrowed in concentration. "Pick your nose," she said, forced charm lacing her voice.

Nora brushed it off. "Seriously?"

Colbie pushed on. "Do a cartwheel."

Nora crossed her arms. "Do better."

"Flash that guy."

Nora's expression cracked. Not from the force of Colbie's charm but from trying to fight a smile. Colbie purposefully quashed it. "Call Topher and apologize."

Nora wasn't expecting that. The hurt reared its head and brought defensiveness along with it. "Are you joking? He took everything from me."

"And where would you be if you'd killed him like you intended?" Colbie took a deep breath, hands clenched at her sides. "Call my brother and tell him you're sorry for everything your pack did to him."

Nora's hand twitched, but again, she brushed Colbie off. "That wasn't me. Try something else."

"Stop me from draining the next human who passes." Colbie didn't put any charm in her voice this time. Nora remembered Lana's light warning as Colbie's bloodlust took over. She hadn't been reading the signs, and Colbie had pushed too hard.

Colbie turned and ran, Nora helpless to follow.

CHAPTER 11

Luckily, Colbie didn't get far. Though she was much faster than Nora remembered. Nora lunged, grabbing Colbie around her waist before she could attack a cluster of humans. Colbie hissed, *actually hissed*, as Nora tugged her back. The group was talking so loudly they didn't even notice.

"I need it," Colbie moaned. "It hurts."

"I know." Adjusting her grip, Nora led Colbie, now breathing through her mouth and trying to control herself, across the street and into an alley. "Wait here. I'll be back in one minute. Just smell the trash so you don't kill anyone, okay?"

"Gross." But Colbie turned to the dumpster. Her entire body tensed, arms crossed tight. And Nora had never seen her like this. As she left the alley, she realized how fortunate she had been to be so attracted to Colbie, of all vampires. Nora had never seen her lose control. She'd never even hinted at coming close to this state. Even at the basement steps those weeks ago, she had passed by Annaliese and Oliver without a glance their way before moving to the humans on the stairs.

Nora stepped back onto the sidewalk. There was a bar next door with fogged windows. A late-night pizza joint on the other side. She didn't have a lot of time, not that she wanted to do this at all. It wasn't an easy decision, but in the end, she hoped what she was doing helped the most people in the short run. Two college-age women walked out of the bar, laughing. One said to the other, "I might have to go to the alley to puke after that tequila."

"Okay!" Her friend was all enthusiastic support.

Nora approached. "Hey! Can I ask you two for a favor?"

They paused, wary. Debating whether or not to keep walking. For the first time, Nora wished for charm and saw the value in it. But she also needed to test a theory.

"My friend is a vampire. She's really hungry, and we don't have time to get to Fourth and—"

"Ohmygod yes!" The potential puker nodded. Her friend's eyes lit up.

"I was just saying we should go to Blank Space next so we're not hungover tomorrow. This will save us the taxi fare."

Nora fought the urge to warn them against such actions. To tell them they shouldn't be so eager and list the dangers. But she needed this. Colbie needed this. And the women were willing. What more could Nora ask for? "Um, okay then."

Nora led them to Colbie, who, fortunately, seemed even more in control, though her smile dimmed when she smelled the women. "Tequila, Nora? Really?"

She didn't give Nora a chance to respond before stepping forward and pressing her lips, then fangs, into the first woman's neck.

Nora watched the woman's face instead of the far too seductive way Colbie was draped along her body. Her features went slack. Eyes sliding shut as she succumbed to Colbie's bliss. Not an ounce of hesitation. And despite Nora trying not to look, she noticed the woman's hand lift, pressing into Colbie's lower back and bringing their bodies even closer. She made an encouraging noise, urging Colbie on. To keep drinking? Or...?

Clearing her throat, Nora tugged at the woman's hand.

"That's good. Drink from both of them so you don't take too much."

With a giggle Nora was not expecting, Colbie released the first woman, licking the holes in her neck to heal them, and stepped into the next. This time, Nora didn't watch.

By the end, Nora couldn't tell who was more grateful. The now high, but not stumbling drunk women, or the fed and, Nora realized, very drunk vampire. Colbie giggled again as they walked off, watching them for too long. "You have great taste, Nora."

Nora couldn't think of anything to say to that. She moved to leave the alley, stopping in surprise when Colbie tripped after her, laughing again.

"God, they were wasted," she muttered. "I could not keep up with them."

Then, seemingly without thought, she slipped her arm into Nora's to steady herself. Nora's world finally settled. She pulled in a breath. This. *This* was the touch she'd been craving.

Nora marveled at the physical contact, so sweet and firm and grounding. It had been *weeks* since anyone so much as hugged her. But Nora also knew that wasn't entirely what this was. This wasn't affection. Even so, Colbie's touch had always been exquisite. It had always made Nora feel more. So much more.

And when Colbie dropped her head, resting her temple on Nora's shoulder, Nora held her breath and dared not jostle her. "I don't think I should practice charming anymore tonight. If Lana's mad, I'm telling her it's your fault for getting me drunk."

"I don't think I want Lana mad at me."

"I don't think Lana can get mad at you. She wants your name on the club too badly."

"Why me? Why doesn't she ask Henry?"

"Well, she hates Gabriel for one. Lana can hold a grudge like no one else and blames him more than anyone for what happened. Lana loved Grace, as weird as it may sound for her to be capable of such a feeling."

"Then why does she want me? I'm the one who killed him."

"Because she understands supernatural instinct. She feels for you, being shoved in a room on your first change when you should have had space to run under a full moon. She wouldn't have expected you to act differently than a wild wolf." Nora's heart raced the longer Colbie talked. Was this only how Lana felt? Or could Colbie…

"Gabriel did that to you. Gabriel has spoken out against vampires at every turn. He's been careless in his hunt for unclaimed, killing even claimed vampires and making more enemies in the last weeks. Not that they haven't been killing claimed all along. Poor Brady." Colbie tipped her head back, shooting a glance at Nora. Their faces were so close it took Nora a second to realize the significance of the look. That was what Nora had been doing when they met. Hunting for a vampire. All for Gabriel. Willing to kill.

Because of a lie.

They were walking past the pizza place. Still resting her head on Nora's shoulder, Colbie stared upward. The moon was bright and soothing. Colbie's grip tightened on Nora's arm. "Lana wants you because she thinks we're the future. Young people. She thinks if Morales's daughter can align herself with vampires and witches, it will be a bigger statement than anyone else could make. Henry is already open-minded, but he isn't an institution in the city like Morales. People expect him to leave as soon as things get too dicey. Lana wants you to build a pack and knows you aren't going anywhere. It'll be a pack like Henry's but younger and maybe less peacemaking. And also, your pack will know the city as well as Gabriel's. The opposite of him and a statement to the world that times are changing. Lana wants her name written in history. It's why she came to New Brecken.

It's why she changed. It's why she's so proud to have created Topher."

Colbie was drunk enough that Nora struggled to follow her quick, slurring words and line of thought. "Do you think she'll do it? Do you think this could work?"

"I know I'm drunk, and a big part of me wants to push you into the river right now, but look at us." Colbie straightened to gesture between them. "It's already working. As much as I swore to myself I wouldn't let it."

"You don't even want to be friends?" Nora asked. She tried for a smile.

"How the tables turned," Colbie said with her own half-hearted smile. Hope was a glorious burst in Nora's chest. "I think you know I've never wanted friendship with you, even when I asked for it."

"Colbs!"

Colbie twisted to answer the shout, grinning at Topher as he came upon them. She wasn't surprised, though Nora hadn't heard his approach. He held a hand out for Colbie. "Drunk?"

"Very." And Colbie left Nora for Topher, looking grateful. Nora's heart twisted, dimmed. "Take me home?"

"Of course." Topher didn't spare Nora a glance as he pulled Colbie under his arm, and they walked off, leaving her alone on the street.

But then, right before they rounded the corner, Colbie glanced back. Happiness exploded in Nora's cells. She knew what that look meant. Nora stepped as if to follow, but Josh pushed off the brick wall next to her. She hadn't even taken notice of his smell in the air or how he watched her. She'd been too fixated on Colbie.

"I called him," Josh admitted.

"Why?" Nora didn't know what would have happened if she'd had more time with a drunk Colbie, but she felt bereft without Colbie's presence beside her—the moment had been so fleeting. Already she craved more.

"Because you're going to hurt her again," Josh stated.

Nora glared at him. "You don't know that."

"I know plenty. If you want Colbie, really want her, you have to choose. And I mean *really* decide this is what you want. You have to give up on your old pack. Apologize for the harm you caused and step up to make things right. You have to give it thought, not just pounce on opportunities. You have to make her feel safe. Make her family feel safe with you. You can't just let Lana throw the two of you together. And for it to matter, you have to be in a place where you have something to offer Colbie aside from the wounds you're still licking."

An argument or protest or whine rose in Nora's throat. She swallowed. Threw her shoulders back and turned away.

Walking home, her hand itched to pull out her phone and call Matt. It was habit. Josh's admonishment reminded her of her once best friend. But Josh had talked like Nora was capable of making choices and standing firm. He looked at her like she was an alpha. Matt never would.

Josh made it sound like Nora had a chance to change things. She was terrified of that hope. But not reaching for her phone to call her old pack seemed like a good first step.

As soon as she found a shadowed corner, Nora stripped and let the change rip through her. Running through the city as a wolf for the first time, she smelled how many members of Henry's pack lined the street. More than she thought he had following him. More than he'd shown last March. Nora smelled the vibrant life of the humans. She smelled the potential and the power that lined this street. She knew it could be hers. If she chose it.

Colbie was quiet, never a good thing. Topher hadn't recovered enough from the dead drainer help to anyone on an emotional level. Maybe physical, though. A quick flare of charm allowed Topher to pull aside a sober human for Colbie to drink from and cut some of the alcohol effects. She smiled in thanks after but kept walking. Topher knew where she was going. Wincing, he stopped trying to make conversation as they continued, block after block. Finally, they began to slow from the quick pace Colbie set.

They passed a high school. It was brick with rusty red accents. Older and smaller than Topher remembered. Colbie stopped and faced it fully, curling her fingers in the chain-link that was twice as tall as she was but offered no proper protection from the likes of them.

"How many days do you think you actually attended?" Colbie asked.

The smirk that came over Topher's face felt foreign and familiar at the same time. It was how he used to smile. Being here reminded him of who he once was. The smile died. Reminded of Julia, too. "Oh, when I was a wet behind the ears freshman, I once attended a whole week without skipping."

"Why did you hate it so much?"

Topher leaned back against the fence. It rattled, the loudest noise in the night. Topher curled his shoulders as if to hide from the school behind him. From it all. The human life and the problems that ate at him now seemed as easy to brush off as ants. Why hadn't he just brushed them off? How could he never have imagined how much harder things would get?

"I hated the world, Colbie. I just wanted to escape it all."

"Did you ever feel like you had?"

Hands suddenly in need of a task, Topher pulled out the pack of cigarettes he kept in his back pocket. He lit up and inhaled long enough for Colbie to ask again. She hated unanswered questions. "Did you, Topher?"

He spoke out of the corner of his mouth, smoking trailing upward. "Yes. There were moments of escape. When the world slowed, and I could breathe."

Colbie examined Topher's profile. She grabbed his arm, trailing her fingers up his rose tattoo before pressing her nail into one of the small scars inside his elbow. "When you did this?"

"When I did that, I wasn't a human who needed to escape. I didn't even need to breathe. I was nothing but a heartbeat and it was wonderful, but not the escape I mean."

Colbie sighed and mirrored Topher's posture, the fence dipping under her weight. "You mean Dylan."

"I mean Dylan."

"Do you think you'll ever be happy like that again?"

That wasn't a question he could contemplate. Something occurred to Topher then. He breathed out a puff of smoke, letting his head fall back. "Colbie, do you think Nora is your Dylan?"

"If I were sober, I would say no."

It was the feeling of the hair rising on your arms, only Topher's hair no longer did that. His next breath was shaky around the cigarette. He couldn't think of a single thing to say. Dylan hurt. So, so badly. Topher didn't want Colbie to ever feel like he did now.

Colbie kept going, shuffling her feet restlessly. "Mom and Dad fucked each other up. They stayed together, but… the games. The plotting. The competition and just… they stayed together. Like they were stuck. I can't imagine either of them in love with someone else. Do you think that's our family? Do you think we fall once? And fall hard? And then it ruins us one way or another?"

"You aren't ruined, Colbie. You're too strong to let yourself be ruined."

"What about you?"

"Sometimes I think I was just born ruined."

"God, Topher." Colbie snatched the cigarette from his hand. "You give me secondhand embarrassment when you talk all emo like that."

His lips quirked. It was moments like these that he felt the healing. When Colbie could make him smile in the same conversation in which he'd said Dylan's name. "What else are little brothers for?"

"Giving me awesome night vision and sexy fangs."

And it was either feel sick to his stomach or laugh. It wasn't a full laugh, but the sound he made was enough to make Colbie grin again. She had said all the words to lighten the conversation, but it was as if she needed his permission to let the darkness ease off even a little.

But Topher's mood couldn't be shaken so easily. "Colbie, Zayn and I caught another unclaimed. We brought it to the apartment, and... the drainer in the first room was dead. They're dying. Julia's dying."

Colbie's hand trembled as she studied the cigarette. "Topher, I think we knew this was coming. Unless you're willing to let them kill, we can't sustain them on packets of blood. I've been preparing myself for the worst since she got changed. We might just have to face reality."

"It's not... okay. I..."

"I'm not saying it's okay!" Colbie's voice cracked with emotion. "*None* of this has *ever* been okay! I'm just saying it might be out of our hands. I'm saying, Topher, that you can't let this ruin you further because it isn't your fault!"

"It is! Who else could be blamed?"

"Who turned you? Who made you feel worthless all our lives until you went searching for validation from rotten people like Hunter? Who controls this fucked up world? Topher, you're a victim here as much as Julia. As much as Dylan. The only reason you think you aren't is because you're surviving."

Topher's entire being rejected her words, but he could never argue with Colbie. They stood, side by side, until the worst of the feeling passed. Until the cigarette had burned nearly to the filter, and they were breathing steadily, drawing comfort from each other.

"Maybe we'll figure something out, or maybe Julia has been gone for weeks." Colbie handed him back the cigarette, talking through a stream of rolling smoke. "I want to go see it. Will you come with me?"

"Do you go there a lot?"

"Sometimes. Not a lot."

Topher's hesitation was the amount of time he needed to decide if he could handle more hurt tonight. "Sure, I'll come." As long as Colbie stayed close, he could take anything.

They pushed off the fence and started off again, both knowing this path intimately. Colbie linked their arms as they took Reynolds and found Havings Loop. There, at the end of the cul-de-sac of trimmed green lawns and white picket fences, was the world that had smothered Topher for years. The world that pressed Colbie so small.

A tall blue house with the bright yellow trim their mom painted when she was angry with their father and knew he'd hate the color. A place with smears of black on the light gray concrete drive where they had used magnifying glasses to burn homework. A house with a tree standing guard next to it. The tree Topher had once climbed to get into Colbie's window and attempt to drink the life out of her. Only stopping at the last minute, when rather than screaming or fighting him off, she had reached to squeeze his hand.

She did so now as they stopped at the end of the drive. Their parent's matching cars were parked side by side. Black his and hers Volvos.

"Cringe," Colbie said, grimacing at the new license plates.

"And you think *I'm* embarrassing. At least people thought I was cool."

"You aren't dead, Topher. If you went on social media or even just walk around here when people are out, they would all think it was super cool that you are what we are."

"Not that many people want to be vampires."

"Maybe, but they'd all want to be you if they were."

"Have you? Been on social media, I mean?"

Colbie shrugged, pulling at her flannel. "No. I didn't have

real friends, you know that. I wasn't all that happy with life here, either."

"You were popular."

"I barely ate to stay thin enough to be beautiful enough to be popular enough for anyone to notice me. For *them* to notice me." Colbie jerked her chin in the direction of the matching plates.

"They never did, did they? Either of us, with our opposite attempts."

"No. They got their golden child. Why would they need us?"

Topher wanted to retreat from this turn in the conversation. He wanted to run from this house and the choke of memories. He wanted to run inside and charm their parents into forgetting everything about him and Colbie. He wanted to charm them into loving them.

It felt like he was actively practicing bravery when he asked, "Have you talked to him?"

"No. I'm pretty sure they all think we're dead. Those first few weeks after the change, he used to call. He left voicemails and asked where we were."

"Asked where *you* were," Topher said. No doubt their family blamed Topher for Colbie's disappearance. *He* never got the phone calls. "Why didn't you answer?"

"It felt too hard. Too painful. Then my phone stopped working, and we had to get new ones. Now, I'm scared to face how I left him to worry. I don't even want to see what it did or didn't do to Mom and Dad. With our lives now, it seems safer to keep them separate."

"I agree."

"Of course you do." Colbie squeezed his arm and turned him from the house. The reality of Julia's situation right there. "Things will get better, Toph. For us and New Brecken, once we figure out what's happening. We'll grieve and have dark days, but one day, we'll be happy."

"You think so?" Topher had a hard time imaging further than the next night he had to survive. When survival wasn't such an issue, Topher dreaded the time that would be left to grieve. A big part of Topher thought being Lana's second meant he'd never have to face what happened, but it kept creeping in, looming over him. In quiet moments. The knowledge that Dylan was gone gone gone. That Topher would never be human again. That he would always miss sunlight and the heat of Dylan's touch.

Now, Julia was following. Maybe they were poor lovers, but they *had* been best friends. As long as she was alive, there was still hope. The hope was in equal parts devastating and what kept him upright.

Topher had Poppy and Ru and Colbie and Oliver and Zayn. He had his people, no matter their magic. But he didn't know what to do with the fact that he would never have Dylan. That there was no hope there.

"Tell me how training is going," he told Colbie. He needed another distraction like he needed her to be happy with this life he'd thrust them into.

A motion light flicked on behind them, but neither checked to see if someone had set it off. They only quickened their steps, Colbie updating him quietly as they slipped into the shadows of night.

Once they reached the river, Topher stopped Colbie. The guarded look on her face meant she was equally unprepared to talk about the fact that they might have been seen.

"Lana wants me with her at the Alpha's Den for the day."

Colbie's lips dropped into a pout. "Again? Isn't it Zayn's day to stay with her?"

"He and Oliver are celebrating Oliver's last final being over."

"Fine. Go. Text me when you wake up. Be safe."

"I don't have much control over that."

Colbie frowned. "Poppy warded it today. You'll be fine, right?"

"I'm sure Poppy's working on it more today, and Raven will be around, watching the cameras. We'll be fine."

"I miss Poppy. These summer hours suck."

Topher licked his thumb and pressed it into the furrow of Colbie's brows. "Pick a different word."

Colbie swatted him away, releasing a laugh. Topher turned to go but Colbie caught him in a tight hug first. With her face pressed into his chest, she asked, "Do you ever think we'll go back inside? Do you think you'll ever want to try talking to them again?"

"If you ever decide you want to and you want me with you, I'll go."

"That doesn't answer my question."

"I don't know what I want these days." Topher shrugged, jostling his sister. "That's the best I have."

Colbie stepped back, nodding. "Can we talk about it more?"

"Of course. You can talk to me about anything. Including whatever happened with Nora earlier."

"Whatever did happen?" Colbie seemed to be asking herself more than Topher, so he stayed quiet.

The end of night was tugging at him. Dawn not far off. With reluctant goodbyes, the siblings separated. Topher answered his maker's summons. He didn't know what he wanted, but he was getting better at identifying what he didn't.

He didn't want to spend the day sleeping in Lana's bed.

CHAPTER 12

Poppy woke up far too aware someone was watching her. Regret was a nauseating weight filing the back of her mouth. Why had she given in? Why had she acknowledged him?

Fear of what he would report mirrored the fear that her roommates would discover her spying. When she opened her eyes, the poltergeist would tell her what he'd seen Topher doing the night before. Poppy would have so many questions answered. Shame made her reluctant to face her decision, but… she wanted to know.

Poppy sat up, missing the mornings when she woke to cuddles with Mouse, the sound of her roommates getting ready to sleep for the day, soft voices and soft light, and that gentle undertone of being *home*. So much warmer than the shadowy, cold presence of the dead.

He stood over her, smirking. "You won't believe what your boyfriend gets up to."

"He isn't my boyfriend."

"Do you wish he was?"

Sometimes. Not as much lately. Mostly when she felt the fluttering of her old crush, she remembered watching Dylan die. She remembered how bad she felt for conjuring that memory for all of them to watch. Yet, here she was, invading Topher's privacy again. "Tell me what happened last night."

The poltergeist did. Poppy's body sank into horror as he described the summoning circle, the capture of the unclaimed, and the small apartment building filled with the monsters wasting away. The one found dead. "It was awful. You should have seen it. I could barely stand to be in there. The girl in the last room… The boy must have known her before. Kept asking her to remember him and using his charm before he fed her. Seemed worried about her after finding the dead one."

"Why? How would he know one?"

The poltergeist shrugged. "He kept saying, 'Give me one memory, Jules.'"

A chill flooded so viscerally into Poppy's bones that her bottled blue lights flickered above her plants. The poltergeist had said the words in a perfect imitation of Topher's voice laced with charm. He had no way of knowing who Julia was. Poppy had barely thought about Topher's human ex-girlfriend with everything else happening. Not since she'd learned about Dylan.

And now… Julia was one of the unclaimed? When had she been attacked? How long had Topher been keeping her hidden, feeding her stale blood? Why hadn't he told her or Colbie—unless Colbie did know?

With a snap, Poppy summoned Colbie's phone. Emotion backed the spell, making it so she hardly had to focus on sliding it off Colbie's nightstand, across the floor, under Colbie's door, and then under Poppy's. She scooped it off the ground with a shaking hand and quickly put in Colbie's passcode.

It didn't work. Colbie— open, honest, brutal, and blunt Colbie, had changed it from 1111. She'd changed it from the passcode she knew Poppy knew. Unable to even name all the emotions pounding at her temples and swirling in her gut, Poppy tried a 1234. She tried Topher's birthday, Colbie's birthday, and even her own. She was running out of attempts. In a frustrated flare of magic, Poppy closed her eyes, drew from the pothos plant that was so long its vines draped over her ceiling, and used the Sight in an attempt to uncover the code. Two bulbs of blue light burst, and dead leaves rained, but Poppy found the numbers imprinted on the device's physical memory from Oliver tapping them in. Did he know too? Teeth gritted, Poppy unlocked the phone.

Colbie's last screen was her messages to Zayn and the answer Poppy needed.

Zayn: *Is it my night or T's?*
    Colbie: *Topher is on feeding duty tonight. Have fun with O*
    Colbie: *As in Oliver. Not the other big O*
    Zayn: *Can't I have both?*
    Colbie: *I don't know, can you?*
    Zayn: *I'm about to find out*
    Colbie: *ewwwwwwwwww*

Poppy stared at the words. Clearly, Colbie, Zayn, and Topher had been doing this long enough to have a nightly routine. Clearly, Oliver knew if Zayn was in on it. Clearly, the vampires were blatantly keeping secrets and hiding this from Poppy. Right when she thought they were inviting her in. She was going to work with Lana for the Mother's sake. Poppy had been there last winter. She was supposed to be part of the group. Why would they hide what happened to Julia?

The reason Topher was taken to be killed by Nora crept in. They never found out who or what was making the unclaimed. Why would Topher hide this if he wasn't feeling guilty?

What if Gabriel had been right?

Squeezing her eyes shut, Poppy lowered the phone into her lap. She *trusted* Topher. Whatever this was, it wasn't that. He wasn't making the lowers. He would never. He'd found the circle. He hadn't made it.

But what else was he hiding? Poppy turned back to the poltergeist, voice flat when she asked, "Was that all?"

"After feeding those poor creatures, his phone rang. I wasn't close enough to hear the other person, but he hurried off toward Twenty-Fifth Street after. There, he found the girl vampire—"

"They do have names. That you know. It would be much less confusing if you just used them," Poppy snapped.

He rolled his clouded eyes. "There, he met with *Colbie*. She was hanging on the arm of that wolf gi— Nora. Topher collected his sister, and they appeared to be walking her drunkenness off. They stopped to talk outside a high school in the southeast part of town. Some sad stuff and about feeling like teenagers and the boy Tiff killed. They went on toward some houses and stopped to talk about their past lives at their childhood home. All very sentimental. I got the impression their parents weren't nice to them and their brother."

"Their *brother*?!"

"Well, they were very vague but mentioned a *he* that they aren't in touch with and feel is better off without them. At least, that's what I took away from the conversation." He shrugged like it was nothing. It wasn't nothing. It was another, huge secret. The West siblings never talked about their human lives.

They kept so much from her. Hidden lowers, Julia, a brother…

Poppy was speechless. The poltergeist filled her stunned quiet. "They ran back toward here but split up when Topher had to join Lana for the day. It appears they rotate who keeps her company, thought Topher stays with her more."

The bedroom door burst open, and Poppy jumped so hard she sent Colbie's phone clattering to the floor. With a lazy flick of her wrist, Ru banished the poltergeist, not noticing he and Poppy were talking. "What's wrong with you?" Ru asked, far too cheerful after the last few minutes. "You look like you've seen a ghost."

Laughing to herself, Ru gathered a change of clothes and went to shower off the smell of dogs, leaving Poppy alone with her darkening thoughts. At least Ru didn't know Poppy had acknowledged the poltergeist. She hadn't found out about the spying. With this new information and the secrets exposed, Poppy couldn't regret her actions.

She just had no idea where to go from here.

With her thoughts circling, it didn't take Poppy long to clear up the dead leaves, trim the pothos, and water it with a life brew. New vines were unfurled to replace the ones Poppy used to open Colbie's phone. That had been a lot of magic for Poppy to expel, and the day had just begun. She needed to be careful casting wards when she got to the Alpha's Den. Poppy's stomach dropped. That's where Topher was. Topher and Lana and all the secrets they held between them. Did Lana know about the third West sibling? Had Topher and Colbie managed to keep him hidden from the entire community?

Poppy paused and stared at the empty vial in her hand before shaking her head and dressing for the day.

Ru was still showering, and Poppy was reluctant to give her sister enough time to pick up that she was upset and ask questions. She also didn't want Ru to notice how quickly the poltergeist overcame Ru's banishment. He was already back in the room, spinning Poppy's brush around and around on her vanity.

Ignoring him, an easy task with him subdued now that he spent the night busy and had almost as much to contemplate as she did, Poppy quickly and carefully packed all the brews, chalks, and materials she would need today. She didn't even make coffee before hurrying out the door and successfully avoiding Ru. Doing the math as she got on her bike, Poppy figured she had enough money for coffee and breakfast at the vegan bakery, though she winced at the idea of splurging two days in a row. Then she remembered Josh paid yesterday, which led to her remembering their conversation, and her mood lightened just a touch.

Poppy stopped at a red light and watched the poltergeist gliding beside her. He glanced into the car beside her, shaking his head as he pulled it out of the windshield. "Black-out windows were a good call for that one. He's really digging for gold."

"I didn't need to know that," Poppy said.

He smirked. "It's always good to remember how human we all are. Even someone with enough money to buy that privacy acts like anyone else when he has it."

"I do not pick my nose."

"Penelope. I've been stuck to you for weeks."

Poppy felt the urge to gag. He was nearly always there, though she'd noticed early on he faded when she went toward the bathroom or moved to change. At least he had allowed her that much.

She changed the topic. "Will you tell me more about what my mother was doing?"

"Are you certain you want to know?"

The light turned green, and Poppy began peddling again instead of answering. Did she?

Eventually, she stopped between the Vegan Your Day and Alpha's Den. There was only the thrift store between the two buildings. As Poppy entered the café, the poltergeist seemed content to stand beside her instead of causing small acts of chaos. Apparently, curing his boredom truly rid him of his restless energy. For now.

Poppy approached the counter. The person working the register wasn't someone she had seen before. They had half their hair buzzed, the other half a sharp line down to their chin. They wore bright green glasses over their matte green eyes, somehow bringing *out* the color rather than making it clash. That was true magic. Their skin tone was bronze, their race as ambiguous as their gender.

Poppy ordered her usual. They nodded but seemed distracted and continually glanced behind Poppy, making her hair stand up. Coming to a decision, they glanced behind them into the bakery, and when they saw no one around, faced Poppy with an expression that made her stomach drop.

"My name is Jay. I don't want to make you uncomfortable." By now, Poppy was already flexing her wards to ensure no one was following her or about to attack. "But I'm a medium. Would you be open to a reading?"

Poppy relaxed. Jay saw the poltergeist, not a danger following her.

It was so… innocent. Compared to the world she lived in. Introductions and asking permission were acts of respect Poppy wasn't used to. "That's alright. I know he's here," she said, gesturing toward her grandfather. "Won't leave me alone."

Jay's dark, thick eyebrows rose. "You see him? He's haunting you?"

"Yeah, it's fine. I—" Poppy stopped herself before she admitted to the shoddy spell that had landed her in this position. Just because the human saw ghosts didn't mean they fully knew magic. Best keep the innocence intact.

"Would you like me to pass a message on to him?"

"I would love that," the poltergeist broke in far too gleefully. "Tell her she's wasting everyone's time going after her degree, but now that the school year is over, we need to focus on finding her mother and ridding the city of those demons. *That* should be the priority. Not this bullshit she's contemplating aligning herself with even more vam—"

Poppy swiped her hand at him, hissing, "Get out!"

The poltergeist wouldn't normally have listened, but Poppy reached into her bag. He watched her pack this morning and had been on the receiving end of her potions when she'd experimented how best to get rid of him. With an eye roll, he faded slightly, stepping back and falling silent. None of the potions worked, but they weren't pleasant.

Wincing, Poppy turned back to the human staring at her, mouth agape, the stud in their tongue on full display. "Sorry about that. He doesn't know what he's talking about."

"You can hear him… You talk to him… *Demons?*"

"Shit. It's nothing. Really. Please forget about it."

Jay recovered their facial expression, squinting at Poppy now. "What are you? Do you have the Sight?"

Poppy tilted her head. She knew humans possessed their own stories and methods of witchcraft. Being passed through birth, the witch bloodlines were blurred. Some humans had more magic in them than others. Was this someone who dappled, or was the emphasis they put on the word Sight a sign they knew more than most? "Do you?"

"Yeah. I train with a witch in town when she lets me in."

"A witch? Who?"

Jay clicked their tongue. "You can't just ask about the witches. They live in secret. Is it just that man that you see?"

Poppy nodded. Sometimes Ru, with her superior Sight, would find a ghost here and there, having to reinforce her wards so they weren't drawn to her power. Poppy didn't have that problem. Nothing was drawn to her scant magic. In fact, the poltergeist complained often about how much weaker he was now that he was tied to her. "Did the witch ever teach you how to get rid of them?"

Jay shook their head. "Never had a problem with one sticking around. I can try asking if she'll let me see her again soon."

"Please do."

An awkward silence, full of secrets and distrust, settled between them. Jay remembered themself first. "I'll just get started on your order."

Poppy nodded and backed away from the counter, relieved when another customer came in, and Jay yelled they would be right with them. Poppy sat at the nearest table, mind spinning yet again this morning. One of the biggest draws to helping Lana was access to other supernaturals and their knowledge. What if she didn't need to get in further with this side of New Brecken, though? Especially with ghosts, humans had been collecting knowledge for centuries *and* Poppy knew this one in particular was good with secrets. They had proven that by not exposing their witch friend. What if Poppy could ask Jay her questions or ask Jay to be the go-between and ask their witch friend?

The bell on the door rang again. "Poppy."

Poppy couldn't help but smile, relieved at the interruption from her thoughts. Annaliese wasn't smiling back, but it wasn't an unfriendly greeting. She dropped her small, bright purple backpack onto the chair opposite Poppy and went up to the counter as the other customer accepted their black coffee and left. "Hey, Jay."

Jay smiled, recovered from their strange conversation with Poppy. "Hey! Haven't seen you in a while. How are you?"

"Good. You?"

"Also good. Are you happy the semester is over?"

Annaliese shrugged. "You?" It was almost amusing how steady Annaliese's personality could be. Jay was likely someone she'd known far longer than she knew Poppy, yet the casual lack of enthusiasm was the same.

"I dropped out. Need to save up some money and do what's healthier for me."

"Probably smart. Is Taylor still in?"

"Yeah, she loves school. She'd never leave if she could afford to take classes the rest of her life."

Annaliese let out a small laugh, but it was clear she needed the coffee she hadn't ordered yet. "You two always did insist on being opposites."

Jay shrugged. They spotted Annaliese's bag next to Poppy. "You two friends?"

"Eh. At the moment, it seems."

Poppy snorted. "Shut up, or I won't bring you along today."

Annaliese gave a mock gasp of indignation. "You wouldn't dare."

"How do you two know each other?" Poppy asked. Were they close enough for Jay to loosen up their secrecy and tell Annaliese who the witch was?

"Annaliese and I go way back. We were in kindergarten together."

And once again, that familiar jealousy rose in Poppy's chest, taking her breath away in its sudden force. Besides Ru, there was no one in Poppy's life that she had known for a significant amount of time. She longed for friendships that stretched through time and growth. Consistency and *knowing*. Poppy couldn't even count on her sisters. They'd abandoned her without thought as soon as the wards fell. If Ru had the choice between staying with Poppy or their other siblings, Poppy couldn't be sure who Ru would pick. She didn't have people in her life that were just *there*. Annaliese, for all her grumpy and scratchy exterior, had people in this city who were her childhood and home. She was a great friend to Nora and, from Jay's ease, even to people she didn't know as well.

There was something about Annaliese that was so grounding. Her stony expressions alone were comforting in their reliability. Poppy would bet her plant collection that Annaliese was an earth sign. Annaliese kept friends. She made people comfortable. None of her grouchiness was taken personally, while Poppy fought the need to keep up her cheerful exterior for fear of rubbing people the wrong way and losing them.

Jay got busy making Annaliese's latte, Poppy's tea, and gathering the baked goods they ordered. Annaliese leaned sideways on the counter so she could face them both. "Nora dated

Poppy's roommate last winter. That's how we know each other."

Jay's brow pinched. "Nora? As in Nora Morales? I didn't think she ever dated."

"Yeah, it was a pretty rough first go."

Poppy snorted. "That's one way to put it."

"I guess I always thought she had a thing with that red-haired guy," Jay said, scratching at their memory.

"Matt? No way. Well, I think he might have had feelings for her, but they grew up so close that Nora considered him more of a brother."

Jay wiggled their eyebrows. "I'll have to tell Taylor he's still around and single."

Annaliese widened her eyes. "I wouldn't. Nora was messy trying to date. I can't imagine how bad Matt would be at it."

It was shocking, all that was left unsaid, but also seeing how easily werewolves fit into human lives. Matt and Nora were known in this city just like Annaliese. Would it have been possible for Poppy and her sisters to integrate if their mother hadn't been so wary of humans? Witches showed more signs of magic at a young age, but that wasn't something Poppy struggled with, unlike Ru, who glowed until she was four and learned to dim it. But maybe Poppy could have had these friendships. It was another thing her mother had taken from her.

"So, how well do you know each other?" Jay finally asked, nodding between Annaliese and Poppy and then, for Poppy, flicking their eyes significantly toward the ghost.

"Not *that* well," Poppy said in response to the unspoken.

Jay looked disappointed but nodded. No more talk of hauntings for the moment. They set the goods on the counter, and Annaliese took them. "I'm sure we'll be back a lot," Annaliese said. "We just got a job a couple doors down at a new club opening up."

Jay's eyebrows rose. They had an incredibly expressive face. "My boss said it was supposed to be a speakeasy?"

Annaliese nodded. "Nora's working there too."

"I've heard lots of rumors about that place." Another glance at the poltergeist. "Fourth Street type of rumors."

Annaliese winked. "I guess you'll have to come by to find out."

Poppy stared at her human friend. "We better be going," she said, standing quickly and grabbing her things and Annaliese's arm, leaving her no choice but to follow. Jay's hasty goodbye was shut off by the closing door.

On the street, Annaliese yanked out of Poppy's grip as aggressively as one could while holding a coffee in each hand. "What was that?"

Fortunately, the street was fairly empty this early in the morning. No one, except the poltergeist, was nearby to hear Poppy. "You can't just go around telling people we're supernatural!"

"Why not? Isn't that Lana's goal? To be more open about it?"

"No! I can't... witches... Annaliese, it's dangerous to confirm the stories. Stories bring people in. Confirmation brings danger."

"And you're here to keep us all safe."

Poppy gaped at Annaliese, the protest painful in her throat. *Who's here to keep me safe?* But Poppy swallowed. Annaliese, hard as it was to accept, had a point. Without another word, Poppy led the way down the street, reaching into her pocket for her phone to call Raven. As Annaliese kindly reminded her, Poppy had a job to do.

Minutes later, Raven pushed the front door open, squinting at the sunlight. Raven was tall, almost as tall as Topher. Her hair was more orange than red, and she was dowsed in freckles. Her smile was easy when she opened the door in a hoodie and leggings. She seemed less exhausted today. A little less stressed. "We finished up construction last night. Everything is in place, but Lana said she's fine with it if you have to move things around."

"Okay."

"I'm going to head home if you're all set here. Call me if I need to come back and keep an eye on the place, but it would be ideal if you could have the wards done today. We have the first round of training for the bartenders tonight."

"I should be able to get it done. I can leave some of the smaller details for later."

"Great, just as long as Lana and Topher are safe upstairs." Worry pinched Raven's brow.

"They will be." Even if the thought made bile rise in Poppy's throat.

By the expression on Annaliese's face, she felt similarly about the sleeping arrangement.

Raven left, and the door closed, cutting out the noises of the wakening street outside. Poppy took a large drink of her tea. She and Annaliese looked at each other for a moment, Annaliese waiting to see where they would begin when a knock on the front door startled them both.

Josh stood outside, his arms full of three plants. Poppy smiled. Henry had offered to help pay for some of the greenery she would need when she realized her proportions wouldn't be enough. Hopefully, Josh had brought enough pots and soil. "More plants?" Annaliese asked.

"You have no idea," Poppy said as another pack member followed Josh inside. And another.

Josh set his monsteras off to the side. "We found most of what you had on the list. I seriously had no idea plants were so expensive."

Poppy nodded. "That's why we're mostly using what I already have. You got the pots and soil?"

"Danny's on his way in with them."

Without a word, the other pack members left. Daniel stuck

around, grinning at Poppy and Annaliese. "It's nice to be reunited. Is Nora coming?" he asked with apparent interest. The new alpha was big news in the wolf community.

"She might later. I snuck out while she was sleeping off her run from last night," Annalise said.

Poppy clapped, drawing the attention from Annaliese. "We have a lot to do today. Luckily, it's not a lot of casting, so if you are sticking around, you can help. I need someone to pot the propagations I have, someone to chalk all the entrances, as in door and window frames, and someone to help me get all these plants situated. I have lots of herb bundles to put above doors and things to burn, too."

"I'm not good with plants," Annaliese claimed immediately, even though she'd done fine planting yesterday. She was probably tired of digging in the dirt.

"Daniel should handle the propagations." Josh pushed his brother forward.

"You like plants?" Poppy asked.

Daniel blushed a little but nodded. "I've been dabbling in the last couple of years."

"We would still be stuck in that nursery if not for him," Josh laughed, sweetly proud as he wrapped an arm around Daniel's neck.

Poppy smiled and got Daniel set up. She picked up the newly purchased snake plant and philodendron and told the others to follow her. She wanted to get the top floor over with first so she wouldn't have to spend the day watching Topher and Lana sleep.

CHAPTER 13

Nora woke up with a jolt. The silence in the apartment betrayed Annaliese's absence. It was surprising that her roommate had left already, no doubt to join Poppy, and Nora hadn't woken up from the noise.

But Nora had been immersed in her dream. One of the first she'd had since changing that wasn't a nightmare, though it wasn't exactly happy either. It featured Colbie. Heavily.

Colbie's hands and teeth and lips and weight. Part of Nora wanted to rush off and make sure Annaliese wasn't inexorably entrenching herself into supernatural matters, but a much larger part was still warm and buzzing. So Nora lay still for just a little longer. She felt the heat in her core and softening of her body, and it was so good. Better than she had felt for weeks.

Nora wasn't numb. How long had she gone without really letting herself feel? Nora knew grief and loss and fierce loyalty, but *this* was new. It was wanting. Wistful. Hope.

These feelings had been there last winter, but Nora had constantly shoved them aside. Over and over, telling herself it wasn't possible considering her pack. But the dream had woken it all back up, and Nora found she didn't want to stifle it this time.

After last night—after Josh told her what she would have to do, maybe there *was* hope.

And this meant she'd have to change.

It was a hot day, so Nora put her thick, black hair into a ponytail and dressed in a tank top and her favorite jean shorts. White sneakers and sunglasses on, she left the apartment. There was still a faint urgency to get to Annaliese, but Nora knew once she was surrounded by people, these butterflies and thoughts of Colbie, of that damn dream, would vanish. So Nora walked and let them linger until she reached Twenty-Fifth Street. Josh and his pack members had been around, though Josh and Daniel were the only two she could tell were in the Alpha's Den.

It was strange how their scents were hard to pick out. Poppy told her that other wolves or vampires would smell the marked territory, but no one else could smell who was inside the Alpha's Den at a given time. Nora was able to because she was woven into the wards, but even so, her ability was muted. The wards were working.

Even more incredibly, the plants the witch had planted yesterday were thriving. Nora didn't know plants, but she thought it was ivy or something like it already crawled up the brick wall, sticking to the building as if by magic itself. She stepped up and knocked on the front door. A very dirt-covered Daniel let her in. Nora felt the wards let her through, just like they had at Colbie's apartment. It was a comforting sensation. A welcoming. Safe and known.

"They all went upstairs. I'm potting some plants if you want to help me. Oliver said he'd join me, though, if you want to go see if Poppy needs you upstairs."

"Oliver is coming?"

"Yeah. Annaliese put on the group chat that we were meeting here today."

"Group chat?"

Daniel's face flashed with surprise. "Sorry. I thought you were on it. I'm sure she'll add you."

"Sure." But Nora knew why Annaliese hadn't. The same reason Annaliese had left today without waking her. And Nora knew she had to cut the crap with her protective instincts. She was pushing Annaliese away.

Stomach rolling with fresh worry, Nora took the stairs and found Annaliese, Poppy, and Josh shutting the door to the top-floor apartment behind them. Poppy seemed to be in a low mood, though Josh and Annaliese acted like nothing was amiss. In fact, Annaliese was laughing so hard that there were tears in her eyes.

"I just… I haven't seen someone do that since middle school."

"Well, Topher shouldn't have made himself such a target, sleeping on the couch like that. What was I supposed to do? Not draw on his face?"

Annaliese doubled over. Josh caught Nora's scent, spinning around with a smile. "Nora! You made it!"

Nora blinked, momentarily stunned by the pleased greeting, especially after his stern words the night before. "Um, hi. What's going on?"

By way of answer, Annaliese offered Nora her phone. A startled laugh left Nora immediately. Josh had taken a black marker to Topher's sleeping face. He now looked like every cartoon portrayal of Dracula. A heavy widow's peak, sideburns, uneven fangs on his chin, and then, to top it off, a little penis-shaped beauty mark under Topher's right eye.

"Damn. I want to be there to see him when he wakes up. Or see Lana's face."

Even Poppy, for her dark mood, giggled at that.

"I can't remember the last time I've laughed this much," Annaliese said, rubbing her cheeks as though they ached.

When everyone had caught their breath, Poppy pulled out a piece of bulky, green chalk. She handed it to Nora. "Any threshold or potential entrance needs to be marked completely."

Annaliese wiggled her own piece of chalk, already half-used. "It's almost less fun than planting bushes in the heat."

Poppy and Josh went to the lower level, discussing what plants they should bring up this time. Nora turned to Annaliese. "I think we should talk."

Annaliese stiffened, but she nodded as she went to the window at the end of the hall. As Annaliese began marking the base, Nora reached to get the top.

"I… I've been thinking I need to learn how one makes a pack."

Annaliese stepped back so she could study Nora's face. "You weren't sure yesterday. What changed?"

Nora fiddled with her chalk. The dust on her fingers tingled and smelled like salt, sage, and a few other scents Nora didn't recognize. "I saw Colbie last night and talked to Josh. I don't think I'm ready to try with her again, but I want to be the type of person who could. I want to move forward. I want to stop calling Matt every free second and feeling like if I lose you, I'll have lost the last thing tethering me to this earth. I need to focus on this to stop smothering you."

Annaliese nodded slowly, not nearly as relieved as Nora expected. "You understand that if you do this and build a pack, you can't just do it so you're better? You can't do it to make me happy or make Colbie notice you? The responsibility you'll accept is almost like… parenthood, but not. I just mean, it shouldn't be for you. You should be doing this for your future pack."

"I know. I get that. I want to make a place for people to feel accepted and loved. Like what I always imagined my pack would feel like. Can't it benefit me too?"

"Of course it will. I just want to make sure you're doing this for the right reasons. And that you understand the risk."

"I want to understand. Will you come with me if I meet with Henry?"

Annaliese squeezed Nora's arm, leaving dust and tingling magic. "Of course. When?"

"I'll ask Josh. And one more thing…"

"Yes?"

"Can I get on the group chat?"

Annaliese rolled her eyes. "You are. Where's your phone?"

Only then did Nora realize she hadn't taken it with her this morning. Her thoughts had been so consumed with Colbie and warmth that no part of her had reached for it to call Matt.

Unlike the last few weeks, tonight was strangely open for Topher and Colbie. Zayn had feeding duty. Lana was busy meeting with one of Grace's other seconds in secret. When Topher woke in the Alpha's Den by himself, he'd taken a minute to tour the building. Every room now had plants in the corner. Lines of chalk spells were fading into entrances. It smelled like humans, magic, and wolves. There were pizza boxes in one of the trash cans. All his friends had spent the day here, pouring their work into making this place safe. Making him safe.

The sensation that spread in Topher's chest was addictive and sweet. He went to the window to examine the chalk and caught a glimpse of himself. He started. Laughed. Then, like a dam had broken, laughed harder. He ran to the bathroom and was soon clutching his side as he sank against the door and down to the floor. He felt hysterical, but he couldn't remember the last time all this negative tension inside him had been released like this.

It felt like getting high.

Topher took out his phone, the warmth only burrowing deeper when he saw the new group chat and messages filling his screen. Through them, he could walk through the day his friends had spent without him. One of the more recent messages was of his sleeping face and the marker drawn on it.

Annaliese: *Josh is an *artist**

Josh: *I can't wait until he wakes up*

Colbie: *NO ONE TOLD ME VAMPIRES SHOW UP IN PICTURES DOES THIS MEAN I CAN STILL USE A MIRROR*

Poppy: *Sorry all, she woke up with way too much energy*

Colbie: *IS HE AWAKE YET????????*

Topher dropped his real fangs and took a selfie to send to the group chat.

Annaliese: *The double fangs make it even better*

And Topher smiled at the message until the cold press of the bathroom tile had him getting up. After vigorously scrubbing his face, he ran home. His feet kissed the pavement, and the moon sparkled off the river.

Colbie was cuddled up to Ru on the couch, and Poppy was in their kitchen area. She looked exhausted, her hair coming out of her braids and a smear of a mud-colored potion on her cheek. But that wasn't why their eyes caught and held. Topher could tell immediately something was off. Something bad. His good mood instantly vanished.

"What's up, Popsicle? Rhubarb?" he asked, pretending at casualness like it was a lifeline.

Ru laughed at the nickname. Poppy shrugged, her smile forced. "Not a lot."

Topher sat on one of the stools at the island, across from Poppy. She kept fiddling with the ingredients spread across the counter between them, unwilling to meet his eyes. Topher paid closer attention than usual, knowing it was a violation of privacy but needing some clue. Her heart and scent weren't reacting with attraction to his proximity. They were over the worst of that. So why was she being so weird?

Anxiety crawled at Topher's throat, and he fought the urge to reach for his cigarettes. "Seriously, Poppy, what's up?"

"Nothing!" The forced breeziness wasn't like Poppy.

By now, Ru and Colbie had fallen quiet on the couch, watching the two of them. Colbie spoke up, voice light like Poppy's. Mimicking the forced tone. "The vibes are not it right now, Popcorn."

Ru's eyes were wide and darted between them all. Topher hated to bring any conflict in front of her or Poppy after they'd experienced little security in their childhood home. Not that Topher was an expert, but this apartment was his safe place. He had to make sure everyone within it was okay. "What's going on?" he tried again. "You said it was just school making you distracted and stressed before. Now you seem even more worried, and from the way you won't meet my eyes, it feels like it has to do with me. Did Lana say something? Do you not want to work with us anymore? I can get you out. You just have to tell me what you need."

Poppy shook her head, voice still an octave too high. "I'm fine!"

Disappointment settled between Topher's shoulder blades. He glanced back at Colbie, and she shrugged to the question in his eyes. She had no idea why Poppy was being weird. Likely, Colbie had been too entertained by the group chat to notice.

"You don't want to talk about anything? Everything went okay today?"

"I. Am. Fine."

What could he do? Force her to talk to him? Topher stood. "Alright. I'm just going to shower."

No one said anything as he grabbed a change of clothes from his room. It was still silent as he went to the bathroom and turned on the water. Topher couldn't relax under the hot spray, so he kept his time there short. How quickly he went from laughing at Josh's antics to sinking back into the anxious, dread-filled dark. Topher dried off and dressed. The scene was much the same when he left the bathroom. Like an unwanted guest, Topher tried to slip back into his bedroom unnoticed, crouching to pet Mouse. When the cat was done with him, Topher stomped into his shoes.

Colbie straightened when he came back out. "Where are you going?"

Topher didn't know. He just couldn't be here. He searched for a lie, anything he'd been neglecting in the last few weeks. "Just going to see some people and feed. Check up on Rebecca and all of them."

Topher only glanced back long enough to see Colbie and Ru's eyes knit in similar expressions before he swept back out the door. So much for his night off to spend at home. He texted Rebecca and went to meet her, but his visit was quick. She was brimming with health and stories about her kids. It was enough to lighten Topher's mood briefly. She didn't even ask to be fed from; just hugged him and went on her way like it was old times. Like she didn't only agree to meet because of what he was.

Lost in thought, Topher found himself wandering back toward the river. How was it that Rebecca was done with his saliva when it had consumed Julia? Had he fed on his ex too often? What was different there? Were some people just more easily addicted to vampire saliva? But everyone he used to feed from had possessed self-proclaimed addictive personalities. Why had he ruined Jules and not them?

He started toward the drainer apartment building, thinking he might go see her. Check if she'd gotten any worse. But then Zayn texted an update, reporting no changes. No new information from the latest drainer either. Lana had arrived to question him.

Topher didn't want to see Lana, but he desperately didn't want to be alone tonight. Maybe he'd text Josh, although the wolf was probably sleeping off the day of helping build wards. He could call Colbie, but she deserved a night off at home. Plus, they'd talked about the heavy things last night. Topher wasn't eager to do so again. Colbie thought about the family they'd left behind more than he did, and the more they talked about it, the more certain he was that it was only a matter of time before she wanted to go home. Topher would give his left thumb to prolong that as long as possible.

Weeks ago, Topher would have gone to the Maker in this situation. Would have found the other lowers. They would have danced or played soccer or complained about Lana for hours. Topher pulsed with a fresh pang of grief. Even the lowers of other vampires were off the table. Topher avoided Fourth Street at all costs these days. He still had friends there, but they would follow the orders of their makers. They would report back every word he said and watch him close to catch him in any type of confession. Even after everything, the rumor lingered that Topher created the drainers.

Topher itched for a soccer game but wanted Poppy there, and she needed space. Sighing, he slowed to a stop at an empty park. His mind kept trying to derail, to slip into grief during this rare moment of solitude. The very reason he never let himself be alone. Bringing out his phone, Topher thought about calling Oliver, but he was starting a new job soon. He would be busy or sleeping. Another pang slipped in as Topher scrolled through his messages. Tamera. Sammy. Jaeger. Muscles, Brady…. All dead. And he missed them.

He missed so many. So much.

A name jumped out as Topher was beginning to accept the encroaching, lonely darkness. Without giving himself time to hesitate, he called the number.

Annaliese answered on the third ring. She didn't even sound surprised. "Hey, what's up?"

And Topher froze. There were so many things "up" that he couldn't pick one. "Um, I was just… I—" He cleared his throat. "Are you free? To hang out?" He barely got the words out.

"One second." Topher heard Annaliese's muffled voice and Nora's response. They went back and forth for a time,

Annaliese's voice growing sharper before Nora mumbled in assent. "Sorry. Nora and I were going to go meet with Henry. Want to join us?"

"Oh, sure." The wash of relief was so nice and cool that he didn't question it as his feet turned toward Henry's. "I can be there in five."

"Sounds perfect. See you soon."

Minutes later, Topher stood outside Henry's newly refurbished apartment building, wrinkling his nose at the smell of fresh paint, as Annaliese and Nora rounded the corner. Topher examined Nora closely, unable to stop thinking about how he'd found her and Colbie. He *knew* there was too much unsaid and unfinished between the two of them.

Nora smelled sour with nerves, rubbing her hands up and down her biceps as they approached, though Topher knew wolves rarely suffered from the cold. In her t-shirt, he could see the band of moons tattooed around her bicep. Would she keep that mark of the pack that was now Gabriel's? Would she claim it as her own since it started with her father? Topher looked down at his own tattoos. He didn't regret them, the smoking skull or the rose bush, but they meant so much less than they used to.

He opened his mouth to greet them when the door whooshed open, and the twins spilled out. "Topher!" Cora said, almost sounding happy to see him. "Here for Josh?"

"No. We were hoping to see Henry. Is he in?"

Cora narrowed her eyes at Annaliese and Nora, but her expression softened when she addressed Topher. "I'll just go ask him if he's free."

"I appreciate it."

The twins went back inside, leaving Topher, Annaliese, and Nora in a triangle. Nora broke the quiet. "They all know you?"

Topher shrugged. "I hang out with Josh here sometimes. Henry likes to ask me things about Fourth Street and my, um, vampire gifts. He's like Lana, studying all this, but with more experience and traveling. We're trying to figure out what made me so strong."

"What do you think it was?"

Dylan. But Topher was hiding from the grief. "Wrong place, wrong time. Or right place, right time, depending on who you ask."

Annaliese nodded, eyes clouding with sympathy. Nora hadn't been there to view the worst night of his life, so she looked confused. But she was also distracted. If she were in wolf form, her hackles would no doubt be raised. She kept sniffing the air of the other werewolf territory, head twisting so she didn't miss anything or anyone. Topher wondered if this was an alpha thing or a new wolf thing. Either way, it was good she was finally here. Finally asking someone besides Gabriel questions. At least, he assumed that was why they were here.

"It's not just Henry, though, is it?" Annaliese asked after a beat.

Topher raised an eyebrow. "What do you mean? I said I see Josh too."

"No. As in, you could probably get a meeting with anyone in the city like this. Just showing up and asking to talk."

"Well, maybe. Most people still don't entirely know what I am, but Lana has hinted and shown enough that they might out of fear. Or if I used her name. Even people who hate her still meet with her."

"Because of you?"

Topher fought the urge to squirm, skin crawling like it did whenever his strange abilities were the topic of conversation. "Why does it matter?"

"I'm trying to fully understand the power dynamics here. Lana thinks Nora is strong and wants to be on our side, but we don't know what will happen when push comes to shove. We don't know how much we can count on her. But, as far as I can tell, Lana's greatest source of influence and strength is *you*. And I feel like, if we're allies, until Nora figures out her pack situation, the same is true for us. This begs the question of whether Lana has your loyalty or we do. Because, like I said, you're where we can expect the most support. Then, given how Nora treated Colbie, we should be wary and try to get on your good side if we want to solidify our ability to count on you."

Topher didn't respond. The way he'd felt toward Annaliese since she told him they were friends wilted to yet another cold weight in his gut. Suddenly, he wanted to leave, but the door opened, and Josh's smile welcomed them inside. "Hey, y'all! Henry's free right now. I said I'd walk you up."

Nora gave a stiff nod. Topher let her and Annaliese go up first. He hated that what stopped him from slipping away into the shadows was knowing now that Nora and Annaliese would take it as a slight. A supernaturally political slight. A slight that would reflect poorly on Lana and might impact his maker's plans.

So Topher followed, feeling empty and distant. One of Lana's darlings, performing to keep peace. Making Nora and Annaliese happy so they didn't think he was disloyal.

He hadn't realized this was what Annaliese meant before when she said they were friends. He felt foolish for thinking otherwise.

CHAPTER 14

Josh led them upstairs to what might have been a penthouse in another apartment complex but appeared to be a shared office space and nap center. Huge dog beds and bean bag chairs dotted the floor, drawing a laugh from Annaliese. Daniel, in human form, looked up from the one he was lying on, his laptop open on the floor in front of him.

"Don't knock it until you try it," he said.

Josh bent to ruffle his brother's hair as they walked by. In the far corner of the room was a well-worn mahogany dining table. This was where Henry was seated in front of a laptop and a stack of papers. Quinn sat beside him, headphones in as she worked on her own computer.

Henry stood with a smile as they approached. "Hello! It's a pleasure to see you again, Nora. Christopher. And I'm sorry, I don't know you."

Annaliese offered her hand with easy confidence despite being up close with someone who was quickly becoming one of the most influential supernatural leaders in the city. "Annaliese."

"I've always loved that name."

Annaliese nodded as if this was a given.

Henry turned back to Nora. "You have some questions for me?"

The alpha gestured to the seats around the table. Topher could tell he was trying not to betray too much eagerness, but his eyes lit when he looked at Nora. There was a background here or a wolf thing that Topher was missing.

Nora sat. She glanced at Annaliese, and when her friend gave her a supportive nod, she started. "I do have questions, but I don't feel comfortable talking about my mom yet. I want to talk about being an alpha."

"That's fine. Any questions you have, I'm happy to do my best to answer."

Picking at the hole in her jeans, Nora nodded and gathered her thoughts. Everyone was quiet as if they feared spooking Nora from this new step. Even Quinn kept glancing over; curiosity and concern splashed across her features. Topher was aware of the other werewolves around them listening in. The entire room was still. The drone of the overworked AC in the window the only sound.

"How did everyone know I was an alpha?" Nora asked.

"We weren't sure. Before the change, many people show characteristics of alphas. It's a confidence, a faint scent, and a way of speaking. Even after the change, they can continue showing those characteristics, but because they are willingly under the charge of another alpha, those features get tamped down. To break out from under an alpha's wing, one must fight and gain control over the alpha and current pack, step up after the alpha's death, *or* have a strong enough will to peacefully break themselves from the alpha and begin an entirely new pack. This last option requires incredible strength and connection to their human mind and will, even in wolf form. Breaking the other alpha's control and ties to their pack takes almost total separation from the wolf's instincts. It is very rare, and you must possess incredible strength to have achieved it. Especially on your first change. That's unheard of."

Topher hid a wince when Nora shot a look his way. Few knew he'd charmed Nora into breaking out from under Gabriel's will. There was no telling what kind of fear Topher's charm had the potential to induce among the wolves. Not to mention anger. He didn't need to give Gabriel more cause to hate him, and if the alpha felt Topher had taken Nora from him… If Henry knew he was capable of breaking wolves from under his wing… The implications of this information getting out were disastrous.

"So, the alpha traits were there before I got out of Gabriel's influence? I couldn't be an alpha now if they weren't?" Luckily, Nora realized the risk of exposing what really happened and was playing along.

"Oh, yes. I'm assuming you and Gabriel had tension before that? Maybe his directions and orders rubbed you the wrong way? Perhaps you felt you could choose, on some level, to listen to him or found it easy to shake off orders? You probably asked more questions than most of your packmates?"

Nora's expression betrayed the cord that struck. "I wanted to be his beta. To rule next to him."

Henry's smile was crooked. "So did I. With my first alpha."

Nora's eyes widened. "You broke out like I did?"

"Yes. It took me more time and a lot of learning and practice, but that was how I became an alpha and started my pack."

"How? I mean, how did you start a pack?"

"Ah. I feel we're reaching the crux of the matter now." Henry's tone gentled as he leaned toward Nora. "It must be so hard for you. Dealing with this without fellow wolves at your side. You are fortunate to have your friends, but to be a werewolf is to possess magic, and our magic is meant to be shared. It can be overwhelming to carry the weight of it alone."

Nora looked down, blinking.

"Fortunately, you are in touch with your human side enough to bear it. It's been very impressive to see. If you didn't have the will it took to break out from under Gabriel, you likely would have gone deep into your wolf self in this loneliness. You may not have made it back."

Nora blinked harder now, the words touching a nerve. "Can someone make it back after that?"

"Someone like you, maybe. I haven't seen it. To be a wolf is much easier, as I'm sure you noticed. We flow as nature does down the path of least resistance in our wolf form. That's why so few balk at answering to an alpha, why we let the moon guide our changes, and why returning to human form brings back our intellectual side and makes emotion harder to bear. Those who don't change back are usually doing what is easiest to their nature. It's hard to fight nature as a wolf."

Nora pulled in a shaking breath. Annaliese watched her friend close, her brow furrowed. Nora shook off whatever she was feeling, sitting up straighter in her chair. "You didn't answer my question about building a pack."

"You're right. Let's see. How to explain." Henry sat back, rubbing his hands together as he considered. His eyes swept over the members of his pack surrounding him, fondness brimming in his gaze. "You grew up among many family members, right? The pack your father took over was premade and inherited?"

"Yes. Now, it's more people outside the Morales family, though. I only had my uncle and some cousins left."

"And where did the new members come from?"

Nora frowned. "I'm not sure. My father would always bring them in. He found them somehow. Gabriel hasn't brought in any new members."

"He may not have a knack for finding or drawing them. Some alphas are better at it than others." In his gray cardigan and surrounded by papers, Henry suddenly reminded Topher of a professor on TV. "You probably know werewolves, like witches, are born into their power. As it is a hereditary trait, few of us are born outside of an established pack. However, there are those random dalliances by uncaring wolves who consider humans inferior and don't stick around, but we can get into that later. There are anomalies: wolves born to human parents who have forgotten any werewolf ancestry or have had it purposefully left out of their histories. And then, there is the weakening of pack bonds when alphaship is changed. You say there are fewer family members of yours in Gabriel's current pack. Did some leave after your father's death?"

Nora blinked as if she'd never considered. "It was a big fight. They said when my," she stopped to clear her throat, eyes dropping, "when my father was killed, they died trying to protect him… but I thought I saw one of my aunts standing outside my school a few years ago. A month after it happened. Gabriel said I imagined it. That she was dead."

Henry nodded. "An alpha is never weaker than when they first break from another alpha. This makes it difficult to claim a pack. It takes so much power to slip out from under another alpha or fight the alpha that the bond they have with other pack members lessens. This moment when leadership shifts is when pack members can leave."

"And if they leave and don't find a new alpha, they can get stuck in wolf form?"

"Exactly. Or, if they are more in touch with their goals and human side, they may last a few months, even years, in their search for a new pack and an alpha to follow."

Nora's hands shook in her lap. Annaliese seemed to know her friend needed a moment and broke in. "So, an alpha building a pack finds people who don't have packs yet, like the ones with human parents, or wolves whose packs have recently changed leadership?"

"Yes. Or by challenging another alpha for their pack."

"That's not something she would be interested in right now. How does Nora find these alphaless people?"

"By paying close attention. Just like we learn instinctually to identify potential alphas, alphas can identify wolves without a pack. It is a certain… smell is the closest sense I can connect it to. Like an aura. A lostness. A searching that reaches out to me and hopefully Nora. They tend to gravitate toward us. I've had humans approach me without even knowing they were going to make the change. Two students just last week were watching me closely at the grocery store. My pack is so large that I wait and vet potential members. Packs aren't supposed to spread their magic too thin between members. So now, people need to actively choose and approach me, then I ask my pack if they want me to accept another member. But with how strong Nora is, those same people will likely shift their attention to her. They might have done so already, and she didn't know what to look for and missed them."

Nora appeared stunned. "It's that easy?"

"Nothing about this is easy. Once they've caught your notice, they will test you. Push your buttons and see if they can find safety in the boundaries you set. If you seem weak in your interactions with them, they won't feel secure and will move on to the next alpha. But we live in the only city in the US to legalize and promote supernatural living. Anyone desperate for a pack will likely try here first. I've seen many, and if Gabriel hasn't been accepting new members, they've been searching for a home for a long time. The problem, Nora, is you have to decide if and when you are ready for that responsibility. It's a huge undertaking to accept. Living in a pack is easier, financially and safety-wise, but you must be the rock, especially at the beginning. The peacemaker, the person who answers questions, the organizer. You're so young and new to this. Your very education on supernatural matters is severely lacking. But, somehow, you are sitting beside one of the strongest vampires ever seen. You have retained your childhood friendship with a human despite the change. You are aligned with Lana and know witches and all the other packs in the city. You had a great example of leadership in your father and family name. Maybe your aunt and others are *still* out there, searching for their alpha. If anyone your age can take this on, it's you."

Topher and Annaliese shared a shocked look, neither knowing what to do as Nora burst into tears.

Nora left the meeting in a daze. Topher and Annaliese watched her intently. Warily. Their mutual concern was almost as unnerving as everything Nora had just learned.

They walked a few blocks, Annaliese and Topher trailing Nora as she went to the river. Her phone buzzed, a needed distraction. Nora blinked in surprise at the message.

Ricky: *Nora! I heard you quit? What happened?*

Ricky had been so friendly and welcoming. She should have told him she was quitting instead of letting him find out through someone else, but the guilt was minimal with all her other emotions so heightened.

Nora: *Nothing bad! I had another opportunity come up and took it. Sorry I didn't tell you*

Ricky: *That's okay*

Ricky: *I'd still love to hang out sometime. Can we get drinks or coffee?*

Ricky: *Whenever you have time*

Nora frowned. Did Ricky actually want to be friends outside of work? Or more? She hadn't noticed any attraction or interest from him, but maybe she just hadn't been paying attention. Annaliese and Topher were watching Nora. She settled her expression and walked a bit faster.

Hoping he was only seeking friendship, Nora responded: *I should be able to get drinks. What night works best for you?*

Ricky texted her some options. With the club opening Saturday TK Tomorrow?, Nora didn't have much time. She promised to let him know when she got her new schedule as she came to the overlook on the river walk. The texting wasn't working. The repercussions of talking with Henry were breaking through the fog of feeling. Nora stared into the water, then back and down the street toward the Alpha's Den. If Henry was right, that was where her pack would likely come to find her. She'd marked the building, a signal to any wanting an alpha. That place… It was going to become her everything, and it was all tied up with Lana.

Topher followed her gaze and somehow read her thoughts. "Lana imagines you moving into the upper floors there. She wants you and your pack's protection during the day."

Annaliese laughed. "That's audacious. She trusts a werewolf pack not to attack her in her sleep?"

"Not when they owe her enough." There was something Topher wasn't saying.

Nora crossed her arms. "Like what? This is an equal partnership. What should I owe her?"

"The building. You protect it, we protect it, and we all profit from it, but she's the one who bought it with the insurance money from the fire. She came up with the idea and offered it to you. And she thinks you should feel grateful for her for—" Topher stumbled, dropping his eyes. "She thinks because she made me, you should feel grateful to *her* for your alphaship."

A dull roar in Nora's ears. "She thinks I'm grateful for how you ripped me from my family?"

Topher stayed quiet, but Nora couldn't let it drop. She wouldn't be dealing with any of this if it weren't for him. Her life would be stable. She'd be loved and taken care of. She'd be smothered and powerless, but still. It should have been her choice. "Well?"

"These are her words, Nora. I understand how complicated family can be. But Lana would say my actions freed you."

"Oh, fuck off."

Nora rolled her eyes and turned. Too quickly, Topher caught her arm. Nora yanked out of his grip but didn't move.

She refused to look at him as he spoke. "Gabriel lied to you. Over and over. Isn't some part of you at least hopeful now? You might have family out there that he was keeping away from you. That might have been your aunt you saw."

"I don't. They're dead. They would have approached me." But she'd *seen* Maria and her words felt like more of Gabriel's. It was all so much.

"They wouldn't have. It would have been risky. Gabriel could have challenged them, and for all he may do wrong, he's a very dangerous wolf."

"Gabriel lied about me having to kill a vampire to make the change. That was it. I don't think he lied about—"

"There wasn't a big fight."

"What?" Nora spun back to face him. The dull roar was getting louder. The urge to shift, to lunge at Topher's neck, was strong.

"Who told you there was a big fight when your dad died?"

"Gabriel! But he wouldn't lie about this! My family died! Reelings killed my dad and—" This time, the confusion on Topher's face cut off Nora's words.

His eyes flicked over Nora's shoulder, and his face dropped into an expressionless mask. Nora glanced behind her. Lana approached, and she'd heard everything.

"Your father killed Reelings, Morales. Not the other way around."

Silence. The roaring ceased. The information was too much. Whatever expression was on Nora's face, it must have been bad for Annaliese to step forward and put a hand on her arm.

"What do you mean?" Annaliese asked. "What happened?"

For once, Lana wasn't smug. Wasn't haughty. She met Nora's eyes and explained, "Grace told me what happened. He was there. Patter and Solas's stories match exactly. It was one of what felt like hundreds of meetings by that time. Grace,

Patter, and Solas had gotten the humans to agree to the laws, but the supernaturals were slower to decide. Reelings hated the thought of coming out of the shadows. He refused to comply with any system of checks and balances. He thought himself far above the humans and was disgusted by wolves and distrustful of witches. Ironic, seeing as the witches were the only ones on his side. But all the supernaturals would need to agree to follow and uphold the laws to get them passed. There was a split."

Lana paused. Nora had only vague memories of this time. There was fighting within the pack, and her father listening to everyone's opinion, stopping any bickering before it could escalate to physical blows. But he'd never told Nora where he fell in the conversation. The question burst out of her. "Who did my dad align with?"

Lana looked her straight in the eyes. "With the Big Three, darling. He wanted the supernatural legalized. His agreement to keep tabs on the vampires swayed the humans to agree to the laws."

Annaliese gasped. "He wanted the laws? But that would mean his pack would have to—"

"Stop killing us as an initiation?" Lana finished for her, nodding already. "He was a father now. A father with a daughter asking questions and only a few years from the change. A daughter who inspired him to think the world could be different. He didn't want her to feel she had to become a murderer to join her pack. He agreed to let the tradition go and succumb to the regulations the laws would set in hopes of making a better world. Grace admired him greatly for it. He was a father himself, you know."

Their silence was shocked. Lana kept going, earnest, despite speaking with Grace's killer. "He met with Grace regularly. I was in the process of appealing to Grace to change me. Since I was often around, I also talked with your father. He was trying to understand what fueled my desire to make the change. I told him about the illnesses in my family. I had genes that would kill me slowly like they did my mother. I told him about my vision of the future, Nora. He agreed with it.

"The next time they met, they cast the vote. Reelings was enraged his lowers had plotted against him and sided with the humans. Morales stepped between. He killed Reelings and freed the Big Three. The witches, Hall, Jennings, and others who refused to give their names, were angry. Soon after, your father was found dead. It appeared to be a vampire mauling, but all the vampires were under the Big Three and it wasn't by their order. We could never tell Gabriel who was responsible. But Topher floated the idea that it was something else. All these monsters, the unclaimed. What if they were a response to the laws? To the outing of our people and a pushback to the future? What if whoever made the monsters, the drainers, started with your father?"

"Why?" Nora whispered. "How could one unclaimed kill him?"

"That's the mystery we've been trying to solve. Where did these things come from? Who is summoning or making them? Why bring in demons, too? How did one manage to kill the strongest werewolf leader in the city? And where did all the other werewolf packs go?"

"This doesn't make any sense," Nora's voice was a weak whisper. The protest rose as quickly as it was being quashed. Her ingrained knowledge fought against this new view of the world and the biggest tragedy of her life. "Why should I trust you over Gabriel?"

"Go ask Solas. Ask Patter. Ask Jennings or Kallow or track down the other packs. Anyone at that meeting saw Morales kill Reelings and make way for this new future. The only person to say otherwise is Gabriel, a lower werewolf who had been on Reelings's side. He hadn't wanted the vampires to have any power; he wanted to hunt them freely. Strange how that would be what allied them."

Just like that, it was too much. Nora ran, ignoring Annaliese shouting at her back. Nora went to the alley and then the lot behind the Alpha's Den, the name mocking her. It was a strong name—a proclamation. Nora didn't deserve it, not now, at her weakest. Before she made the change, Nora called Matt, desperate for anyone to say what she'd just heard wasn't true.

When his voicemail picked up, she asked, "Is it true? Did Dad kill Reelings? Not the other way around?" Then she hung up and shifted to wolf in the next breath.

It was so much easier this way, but anger nipped at her heels, spurring her on as she ran through the crowded streets, shouting and awe in her wake. Nora followed the river out of the city, across the fields, into the park. All Nora wanted was her mother.

Of course, tonight, she wouldn't find her.

CHAPTER 15

Nora returned home beyond drained. When the door clicked shut behind her, she rested against it, letting her eyes slide closed and rubbing her forehead. She'd wanted to see her mother so badly. There was little way of knowing if Gabriel's story or the vampire's version of the events that led to her father's death were true, but at least what Henry said happened to her mother made perfect sense. Maybe if she could figure out how to get her mother to remember her human side or even just communicate on some level, Nora could find out the truth. Her mother wouldn't lie.

Had her father truly wanted peace among the supernaturals? A system of willing checks and balances? Would he approve of her alliance with Lana? What would he say about her being alpha? What would he say about Topher making her one?

It took a great deal of effort not to spiral into imagining what might have happened. Nora's grief when he died had been… consuming. Now, not even the closure she'd felt over knowing who killed him remained. It rocked her, bringing back the pain in fresh waves. Every ignored phone call from her pack now felt like confirmation of the story Topher had laid out. Nora wanted the truth, but there was no one she trusted enough to verify the events. Whichever way the story was told could benefit whoever was telling it and sway Nora to their side.

She was hurt. She was confused. None of her thoughts made sense. But… The possibility that Gabriel's lies went deeper than she'd previously imagined freed the weight in Nora's chest fighting desperately against the urge to find a new pack. *If* Topher was right and Gabriel had lied about this too, it removed the last wisps of hope she'd held that she might be accepted back into her family.

That she was still thinking in "ifs" meant there was still a tiny kindling, but maybe it was time to move forward as if there weren't.

"I can hear you thinking from here," Annaliese said.

Nora let out a yelp that sounded as if her throat had momentarily made the change to wolf. "I didn't see you!"

"For a second, I thought you fell asleep standing up," Annaliese said, that gentle tone that Nora hated and loved creeping in. Annaliese left the kitchen area and went to the couch with two mugs. She sat and patted the space next to her. "If you're already thinking so hard about all this, it'll help to talk it out."

Nora pushed off the door and toed out of her sneakers. She approached Annaliese cautiously enough that her friend rolled her eyes. "I'm not going anywhere, Nora."

Somehow, she'd known just what to say. Nora's shoulders dropped, and tears flooded her eyes. Annaliese held up the mug of coffee. Nora took it as she sat, and Annaliese waited for her to get through the majority of her tears until she could talk. "I didn't find my mom. I looked all night."

Annaliese nodded.

Nora hiccupped. "I've called Matt every day. Now I can't stop thinking about my d-dad and…"

And Annaliese waited. She stayed close, not shying from

Nora's sobs, face patient enough that Nora felt like screaming. She just wanted a hug. A pack. The weight of someone else's body pressed close. Warm or cold.

Instead, she sipped her coffee, the heat burning her throat and the act of swallowing pausing her gasping breaths. Eventually, the tears slowed enough to talk again. "I've been holding out hope of going back. I know you wouldn't approve, but…" Nora shrugged.

"But they're your family. That is your childhood home."

"Yeah."

"Is it under your name?"

Nora blinked. "What?"

"That was your dad's house, right? I've always wondered if you should have inherited it."

"I… don't know… probably not without my mom."

"What if you listed her as a missing person? Say she went on a hike and never came back?"

"Years later? Sounds suspicious."

"They don't know it's years later. Or maybe with the supernatural laws, you could explain that situation. Henry could vouch for you."

Nora shook her head. She couldn't think about this right now. "I don't want to challenge Gabriel. Not for the house or the pack. I like where we live now, and I don't want to fight."

"But we can't fit a whole pack here."

Nora rolled her eyes. "With my luck, I won't even be able to build one."

"But do you want to? Do you feel ready?"

Nora swirled her coffee, unable to meet Annaliese's eyes as she considered.

"Stop thinking so hard, Nora. You're half wolf. What does your gut say? Aren't you supposed to be all about instincts now?"

Nora studied Annaliese's bottomless dark eyes. Her friend believed in her, wanted her to do this, and was excited by the prospect of progress. "Yes. I want to start looking."

Annaliese smiled and reached over to shake Nora's shoulder. "Yes! Now, keep listening to your gut; where do we start?"

Relief was bliss. Nora should have expected Annaliese to want to be involved in this, but she hadn't. She'd been daunted by the idea of starting this on her own. Venturing into alphaship where everything rested on her shoulders alone. But Annaliese would be there for her in this, too. Suddenly, it didn't sound so intimidating a task.

"Henry said it was a… smell? Right?" There had been maybe too much information flying at Nora during that meeting. Thank god Annaliese had been there and could help Nora sort it through now.

"A smell," Annaliese confirmed. "Do I smell weird? Any latent wolves in my ancestry?"

Nora laughed, taking a big sniff. "Just human and coffee breath."

Annaliese mock pouted. "Damn."

"You hate when I go alpha on you. No way you're disappointed."

Laughing, Annaliese shot her double finger guns, exaggerated enough to make Nora smile again.

"Henry also said they would approach you, right? Kind of makes it seem too easy if you're just supposed to be smelling humans that come up to you."

A name itched in the back of Nora's mind, but she didn't know who the words reminded her of. She deflated. "I was honestly hoping for more actionable steps."

"It'll happen. Now that you're looking, I guarantee they'll be everywhere."

"I just… Annaliese, what if you're right?" As quickly as the hope consumed her, doubt rushed to meet it. "What if I'm not ready?"

Annaliese thought about it. After a beat, she sat up straight, setting down her mug. "If you want my opinion," she waited for Nora's nod, "I think what you lack most is knowledge, and I've had an idea. Something that will be good for both of us."

"What is it?"

"We've gotten all our supernatural information from the werewolves, vampires, and witches directly. This isn't necessarily bad, but they're biased and ingrained within each of their cultures. But I saw Jay the other day and have been texting with Oliver, and I think we have an untapped resource of knowledge. Less biased knowledge. Remember how Jay was really into witchy things? There's no way they haven't gotten more involved as more supernaturals come out of hiding. Oliver knows the most about what impact the vampires have on humans, and I know about wolves from watching you and the pack from the outside. We need to talk to *humans* to learn what cautions to have against each group. I want to know how *they* navigate those spaces because it's where I'll be, and then maybe you won't feel so desperate to protect me. And I think, if you're going to become a leader in this city, you should have their ear and perspective."

"What exactly do you have in mind?"

"A meeting of humans. Maybe I shouldn't even invite you, but considering you know as much as I do, I think you can be the exception. I'll call Jay and Oliver. Maybe we can meet for lunch or something. Maybe we even get Raven there or see if Jay knows more witchy humans."

Nora's nod was hesitant, but she trusted Annaliese, and this seemed a step better than being lied to by supernaturals who would benefit from her alliance. This was something she could do to make her a better leader when the time came.

This seemed like an idea Colbie would approve of.

"This actually feels right. In a wolfy, gut instinct way."

Annaliese's smile was one of the biggest Nora had recently seen on her friend's face. How had the conversation gone so quickly from helpless sobs to genuine grins? Hope. Having a plan. Doing something. Nora needed more of this in her life.

"Great. I'll go make some calls."

Annaliese needed this, too. She wanted to be involved, and she wanted to learn where she stood as a human. Where better to start than with the other humans in similar situations? It had to be better than her befriending supernaturals, right?

Annaliese and Nora set up at Hill's Brewing. The wooden picnic-style benches were almost full when they arrived early in the afternoon and claimed their spot. In a back corner, a blooming lilac bush brought out the lavender of Annaliese's inner braids and perfumed the air. Nora drank her first shandy too quickly. They might to be here for a while, and even with her higher tolerance, Nora needed to pace herself. But the beer was smooth, and she was nervous and still on edge from the talk with Henry.

Annaliese sipped a cider, taking in the patio. Brimming with panting dogs lying in the shadier areas, cornhole, and humans in sunglasses. "I feel like I need a pair of colorful sandals if we're going to keep hanging out in this neighborhood," Annaliese muttered.

"I need to break out my flannels. Who cares that it's eighty degrees?"

"Definitely not crunchy enough."

They shared a smile. No matter their joking, it was a comfortable place to sit. Someone had a Kallow For Governor shirt on. Another person sitting near the brick building had a worn Happenstance sticker on their colossal water bottle. The supernatural paraphernalia was sprinkled in as liberally as logos for queer bands, backcountry brands, and progressive political statements. Nora stared at the representation. When would she ever grow comfortable with any aspect of her personality enough to broadcast it? Even just a singer she enjoyed?

Maybe after she'd kept spending time in this neighborhood.

For a second, Nora let her mind drift. She could bring Colbie here. They could sit at a wooden table, and no one would give them a second glance. Colbie would fit in with the other white people, maybe wearing a—

Nora jolted from her reveling. She'd so quickly put Colbie here with her. So effortlessly slipped into thoughts of her. Nora's mind was usually more disciplined than that. The proximity to the vampires was ruining her control. The hope of building a new pack and family was infecting other aspects of her life.

But Nora had ruined her chances with Colbie. Daydreams and hope wouldn't change that and she needed to keep that in mind.

Fortunately, this was when Oliver showed up. In his Polo and short shorts and colorful sandals, it took a minute to distinguish him from the crowd.

He sat beside Annaliese, pulling her into a quick side hug. He looked good. Sun bronzed and better rested than last winter. "Sorry, I'm late. Your call woke me up. I'm about to switch over almost fully to evening shifts and let myself become another creature of the night."

Annaliese laughed and pressed briefly into Oliver's embrace. Nora blinked at the contact and Annaliese's ease. Was this something only Oliver brought out of her friend, or had Annaliese gotten less touchy about touch without Nora realizing?

"You're fine. Jay doesn't get off until two, so they need a minute to get over here."

"Oh, perfect. Are you going to explain what this is about yet?"

"No. I'm not going to explain it twice."

Oliver smiled, eyes slipping past Nora to take in the people walking by on the sidewalk. It was only then Nora realized how thoroughly he was hiding his discomfort. Discomfort at being around *her*. Had Annaliese warned him she would be here too?

Nora swallowed hard. "Oliver?"

He finally met her eyes, expression wary. "Nora?"

"I'm sorry. About what happened last winter. I'm sorry Zayn was caught up in it too."

His gaze dropped to the table. He hadn't picked up a beer before joining them. "I know it wasn't your fault. Gabriel put you there. But I also know you hurt Colbie. I know you abandoned Annaliese. I know Topher has trouble relaxing now. He flinches at loud noises and sticks close to Zayn whenever Lana makes them go higher than Seventh Street. None of this is your fault, but it started with you, and you left a world of ruin in your path and never glanced back when things were at their worst. Now, when everyone seems to be in the process of rebuilding, you've shown back up. Like I said, I know it wasn't your fault entirely. In a big way, you were a victim, too, so I'm trying to be fair. But I love my friends, so it's going to take me a while. I accept your apology, but I need to work at forgiving you. And if my boyfriend is ever at risk again because of you, it will take much more than a sorry."

Nora swallowed, her face burning. "That's... fair. It's not an excuse, but I was in a dark place for a long time. I feel like I'm coming out of it, but I don't really know who I am now. So I won't make any promises yet, but I want to be the type of person who could."

Oliver shrugged. "So be that person. Only you can decide how things go from now on. But I'm done lecturing and only being nice and forgiving now. Fake it til you make it and all that." He kicked her gently under the table. It was going to be okay between them. She'd never been that close with Oliver, but Nora knew she'd be lucky to have him as a friend.

"Here comes Jay," Annaliese said gently, like she could ease out the conflict from the conversation.

Nora watched Jay approach. She hadn't seen Jay since graduation, and the sensation of being a teenage outcast made a strange revival at the sight of them. Annaliese and Nora had been friends on the outskirts of typical high school society. Nora too animal. Annaliese refusing to give into the sunshine nature of their classmates. Then there was Jay, who could go between the groups but was loudly queer and highly interested in witchcraft, so they couldn't quite fit in either. Too many stories followed Jay regarding ghost sightings and casting ridiculous curses on classmates.

Jay had been branded the lover of supernatural and bullied for it while Nora stood right there, a hidden werewolf among them. High school was weird like that.

Now, Jay approached with a wide smile, primarily for Annaliese. Nora sighed. The standoffish attitude toward humans that her former pack ingrained in her had a lasting effect on all her relationships. Jay slid onto the bench beside Nora with their amber-colored beer, as confused as Oliver had over the subject of the meeting. They only gave Nora a brief greeting that she awkwardly returned. Annaliese straightened in her seat, taking control.

"Jay, this is our friend Oliver. Oliver, Jay. I invited you two because—and I'm going to leave it up to you both how much you explain your relationships—but because we all have a foot in the supernatural world, and I want to learn more about it in order to protect myself better."

Oliver raised an eyebrow, glancing at Jay, "And you didn't ask our *friends* because…?"

"Because, as much as I might like our *friends*, I want to know what it's like to be a human in closer relationships. My education, and Nora's, has been severely lacking in regarding other supernatural groups. I want to learn from people who aren't as biased and—" Annaliese cut off, raising an eyebrow. Nora glanced over her shoulder as she took a drink of her beer, choking when she saw Raven weaving through the tables, coming their way.

"I'd say I'm as biased as Zayn is," Oliver said. He followed their gaze and grinned. "And Raven's even worse. Hey Ray Ray! I didn't think you were coming."

"I swear to god, Oliver, if you keep calling me that..." Raven left any threat unsaid. She slid onto the bench next to him.

"You never responded," Annaliese said, "I didn't think you were coming."

"Well, I've got to keep an eye on Lana's allies, don't I?"

"You aren't here as Lana's assistant," Annaliese reminded her.

Raven shrugged. After a pause, Annaliese turned back to Oliver. "I think to me and Nora, learning about the vampires through your experiences will be more helpful than learning directly from vampires. Your perspective as a human means you've learned how to survive them. You've learned what to be wary of and seen their power compared to what humans can do. You two know better than anyone how vampires affect humans. I bet you know more about navigating their world as a non-vampire than any vampire does."

Oliver considered. "That's true. The less powerful always have to learn more about the, um, more powerful."

Raven patted his cheek. "So eloquent as always."

Oliver shoved her hard enough that Raven had to grab the table to avoid falling off the bench.

"And I'm here because?" Jay asked.

Annaliese raised an eyebrow. "Your Sight. Your involvement with witches. I know you're open about it. I just recognize now that I never told you I believed you. I did in school, and now I've seen way more. I want to know what magic humans are capable of and how you interact with the supernatural."

Jay appeared satisfied by that answer. "But I can't tell you anything about the witch I know."

"Oh, we know. Our witchy friend has given us the whole rundown," Oliver said. Without pausing to address Jay's apparent shock that they know a witch, he asked Annaliese, "So, what do you want to know?"

Annaliese sat up straighter. "I want to start with what will be more relevant for Nora."

Jay raised an eyebrow, and Nora sighed. It was time to come clean. "I'm a werewolf."

"Get the fuck out."

Nora knew it wasn't fair for Jay's shock to rub the way it did, but she felt her face heat and shoulders creep up. Yes, they'd known each other a long time, but the worry that Nora wasn't good enough to be alpha, let alone a werewolf, felt confirmed by the utter disbelief in Jay's eyes. "Well," was all Nora could say, shrugging.

"All this time, you let me ramble on trying to convince the two of you that the supernatural was real and you were changing into a wolf at night?"

"Not exactly. Yes, I lived in a pack and always knew what you were saying was true, but the first time I made the shift was last March. During that time, I learned how much my pack hid from me about other supernatural groups. Now I'm trying to get more information about them before I start my own pack."

Oliver looked... proud? Jay was still insultingly shocked. Raven appeared to be bored. Annaliese tried to get them back on track. "Oliver, what do you know about vampire abilities and how they work on werewolves?"

He considered the question for a beat before ticking the abilities off his fingers as he went through them. "As we know, for the *most* part, charm doesn't work on werewolves. For physical strength, a werewolf is probably stronger, but only in wolf form. In human form, I don't actually know how they compare. And, of course, that's depending on the vampire and werewolf. They're for sure stronger than humans. With senses, we know from last winter that wolves can't smell vampires. Wolves have more freedom, but they are still dependent on the time of day in a sense with the lunar movements, while vampires are affected by the sun."

"Can a vampire feed off a werewolf? Can a werewolf get blissed?"

Oliver squirmed. "Topher said…" he glanced at Nora, and she tried very, very hard to keep disgust from her face. "He said werewolves taste horrible, but when a certain someone took him, he fought back and got blood on his knuckles. He licked it off and thinks it helped sustain him just a bit. What do you think, Nora? Did you feel the spit?"

"Feel the spit," Jay repeated, laughing at how it sounded. Then, "Wait, how would you know what a vampire's spit feels like?"

Now, Nora shifted with discomfort. "I felt… a tingling when we kissed. A little lightheaded, but nothing too strong. Like maybe taking a shot of tequila level of a buzz."

Oliver was nodding. "I'd say I probably feel that more exaggerated when I kiss Zayn. Two mind erasers amount of buzz. I get all wobbly kneed and tongue-tied, though debatably that could just be Zayn." Raven scoffed, and Oliver grinned as he continued. "Sounds like maybe you could get blissed, but not to the extent humans do. I wonder what Topher's spit would do for you."

"Topher's spit would do nothing for me," Nora said, her face scrunching into a grimace at the thought.

Annaliese laughed. "I can't believe we didn't know you liked girls."

Jay's shock was more feigned this time. "You're a supernatural *and* gay? Why weren't we closer friends?"

Nora shrugged. "You just weren't cool enough."

Again, Annaliese doggedly kept them on track. "Jay, do you

talk with witches enough to know how their magic works on wolves?"

Poppy had been tight-lipped about it with Nora, but she knew Poppy's magic didn't work on her like it did everyone else.

"I know a little," Jay said. "Mostly, that magic has a hard time against vampires and werewolves. I've never seen a spirit that wasn't originally human, and I know witches have charms and wards to protect against vampire influence. The witch I talk with mostly just works with me on my abilities. We don't talk about what their magic is like. Let me try something, though." Jay reached into their bag and pulled out a set of worn tarot cards.

Nora had never let Jay do a reading on her in high school. They clearly intended to do one now. They expertly shuffled, cards stacking with a satisfying clatter of snaps. "May I?" they asked.

Feeling uneasy, Nora nodded. Jay fanned their cards face down on the wooden table. Oliver and Annaliese leaned forward with interest. Nora felt like running as far as she could get. Her past was so messy and raw. No way her future wouldn't also be. How embarrassing to have it spread out for everyone to see.

"We'll just check if this even works for you. No big deal."

Annaliese whispered in Nora's ear. "Poppy saw you in the tea leaves. And Josh."

Nora hadn't needed the reminder. It only made her more nervous that this would work.

"Run your fingers over the cards. Pick out the three that call you. They might feel warm, tingly, or softer than the others. You might get a buzz in your ear or a pull in your gut. Your heart might skip a beat. Just take your time and find the three that are yours."

"I thought people drew one?" Oliver asked, making Nora pause as she reached.

Jay shot him a glance. "It depends. For right now, we're going to do a three-card reading. Past, present, and future and Nora's going to pull them."

Nora did so now. It wasn't quite what Jay described. Nora ran her fingers over the deck a second and third time. Finally, sighing, she pulled out the three that felt cold and smooth.

Because of course they did.

"What do they say? What do they say?!" Oliver asked, almost standing to see them better and gripping Annaliese's arm excitedly. Even Annaliese was entertained by the whole situation.

Jay stacked the cards not in use. They set them aside and frowned at the three Nora had pulled, green eyes darting from one to the next. Nora didn't like the dark expression on their face.

"Um, the skeleton guy seems cheerful. That's not bad, right? They say the Death card isn't bad." Oliver did his best to sound upbeat.

"Not at all. The Death card is usually about change. This isn't the Death card, though. The eight goblets the skeleton is standing on make this the Eight of Cups. This card usually indicates it's time to move forward. That certain situations have been outgrown. It can be a call to break out of a comfort zone."

A weighted silence fell. Nora knew what Annaliese and Oliver were thinking. The pack. Gabriel. Her family. How Nora had left behind what used to make her comfortable. She hated to see the situation spun out like a positive occurrence, as if Nora had chosen this. It felt at once reductive of her grief and also like they were giving her too much credit.

"What does the next one mean?" Annaliese said quickly, likely feeling how Nora was pulling away from the situation.

"That's the Seven of Wands," Jay said. "It's one of my favorites, actually—the blues in the painting call to me. An interpretation of it calls for action. Taking a stand. Asserting yourself and doing what you believe to be right."

"Like working with Lana," Annaliese said.

Oliver clapped. "Or doing a grand gesture! Oh, wait, I forgot I'm on Colbie's side, sorry. We only encourage what she wants, and I don't know what she wants, so forget I said anything."

"Or making a pack," Nora murmured. That felt more accurate. To build a pack would show the entire city that Nora was a force to be reckoned with. The stance she took with a pack supporting her would be assertive, to say the least.

"And the last card?" Raven asked.

"The Tower," Jay said. They studied it for a moment, then shot Nora a sympathetic look. "It can be read a few ways, but generally means revolution. Taking down the old and finding a fresh start. Big changes that shouldn't be resisted. Razing the ground and building something new. If used correctly, enlightenment and peace can be found after."

"And incorrectly?"

Jay frowned, holding back. "Maybe you should pull another card. Just to help me get clarity."

"We're just doing this to see if the Sight works on wolves. I think we can say it does," Nora protested. She didn't like that Jay was hiding things. Suddenly, Nora didn't want to know the potential consequences of her choices. The ones she'd made in the past were already feeling bad enough, the regrets so fresh from the reading.

Annaliese quirked an eyebrow. "Just see, Nora. Try one more."

Annaliese's encouragement was all it took. Nora did as she said, slowly, goosebumps up and down her arms. She flipped the cold card, and they fell silent in the face of the dark colors.

"Oh," Oliver breathed. "*That* one is Death."

CHAPTER 16

Nora was four more beers in and finally getting comfortable at the brewery. They'd moved on to discussing the Alpha's Den. Raven had put a ton of work into the club and was all too happy to talk about it, only leaving when it was time for her to train the new bartenders. Jay was drunk enough to begin fantasizing about quitting their bakery job to work with them.

Oliver was laughing about it. "Go crash the training! I told Zayn I would quit my other job to bartend with him. He didn't like that."

"Why not?" Jay asked, more intrigued than anything else.

"It might be as protected as possible, but it's still Lana. Still welcoming of other vampires and supernaturals. He doesn't want me in the middle of it."

"So, it's not completely safe?"

Nora was tipsy enough to lift her chin. "We'll make it safe. *I'll* make it safe."

"There's that Eight of Cups talking!" Jay said, lifting a hand for a high five that Nora returned. This many beers in meant she felt much more optimistic about the reading.

"I'm thinking about bartending," Annaliese admitted.

Nora clenched her jaw to keep from saying anything about that. Especially right now. Oliver saved Nora from a potential fight. "Well, let's see how busy it gets first. Could be swamped, and then it'll be way more fun not to be stuck behind the bar."

Annaliese shrugged like this was a valid suggestion. "Do you want to leave the bakery?" she asked Jay.

"Not in the slightest, but the Den sounds exciting!"

Nora winced at the shortening of the name. The Den was her childhood home, not the club she would help run.

"Then why don't you just come to be a customer?" Oliver asked. His cheeks were flushed from drinking, his words slightly slurred. It was getting later, but the sun was at least an hour from setting. Oliver kept glancing from its progress to his watch as he waited for his boyfriend to wake up and lessen the alcohol's effects.

"That's a good point," Jay admitted, pointing at Oliver with the hand holding their beer and sloshing some on the wooden table.

Annaliese asked Oliver, "You are coming tomorrow night, right? You'll still be at the club even though Zayn doesn't want you working there?"

"Of course! I went to the Maker, didn't I? He just doesn't want me working there. We aren't on Fourth, so he's already happier about me being around this club. Plus, he's had to tone down his protectiveness since he was humbled last March. He has no right to act like I'm some fragile flower when he's the only one whose life has been in danger between the two of us."

Annaliese's laugh was too loud for the topic. Oliver grinned.

"I texted my witch friend about it," Jay said. "And while she thinks you're all crazy, she does think this is probably going to be the safest block in the city with Henry's pack so close. She offered to walk by tomorrow and make sure your witch friend's wards are good."

Oliver shrugged. "If she wants to, but our friend is the best at what she does. None of us are worried."

Jay lifted a skeptical eyebrow before responding to the message on their phone. No one had named Poppy; they only talked with Jay about some of what they'd learned about magic from her. Jay's understanding was different from Poppy's. It had much more to do with instincts and the Sight, aspects of magic that Poppy rarely mentioned without a grimace.

Oliver asked about the tarot cards again, the conversation shifting and blurring with the speed of drunk thoughts. Jay began giving him a reading when Nora's phone rang. She didn't recognize the number, but her mind immediately went to Matt. Maybe he had a new phone, or Gabriel was watching his old one. Nora pivoted slightly from the table to answer, heart in her throat. "Hello?"

"Nora, this is Henry!"

Abruptly, Nora's heart left her throat and plummeted into her stomach. She tried to hide the illogical disappointment. "Oh." She didn't do a good job.

"Sorry to call like this. I got your number from Josh. This is strange timing, but such is the way of our world. I was approached just now by someone in need of an alpha. I was wondering if you would want a meeting? If things don't click between the two of you, I'll consider her, but after our conversation, I thought you might at least want to experience a wolf in search of a pack."

Alarmed, Nora turned to Annaliese, but she was in the midst of assuring a horrified Oliver the three cards bearing skeletons he dropped when he grabbed the deck didn't mean anything while Jay laughed so hard tears were in their eyes.

This conversation was for Nora. It was about her future pack and the life she would build with them. After last winter, Nora would never cut Annaliese out again, but these decisions needed to be made by her alone.

"Nora?"

She'd been quiet too long. Nora cleared her throat. "I… I am interested. I just, I have no idea what to do."

Henry made a comforting noise that was all wolf and immediately settled Nora's nerves. "She's in the other room here now. You could come by or meet somewhere casual. Ask her what she wants from a pack or alpha. Explain your situation. It wouldn't be fair for her to go in blind, given your ties to Gabriel. Tell her you're in an uncertain place in life right now. She needs an alpha and can't be too picky, but you need to be honest and start your alphaship in that vein."

"Right."

"Your instincts will do most of the communicating. Lean into them. Keep up your walls so you don't invite her into your pack unintentionally, but know even if you are welcoming, she has to consciously align herself with you. This is just a conversation. When you're both ready, things will happen, but it won't happen accidentally."

A brief pause. Nora nodded even though Henry couldn't see her. She wished she would have called him earlier. She wished she would have called him while living with her old pack and had his number hidden under her pillow. There was so much she needed to know, and he was the only one willing to give her answers. Now, she was out of time.

"Nora, you also have to understand that as soon as she meets you, she will be tempted to join. You have a very compelling and raw energy. Now that you're searching for a pack, it's going to be even stronger. Remember, you are not meeting with humans. You're meeting with free wolves. This conflict with Gabriel might attract them to you as much as it might deter them. They're going to want a territory, something to fight for, a strong leader with passion to follow. Your work with Lana might be exactly that for some of them. You have much to offer, even with the risk involved. Don't lose confidence, don't hide anything, and stop holding back. You're going to be a great alpha. An irresistible leader because of your character, and your pack will follow you to the end of the earth if you warned them that was what was coming."

"You think so?" Henry's voice was in her ear, but the feelings he inspired in her core reminded Nora of her father. The conviction was the same. It was enough to make her throat tight and chest squeeze. He believed in her. An alpha.

"Yes. I really do. Now, would you like to meet Janelle?"

It was a huge, life-changing, and heavy question—a question brought on by the Seven of Wands. The answer shouldn't have felt so effortless.

"Yes."

Nora shifted. The chair at the high-top table she'd chosen squeaked in protest. Nora almost moved to another table because of it, but she wanted to be in view of the door so the werewolf could find her easily.

Annaliese was maybe too drunk for this, but after Henry stressed how essential honesty would be, Nora needed her friend here. No one would call Nora out faster for a half-truth, and whoever this person was should know how important Annaliese was to her. How important she would be to the pack. At the first sign any new wolf showed a sense of superiority to humans, Nora had already decided not to let them in.

"I'm kind of shocked this is already happening," Annaliese said. "We've had the most productive day."

"Look at us go," Nora tried to match Annaliese's excited tone, but now that this was suddenly real, the nerves stuck uncomfortably in her throat.

"This is just a conversation, Nor. No pressure."

Nora rubbed her eyebrows. "It's a lot of pressure."

Someone stepped into the open double doors of the bar, and Nora knew immediately it was the alphaless wolf. Her smell was heavy, comforting, and drew Nora's attention. She committed it to memory without hesitation. If this person ever joined her pack, Nora would need to know her anywhere.

The werewolf obviously felt drawn in the same way. She walked directly to their table with her eyes wide. She looked over Nora and Annaliese, stiff posture loosening. "You're younger than I thought. And a woman. And not white. I wasn't expecting that."

Annaliese smirked, sipping from her second glass of water. It didn't seem to be doing anything to sober her up. "I like her already," she muttered, loud enough that the wolf heard.

She was tall. Taller than Nora but more willowy. Her movements were sure and strong, like any other wolf Nora had encountered. Her skin was a few shades darker than Annaliese's, but her eyes were a lighter brown. Her hair was shaved close to her head, showing off the lines of earrings dotting her ears.

She sat, and Nora held out a hand. "Nora Morales."

"Janelle Wright."

"And I'm Annaliese. But I'm only here for moral support, so don't mind me."

Janelle snorted and shifted her full attention to Nora, who found herself sitting taller. She did as Henry said and didn't allow herself to open up, to be too welcoming with her energy, but the urge to do it was right there. She could easily pull Janelle in, invite her into her life, and soothe this throbbing ache of loneliness that was hurting even more than usual with a possible solution within reach.

But this wasn't about Nora. This wasn't about making herself more comfortable and collecting followers. This was about giving Janelle a choice.

"So, I'll get right to it," Nora said.

Janelle nodded, leaning back in her chair.

And Nora told the story. How she grew up here, how her father and mother led, and how Nora always wanted to be like them.

Hurting, Nora explained how her father had died, but she learned recently she didn't know the whole story, only that Gabriel became the next alpha, and Nora had hoped he would make her beta. She told Janelle about the rule that she had to kill a vampire and how she met one but fell for her, ruining everything she thought she knew about being a werewolf. How it came down to killing the vampire or breaking from the pack. She left out how Topher had made the break possible and specific names, but she got through the entire story, ending with her new alliance with Lana.

And felt a hundred pounds lighter. Nora glanced at Annalise and basked in the pride in her friend's face.

They both turned to Janelle, watching her careful expression. Nora held her breath.

After taking a moment to process, Janelle cleared her throat. "My parents found my old pack. We lived in the south, and the pack leader there was… traditional. Even worse than your Gabriel, I'm guessing. Honestly, I thought Henry was the most progressive alpha there could be, and he's still an older, straight, white guy. I won't lie; this drama is more than I was expecting, but I also wasn't expecting a story like that. I think… I need to think more about this."

"That's fine," Nora said quickly. "We can exchange information, and you can get in touch with any questions."

"And you should come by Alpha's Den tomorrow night," Annaliese said. "Meet everyone you'd be working with and see for yourself what we hope the future looks like."

Janelle nodded. "I think that would help. And I'd be your first packmate?"

"Yes. I haven't done this before," Nora admitted.

"That's fine. I kind of like the idea of being part of building a pack from the ground up. Figuring this out together."

Annaliese was smiling. She tilted forward, chair tipping dangerously. "No pressure, but I think this will be great. Nora is amazing. She'll listen to you and be such a good alpha. I'd be happy to get to know you better, too."

Nora was blushing now. She put a hand on the back of Annaliese's chair and pushed down so all four legs were back on the ground. "She's drunk."

And for the first time, Janelle smiled. Nora's chest flared with knowing. This would be the start of her new pack. She could feel it.

CHAPTER 17

I t wasn't sunset, but it was getting close. Poppy hadn't meant to leave this late, but she'd wanted to finish setting up her wards today so that tomorrow they would have the day to sink in before opening. Josh, Daniel, and a pack member Poppy had never met before named Ari had shown up to help. Surprisingly, Annaliese and Nora had other plans. It had just been Poppy and the wolves. A sleeping Lana and Zayn upstairs.

Together, they'd strung up plants across the ceiling in the basement, out of the way of spilled alcohol and dancing feet, but still enough to hold a web of magic and charms to promote good behavior and cheer. Hopefully, even by human standards, Alpha's Den would be a safe place for everyone no matter gender, sexuality, or affinity to magic.

Poppy left the Alpha's Den confident with her wards, but everything she had went into them for the last three days, meaning she shouldn't be here. Alone, save the poltergeist, and so spell spent that she saw stars when she blinked. The poltergeist was not happy with her. She'd been too tired to bike, so he sat in her passenger's seat, studying the building she'd just parked in front of and then turning his glare onto her. "This is stupid. Reckless."

"I'm not going inside. I just need to make sure you weren't lying."

If the poltergeist had lied and Topher and Colbie weren't keeping this secret, Poppy would feel awful for how she'd acted last night. Even Colbie hadn't been able to deal with her for long and had left after Ru went to sleep to do who knew what.

"You could just command me to tell you if I'm lying."

"Tell me if you were lying," Poppy said. The wind shifted, and the smell of the apartment building blew in through Poppy's open window. She stiffened at the rot. The cloying dark magic scent that even she could pick up with her limited magical instincts. Poppy fiddled with her charms, the magic in them full and warm.

"I'm not lying."

"Commands work better if I know your name," she said, still unable to trust. Still refusing to believe what she had heard. What she was currently seeing and smelling.

"Are you asking me my name, Penelope?"

It was another way to strengthen their connection. To tie him to herself even more thoroughly. "Yes."

"It's Gus."

She raised an eyebrow. "Gus?"

"Well, Fergus. But no one called me that. Just Gus."

And so it was done. His faded, cloudy colors deepened. Poppy could even see the ruddy shade of his cheeks and the light blue of his tie. "Tell me if you're lying, Gus."

"I'm not lying about this, Penelope."

Poppy noted the specificity. He couldn't promise he hadn't lied to her at all, but she'd worry about that later. "I'm going to check it out."

He groaned but followed her. "You're trouble. Your mother never said you caused trouble."

"Did my mother ever talk about me?"

He muttered something that sounded too much like "Of all the daughters to find…"

Poppy walked up the sidewalk to the front door. The street-lights flickered on behind her, casting a burst of shadows. Grass spilled into the cracks under Poppy's boots. It hid the concrete in places. Poppy felt her magic pulling from the grass and weeds, bolstering her strength and leaving a trail of dried-out vegetation in her wake. She planned to circle the building and peek inside the windows, but of course, they were covered in blackout curtains to protect the occupants from the daylight. Poppy hesitated at the base of the front steps. This was point-less. Gus was right. She should go home. Holding tight to the last of her magic, she searched the stairs and found Raven's impression on them, carrying a small cooler inside every day. The blood. Hopefully, Lana paid the human well to make her interact with these creatures.

"Maybe I *will* just ask Topher about—"

A scream ripped through the air.

Poppy didn't think. She ran at the front door, staggering when she snapped to unlock it and lost another wave of energy. Only Gus's hand, cold and far too solid, kept her from falling. Poppy didn't acknowledge the touch or the jolt of fear to her spine. The adrenaline spike was as much from him as the screaming that continued upstairs. Poppy kept going, taking the stairs as fast as she could.

Had the unclaimed found a human? Was Raven still here? Was there someone else here when they shouldn't be? Was it Julia?

"Let me check the room first," Gus said as they approached the locked door.

Poppy was about to agree when whoever was on the inside gasped. "Is someone there? *Help me! Please, please, you have to—*"

The voice was too frantic. Too human. Poppy didn't think. She snapped, heard the door open but swayed as black crowded her vision. She stumbled into the wall, sliding. Gus shouted, and through the blur, Poppy saw Julia's face. But not.

This face was cast in gray, shrunken, eyes black and wild.

Soulless. All of Poppy's magic cringed from the lack of life. The void that was her being. Julia caught Poppy's arm and, with too much strength, threw Poppy against the opposite wall of the hallway. Julia's smile was triumphant; her hiss flecked with spittle.

Poppy's wards protected her from injury, but the blow knocked the air out of her. She threw up her hands when Julia pounced, but Poppy's magic was a wisp of a spark. Nothing happened, and Julia knocked Poppy's hands away as she lunged for Poppy's neck.

And encountered the charmed necklaces, the wards in place, and beneath all that, Poppy's poisonous witch blood. It gave Julia pause. A beat of stillness in the chaos allowed for the horror to wind up Poppy's throat. She let out a choked noise.

With a shout, Gus ripped Julia off of Poppy and tried to wrangle her back into the room. Julia caught the doorframe, hissing as her nails broke and dug into the wall. Gus's strength fled, as dependent on Poppy's energy as her magic was. Poppy stared, still trying to catch her breath, as Julia shook Gus off, pulled herself out of the room, and scuttled down the hall, movements all demon. Julia's gasping, unpracticed, and wild laugh set another cold wash through Poppy's body.

That was not Topher's pitiable ex-girlfriend. Not the girl who had stormed into their apartment months ago filled with worry for Topher. *That* was a monster. What was Topher doing, feeding it and hiding it away?

The laughing grew distant, and Poppy pushed to her feet. Julia shouldn't have—

Too late, Poppy realized she'd left the door open at the base of the stairs. She turned to Gus. "What have I done?"

He shook his head at her. Even faded, his expression said it all. She'd fucked up.

. . .

Poppy ran down the stairs as quickly as she could. As she reached the base, a dark figure filled the open front door between one blink and the next. Poppy screamed, falling back and landing painfully on her wrist.

Solid and cold hands pulled her to her feet before frantically patting her down. "Poppy! Are you hurt?"

It was Topher. Relief, then overwhelming guilt, flooded her. "Topher. I, I didn't mean to. She—"

"I know." Poppy couldn't read Topher's expression. He had to be angry, though, right? "Lana saw you come in on the cameras. I got here as fast as I could. If you're fine, I'm going to find her."

"I'm fine. I'll help you."

The expression slipped, a slice of the storm within Topher breaking through. Poppy cringed from the glare, and Topher huffed a frustrated breath. "You've helped enough."

And as quickly as he appeared, he was gone again. "We should help him find her," she said to Gus.

"You're too spell-spent to do anything."

"I have a potion in the car."

"You've been drawing from wolves and taking potions all day! All week! Let the vampire handle this. It's his problem to begin with."

Poppy glared at Gus as her mind raced, trying desperately to devise a solution. The night outside was silent, too peaceful considering the nightmare Poppy unleashed. The monsters in the rooms on the first floor started to call out. They spoke to her cautiously, begging for help. Telling her they were confused. Trapped. Kidnapped. So, so hungry.

Julia's screams echoed in Poppy's ears, overlapping with the pleas. This was... so unbearably dark. Bloodcurdling. The reality Topher and Colbie had been hiding from her. *Why?* What hadn't they asked for help? These creatures weren't vampires. Weren't only their problem. Some horrid, unthinkable magic made the monsters. It wasn't something one vampire group could solve on their own. They couldn't charm this situation away.

These creatures were similar to vampires in that they were a void in need of life to fill them. Poppy could feel the black-holes of their energies, but it was so much worse for them than the vampires. They needed to steal a life, not just taste it.

An idea struck. Poppy sprinted to her car, side immediately stitching. She had one plant left, and a few life brews in her bag. She carried it back inside, staggering under the weight but determined. So much of her stamina went into her new task that Gus faded into a quieted shadow, shaking his head with disappointment. Poppy took the stairs, breathing hard. Inside Julia's ruined apartment, Poppy found the stove and an old, battered pot. The cabinets held the bare essentials, but Poppy only needed water. With the pot half-full, she set it on the stove and turned up the heat. Poppy withdrew a sunlight brew from her bag, then a quartz stone that she dropped with a plop into the pot. Once there were bubbles and movement, she turned down the heat to keep it steady at that temperature before going to the fridge, remembering the cooler Raven had brought in. Poppy sipped the sunlight brew; the small burst of power made her head hurt worse but her hands steadied. Using the new energy, Poppy broke open the fridge lock and pulled out the packet of blood. She poured it into the pot, willing the water and blood to mix until they reached body temp.

This magic was eerie. Borderline dark magic. Nothing like anything Poppy had attempted before. It was… exciting. She lost herself to the potion. Whispering to the brew what she wanted it to do as she poured more ingredients from her bag inside. She stayed away from salt or anything that repelled. For once, she wanted to do the opposite. Poppy cut her palm but concentrated on the pooling blood, separating everything that was protection against the creatures of the night. Her witch's life force, dulled with how little power she had, stayed behind while she drew out what made her human. It was a complicated request. Poppy barely had the words to ask for it, but the magic behaved.

Poppy suspended these life particles in the air and wiped the strange navy blue left on her palm off on her pants. When Poppy directed these human bits of her essence into the pot, it flashed. The creature next door began pounding on the wall.

Poppy was close.

She tried the same thing with the remainder of her sunlight brew, holding the liquid in the air and attempting to bring out the magnesium and the essences of sunlight. When she realized it wouldn't work, Poppy shrugged, directed the brew into the cut on her palm, and kept going. She moved the pot so it was simmering in the moonlight coming through the window and then shifted her attention to enhancing the smell of human blood and the vitality of life she'd added.

She was so focused on the brew she jumped when she felt Gus stir next to her. "It smells delicious…" He put his face to the steam, teeth bared, body vibrating.

Ignoring him, Poppy kept stirring. If this was going to work, she needed to add one last element. This magic was tinged with darkness and the shadows always required sacrifice. Poppy could feel the potion calling for one.

Breathing in deep, Poppy found a memory of Julia. The first time they had met. The choking jealousy Poppy had experienced when she met the beautiful girl who stared at Topher like she wanted to eat him. Or for him to eat her. Her confidence. Julia knew she was going to get what she wanted either way. Poppy squeezed her eyes shut with concentration and stirred in consistent circles. She directed the memory and the strength of her emotions at the time into the brew.

In the next breath, Poppy had no idea what memory she'd sacrificed, but the brew smelled like the perfume Julia wore. "This is for you, Julia. Come get it. Julia…" Poppy murmured into the liquid. She became lulled by the consistent scraping of the quartz against the bottom, the purr of bubbles, the whoosh of the wooden spoon, and the gentle tug of potion magic. The magic was hypnotic. Strong. *This* was what Poppy excelled at.

She was so enthralled with the brew she almost didn't hear it when Julia returned to the door with a hiss. Relief swam when Poppy realized she'd succeeded. She let the spell go, hoping Topher was near. Then, she collapsed into the dead leaves of the mint plant she'd brought up with her.

Topher caught the scent, and his stomach dropped. A human was close to where he trailed Julia. She shouldn't be so fast after these weeks of confinement. When Topher finally caught up to her, she didn't notice him or the human smell in the wind growing more fragrant by the second. Topher's mouth watered.

Whoever they were must be young. In peak health.

Julia stood in a fenced yard, scoffing in disgust as she cast a small body aside. A raccoon. Its neck was mangled and bloody. Topher's stomach twisted, but at least it wasn't a human. He had to catch her now before whoever approached got any closer.

Topher had woken up to Lana's frantic call. Their apartment was closer to Seventh Street, where they kept the drainers. He'd barely heard her explain the situation before Topher took off, thoughts on Poppy. On the humans at risk. He had to stop more tragedy.

All this was to say, Topher hadn't eaten. He wasn't as strong as he preferred to be when dealing with the drainers. Still, he had to be strong enough for this. Carrying Julia, screaming and fighting, through the streets did not sound appealing. "Jules…"

Julia waved a hand as if the sound and sway of Topher's charm were an annoying fly she could shoo away. Clenching his hands tight enough for his nails to dig into his palms, Topher prepared to try again. The smell was getting closer, and Julia wouldn't stay distracted by closed, locked doors of the nearby houses and raccoons for long.

"J—" Topher froze at the same time Julia did. That smell…it wasn't… it couldn't be.

Whoever approached smelled exactly like Julia before she was changed into this monster. Julia's head twitched, and she sniffed the air, pinpointing the direction it came from. Topher was too stunned to do anything as she crouched and cautiously followed the perfumed aroma.

There was no way two people smelled the exact same. Topher had never experienced it. For a second, hope flared. Maybe this monster in front of him *wasn't* Julia. Maybe it was a sick ploy of Lana's to keep Topher in her grip after Colbie had revealed herself to the supernatural community. Maybe it was Julia approaching now…

Only the smell was right there, and Topher heard no footsteps. No heartbeat. The drainer's head tilted, listening. Whatever the monster heard, it wasn't for Topher's ears. The hope, a small bubble, all things considered, popped as Topher finally caught the earthy undertones of Poppy's magic tied to the trail. Luckily, the drainer didn't seem to pick up on it. Her pace quickened, running back toward the apartment building, her breath rapid and black eyes shining.

Topher's heart twisted as they entered the apartment building. Julia's human scent, mixed with the rot and darkness of this place, only served to remind Topher how bad things had gotten. Julia ran up the stairs, and Topher followed, weary and hurting. They reached Julia's open door, and Topher saw Poppy at the stove. She always brewed standing straight, lost in the potion before her and whatever strains of magic only she could see. Because of this, Topher immediately knew something was wrong from Poppy's slumped posture. The witch's palm dripped blood and her blue glow was muted and flickering. She didn't turn when Julia banged the door against the wall, but from his view of her profile as he ran into the apartment, Topher saw Poppy's eyes roll back into her head.

Topher had no choice but to let Poppy fall, wincing at the sound of the thud as he quickly shut and locked the door instead of running to catch her. If Julia escaped, it would all be for nothing. Julia went directly to the stove, stepping over Poppy's limp form to grab the pot by the sides. She hissed at the heat but didn't slow as she lifted it directly from the burner and began drinking. The red liquid sloshing down Julia's shirt steamed with heat, but still, she didn't slow.

Poppy moaned when Topher reached to her. He lifted her head carefully and feeling to make sure she didn't hit it too hard. There wasn't a bump, but Poppy's nose was bleeding. "Popsicle?" he whispered. Poppy stirred but didn't wake.

Heart ready to explode, Topher lifted Poppy and held her close. He left the room, locking Julia back inside. As he descended the stairs, a car screeched to a halt outside. Lana and Colbie's bickering was audible as soon as they were on the sidewalk. Topher met them at the door.

Lana's glare was unnecessary. "How in the hell did she find out about this place?"

Colbie was right behind her, Zayn quiet in the rear. At least the two of them looked to Poppy with concern first and foremost.

Topher didn't feel like defusing Lana's rage. He could only focus on Poppy and how good it was to hear her breathing regularly. He'd never seen her run out of magic and energy so entirely. Wishing he'd asked her what to do in this situation, Topher pushed past Lana to get outside. Sleep seemed to be what Poppy needed, but plants or life energy had to help. The building at his back had none of that to offer. Topher had to get her home.

"Christopher! Did you tell her about this place?" Topher kept walking, only pausing when Lana ran forward and caught his bicep, fingernails digging in.

He returned his maker's glare. He had nothing to say to her. Colbie was the one to step forward. "Of course, he didn't tell Poppy! He's been wanting to for weeks, but you hold this place over his head, keeping him in line. Why would he tell Poppy to show up right when he knew you would check the cameras?"

"Then how did she find out?"

"She's a witch! I'm sure she has her ways."

Lana wasn't persuaded. She glared between them as if even Zayn, with his silent support and crossed arms, were ganging up on her. Lana released Topher to point at Poppy. "You do the damage control. Make sure she understands exactly what's going on here. If the other supernaturals discover this, your girlfriend is dead. They all are, and we'll be no closer to answers."

Topher held his glare long enough for Lana to know he didn't appreciate the reminder before he nodded. This time, Lana let him go, turning her attention to Colbie and Zayn and ordering them to make sure Julia's was the only door opened and everyone else was still behaving. Topher and Colbie caught eyes over Poppy's head for a beat before he went to Poppy's car and gently set her in the passenger's seat. He drove home, scaring Ru shitless when he burst through the door with her unconscious sister in his arms.

"What happened?" Ru demanded, jumping off the couch. Her magic flared, popping the lightbulbs and short-circuiting the TV for the first time in two months.

"She'd okay. I think she used up all her magic."

Hands trembling, Ru held her palms over Poppy's chest, letting them hover for a beat before brushing her fingertips over all of Poppy's necklaces, rings, and bracelets. "She used it all..." Ru muttered. Poppy's breathing eased as Ru kept touching her, sharing her power somehow and refilling the charms. He held Poppy tight and waited until Ru stumbled back. She frowned at a point behind Topher's right shoulder, and he spun around to face the threat.

No one was there.

Ru didn't seem to notice or care about Topher's confusion. She waved a hand in that direction flippantly. "I've only seen this a couple times, but when it happened to Jane, sleep helped more than anything. Poppy will wake up super hungry."

Topher nodded. He maneuvered Poppy enough to free his hand and pull out the wallet in his back pocket. "Order her something to eat when she wakes up. I'll put her to bed."

Ru started looking up options on her phone. Topher bent to kiss her forehead as he passed, noting how much tension remained in her shoulders. "It'll be okay. Poppy's going furious with me when she wakes up, but it will be okay."

Ru relaxed a touch. "What happened?"

"I can't say. Not yet."

"But everyone is okay?"

"Everyone is okay."

Topher took Poppy to his room, laying her on the sheets to remove her shoes and find a bandage for her palm. When he couldn't locate any, he braced himself and licked the wound clean. Trying not to gag, he watched it heal with satisfaction. Topher tucked her in as comfortably as possible. Once she was comfortable, Topher sat at the end of the bed and dropped his head into his hands.

That had been far too close a call.

Topher's phone buzzed with a call three hours later. Ru slept beside her sister, undisturbed Topher's position at the foot of the mattress.

He'd been texting Lana almost nonstop, their conversation taking on multiple threads as she did the finishing touches around the Alpha's Den without him, and they both mused over what Poppy had accomplished. According to Lana and Colbie, Julia looked better than she had a month ago. Whatever potion Poppy brewed had given Julia strength without needing to kill.

Topher didn't want to hope. It was there anyway, rising and rising in his throat. He stared at Poppy, the bitter taste of her blood still burning his tongue. The magic she was capable of... She was incredible, and Topher kicked himself for wanting to protect her from this, too. Maybe Colbie was right. These secrets he kept seemed only to make things worse.

But Poppy knew now. Topher could only imagine what this would mean for them as they tried to help the drainers.

If she was willing to help at all.

Ru stirred as the vibrating continued. Topher answered his phone as quietly as he could. "Hey, Josh."

Josh copied his whispering. "Hi, Topher. You busy?"

"A bit, yes. Poppy ran into some trouble and used up all her magic. She's sleeping now, but I don't want to leave her."

Josh was no longer lightly whispering. "What happened?" he demanded.

"I... I fucked up. I don't want to explain it on the phone, but if you come ov—"

"On my way." Josh hung up.

Nerves twisted Topher's stomach, making the wait feel far longer than it should. Ten minutes later, the front door opened and brought in Josh's scent.

He came into Topher's room, noting the strange sleeping arrangement. "You creep," he whispered, but the joke was forced.

Topher watched Josh toe off his shoes and settle on the mattress in front of him, legs crossed and back stiff. Ru rolled into Poppy and drew up her legs to make room. Josh leaned forward, touching Poppy's leg. Topher didn't see what he did, but Josh's scent grew more potent, and Poppy flushed. She blinked, and Topher had never been happier to see the green of her eyes.

Poppy tried to sit up. Topher offered a hand when the layers of blankets made it difficult for her. Topher's stomach, already churning and low, dropped further when Poppy ignored him and sat on her own. Frowning at the two of them at the end of the bed, Poppy woke her sister. "Hey, go to our room. I'll be there in a little."

Half asleep, Ru didn't bother to argue. Poppy turned to Topher when her bedroom door clicked shut on the other side of the apartment. "Where's Colbie?"

Topher pulled out his phone to check. "She's on her way."

"Good. I want to talk to both of you." Her eyes were still dimmed with exhaustion. Topher wanted to insist they do this tomorrow night, but there was little chance they would have time with the club opening. "Did you know about this?" she asked Josh.

"About what? What happened?" Josh still held Poppy's leg. She sighed, blinking up at the ceiling. "We'll wait for Colbie. I want to hear it from both of them."

And suddenly, Topher had a new worry. What if Poppy was too angry about this? What if she wanted to move out? What if she decided it was too dangerous for her and Ru to stay with them?

Topher closed his eyes as they waited and worked to calm himself. When Colbie finally walked into the room, she glanced around, and quirked an eyebrow. "You alright, Soda Pop?"

Poppy glared. "This isn't... what the fuck was that place?"

Topher cleared his throat when his next inhale shook. Stepping forward, Colbie took Ru's vacant spot on the bed. How did she appear so at ease? Not a hint of worry in her features. Topher let out a cautious breath. Maybe it would be okay.

Colbie wasn't scared, so it couldn't be as bad as his brain was making it out to be.

Colbie took over the explanation, "As you know, Topher and Lana have been hunting these drainers since they first showed up. Now that we've lost contact with the other vampires, it has fallen even more on us to figure this out. They truly believe the only way to solve this is by killing off the drainers and hunting them until they catch whoever is making them. If you talk to people like Gabriel, he's certain that whoever this is will end up being a vampire and a corrupted witch. But no one is trying to reverse it. We never even considered the option until Julia got turned."

"What do you mean, reverse it?" Josh asked.

Topher's voice was rough when he answered. "Lana found Julia after everything that happened last winter. Found her right after she'd been turned into a drainer. Lana captured and kept her, knowing Julia is important to me. We've caught more since, but we're barely able to keep them alive without allowing them to kill, and we're no closer to curing them."

Poppy sat up, pointing in Topher's face. "Because you didn't ask for help! What would vampires know about any of this!"

"Lana was hoping with the club and building relationships, we could work our way to asking—"

"And you trusted Lana over me?!"

"Poppy!" The witch started at Colbie's sharp tone. Topher equally hated and appreciated the look on Colbie's face. Even at twenty-one, he never felt safer than when his older sister stood up for him. "*Lana* found Julia. Right after I told the entire supernatural community I was a vampire and Lana lost the hold she had on Topher. Do you think Topher or I chose not to tell you? Do you think we wanted to keep Jules locked up and wasting away? No. This isn't what we want, but you know what will happen if we step out of line? Lana lets Julia go. Lana tells everyone what happened. Lana kills Julia. Or, if Topher gets too far out of line, Lana tells everyone he's gone rogue and made me and the other drainers."

Poppy's face paled. Colbie kept pushing. "We're desperately holding onto hope as it is. We couldn't risk Lana's anger. Even now, I spent the entire night convincing Lana we didn't tell you about that place. She's fucking pissed. This situation, as much as we wanted your help, isn't about you. It's about Lana's abuse and what she's been holding over Topher this whole time. Even if Lana doesn't confirm them, the rumors are still spreading that Topher's the one making these monsters. What will happen if people learn who Julia is to him, and it ties him to the problem even further? Lana loves Topher's power but would ruin him in a heartbeat if it served her."

Poppy and Josh fell quiet. Topher couldn't take the quiet for long. "I did want to tell you. Both of you."

Josh's eyes softened. "I mean, I feel like you kept trying to. You've been asking me for weeks to reach out to other supernaturals to see if this has only happened here and if it's curable. I just didn't know you had specific drainers in mind that needed curing."

Topher nodded. "Can you... will you not tell Henry? Not yet."

Josh stiffened, staring at Topher for a drawn out moment as he considered keeping this from his alpha. "I'll wait. But if we don't make any progress and the situation turns dangerous, I'm telling him."

Nudging Josh's knee, Topher thanked him, knowing how much this went against Josh's priorities and bonds.

Poppy's eyes shifted between them all, her shoulders still tensed. It only made Colbie's face harden further. "Look, Poppy, you only just agreed to work with Lana. You dropped Josh, and you've been busy with Ru. You've done the witch thing and made it clear you want to stay out of things. If that's changed now, we'll involve you more, but it's been hard to know where your lines were."

Poppy blinked, taken aback. "You thought I wouldn't want to help?"

Colbie shrugged like it wasn't unreasonable. Topher shook his head, one thought catching. He couldn't release it. "Do you think you can help?"

Poppy frowned. "I don't know. I'd have to study them more and see what my potion tonight did. For now, I'm too tired to even think about all this."

Everyone nodded. Topher got up to leave, but Poppy stilled him. "I'm going to go sleep with Ru. I'll be there tomorrow night, but I need time to think. I don't know if…" *I can trust you.* She didn't say the words, but Topher read them plainly on her face.

Colbie watched Poppy rise. "Sure, Pop Tart. Just remember, we aren't the only ones. I had to work my ass off convincing Lana you traced us with magic when we all know you would have done that to find us last March if you could. I'd be interested to learn more about the tricks up *your* sleeves if we're going to all come out of this together."

Shockingly, Poppy's shoulders slumped, guilt etching into her features before she blinked it away.

It was enough to convince Topher that Colbie was right. Poppy was hiding something.

CHAPTER 19

Nora woke late and stayed in bed for too long, thoughts spiraling and phone buzzing sporadically with messages. Janelle had question after question. Ricky asked if they could do drinks on Monday since the weekend was busy for Nora. The group chat named Alpha's Den was blowing up with last-minute plans for opening day. Even Colbie still contributed, her name on Nora's screen making her heart race while Colbie's messages grew more nonsensical as she fought the lull of sunlight.

Nora couldn't help remembering how Colbie had cuddled up close when sleep overcame her. Like she was trying to squeeze out every bit of warmth. Nora longed to talk to her about Janelle and the conversation with Henry. She missed having Colbie a text away. She missed how Colbie's mind ran on a completely different track to Nora's. She longed for Colbie's insights. The ideas that came to her so easily were never what Nora would have considered. What would Colbie say to all this? Would she be proud of Nora's progress? Would she think Nora could do it? Start a pack? Follow her own path?

Or had Nora ruined all of Colbie's faith in her?

There was a meeting set for noon. All the new bartenders

hired would meet to run through drinks one last time. Everyone else, including Annaliese and Oliver, would learn the basics and other tasks that might be asked of them. Raven would give Nora a sense of what to expect as resident werewolf.

Nora had an hour to get ready. She could hear Annaliese bustling around the kitchen and smelled fried eggs. She was getting dressed when Janelle sent another message. *Can we meet again today?*

Nora: *Of course, only we'll be pretty busy with all the Alpha Den things.*

Janelle: *I was actually hoping to see the place. Can I join?*

Nora: *Absolutely.*

So, Nora sent Janelle the information and left her room with a smile. She was stunned by the progress and the possibilities. Her world seemed brighter than it had in years.

Nora wished her father could see it. Her steps faltered when she wondered what he would say about Colbie. There was no way for her to know.

When the time came, they met in the back lot of the Alpha's Den. Janelle stood off the side, eyeing an exhausted Poppy, a hungover Oliver complaining about how his boyfriend refused to get drunk last night and save Oliver from his choices at the brewery, a wary Josh, a few humans Nora didn't know, and a haggard-looking Raven. Josh stared intently at Poppy. Nora got the feeling something had happened. Something big, but she didn't have time to ask before Raven opened the back door and waved them all inside.

It was truly amazing what Poppy's plants had done. At once, they crowded the space and opened the aesthetic. The black steel of the walls was now a backdrop to rows and rows of vines. The neon signs and chandeliers weren't nearly as jarring with the green to soak up the light. They were infused with a blue glow the shade of Poppy's magic.

"You did a great job, Poppy," Josh said, earning himself a small smile, though it failed to reach Poppy's eyes.

"It was a lot of magic, but it should hold for a while."

The humans were taking all this in a stride. "You've been around witches?" Annaliese asked them, noticing this as well.

"Not so much. I've seen Kallow," one supplied, not overly helpful. He seemed tired and muted. Oliver patted the other man's arm familiarly.

One of the women spoke up. "Grace had her come by Happenstance a few times. That's where we worked before."

"Oh," Annaliese said. Nora stiffened at the former maker's name. The humans' eyes were nearly blank. Their features drawn. Skin pale like they'd seen as much sunlight as the vampires they worked for. The man kept fidgeting and pulling at the lifeless curls in his light brown hair.

Lana had sworn before that vampire saliva wasn't addictive. Topher suspected otherwise. Studying at the lost, former inhabitants of Fourth Street, Nora was even more swayed toward Topher's view of things.

"Why don't you anymore?" Janelle asked.

Nora found herself cringing from the answer as the woman provided it. "Grace died, and his seconds running the club now decided to employ all the lowers as bartenders."

"To keep an eye on them," the man finished.

"Are they not behaving?" Josh asked.

The three humans shared a look but didn't comment further.

"Whatever the reason, we're fortunate to have them," Raven broke in. "And since no one feels like introducing themselves, this is Iris, Mik, and another Josh. We'll have to figure that confusion out."

"Wow, I've never met another Josh," Josh said. Even

Poppy's smile stuck at that. Oliver laughed and winced, rubbing at the spot above his right eyebrow. Pitiful.

Raven glanced expectantly at Janelle, who offered her name quickly. She was paying close attention to Josh (the werewolf one) and when they moved to go downstairs, Janelle spoke in Nora's ear. "I know you know Henry, but I didn't realize you worked so close with his pack."

Nora shrugged. "Yeah. And we'll keep working with him if this all goes well. Plus, Josh is harmless and always seems to be around either way."

They entered the basement. It was getting easier for Nora to go down the stairs. Especially when she was conscious of Janelle's proximity and how she was judging Nora's strength, deciding if she was a worthy alpha. Nora couldn't falter.

Raven turned to Poppy. "Can you tell us more about the wards? Anything we need to do? Anything specific we should still worry about?"

Poppy nodded and explained how they would first and foremost keep out dark magic like that infecting demons and the unclaimed. It would also block weapons and people entering with ill, violent intent. Truly dark souls would just keep walking by. During closing hours, only the few people Poppy had opened the space to would be allowed. Poppy couldn't make any promises on how the wards would work against werewolves or other vampires, but the magic would alert them of any other supernatural's presence.

Then, there were the wards she used to protect the building itself. No one could leave with anything that didn't belong to them. Fires would be snuffed out immediately. Power outages and other issues would get rerouted. The doors couldn't be broken, nor the locks. "Maybe a strong earthquake could knock the place down, but with Nora and Josh funneling their strength to me while I was casting, I doubt even that."

Janelle's eyes widened, glancing between Nora and Poppy. "You lent your strength?"

It was the first hard proof that Nora was serious about aligning with the other supernaturals. She tipped her chin up, meeting Janelle's eyes, surprised at herself for the lack of shame. Adriana would have mocked her, but Janelle just gazed right back as Nora said, without offering any explanation or defense, "Yes."

Raven took her position behind the bar, and they all sat down on the stools opposite. The shelves were now fully stocked, ice machine clacking in the stock room behind the door to the right. Nora stared at them all lined up, their reflections glistening in the polished mirrors behind the bar. There were gaps between them as if seats had been left for the missing vampires in their group. Nora was sandwiched between Janelle and Annaliese but still felt Colbie's absence as if there should be coolness beside her, not a warm body.

Now that her defenses were down, Nora couldn't get the vampire out of her head.

"Alright. We've printed up a schedule and other paperwork for you all to fill out so we can officially start on payroll, but your checks for working on the wards are here too," Raven began, getting straight to business. "We should be covered in terms of bartenders with myself, these three, and Topher and Zayn when they wake up, but that's still a barebones staff. Anyone else interested in making drinks?"

Raven quirked an eyebrow at Oliver, but he only shrugged and passed on the paperwork. To Nora's surprise, it was Janelle who spoke up. "I'm not sure where I'll be after this full moon, but I have bartending experience. I can help out while I'm around."

"I'll take it," Raven slid Oliver's blank papers to Janelle.

"I wouldn't mind learning," Annaliese put in. "I don't know if I can keep working when the school year starts, though."

"That's fine. The vampires will be awake most of our

opening hours during fall and winter. We just need more afternoon help for the summer."

So, Annaliese filled out all the papers. Nora sat silently beside her, jaw clenched. Hopefully, Janelle would choose Nora and continue to work the bar with Annaliese. It would be ideal to have someone trusted on hand to keep an eye out.

"And what do you expect of me?" Nora asked once her own paperwork was completed.

"You'll learn from Lana about the business end of things and meet with the supernaturals who stop by. I'm sure you'll be needed for backup in the bar occasionally, but Lana wants you free to network and step in as protection. You could bounce and watch the door or just wander around, making sure everyone is in line."

That sounded like a lot of aimless free time until other supernaturals began showing up, but Nora nodded. She needed time to figure things out. To learn about this community that she was finally diving into headfirst.

"Let's go through our signature cocktails then," Raven said. She pulled out a few bottles and syrups, movements quick and sure. "This first one is a Colbie creation, the Bliss."

And the crash course in bartending commenced. Nora tried to pay attention, but the reality of the situation was dawning on her. She was sitting in her own supernatural club, about to stake a claim in this city like some new leader. A potential packmate sat on her left, watching Nora's every move and judging. On top of all that, Nora would be working with Colbie every night.

Was she ready for this?

Opening night. It was finally happening, and Poppy couldn't get herself to feel anything other than dread. Dread that other supernaturals could see her face and tie her to the magic. Her gut tightened with nerves every time she thought of seeing

Topher after nearly letting Julia loose. Poppy didn't want to see either of her roommates with their lies exposed. She was anxious to see how Colbie would fare working alongside Nora. Above all, Poppy feared her wards would crash, and she would fail.

The only bright spot was how, with Nora's power, the wards overcame her ties to Gus and kept the poltergeist out. Yet even thoughts of him made Poppy's stomach turn, remembering how Colbie knew she was hiding something.

The clocks ticked ever closer to opening. At five, Josh and Nora took positions at the front door in their uniforms. Lana wanted to keep a speakeasy/cocktail lounge theme. Josh's black shirt was tucked neatly into his black pants, a red bowtie the only splash of color. Nora wore straight-leg red pants and a button-up black shirt. The alpha appeared slightly overstimulated but seemed to draw comfort from glancing back at Annaliese and Janelle behind the upstairs bar.

The werewolves began checking IDs. They didn't answer the human patrons' questions about this place being a speakeasy or supernatural, pretending not to hear. It lit up the guests' faces. They examined each person working and every door, trying to figure out the mystery for themselves.

Poppy hated it when they examined her where she sat in her flapper dress at the bar. She they were seeing far too much.

Poppy hadn't expected the black and metallic walls and floors to lend to a twenties styling, but everything had come together with the rugs and furniture in place. Plus, the basement was all modern, including the uniforms for the bartenders working below, where it would be hotter and faster pace. Black t-shirts and, for Mik, a red bodysuit and skirt combo. All the clothing was paid for by Lana, with multiple outfits for them to bring home.

The maker was sparing no expense. She expected her investment to pay off.

Around six thirty, there was a burst of excitement when the

first human ventured toward the walk-in cooler door, watching Annaliese and Janelle to see if they would stop her, and then squealing when opening the door revealed the stairs and hidden layer of the club. They ran down the stairs, for all the world feeling like the cleverest drunk people alive. From that point, word of mouth contributed to a near-constant stream of people venturing into the basement. The line only waned when Raven brought Nora a clicker counter to keep track of the number of people going in and out. Nora was overwhelmed with the task, but Raven was too frazzled to do it herself. She glanced one more time at the door on her way back down before shouting to Poppy, "Text me as soon as Topher and Zayn get here. We need them behind the bar."

Even the bar in the cocktail lounge with its ten seats and four high-top tables was getting so overcome that Poppy left her barstool to help in whatever way she could along with Oliver.

Admittedly, they were probably more of a hindrance, but Poppy could pour the simpler drinks at least, and Oliver was great at changing out empty bottles and grabbing ice from downstairs.

Poppy's job tonight was simple, but trying to multitask was wearing on her. She was supposed to monitor her wards. Made sure they let in everyone they were supposed to and no one else. What she hadn't accounted for was the excess energy pouring from the humans. The magic kept glowing, different vines and plants flaring with blue, causing a round of cheers each time. Poppy was trying to siphon it into herself or Nora or Josh to keep the plants from glowing, but eventually, she had to give up and let the magic show, as much as it went against her instincts.

The wards were more fortified than ever. Nora and Josh tried to wave in at least three people that the magic didn't approve of. Nora told them to do some personal work and moved on to the next person, not having time or wanting to explain why they couldn't get in.

People were curious about the staff at Alpha's Den before, but as the sun set, in came the humans who eyed everyone working with wide, shifting eyes. One girl stroked her neck suggestively, making Janelle roll her eyes. "You think the vampires are up this early?" the werewolf asked.

The girl gasped and turned away, but a light was in her eyes. A twist to her lips as she reconvened with her friends, and they bent their heads to whisper together. Janelle had basically confirmed the vampires would be coming.

They hit max capacity by the time Lana texted the group chat that she and Zayn were awake. Lana needed a minute to get ready but would head down soon. Poppy's stomach stirred with nerves, bringing her out of the moment. She was surprised to realize she'd been enjoying herself. She and Oliver had been doing laps, checking in with the bartenders, grabbing snacks or a change of shoes, or just hanging around to talk in slower moments. Nora seemed nervous around Janelle, but every time they spoke, Janelle watched Nora walk away with more interest. Janelle asked Poppy questions during the lulls about Gabriel's pack and how big of a danger they might be to the club. Poppy didn't have many answers, only an assurance that Henry's pack was larger and dependable.

"They might come check it out, but they'll probably be more interested in dealing with Lana. I'm more worried about Solas and Patter, anyway. They've been too quiet."

Janelle nodded. She was new to the city but had already learned all the supernatural leaders' names.

When Lana finally made her way downstairs, a hush dropped over the lounge.

Lana was dressed in red. She had black jewels strung in her hair and dipping over her forehead. Her hair was styled perfectly so she looked like a Gatsby character. Ageless, she'd stepped directly out of the twenties. The fangs she had on full display made it seem even more likely.

Lana smiled, showing her slim, pointed teeth to the fullest extent. "I see things are going well!" She beamed around the place, eyes lingering on the very stiff Janelle. "A new wolf! Are you planning to join our Nora?"

"I'm considering," Janelle said carefully as Lana came to lean on the bar between two humans who fell quiet, enthralled in Lana's unchecked charm.

"You think you'd like this place?"

"Maybe. I don't know about you, though," Janelle said, glancing pointedly at the slack-jawed humans.

Lana's eyes lit. "Good. I like my people to challenge me. As long as you know this place wouldn't exist without me. You saw the upstairs rooms when you got your uniform?"

Janelle gave a curt nod. Lana's smile grew. "Follow Nora, and those rooms will be open for you and your packmates. The only payment I need is complete protection when me and my darlings sleep upstairs. Room and board and a nice job," Lana spread her hands, smiling without fang now, "What more could a pack ask for?"

A good leader... Poppy couldn't help the uncharitable thought, but at least she didn't voice it. After everything last winter, Poppy wasn't sure how Nora would do as an alpha. The girl had been raised in a messed-up situation, and Gabriel was deep in her head. Hopefully, the time apart would help, but as far as Poppy knew, Nora hadn't seen her old alpha since everything happened. How would she react? Would her shoulders fold in again like they do whenever Gabriel was mentioned? Would she ignore Colbie in favor of him, though everyone saw how Nora still looked at Poppy's roommate? Would Nora leave the club, abandon this whole endeavor the moment his alpha commands reached her ears?

Or was it possible Nora recognized the manipulation she'd escaped? Could she feel her own power? Poppy had never felt so much raw energy, not even from Ru. Nora almost seemed equivalent to Topher's power but kept it all on a tight leash. She'd inherently learned control, either through making herself small for Gabriel or watching the wolves in her life. Poppy wasn't even sure how that kind of power translated into a werewolf in terms of abilities, but the part of Poppy drawn to life energy was eager to see what Nora could do if she let loose. Maybe Nora couldn't until she had her pack. Maybe that would be the final step in healing Nora needed to overcome how Gabriel had fucked with her mind.

Colbie dashed inside from the back, hair in its usual bun and dressed in a black cropped, strappy top and baggy blue jeans. Colbie was wearing makeup for once, Ru's hand in the tight lines and crisp colors. Her blue eyes popped, bright with excitement.

"Colbie! I gave you your uniform yesterday!" Lana exclaimed, sounding far too distraught and making the situation abruptly ridiculous.

Poppy hid a smile behind her hand, and Colbie winked at her. It was so difficult to stay mad at her. "Was that what that was? I thought it was Topher's and left it for him to wear."

Lana rolled her eyes, but Zayn laughed. He looked incredible in the same tux Janelle wore. Her eyes followed him as he stepped behind their bar. "I can take over if you want to go check out downstairs with Colbie, Poppyseed."

Poppy smiled, set free. She bounced up to kiss Zayn's cheek in gratitude as she passed, and he pushed her off with a groan.

"Hands off, Jennings!" Oliver said with mock outrage as he came up from the basement, a faint sheen of sweat covering his face. He was *still* a touch green. Poppy wondered when he'd last experienced a hangover. "Babe, I think I've suffered enough. Put me out of my misery so I can keep something down."

Zayn opened his arms to Oliver and dipped down to bite his neck in front of everyone. Janelle sucked in a breath. Lana laughed into the shocked silence. Colbie grabbed Poppy, already bored of the spectacle.

Poppy picked up the tequila soda she'd hidden under the lip of the bar and followed Colbie downstairs. Even though Lana claimed she had no desire to hide the supernatural happenings here, it was still shocking. Vampires feeding. Plants glowing. Soon, they'd probably have Josh or Nora in wolf form running around.

Yet the dread from earlier was a quiet hum. The excitement and life in the air were getting to Poppy. When Colbie checked over her shoulder with a smile, Poppy smiled back. She felt the energy surging, and the urge came to tramp it down. Poppy ignored it. She let the blue flush come over her, lighting the narrow stairs as they entered the sweaty noise of the basement club. Her sound wards had held so no one upstairs could hear the thumping base and shouted conversations. It was an entirely different world down here.

Behind the bar, the three bartenders and Raven worked quickly. Raven flirted and smiled her way back and forth across her section. Iris's face was drawn in concentration, but she moved with confidence. Human Josh was swamped, soaked with sweat as he shook drinks. Poppy was surprised to find Nora in front of his section. She passed him a water bottle and shouted something. He shook his head, yelling back and making her laugh. It was the fastest Poppy had ever seen Nora warm up to someone.

Colbie said something that sounded like "That bitch." But her smile was worryingly fond as she watched Nora laughing.

Poppy felt so powerful, surrounded by people she trusted, the energy of the club, and the strongest wards she'd ever set. In that moment, she knew the biggest danger in this place was the look Colbie was giving Nora. Poppy could do nothing to protect any of them against it.

CHAPTER 20

Topher would be the last to arrive at the club. He'd woken with his alarm an hour ago but was dragged back into sleep so hard he didn't even wake up again for his snooze.

Yet, he couldn't muster the energy to care. He was so tired. Even the remnants of the sunlit day urged his mind to sleep. Topher didn't remembered it being quite this bad last summer, but at that time, he'd welcomed the bliss of sleep. It meant avoiding having to feed. It meant no thoughts. Then, when Poppy joined them and introduced him to potions, it meant an escape from grief with the dreams smothered by magic.

Topher silenced his alarm, groaning at the notifications on his phone. Lana had sent him multiple messages. One insisted he bring Colbie's uniform with him, another threatened him if he didn't wear his own. Topher rolled his eyes, but with everything on shaky ground after last night, he pulled on her suit. However, he refused to wear the shiny black shoes Lana had given him to fit the era and wore black sneakers instead.

Ru was in the living room, listlessly watching TV. "Good morning," she said when he opened his door.

"We need to make you some friends," Topher said, ruffling her hair. She was doing the same thing she'd done last night, sitting on the couch watching reality TV without him. What Topher would give to hang out with her.

Ru shrugged. "I doubt Poppy would let me. Not until I have full control."

Topher came around the couch, sitting on the coffee table to block her view of the screen. He ignored his buzzing phone. "There are members of Henry's pack your age. They aren't even wolves yet. I bet your magic wouldn't affect them."

Ru shifted on the couch, excitement she tried to smother brimming in her dark eyes. "If something happens…"

"You'll be as safe there as you are here. Nothing like what happened to Jane will happen to you or Poppy. Whoever is using the demons won't touch you at Henry's."

"It's my mom using them!"

Topher shifted back, leaning on his palms. He still didn't know all the details about what went down between Poppy and her mother last March. People avoided mentioning the witch in front of him. "If your mom was making the unclaimed, I would probably be one right now. She was gathering the demons, but Poppy is sure she's not killing witches. I believe her."

"How can you even talk about her? It's bad enough she ruined our family, but she murdered people! She killed your boyfriend," Ru whispered the last words like she wasn't sure she was allowed to say them out loud.

It hurt. Mentions of Dylan never failed to rob Topher of breath, but he could tell Ru needed this conversation. "She did. And I don't trust she hasn't done more or worse, but we don't have proof she's still killing humans." Topher left that there. He hadn't been alone with Ru in a while and his questions for the powerful witch gnawed at him. "Ru, what did you feel the night she destroyed your coven?"

"It was the most magic I've ever felt, but it wasn't bright. It felt heavy. It pulled at me and made me tired. Usually, magic is like a breath of fresh air. It feels like the first hot day after winter—Oh, sorry."

Topher snorted. "Keep going."

"It usually *gives* me energy when people use magic around me. Even when I cast, it takes forever to start feeling tired. But when my mom broke our coven, it was like a sudden snap, and then I didn't have the will to get out of the chair I was reading in. Jane was sitting with me, and she gasped and grabbed at her chest like she was having a heart attack or something. She felt it more than me. We'd all poured magic into the wards since we were seven. She'd been doing it for years when our mother used the wards." Ru paused. "Personally, I think that was all Mom did. Poppy thinks she broke whatever had made us a coven, but all that changed for me was how the wards no longer protected the home we lived in. I felt the same sister bond with Jane before and after. Same with Poppy."

"So it was a taking. Not a giving."

Ru nodded.

"Can I tell you something I've never told anyone?" Topher asked. He'd thought maybe Poppy would have felt what Dylan had done for him by now, but she'd admitted multiple times her work with the Sight wasn't strong.

Maybe Ru would be able to feel him. Maybe Ru could tell Topher if there was still a part of Dylan clinging to him.

Ru studied him. "What is it?"

Topher opened his mouth to put words to the suspicions in his head, but his phone began to ring. He sighed, pulling it out to silence it as Ru glanced at the clock and gasped. "Topher! You have to go! Oh my god, you're so late!"

He laughed at Ru's concern. She was a supremely punctual person. He pointed in her face. "I'll call Henry or talk to Josh about you going to their place tomorrow, alright?"

Her cheeks reddened, but he saw the spark of longing in her eyes. "You think they'd like me?"

"If they don't, I'll deal with them." Topher kissed his

fingertips and pressed them to Ru's forehead. "Be good, Roux —but like the sauce."

Her laughter followed Topher out. His questions were still caught in his throat, but Topher swallowed them down again, the mystery of the drainers, demons, and deaths surrounding New Brecken making his skin crawl.

It was a Saturday night and still relatively early. The streets were crowded with those exiting dinner plans and those entering drinking plans. As Topher moved north toward Fourth Street, it was quiet. The vampire clubs mostly drew in a late-night crowd.

As soon as the camera found him entering the drainer apartment building, Lana texted. *I see you're up. Next time, just answer your damn phone.*

Topher made a point of stopping in front of the camera, reading the message, and putting his phone back in his pocket without responding. He almost wished he could see Lana's face when he did that. Going into the first room, Topher drew on his charm, but the latest drainer sat quietly on the couch, staring across the room. "I'm so hungry. It smells human."

"Someone comes by in the day to bring this," Topher said as he opened the fridge. He hated how human the drainer still seemed, so fresh from the change.

Topher threw him the blood packet. It was empty in a second, and the drainer groaned. "Not enough."

"I know, but we can't let you kill anyone."

The drainer glared and hissed. He began to rise. Topher held him in place with a silent burst of charm and moved through the next rooms where the drainers were quiet. Wary, but resigned.

Before Julia's door, Topher paused. Memories of last night were quick and cutting. Poppy could have died. Her magic had been so weak Topher could barely sense it in the air. She hadn't known what she was walking into. What if she'd opened more than just Julia's door?

Why had she opened Julia's door? Julia could have killed someone. They'd gotten so good at finding the drainers early that no one had murdered in weeks. What if some other supernatural group had come across Julia and found it suspicious she'd survived so long? What if that led them here, and all their efforts to study these drainers and save them vanished? What if they'd killed Julia?

Topher wanted to be angry with Poppy about all these risks, but he should have told her about Julia sooner. He'd wanted to ask for her thoughts on saving them. She'd proven last night that her instinctual knowledge of magic could have helped the drainers much sooner. So, the anger went where it was supposed to. Where it always went. First, to himself, for not being strong enough to defy Lana. Then, as always, to Lana for putting him in these situations.

Topher didn't often let himself dwell on how much he hated his maker. How much she'd taken from him and then how she'd identified what little he still had left and effectively hung it above his head.

She'd hid Colbie from the supernatural community until Colbie took that decision from them both. Then, Lana just so happened to find Julia. That still struck Topher as odd. It flared his anger brighter. Lana *must* be hiding something further from him, but if he pressed too deep, she had more threats waiting. Like their childhood home. She'd followed Topher there the night she turned him. She'd charmed him out, Colbie clinging to his hand. Lana asked once who else lived there when Topher was at his angriest with her. The calm curiosity amid an argument was a chilling reminder of what she would do to get her way. Now, he knew he had to swallow the feelings. Accept the helpless situations.

Lana had made him into the perfect vampire lower. Topher felt stuck every day, no matter his strength. Raven was wrapped around Lana's pinky. She could act in whatever way Lana dictated during the day. No one was ever safe.

His phone buzzed again, reminding him that his small acts of rebellion couldn't last. Lana knew how long he was spending here. She'd forbidden him from trying to get answers from Julia and using up his charm before their opening night. Who knew how much he would need to keep the new club safe?

Shaking himself, Topher opened the door. And froze in the entryway. Julia stood at the window, peeking through the curtains and far calmer than he'd seen her in weeks. She turned, and the expression on her grayish face stopped his breath in his chest. "Jules?"

Her head tilted too fast to the side, breaking the illusion of humanity. Topher blinked away the disappointment.

"Where am I?" she asked.

That was a new question. "New Brecken. Seventh Street."

She squinted at him like she couldn't tell if he was lying. He could see the veins in her eyelids, a dark, dark purple. Almost black. But lighter than the last time he'd seen her. Had Poppy's potion worked? What else could it do?

"Where is New Brecken?"

Topher went to the fridge, unlocking the new chain to bring out the human blood. Julia walked up to him and accepted it, sipping rather than guzzling the contents. "What do you mean, where is New Brecken? You grew up here."

"Grew up here?" she asked like she'd never heard the phrase.

But she was talking. Actually engaging. "Julia, what do you remember of being changed?"

Julia's jaw clenched. Working against something. The memory block or stubborn urge not to share. All the drainers had it. Topher didn't want to try his charm against her to see if it was weaker after Poppy's potion. He didn't want to ruin this fragile moment. "Why can't you tell me?" he asked.

"I was told not to. In a voice like yours."

"Like mine? They sounded like me?" From what they had learned, he and Lana suspected the sorcerer making these monsters was a woman. It didn't help their search much if it was a man, but at least they were less likely to capture someone undeserving.

"Not sounded like *you*. They sounded like your…" Julia searched for the right word "…magic."

"You were charmed to forget everything?"

Julia shrugged like she didn't know and didn't care enough to think about it. Topher's head spun. He wanted to call Poppy, see if a vampire could be a sorcerer or if a sorcerer could use charm—

Topher's phone pinged, a different notification than Lana's messages. This was in the supernatural leader email chain. The professional messages were used to keep humans and supernaturals alike in the know. Before last winter, they'd mostly used it to set up meetings. Now, it was used for updates on the drainers. The latest email was from Gabriel, with pictures of the latest summoning circle and the dead drainer nearby.

Two made so close together? Topher's brows furrowed. The rituals had been happening less and less frequently. Why an increase now? What was happening in the city?

Would it get worse, not better, as the summer deepened?

Julia wandered into the bedroom. The door snicked shut behind her. Topher fought the urge to follow her, ask her more questions, demand to know how she was feeling and what the potion had done for her.

But he had places to be. An apology to give Poppy and questions to ask her now that she knew about this place. He saw now they wouldn't get anywhere if they didn't work together. And that's what the Alpha's Den was all about, right?

CHAPTER 21

The moment Topher arrived, the atmosphere of the club shifted. Mik, Iris, and Human Josh froze, eyes tracking him like a celebrity had made an appearance. Topher didn't smile, but Nora knew him well enough now to see he wanted to when he spotted the bartenders. Yet more of Fourth Street that Topher was involved in. Topher stepped behind the bar, ushering Josh toward the ice machine with the empty buckets. The human looked strangely disappointed to be given a break after he'd been drowning in his section. He hadn't wanted Nora's help, but he'd told her not to move. Where she sat directed the flow of traffic. Nora didn't know when humans started shying from her, but it was noticeable in this tight space.

Topher turned to face the humans gathered around Nora, his blue eyes practically glowing in the black light. The effect was immediate. Excitement raised voices, yet the jostling stopped. Everyone was suddenly far more willing to wait their turn. Content to watch Topher bartend while they stood in line.

None of them doubted he was a vampire. He might as well let his fangs down.

Then Topher began serving drinks. Nora remembered

being impressed by the bartenders at the Maker, but that had also been her first time in a club. Now, she was twenty-one and had more knowledge, like how hard it sometimes was to get the glass cup out of the cold metal shaker after slapping it in to mix the drink.

Topher was quick. He was accurate. He didn't have any trouble separating his mixing instruments. He typed in orders and swiped cards without pause while nodding to the next person in line to go. He could hear over the music and ask questions with hand signals Nora picked up while watching him. *Single or double? Do you need water? We don't have that gin, is this okay? Is this guy bothering you?*

The impatient crowd had been moving into Iris's far section of the bar, but now Topher had them coming up and slipping away faster than anyone else. Vampire speed and hearing equated to a perfect bartender.

Then, Lana joined them. She seemed to argue with Topher as they moved efficiently behind the bar, their conversation never slowing them down. In ten minutes, the only people standing around Nora were camping out. The dance floor was packed, everyone with a drink in hand.

Nora turned as Annaliese's scent broke through the crowd. "Zayn told me he's got it covered," she said as she sat beside Nora in one of the only empty barstools.

Topher plopped a light-yellow drink in front of Annaliese without waiting for her to order. He moved to get another round of shots for the group to Nora's left before she could say thank you. Now that Nora had seen Topher a few times without Annaliese near, it was hard not to note how many walls he had up around humans. His face barely shifted, but it was more than the lack of smiles. He dimmed everything so even his eyes were cold and unreadable. Nora had felt the need to hide her thoughts before. Those days of dating Colbie behind her pack's backs were exhausting. How must it feel to keep such a tight at all times?

Nora laughed to herself. Who would have guessed she'd ever be sitting at a bar with Annaliese, feeling sympathy for a vampire? And not just any vampire. The one Gabriel considered the biggest threat in the city. Nora almost hoped Topher's version of what happened to her father was true so she didn't have to consider how big a betrayal she was committing against his memory. If her father truly wanted change, had been about to eschew tradition so Nora wouldn't have to murder a vampire, would he be proud of her now?

That line of questioning felt enormous.

Feeling eyes on her back, Nora looked over her shoulder and easily spotted Colbie in the crowd. Next to Poppy's glow, Colbie's eyes were unnatural, as if the blue was reflecting and not inherent already. Against the dark club backdrop, Colbie's gaze was as mesmerizing as always. Striking. Consuming.

And focused entirely on Nora. Goosebumps erupted down Nora's arms. It was familiar. It was new. That look… it was everything.

Oliver stepped into Nora's line of sight, breaking the stair and taking the stool on her other side. He seemed much better than he had earlier and was eating a sandwich from the food truck down the street. With his company and Topher's watchful eye, Nora turned to Annaliese. "I think I might do a lap."

By then, Annaliese was trying to get Oliver to share with her and barely bothered to wave Nora away. When Nora met his gaze, Topher gave Nora a nod, a silent promise. Shoulders relaxing, Nora pushed away from the bar.

She wanted to go over to Colbie; the chance of her consenting to dance was tempting enough to risk rejection. Yet, Josh's cautions were still in Nora head. Thoughts of her old pack, though brushed aside, too close to the surface. Nora's steps slowed. Maybe she wasn't ready. She didn't trust herself not to hurt Colbie again. Ducking her head and swerving,

Nora took the stairs, intent on finding Janelle. She hadn't checked in on her potential packmate in a while.

The plants lining the stairwells shifted, reaching toward Nora as she climbed the steps. Poppy had warned her that with all the power she'd contributed to the wards, the building might start acting out and trying to return the favor. It made Nora shiver to think of this place as being sentient enough for that. And yet… Nora could feel it. An underlying scent in the air reminded her of her parents' bedroom. The soft smell of their bedsheets, the spice of her father's cologne, the floral undertones of her mother's shampoo, the warmth of their wolf essence heightening it all. This was the smell the Den had even been missing. The smell of home, found in this bustling club that *should* stink of strangers' sweat and alcohol.

It made Nora walk with more confidence. It made her believe in Poppy's magic and the vampires' intentions. Maybe not Lana's, but even if she reneged, this building was loyal to Nora. It sought to please *her*.

Upstairs was busy, but nothing compared to the basement. Down the hall, a line of humans waited for the bathrooms. The water station in the corner was getting attention. The bar was experiencing a quiet moment, and Nora stood to the side to watch Janelle and Zayn chatting. Janelle already appeared comfortable with the vampire, grinning and nodding at whatever he explained. The line to get inside had eased. Human Josh was checking IDs and enjoying the breeze of the open door. Werewolf Josh sat at the bar, looking over his shoulder. He saw Nora and smiled, but Nora could tell she wasn't the person he'd been hoping to see. Poppy was still downstairs with Colbie.

Nora was crossing the room when the air shifted. The world came to an abrupt halt as Nora caught the new scent. Josh stood; his smile disappeared. Zayn was coming out from behind the bar, Janelle following.

And Nora turned, heart a dead weight in her chest. It

hollowed her lungs. She couldn't get that first blast of scent from her nose.

Adriana and Matt stood in the doorway. Adriana was smirking, taking in the small cocktail lounge with an unimpressed eyebrow raised. Matt's expression was dark, his focus entirely on Nora. Human Josh knew supernaturals well enough to set aside, walking quickly until he was behind Zayn's bulk.

So much rose inside Nora. She couldn't name what she felt and simple stood still under the barrage, mildly aware that Janelle had taken up a position at her back. Zayn was watching her for an indication of what he should do. Josh wore an uncharacteristic glare where he stood, but didn't move to step between packs that were not his own.

The sight of Matt and Adriana shouldn't have been so shocking, but it took Nora apart. Old instincts rose. Nora fought the urge to sink back into the submissive, younger pack member. They hurt her, deeply. There two people who were supposed to be her family but hadn't spoken to her in weeks. All because of circumstances mostly beyond her control.

And yet… She felt the alpha, roaring and new, clawing forward on a wave of anger. Saving her from the heartbreak. They had come into *her* space. Uninvited. Unannounced. She heard a soft laugh from Janelle, a response to Nora's curling fists.

The humans noted the tension and made their way downstairs. Nora watched them pass, waiting to react until the room was clear. Even after, the alpha awoken in Nora knew the strength of silence. So, she crossed her arms, met Adriana and Matt's stares, and waited.

It wasn't what they anticipated. Adriana's smug expression slipped, and Matt shifted with discomfort. Nora quirked an eyebrow, inviting them to speak.

Matt cleared his voice, glancing behind Nora. She could smell Poppy fighting her way upstairs against the tide of humans. No doubt the witch had felt Matt and Adriana entering the wards. The fact that she was coming made Nora's heart squeeze. If Poppy had to cast, this would be the first direct exposure of her magic to the supernatural community. Knowing, for all their disagreements, that Poppy had her back gave Nora the confidence to put herself fully in front of Matt and Adriana, a buffer between the stairs and her old packmates.

"Interesting place you have here, Nora Mora," Adriana said, forced lightness in her voice.

"Interesting, I don't remember inviting you."

Another soft laugh from Janelle.

"Come on, Nora. We're family."

Nora blinked. She'd been so distracted by Janelle and Poppy's approach, she almost missed Adriana's words. "No. Family answers their phones. Family forgives and doesn't keep secrets. They don't give ultimatums to determine which members are welcome. You aren't my family anymore. And you aren't welcome."

Matt's face paled. He dropped his glower, stepping forward. "Nora, you have to understand. You aligned with the vampires. How could we just forgive that? It doesn't mean we cut you out forever; you just have to prove you can be part of the pack again."

And Nora faltered. She hated that she did. "I don't think—"

"Nora, is this really what you want? How can you trust these people?" Matt's eyes widened toward Zayn.

"I—"

"It's *me*, Nora. Matt. I know things are screwed up, but we *are* family. Don't you want to make things right? You can still earn your spot; we can figure things out. Gabriel misses you. We all do. I know you miss us too. You've called enough times."

Nora couldn't respond to that. She felt herself shrinking,

and Matt could see it. He struck again. "Nora, come back. Come home. Join the pack. Finally."

Nora trembled. She knew, *knew*, that wasn't an option. She knew she wasn't the only one at fault. She knew that agreeing to see Gabriel was the path of least resistance and went against all the work she'd been doing. She knew that Janelle could feel her wavering, could see the words stuck in Nora's throat—

"Clearly she can't." Colbie's voice was almost Nora's undoing. The fear swept back in, a current so strong it nearly knocked Nora's feet out from under her. Nora had hidden Colbie from the pack. She'd kept their relationship a secret not just for herself, but to keep Colbie safe.

But Colbie didn't falter. Colbie wasn't afraid. She stepped to Nora's side and smiled at Matt's renewed glare. Colbie was fierce, curls framing her face, eyes burning, chipped red nails flashing as she jabbed a finger into Matt's chest. He growled, and Zayn hissed loud enough to cut the sound off. Colbie's smile shifted, taunting. That infuriatingly knowing expression that used to draw Nora in so irresistibly settled on her face. "Nora is making her own pack. She's the one carrying the Morales name. She's the one with allies here—the one with loyal connections. Whatever show of power Gabe thinks he's pulling by sending you two lowers in here, you can go back to him with your tails between your legs. This is the *Alpha's Den*. I know you all don't know much about the other supernatural groups, but you should know how to respect another alpha's territory, at the very least. If Gabriel wants to challenge anyone for it, he can show his little face."

Adriana stepped forward, outrage overtaking her features. "You don't speak for her, and you—"

"And you don't *listen* to her! You never fucking have. She's always deserved so much better than what your worthless pack gave her."

Nora's heart raced. Adriana was speechless. Nora had never seen her cousin at a loss for words. Colbie had done that.

Done it for her. Nora knew it wasn't the time to stare, yet it was so hard not to.

But as words failed, something even more violent crept into Adriana's dark eyes. Even Matt was ready to lunge, but Topher was suddenly, silently, at his sister's side. Their courage stumbled. Power emanated from Topher, so strong they could taste it in the air. He flocked to Colbie, Zayn at his side, and didn't need words. Poppy grabbed Josh's hand and raised her free arm, vines snaking out menacingly. Adriana yelped and stumbled back a step. Josh laughed, an insult all on its own. It sounded like a bark, the change just under his skin.

"Get the fuck out," Colbie said, flicking her fingers toward the front door almost lazily. Then she turned her back as if her words alone were enough to rid the club of the threat. As if the threat was no longer significant enough to require her attention. Colbie strolled down the hallway, and the door clanged as she exited the building entirely.

"Nora..." Matt stepped forward, but Nora was already moving to follow the vampire out. His fingers brushed her arm before closing on empty air. Nora felt it as Poppy, Janelle, Josh, Zayn, and Topher closed the gap she left and blocked Matt's progress. She felt the club settle, the energy returning to normal as the threat was dismissed. She felt it when Matt and Adriana left. She could feel all this, yet still didn't know the emotions in her chest.

"What the hell was that?" Nora demanded as she threw open the metal door facing the alley.

Colbie froze, shoulders raising and hands clenching at her sides. "Just go back in, Nora. I want to be alone."

"That was..." Nora didn't know what that was. Why had Colbie done that? The confusion, the not knowing, was almost painful. No. It was hope. *That* was painful.

Nora knew without a doubt that Colbie acted without thinking. She acted *for* Nora. She had challenged one of the supernatural leaders, aligned herself permanently with Nora, and invited in trouble, all for Nora's sake.

Yes. The hope was painful, and Nora knew it was useless and had nowhere to go. So, she got angry, one emotion moving to the next. "What. The. Hell. Just. Happened."

"I don't know! Okay? Just go back inside. I need a minute."

Nora could not leave her now. Not after that. Not when Colbie wouldn't look at her. "You defended me."

"And you think that's outside my character? To be nice?"

"No. Just…" Annaliese did that. Annaliese was the exception to the rule, and that was why Nora kept her so close. That was why Annaliese was Nora's best friend. When the words failed Nora, Annaliese stepped forward. When words didn't fail her, Annaliese listened better than anyone else.

To have more than one person in her corner wasn't something Nora could fathom right now. Especially not when that person was Colbie. How? "Why would you do that? After everything I did?"

"Maybe it's not really about you. Maybe it's just about how very, very much I hate your old pack."

Nora couldn't even wince. Her reactions were all focused on Colbie. She could barely even think about her old pack when she was consumed by how Colbie had handled them.

Her old pack was no longer an empty space in Nora's soul. It wasn't a pain point that consumed her thoughts. Where once there was nothing, there was now hope. Maybe it would be Janelle. Maybe it would be Annaliese, Oliver, Poppy, Zayn, Topher, and even Colbie. Either way, Nora didn't feel as alone anymore. That was almost as terrifying as trying to understand what was happening currently with Colbie.

Last winter, Colbie was still in hiding. Colbie had never come face to face with Nora's pack until she'd stepped out of that warehouse, but at that moment, no one's attention had been on Colbie. She'd only just been introduced as a lower, and Nora had just become an alpha, taking all the focus.

The bravery it took to step forward and declare a side… Nora was only now realizing she might be capable of it. Colbie did it. Like it was simple and necessary. She'd stepped between Nora and her pack and—

"Why are you out here?" Colbie asked. She finally turned, giving Nora her profile as she let herself fall into the wall, leaning her back against it like she was trying very hard to appear more casual.

Her fists were still clenched.

"Because I don't understand what just happened."

"No, Nora. Why are you out here with me when your pack was right there? Haven't you been trying to talk to them for weeks? Why didn't you go after them?"

Nora blinked. She hadn't even considered following Matt and Adriana. Not after how they'd looked at her. Not after Matt's too-gentle tone and Adriana's smugness. "They shut me out. It's not like they were here to talk to me. Gabriel probably sent them to threaten Lana or something. They weren't looking at me like I was the reason they were here. Like I was significant." The words were too bitter. She wasn't that far past her ache for her pack.

"If they had been, would you be with them now?"

"I don't know."

Colbie seemed to deflate at that. "If Gabriel had shown up, how differently would things have gone for you?"

Nora didn't have an answer for that.

Colbie wrapped her arms around her middle and angled her head away. "Please go back in, Nora. I want to be alone."

Frustration rose in the back of Nora's throat as she turned and reached for the door handle. Why couldn't they just have a conversation? When so little made sense, being with Colbie always had. Nora craved that feeling, but it was unfair to ignore Colbie's wishes. To use her to feel anchored. But why wouldn't Colbie meet her eyes? Even when she'd ripped out Nora's heart, she'd never faltered.

Dropping her hand, Nora spun on her heel again. "No. You know why I'm not with Matt right now? I didn't even think about following him because I was too focused on you."

Colbie went fully, entirely still. She wasn't even breathing. For the first time ever, Nora realized she'd said the right thing. She'd read the moment correctly. "I wanted to follow you," she pushed on when Colbie remained frozen and silent. "I needed to know if you defended me because you still cared. What I saw in there gave me hope. That's why I'm out here with you."

The Alpha's Den was in full swing again on the other side of the wall. The faint, thumping base moved more than Colbie. "Colbie. Say something, please."

Finally, Colbie blew out a breath, fully relaxing into the wall. It was the encouragement Nora needed to take a cautious step toward her. Colbie watched Nora near, her expression raw. Pained. But she didn't protest. Nora kept approaching until Colbie's black boots were settled between Nora's dirty white sneakers. Colbie was shorter as she leaned back. She tipped her head, skull thudding on the bricks. The world stilled as their eyes met.

Colbie drew in a shaky inhale, eye. Her hands twitched at her sides, making Nora's heart skip a beat. "You hurt me, but that doesn't mean I like seeing you hurt. I had to do something."

"But you didn't. Have to, I mean."

"Nora. It isn't as if you mean nothing to me. You hurt me so badly. I gave you the ability to. Because I cared about you. That doesn't just vanish, but neither do the reasons we didn't work. You couldn't stand up to your pack for the same reason I couldn't watch them speak down to you. You still care, and as long as you're trying to be one of them, you'll choose them over me. I can't go through that again."

"But I'm here. I didn't follow them."

"I don't trust you to keep making the same choice. Next time, it might be Gabriel. Next time, you might be alone and start listening to Matt when he hits you with those stupid puppy dog eyes. Do you really think you could just let them go? If they asked, would you tell them no? Can you tell me now that you will never hurt me again for their sake?"

"Colbie, that isn't fair. They're my family as much as Topher is yours. I won't ever do what I did last winter, but if they come again, I'll talk to them. If I could make them listen, it could help everyone."

"And if they decided they were at war with vampires, with Lana, who would you align yourself with? Gabriel and his pack, or Lana and me?"

Nora hesitated a beat too long.

"They LIED to you, Nora!" Colbie straightened with agitation, bringing their faces ever closer. "They used you when you were at your most vulnerable. They won't *ever* respect you as an alpha. As a person. I know you love them, but you *can't* trust them. I trust my brother. I trust the people I've chosen for my family. That's the difference. That's why you choosing your pack is not the same as me standing by Topher."

"But he changed you." That was Nora's last hold-out against him, against all the vampires. The changing. The taking of will. It didn't sit right with Nora even though she knew Topher did what he could to avoid using his charm and hated himself for what he'd done to Colbie. The power was still always there. He could do it again.

"No." Colbie spoke with such firm certainty that Nora couldn't look away. She was desperate to believe she was chasing the right side. "He came to me when he was hurting more than he ever had before. He came to me when he was terrified. He came to me at his lowest point, and then, what Lana did to him without his consent turned into an attack. But I would never tell him not to come to me. If I could go back, I would tell him to do the same thing. I want to be here for him. I forgive him, and we move forward every day together. If you could go back, would you change things? Would you wish they would treat you differently? Have you truly been able to forgive them?"

Nora's thoughts whirled, refusing to settle into words.

Colbie kept going. "If you don't have an answer, you need to figure things out. You don't know what the hell you want, and you're willing to be treated like that until you figure out you deserve better. I hope you figure that out. I hope you learn to choose your family. To choose yourself. But I can't trust you to choose me. That's why this won't work. I want to be chosen. Every time."

Nora swallowed hard as Colbie's words sank in. When Colbie pushed by her to go back inside, Nora let her pass. When the sky opened up and the rain it had been threatening all night finally struck, Nora let it drench her.

Was she capable of choosing herself? What would that mean?

When Nora closed her eyes, she still couldn't quite see past the memories of her old pack, but there was a light at the edge of the sadness marring those memories, almost like if she concentrated, she could put new faces over the old. It felt... hopeful.

The rain washed away the events of the night. Nothing was better because Matt had finally spoken to her, but so much of her was still clinging to the feel of Colbie so close. Nora could go inside and find comfort in Annaliese and maybe everyone else. She loved that. She needed it. She felt closer than ever to convincing herself it was better than what she'd lost.

CHAPTER 22

Nora was so focused on getting to Colbie, surprising though that was, she missed how Annaliese slipped through the crowd toward the front door. Poppy hurried after her, noting a familiar human following on Annaliese's heels. The two of them left the building, but Poppy burst out the doors in time to grab Annaliese's arm and stop her from shouting at the wolves.

"What are you doing?"

Annaliese shook out of Poppy's grip, glaring at the wolves' progress. "I'm going to ask who they think they are showing up like that!"

"Annaliese, they're pissed. They aren't even allies with Nora anymore. You can't just run up to werewolves and—"

"I can and will. What they did to Nora was… I expected them to show up at some point, but not for it to be Matt and her cousin. Not for them to think they can act like that. What the hell is their game plan? What did they think they would gain?"

"I don't know. Maybe they just wanted to check it out. Maybe Gabriel sent them since his presence would be too much of a threat."

Annaliese rolled her eyes. The other human stepped forward. The way their eyes immediately went to Gus reminded Poppy who they were. Jay, the medium from the café.

They also reminded Poppy what Gus could do. She turned to the poltergeist, who had been unhappy with Poppy since the Julia fiasco. He was particularly grumpy after a night of the wards keeping him out. Poppy raised her eyebrows at Gus. He crossed his arms, daring her with an eyebrow raise of his own. He wanted to be acknowledged.

"What was that?" Jay asked, startled. "You talk to him too?"

"Who?" Annaliese asked. She was still on edge, voice harsh, anger stiffening her shoulders.

Poppy gestured for Annaliese and Jay to follow her around the corner and out of hearing range of the people leaving the club. "I might have a way to follow the wolves and hear what they're planning," Poppy said.

"But you said your magic doesn't work on wolves."

"It doesn't, but—"

"You're a witch?!"

Poppy ignored Jay's outburst. "It wouldn't be me going or using magic. It would be, um, the poltergeist haunting me."

Annaliese looked as shocked as Jay. Poppy waited. Jay came out of it first. Understanding cleared their expression. "If he's bonded to you and you're already using him, we could watch."

Now, it was Poppy's turn to be surprised. "What do you mean?"

"Um… the witch that mentors me has a strong Sight. Sometimes she uses spirits to eavesdrop. It's how she helped me catch my sister's ex cheating on her."

"Show me how."

In the next minute, they were holding hands. Annaliese was stiff, no doubt remembering the last time they had done something like this—that horrible memory in the sweatshirt. But Annaliese was too angry to give in to her morals about the spying. Her grip tightened on Poppy's as Jay explained, "If your bond is strong enough to control him, you should be able to follow that link. Have you ever done any type of mind-melding?"

Poppy gave a curt nod, not wanting to think about that instance either.

"It should be easier with a ghost connected to you already. Their defenses have no life force around them to keep you out."

And still, no part of Poppy wanted to force this on someone else. Taking Gus's will appealed to her as little now as it used to. She turned to him, feeling Jay and Annaliese's attention like the heat of flames as she asked, "Will you let us do this?"

Jay's eyes widened. They knew better than to speak directly to ghosts. They gasped when Gus said, "Your mother did it all the time. Go ahead."

Poppy couldn't tell if he was actually okay with this, but she could also feel Annaliese's impatience and her own desire to know what Gabriel was up to. Poppy started a low chant under her breath to help direct the magic. The Alpha's Den at Poppy's back, overflowing with life energy from the humans within, fueled her. It had never been easier for Poppy to cast.

In the next blink, the three of them could see themselves. The shadows cloaked them in the ally. Gus waved a hand in front of Poppy's eyes, laughing when she could still glare, and turned. He swept up the streets, following the direction the wolves had gone. Luckily, they had stopped not too far away. They were caught in the midst of an argument.

Gus hovered beside them, glee filling him over the tense bickering. He loved any source of conflict. Nora's cousin spoke quietly, but Gus slid in close to listen. Far closer than was socially acceptable.

"If she won't rejoin the pack, you can't *treat* her like part of the pack, Matt! We went there to get a feel for how many supernaturals were involved, not to beg her to join us again. We're better off without her."

A growl ripped out of Matt's throat. "How can you say that, Adriana? She's family! She made a mistake!"

"And she's doing nothing to make it right!"

"How was she supposed to do that when none of us were allowed to talk to her?"

"She knew where to find us, Matt. Gabriel never blocked her. All she had to do was submit to him. She killed her vampire. With a good enough apology—"

"—I would have taken her in with open arms," Gabriel agreed, approaching from around the corner. The part of Poppy's mind still connected with her body felt as they all squeezed hands, stiffening at either the sight of Gabriel or the warded, blurred image of the witch at his side. Gus slid back a step, trying to discern if the witch could See him. Or if it would matter. Most witches dismissed the ghosts around them, knowing as long as they didn't acknowledge the dead, nothing would come of their presence. There was still a risk she would banish Gus. Poppy held her breath, hoping she wouldn't.

"You still would, right? If she stopped this, she could come home?" Matt sounded desperate, belying how much he still cared and missed Nora.

Gabriel frowned over Matt's shoulder, where the new neon sign extended off the building down the street. It proudly advertised the club and its name. The Alpha's Den. An insult directed right at Gabriel. Poppy knew no matter what he said to Matt, he wouldn't just let Nora walk back into their lives. Not after she'd put her ownership over a vampire club.

Had Nora known this? Had she already given up her old pack and not admitted it out loud? It gave Poppy hope for Colbie, but the two of them would still have so far to go.

"What was it like in there? What did Lana say when she saw you?" Gabriel asked, choosing not to answer and confirming Poppy's suspicions.

Adriana scoffed. "We didn't make it two steps inside before Nora was there. I think the place is warded."

"Oh, it definitely is," the mysterious witch agreed. "Strong wards. I've never seen any like it." Though they couldn't see her face, Poppy perceived the surprise in the witch's voice. It made Poppy straighten with pride. She'd very rarely heard another witch compliment her casting. Not that this witch knew the crutches Poppy used to achieve the magic.

Gabriel considered this, displeased. It was quiet long enough that his packmates shifted. "And Nora?"

"She seemed… well," Matt said.

Adriana snorted. "I could smell how lonely she was. She still doesn't have a pack and lets the vampires do the talking for her."

"What do you mean?" Gabriel asked sharply.

"One of Lana's lowers got in our face about her."

"The boy?"

"No," Matt answered, "but he was there. His sister did the talking."

Gabriel nodded, though he was puzzled. Shaking his head, he gestured toward the witch. "We think we can get a meeting with Lana. She's interested in talking to witches, even though she has one on staff. The word is, she's hoping to create a group of supernaturals powerful enough to combat the existing leaders."

"What do Solas and Patter have to say about that?" Adriana asked.

"We're meeting tomorrow night. I was supposed to have more to report about the new club."

The dig was enough for Adriana and Matt to drop their eyes. Gabriel scrubbed a hand down his face. "It's good we know Nora hadn't made any bonds. We need her to stay that way. Matt, you were closest to her. Try getting through to her. She has no idea what she's doing or the enemies she's making."

"I can talk to her again?" he asked, hopeful.

"Yes. We never expected Lana to pull this off. Now, we have to keep her from succeeding. She has the West boy and Henry's ear but no real connections to the city. Nothing that would compare to Solas and Patter and Kallow. If she were to have two packs in her pocket, that wouldn't look good. We need to keep Nora from bonding. Eventually, she will come around and agree to submit again."

"And I'll check out the situation with her witch on staff, make sure she isn't a threat and spread the word so the rest of us know better than to approach," the witch said.

Gabriel shrugged. "No one else should be willing to risk it. Not with so many witches getting killed these days. The exposure is foolish. Everyone knows what Lana is trying to pull is just a distraction from the real danger the city is facing. We all need to focus on the unclaimed murdering humans and fixing the laws so whoever is responsible is properly punished."

The witch laughed. "And for all they know, Lana is still the one behind it."

Gabriel nodded. "Matt, call Nora tonight. Set up a coffee date or lunch, something during the day that the vampires won't find out about."

"What about Annaliese?"

Adriana laughed. "You still worry about the human? If Nora has alpha capabilities, there's no way the human will matter for long. Nora is a wolf now, Matt. *Hopefully,* she's learned how to act like it."

Gabriel rolled his eyes. "You'll just have to convince Nora if she wants any sort of pack; she must stop this nonsense. No more vampires. No human besties. Nora needs to toughen up and learn her place to make it in this city."

It didn't sound like advice from a former pack member when Gabriel said those words. It didn't sound like he hoped Nora would find her place.

It sounded like a threat.

Matt nodded slowly. He heard it, too. Nora would collect as

many enemies as Lana if she wasn't careful. But Nora was stronger than Gabriel suspected. If Nora stayed her course and figured things out, he would need to stop underestimating her.

The werewolves and witch went their separate ways. Poppy severed their connection with Gus's view. Annaliese was smirking as they returned to themselves. "Oh, this will be fun," she said. "He has no idea what's coming for him."

Jay rolled their eyes. "Y'all are so dramatic."

"You love it," Annaliese said. "That's why you're sticking around."

"You're one hundred percent correct."

Nora woke to three messages, each spurring a spike of emotion —a roller coaster of a phone screen.

The first one was from Janelle. Nora opened it, heart dropping.

Just want to be upfront. I'm leaning more towards Henry at this point. I told Lana I'd still like to bartend. Hope that's not a problem.

Can I ask what swayed you? Nora sent the message, but the weight in her stomach told her she already knew. It would be nice to think Janelle hadn't liked Nora's friendship with vampires, but that wasn't it if she still wanted to work at Alpha's Den. Janelle wasn't impressed by how Nora had let Matt speak to her. She didn't think Nora would be a strong leader.

Janelle: *I think you know. Who would you choose if you were in my shoes after last night?*

That's fair. Nora couldn't think of anything else to add.

She opened the next message. It was in the Alpha's Den group chat and from Lana. *Great first night, everyone. My darlings, you need to feed more. People left disappointed, thinking there weren't any vampires around. I carried the team in that aspect. However, we did have a successful first night, and the news of the werewolf standoff is spreading —with our involvement coming out favorably. Nora, please work on getting your own pack so my darlings aren't risking themselves standing up for you XX*

Colbie had sent a thumbs down for the whole message. Oliver had sent a gif of some TV character doing a strange dance. Topher had thumbs downed that. And Nora was comforted enough that their responses made her smile. She knew what face everyone made as they sent it. She knew how they were pushing Lana's buttons. It was silly to feel like she belonged in a group only because of a conversation thread, but here she was. Nora "loved" Oliver's gif and he quickly thanked her for the show of support.

Which led Nora to the last message. Holding her breath, she opened the text from Matt. After weeks of Nora's messages filling the screen. After last night. After *everything,* his text only read, *Can we talk?*

Part of Nora was seriously tempted to thumbs down the message like the West siblings would. But this was what she'd been waiting for. Apart from the small desire she still carried to make things right, Nora had so many questions. So many words in her head weighing her down.

She hesitated, staring at Matt's message and then her unanswered texts littering the top of the screen. What he said wasn't an adequate response. What he'd said last night shouldn't be acceptable. What happened to her… Nora still couldn't make herself think too hard about it.

Leaving the text on read felt like a momentary victory. With the message burning a hole in her pocket, she got ready for the day.

Annaliese sat at the kitchen island, a cup of coffee in front of her and laptop open. Her bulky glasses were on, and her braids pulled back in a low ponytail. She watched Nora like she'd seen Matt's message and knew Nora was considering responding.

"Do you sleep anymore?" Nora asked. It had only been six hours since they'd closed the Alpha's Den and gotten home.

The night had presented the hiccups expected for an opening. Zayn assured Nora and Annaliese it wouldn't usually take them so long to close, but Lana had yet to hire a cleaning service to come in during the daytime. She wanted to make sure profits could support that number of employees first.

For all of Lana's faults, she seemed a fair business owner. On Monday night, she and Nora had a meeting scheduled. If Nora was going to act as more of a superior, they needed to go through her duties and discuss how her future pack would interact with Lana's lowers. Nora's heart dropped thinking about a future pack after Janelle's rejection. Would she ever prove to another werewolf she was worthy? Would she ever truly believe it herself?

"I wanted to make sure I caught you before you left," Annaliese said, studying Nora's face.

"Left for where?"

Annaliese blew out a breath. "I'm going to tell you something. Just… don't be mad?" And then Annaliese went into a story involving their high school friend, Poppy, and a ghost.

When she was finished, Nora felt like she had been doused in cold water. Gabriel working with a witch? Adriana's dismissive attitude. Matt unsure. And…Annaliese's mildly triumphant expression. She was trying to hide it, maybe didn't even mean for her face to look like it did, but Nora knew how Annaliese felt about her old pack. She knew that Annaliese was rooting for Nora to blow them off. To stop thinking about them and turn off a life's worth of memories. To finally move forward.

And that look in Annaliese's eyes made Nora's hackles rise, no matter her logical reasoning. "Does that make you happy?" she asked, not recognizing her voice. "Do you love hearing about how my pack still thinks so little of me? Should I just get over it now?"

"Nora, no! Of course not. I—"

"You just thought you'd listen in on them with Poppy and

Jay. Feel vindicated with them to back up your story. Everyone knowing exactly how my family thinks of me." Nora's voice cracked. She wanted to cry. She wanted to turn wolf and feel things in an easier way. She wanted a hug from Matt. A comforting hair rustle from Tio Marcus. A hand squeeze from Gabriel.

A pack huddle. Her father's voice. Her mother's scent.

As much as every part of her knew that was all over now, she didn't need Annaliese half smiling as she told her so. She didn't need to know that Poppy and Jay heard it first. Nora felt numb. Even the text from Matt—Annaliese had known Nora would be receiving it. She'd been waiting to tell Nora it didn't mean anything. Matt still hated her and was only following Gabriel's order. Everyone had known except her.

Nora hadn't even realized how much she'd hoped Matt wanted to talk things out. She didn't even need to talk about rejoining the pack. She'd just missed her childhood best friend.

"That's not it, Nora."

"That *is* it, though. Why else would you spy on them? You don't trust me to know they aren't good for me? You have to keep layering on the hurtful stories to prove your point?"

"Oh, what? I can't protect you, too, after dealing with all your alpha bullshit? I'm not allowed to watch your back?"

"You don't get it! Any of it! You don't get lonely. You don't get touch-starved. You don't miss what it feels like to have everyone's love and bonds in your head your whole life and then suddenly live in silence! You don't understand how hurt I was last night and how proud I was of myself for not going after them! For choosing me! You didn't think I was capable of doing it, just like Gabriel didn't. Just like Matt didn't. Just like Colbie doesn't. Sometimes, it feels like Lana and Henry are the only two people who think I can do this. It makes it hard to believe I have a chance at being alpha when the people who know me best have so little faith. And if I can't be alpha, what's left for me but Gabriel?"

Annaliese pulled in a long breath. "Nora, you *know* I believe you can do this. You're upset and grieving, but you know you can do it too. It's going to be—"

"I need some space." Nora didn't know what she wanted, but she couldn't breathe. She left the apartment without another word.

Nora went to the Alpha's Den. She circled the building. Used her key to get inside. Walked the quiet halls. There were so many new scents now. The sweat and vibrancy of humans clung to the walls. It filled even the plants around the room, which were unfurling fresh leaves at too fast a rate. Nora touched one and felt the tingle of magic. Whatever spell Poppy had put on them, it was intense. Pausing, Nora went to the second floor. Lana was likely sleeping above, but it was these bedrooms that drew Nora now. Last night, Lana had brought her in here. She'd explained how she didn't furnish the apartments fully so Nora's pack could move in and decorate how they pleased. If they shared rooms, Nora could easily fit eight pack members. Given a pack's tendency to love sharing space, she could fit even more. Nora would probably move in here, too. These walls could soon echo with the sound of a pack existing. Play fighting in the halls, cooking together, movies at night with all of them piled into one of the living rooms. They would protect and live together like a pack was meant to. Nora, through her alliance with Lana, could provide that for them.

Maybe it was a stubborn response to Annaliese's doubt, but after the success of the club last night, Nora was more confident than ever that this place could thrive. That she wouldn't fail within the walls, and *if* she did, she had people who trusted her around to lift her up. Topher was steady, Josh ready with advice, Poppy examining things from every angle.

And whether or not Colbie loved her, she still cared. She

was still watching Nora's back. At this moment, there was no one Nora trusted more.

Even telling herself all this, feeling the potential of the future within the space, Nora was numb. And she knew what she needed after fighting with Annaliese.

She pulled out her phone, sure that she would regret doing this as much as she would regret not doing it. She messaged Matt back. *Yes.*

Nora expected him to call. Instead, he asked her to meet at the park near their old house. The thought of being so close to home made her skin crawl, but Nora had to believe she could do this. She agreed and left the club, locking up behind her and letting the building pull some energy. It was constantly feeding from her, just a little bit, but enough that Nora noticed. It never significantly impacted her energy levels, and Nora knew she could wall her strength off from it if needed, but she liked the idea of her power protecting the place. She let the building replenish itself before she left.

Matt waited by the fountain in the middle of the park. The water was coming out of a wolf's mouth. Its stone cubs circled beneath. Wolves and werewolves were common in the national park. They were spotted in decorations and architecture throughout the city. Even though her father had been a prominent alpha, he hadn't been here long enough for the wolves to be in honor of him. There used to be other packs here, but they'd all left around the time her father was killed. Gabriel said they weren't in favor of the laws and had left in protest.

If Gabriel had been lying about what happened to Nora's dad, was he lying about that too? No one else knew where the packs had gone. Was all this supernatural dark magic what ran them out?

Could Nora do something to fix it? To make the city a place of welcome again?

Matt watched Nora approach with guarded eyes. His red hair was longer and in his face. His jean jacket hung open to reveal a simple black t-shirt. He was dressed like Gabriel preferred to dress, not the bright colors that Matt used to love, no matter how badly they clashed with his hair. Even though they were ready to talk for the first time in weeks, Nora missed him more than ever. This wasn't her Matt. The friendship they had once shared was gone. They were both so changed from its breaking.

"I wasn't sure you'd come," Matt said when Nora stopped, keeping a good five feet between them.

"Me neither."

Matt smiled at that. Nora fought a cringe. The first words out of her mouth were exactly the type of indecisive statement Matt expected of her. But she didn't backtrack. She waited for him to talk. "How are you?" he asked.

Nora thought about that. She was here, so she was clearly still lonely and hurt. But… she also felt like she could turn around and leave as soon as she didn't like where this was going. "I'm doing better. Getting used to the changes."

"You know you don't have to, right? Get used to anything, I mean. Gabriel wants you back. He'd still let you be beta."

Those were Gabriel's words flowing emotionlessly from Matt's mouth. She tilted her head. "He hasn't made you beta?"

"No. He's waiting for you to come back."

Ah, there was the emotion—the spike of bitterness. Nora nodded slowly, glancing away from Matt and around the park. It was moderately full of families and dog walkers. The Sunday morning calm and warm. Nothing like the conversation happening between the two of them.

Nora turned back to Matt. "What does he have you do? What do you all do during the day?"

"We couldn't tell you that before you joined the pack, Nora. Why would we tell you now? You have to earn—"

"And *that's* the problem. I don't actually think I have to

earn anything at this point. What I've earned is an apology. From you. From Gabriel. What I deserve is the truth about what he's done with my father's pack. With *my* legacy."

Matt reared back. "That's not how things work, and you know it, Nora. We're doing exactly what Morales would have wanted. You're the one deviating. You're the one being difficult."

"You think if Dad could decide, he'd pick Gabriel over me? You think if he'd been able to pass on alphaship peacefully, he wouldn't have trusted me with it?"

Matt *rolled his eyes.* "It doesn't work like that, Nora. The more naive you sound about all this, the more driven by emotion and not what's right, the more I have to think that, yeah, he would have picked Gabriel."

"Hmm." Nora tried not to let that cut too deep. She wasn't surprised, though it still didn't feel good to hear. "And everyone else? You? If I had been there as an alpha when my father died, would they all have picked Gabriel over me?"

"They did pick him, Nora."

"What about Tia Alejandra? Or my mother? Or Ian? Or Miguel? Or Ryan? Or Gabby?"

Matt blinked. "Nora… you know what happened to them. They died trying to protect him. Your mom left because the grief was too painful. Why would you ask me that?"

"Because I saw my tia, Matt. She isn't dead, and the more I learn about this city from people who aren't Gabriel, the more I question everything he ever said."

"Enough!"

Matt cowered, head ducking in compliance. Nora felt the alpha command slide off her like oil over water. She turned, chin lifted, to meet Gabriel's eyes. He blinked at her reaction, and Nora remembered how she'd had to force herself to feel his commands before. Desperate to join the pack, she'd convinced herself his orders affected her like everyone else.

She'd been proud when she felt his words at the base of her spine. Her stomach turned to think of it now.

Gabriel recovered his surprise and tried a different approach, softening his mismatched eyes and stepping forward slowly. "I never lied to you, Nora Mora. Come on. You *know* that. You *know* me. All of us. We're your family."

He sounded like Matt had at the club. Or Matt sounded like him. "Then tell me the truth. Then treat me like family, not a powerful lower you want to submit to you."

Nora glare at Matt when he scoffed. "I am powerful, Matt."

"Powerful people don't go around stating it. You know you aren't, Nora. You have some strength, but it makes no sense that you were able to break out from under Gabriel."

Ignoring the whisper that reminded Nora she'd only done it with Topher's help, Nora set her face. "I didn't come here to be insulted. I came here for an explanation. For an apology."

Gabriel stepped closer. Nora refused to back down. "We were doing what was best for everyone, Nora. And I'm trying to help you now. I can smell the loneliness, the desperation. You *need* a pack. It's been too long. Come home, and everything will be made right. We're close to fixing the city. You can help us."

Nora felt outside the conversation, listening to it all like someone who hadn't grown up thinking this was normal. Listening like a bystander who carried themselves with confidence. Listening to them talk to Nora through Colbie's ears. And Nora hated it for herself for the first time. It made her angry. Whether or not she was only an alpha because of Topher, she deserved better than this. Poppy said she was strong. Henry said she was strong. Nora felt in her core and arms and heartbeat that she was strong.

It made her angry that they were both standing there, taller and older and paler and smug, trying to make her feel weak again. Trying to make her small.

Nora turned her back on Gabriel, intentionally dismissing him and feeling even more of Colbie there in her actions. She looked at Matt and wanted to strike as deeply as he did. "I don't know what all Gabriel has lied about, but I will find out. If you ever want to join a true Morales pack, you can find me at the Alpha's Den."

Nora walked away, head high. Gabriel's parting words still managed to send a chill down her back. "I never lied to you. This is a mistake. You don't know what's happening in the city, Nora. You're in over your head, and you're going to regret this. If you build a pack and realize you're wrong, you'll be bringing them down with you. This isn't just you that you're hurting. None of us will forgive you, nor will anyone foolish enough to follow you."

When she was far enough away so he wouldn't hear Nora whisper, she told herself, "He's lying." She repeated it all the way home.

CHAPTER 23

When Annaliese picked up Poppy, both were humbled by how apparent it was that they'd stayed up far too late the night before. They'd left the Alpha's Den around 2:30 after finishing mopping. Luckily, Lana had approved a cleaning crew after counting the drawers. Poppy was already anticipating the nap she would take after this coffee run and recap session.

Annaliese put the car in reverse.

"Wait!" Ru came running out of the apartment. Poppy blinked. Usually, Ru was dressed in leggings and a T-shirt around the house and for her dog walking. Currently, she had on a pair of Colbie's baggie jeans and a crop top she must have bought recently. Her hair was in two half buns, and she carried a purse. Was that lipstick?

Poppy got out of the car. Ru came to a stop in front of her, breathing hard. "I heard you were going to Vegan Your Day."

"So?"

Ru readied for battle. It made Poppy's body react similarly as instincts bred from a childhood of sisters rose to the surface. She crossed her arms.

"So Topher thinks it would be good for me to make friends.

My wards are solid, and I stocked up on potions just in case. You'll be close by. Topher said I should go hang out with Henry's pack. There are wolves my age I could try to be friends with. I used Topher's phone and texted Josh. He knows I'm coming, and Daniel said I could hang out with them."

"You want to go… make friends?"

"Please, Poppy! It'll be so safe. Josh promised it would be great. And I know Daniel already. I'll probably hang out mostly with him, but he said more high-school-age kids are here now, too."

Poppy blinked. It hadn't occurred to her that Ru was lonely. That she was longing for an excuse to get out of her leggings. Her sister was glowing with excitement. Literally. A gentle white yellow cast off her skin, barely noticeable in the sunlight. "What if you lose control?"

"I won't hurt anyone. Werewolves are safe from my magic. And they know what I am, so I won't expose myself."

"You won't leave their den?"

"Not until you come back to get me." Ru held up her pinky. Poppy couldn't fight a smile as she caught it in her own. She pressed a kiss to her sister's knuckle.

"Okay. I'm sorry we didn't think of this sooner. I should have realized you would want to get out more."

Ru jumped, going a bit too high off the ground with her magic. She squealed and proceeded to dance a few moves she'd picked up on social media. Then, making Poppy's heart feel too close to bursting, Ru bent to speak to Annaliese in the car. "Would you mind giving me a ride to Henry's?"

"Not at all. Hop in."

Ru slid into the back, asking Annaliese if her hair looked okay. Poppy tried not to be offended, knowing she didn't put enough effort into her hair for Ru to want her opinion. The two talked about the difficult process of even space buns, braids, and hair-cutting disasters nearly all the way to Henry's den. Poppy recognized Ru's constant stream of words as nervous chatter and wanted to climb into the back to wrap her little sister in a hug. All of this was so new and foreign to both of them. Poppy remembered well her nervous excitement when meeting Topher and Colbie. She'd been incredibly lucky to find such good friends on the first try, but Poppy liked most of Henry's pack. They would be kind to her sister, which eased some of the risk.

Ru's nerves were familiar, but Poppy's urge to comfort her and the desire to hold her hand when they reached Henry's were new. She wasn't a protective older sister when they lived together. She'd felt too much jealousy toward the youngest Jennings. Now, she wanted to encase Ru in bubble wrap and potions to keep anyone from giving her a sideways glance. Annaliese pulled into the apartment visitor's space, and they got out. As they walked inside, Poppy stopped fighting the urge and reached for Ru, squeezing her sister tight and smelling their room and the tinge of their family magic in Ru's hair as their wards mingled.

"Call me if you get overwhelmed or tired or anything goes slightly wrong."

Ru hugged Poppy back just as tight. "You too."

Poppy laughed, stepping away as Josh came up to greet them. "Hey! Daniel, Ari, and Elsa are in the kitchen making a mess they claim will end up being banana bread."

Ru laughed, and Josh led them inside. Poppy melted to goo, watching how Josh's babble eased the tension in Ru's shoulders. They paused so Ru could meet Henry, who pointed at her and told her to behave with mock severity before continuing with Quinn at his side.

Poppy stiffened when he glanced back with wide eyes, no doubt feeling the power flowing off Ru, but he didn't comment. Poppy muttered in Ru's ear. "Rein it in a touch."

Ru mouthed an apology, concentrated, and ceased glowing.

In the kitchen, the younger wolves accepted Ru into their ranks after barely pausing for introductions. Poppy had never seen her sister so happy. Even Annaliese was grinning as she watched them.

Poppy turned to Josh. "She might… get too excited and slip up with her magic," she whispered. She couldn't just leave without everyone prepared for what might happen.

Josh shook his phone screen at her. "She warned me and asked me to let everyone know. We've spent time around witches before, you know. Maybe not as young and powerful as Ru, but it would still take a lot to surprise us."

The group of bakers burst into laughter over something Ru said. Ru flushed with pride and pleasure. When she caught Poppy's eyes, she made a shooing motion, mouthing, "Go!"

Poppy turned to Annaliese. "I think we should leave them to it."

"Looks like it. Want to join us for coffee, Josh?"

His brown eyes lit with pleased surprise. He'd been at the club as late as they were, though he didn't seem nearly as tired. "I'd love to."

They set out, leaving Annaliese's car parked in the apartment lot and opting to walk the few blocks it took. The quiet between them wasn't uncomfortable. It was nearly as familiar as the quiet moments with Colbie and Topher. More friendship all around.

"How did your first nights go?" Josh eventually asked.

"I think well," Annaliese said. "Besides Matt and Adriana's surprise appearance, I'm actually shocked how well it went." Annaliese kicked at a rock on the sidewalk. It was a hot day. The river flowed by, offering a slight coolness to the air and drawing all the bugs to the path they walked. Poppy cast a light spell to keep them away.

"How was Nora with seeing them? That was her first time since the change, right?" Poppy asked.

"Yeah, it was. She's… well, we fought this morning. I don't know what she's feeling. Upset enough that we got into it. I feel bad."

Josh winced. "I can't imagine. Thinking about losing my pack makes me want to throw up."

Annaliese sighed. She kicked another rock. "I don't think I'm supporting her right. I just want her to stay away from them, but she can tell I feel that way. It makes her all defensive."

"She'll figure it out," Poppy said.

Annaliese paused, bringing them all up short. "Do you think so? Do you think she'll make a pack and not rejoin Gabriel's?"

Josh was nodding before Annaliese finished the question. "I don't know Nora super well, but I can feel her alpha whenever she's near. That part of her will never submit to Gabriel again. What she's struggling with is the grief of losing her pack and family, not any desire to return to how she was before. I doubt it would even take if she tried to rejoin him. It would probably turn into a challenge and I'm sure she even knows that. Acceptance is just hard."

"I don't want to lose her in the process."

Josh slung his arm over Annaliese's shoulder. "Whether or not you like it, Nora considers you pack. That doesn't mean you won't fight. It just means you love each other through it."

Annaliese smiled a bit and allowed Josh to keep his arm there as they continued.

"For what it's worth," Poppy said as they walked, "I think she'll get there too. I've never felt anyone as strong as her. Compared to Nora, I'm surprised Gabriel is even an alpha."

Josh gasped. "Harsh, Poppy!" Then he fell to laughing, clearly in agreement.

Poppy flushed with the simple, pure happiness of making him laugh. When he put his other arm around her, she leaned into his touch and didn't let herself think too hard about how good it felt.

Nor did she pay any attention to the strange expression on Gus's face, always hovering on her periphery.

Oliver waited patiently outside of Vegan Your Day. They were running late with Ru changing their plans, but Oliver wasn't put out about it. Just as tired as the rest of them, he still conjured a bright smile as they approached. "Are you recruiting more members to our supernatural alliance club, Annaliese?" he asked.

Poppy raised an eyebrow, turning under Josh's arm to look at Annaliese and realizing Annaliese had already stepped out from under the werewolf's embrace. Probably a while ago. Josh kept Poppy tucked into his side, and Poppy didn't want to fight it.

Annaliese answered Poppy's unspoken questions. "We can make friends and alliances without Lana. Learning to trust each other takes work and time; time we won't have if we only do this at night and in the club. Also, humans need to be more involved. We're starting small, but the more familiar we get with the different supernatural groups and how humans can interact within them, the better."

Josh grinned. "I know a bunch of humans involved. Within the pack are spouses or members born without the ability to shift. Next time, we'll have to hang out over there."

Annaliese's jaw dropped. "Really?"

"For sure. Wait, there aren't any humans at Gabriel's?"

"I was the only one I know of who ever went there," Annaliese answered.

"Wow. Okay," Josh said. He sounded confused.

Oliver checked his phone. "Jay is off. I can't believe they got up and worked a shift already."

Inside, Jay waved to them from a table in the back corner. When they saw how many people Annaliese had brought, they and the boy they were sitting with started pushing two tables together while everyone went up to the counter. Annaliese, Josh, Poppy, and Oliver ordered drinks with the highest caffeine content they could handle, which was alarming in Oliver's case. Poppy's eyes kept going to the blond-haired, blue-eyed, summer-tanned boy sitting beside Jay. He observed the group carefully, deeply uncomfortable about the situation.

They sat down with their drinks, and Jay took over the introductions. "Everyone, this is Chance. He's interested in vampires and has been studying them, but he doesn't have anyone to ask his questions. I thought this might be a nice way to start, especially since I don't know if his fake is good enough to get him into the club."

"Well, it might have been, but you just told three people who work there he isn't twenty-one, so it'd have to be really, really good at this point," Oliver said.

Annaliese dropped her eyes, not yet twenty-one herself. She recovered quickly and went back to studying Chance intently, making him shift in his seat. Poppy couldn't blame her. There was something familiar about Chance. She and Annaliese traded a glance, neither of them able to put a finger on it.

"He's quiet today," Jay noted, nodding their head toward Gus.

Poppy had momentarily forgotten about the poltergeist. "Whatever we did last night wore him out."

"That's good. That's a really good sign."

Oliver, Chance, and Josh were equally confused, but Annaliese spoke up before any questions could be asked. "What do you want to know, Chance?"

"Can vampires really only go out at night?"

"For the most part, yeah." Oliver fielded the first question. "Especially during the summer."

"Can a vampire be changed back?"

"Back into a human?" Annaliese asked, surprised.

Oliver's brow furrowed. Poppy cleared her voice. "There have been witches who attempted it, but it took them too far into dark magic." The line of thought brushed uncomfortably close to what Topher hoped Poppy could do for Julia. "But most modern vampires choose their path. No one I've heard about has looked into undoing it very deeply."

"And you're a witch?" Chance asked. After a brief pause, Poppy nodded. It felt strange to admit it in public. Josh shifted closer, offering silent support. "Could you figure it out?"

Poppy frowned. Could she? Would Topher be happier if he wasn't a vampire? Or Colbie? Far better witches than Poppy had explored the question with poor results. "I think that's magic beyond me."

"But could you try?"

Suddenly, it didn't feel like they were discussing a hypothetical. This was personal, and Chance appeared worried. His features were drawn, hiding hope.

The pang of familiarity rang again. Poppy had seen this expression before. It made telling him no harder. "I mean, maybe eventually, but there are a lot of things that are more pressing right now." Like Julia.

Chance opened his mouth to protest but lost his nerve at the last minute, sitting back disappointed. Annaliese turned to Jay. "Did you get a chance to meet with your witch?"

"No. When we get closer to the full moon, she goes quiet and deeper in hiding. She hasn't answered my calls."

"Why?" Poppy asked.

Jay squinted at Poppy as if they couldn't tell if she was joking. "To avoid the demons! They're stronger then." At Poppy's blank expression, Jay sat forward. "Don't you? You really should."

"I mean, I know there are demons in the city, but I haven't noticed them being worse on the full moon. Has she seen them?"

They were all ignoring how pale Chance had turned.

"They scratch at her wards almost every night! *Especially* around the full moon. She has to condense her wards to their strongest and can't sleep when the demons are most active. You don't feel that?"

Jay's eyes were wide. Shocked. This must be a huge issue for their witch friend, yet Poppy couldn't say that her wards were ever threatened enough to concern her, especially now that Ru's magic was woven in.

Was it possible this witch Jay knew was weaker than Poppy? That didn't seem at all likely. But then again, Poppy had never met a witch from another coven.

"Sometimes I feel a scratching, but nothing as bad as that."

"We all know now that Poppy is a boss at all things warding," Oliver stated proudly.

"And why are the demons stronger during the full moon?" Annaliese asked.

Poppy shrugged. "Dark powers fueled by their own form of light. I'm stronger in the sun because it feeds life and is the base of my magic. I'm sure it's something similar for vampires, werewolves, and other creatures of the night. *I'm even stronger during full moons than I would be on a normal night.*"

Now, Jay's mouth was fully agape. "You *cast* on full moons? Doesn't that draw the demons even worse?"

Poppy looked to Josh, both thinking about that night in the warehouse when she summoned her mother. "Only when I let down my wards. I've only done that once to draw them."

"*You've drawn them on purpose?*" Jay grew louder the more shocked they got.

Poppy shifted, uncomfortable with all the attention. By now the woman working on her computer two tables over was shooting them looks.

"Poppy only did that once for a specific circumstance, but my pack was there to watch her back."

Jay sat back in their seat, blinking. "You've purposefully summoned demons, and werewolves helped you. But why?"

"To discover why they're here and what's causing the attacks. We didn't get very far."

"What attacks?" Chance asked, eyes bouncing between

them all. His voice was much higher now. "You mean the murders?"

"Yeah. They're supernatural, but we don't know what kind of creatures are causing them. We're trying to track the sorcerer responsible."

Jay was furiously texting on their phone. "My witch friend doesn't know anything about sorcerers in the city. I'm sure she would have mentioned something like that."

"All the vampires and werewolves are already searching for them. But it's good your witch is hiding out. Witches have been turning up dead, too."

Poppy remembered the black that showed up when she and Ru tried to See Natalie with a pang. She didn't want to talk about that right now. But she did need to know how to find her mom again. "What else do you know about using the powers of the dead?" she asked Jay.

Chance suddenly stood, beyond pale, more gray. "I think I've heard enough. I, I have to go."

"Chance, wait!" Jay followed their friend outside.

Josh, Poppy, Annaliese, and Oliver shared a look. Oliver let a small giggle slip out, before he clapped a hand over his mouth. Before they knew it, they were all laughing. Annaliese shook her head. "How did I not even notice how far beyond normal we'd gotten?"

"What the... fuck do you mean, using... the powers of the dead, Poppy!" Oliver was holding his side, speaking between gasping laughs.

Poppy threw up her hands, rings glinting in the bakery lights. "I just have a slight case of being haunted. We're figuring it out."

"Of course you do," Oliver said, shaking his head at all the ridiculousness of the conversation.

Josh's laughter cut off abruptly. "Haunted?"

"By my grandpa."

Oliver let out another laugh, coughing when he saw how

serious Josh was taking this. "And you've been using him? To what?" Josh asked.

"Spy, basically," Annaliese shrugged.

"I'm going to use him to find my mom," Poppy said. "I have to ask her more about the demons and everything going on." If anyone would know how to help Julia, it would be Tiff Jennings.

Josh's jaw clenched. He'd been there the last time Poppy had spoken with her mother. "Don't do this without me there, okay?"

"Okay." Poppy made the promise but wasn't sure she could keep it. Josh knew about Julia, but he hadn't seen the reality. He hadn't felt the danger in the air of the apartment building. She couldn't risk Julia and the other drainers by exposing them to Josh and his wolf. There was no way Josh would stay quiet about the drainers with Henry if he saw them in person.

The uncommitted promise felt horribly like choosing Topher over Josh again.

Jay texted, asking to reschedule for tonight. Chance needed some time to take it all in. Annaliese deflated a bit. "We didn't even get to talk about whatever Jay can do. I want to know what humans are capable of."

"You aren't on the schedule to bartend until later tonight. Just ask them before you come into work," Poppy told her. Part of her was happy to cut things short. She wanted to check on Ru, brew some potions to restore what she'd used earlier this week, take a nap, and think more about full moons—the day had just started but already felt like too much.

They finished their coffees in another companionable silence that gave Poppy too much time to think about all the heat coming off of Josh. It seemed to permeate her skin and sink into her very core.

She didn't used to think about Josh like this. She didn't even know when it shifted, but her body didn't always react like this to him. It differed from the rush of attraction she'd always felt for Topher. This was… nicer. She could breathe in it. But it was still a pleasant twist in her stomach.

How changeable was she? Had Josh been right when he said she'd only liked Topher because he was the first guy she met? Did she only now like Josh because he was the second? *Did* she like him? Was this attraction or more friendship? Was any of this fair when she'd already hurt him?

"You're quiet," Josh said, leaning in to speak in her ear and sending a satisfying chill down her spine. He stayed there, in her space, and after a pause, put his nose into the dip of neck under her ear and inhaled deeply.

Goosebumps erupted down Poppy's arms. She pushed her shoulder into him, hard enough to move him back but not enough to make him leave. "You're feral. Watch it, or I'll ward my scent from you."

Josh just smiled. "You're more open than usual. What are you thinking?"

Annaliese and Oliver were bickering across the table, consumed by whatever nonsense had set him off. Poppy turned to Josh, his brown eyes right there. He had a smattering of summer freckles. His warm energy was present as always, willing Poppy to use it the same way she made her scent accessible to him.

His skin looked soft.

"I'm thinking I'm confused."

His eyes flashed and he fought a smile. "No reason to have to figure it out now."

"You're so sure there's something for me to figure out with you?"

Josh brushed his thumb up and down Poppy's bicep. She hadn't even noticed his arm draped over the back of her seat. "Yes. But I can't stop thinking about you being haunted. Tell me more about that."

Poppy shrugged, looking past Josh to Gus standing off to

the side. "I don't know much about it. Remember when we went back to get my mom, and she was gone?"

Josh nodded. "You were acting weird."

"That was when we realized we were bonded. He was telling me he picked up my vial with blood on it. He's been following me ever since. Talking to me. Trying to get me to join my mom. Throwing things. Now he's calmer because I've sent him on jobs. I don't want to keep using him, though. I'm hoping Jay and their witch friend will help me get rid of him."

Josh's arm tightened around her. "I'll ask Henry. We can call around to people we know and see if something like this has been solved before."

Poppy opened her mouth to refuse. She'd yet to repay Josh and his pack for helping her months ago, but a stubborn expression settled over Josh's face. "Just say okay."

Poppy smirked. "Fine. Okay. Thanks."

He swooped in close to kiss Poppy's cheek. Of course, this was when Oliver paused to take a breath. He and Annaliese both noticed.

"Is this a thing again?" Oliver asked, pointing between the two of them.

Poppy rolled her eyes. "Let's go home. I need a nap." But she did take Josh's hand when she stood up.

CHAPTER 24

Topher woke up slowly, his mouth already watering, but the familiarity of the scent was enough to keep him from reacting. Even before opening his eyes, he knew he was waking earlier than usual. He could feel the sun pulling him back to sleep but fought it.

Topher yanked the comforter over his head, a useless attempt to block out the delicious aroma. "There's a human in my bed," he said.

Annaliese snorted. "That was creepy."

"Creepier than getting into a vampire's bed while they're dead to the world?"

Annaliese stiffened, and Topher regretted his words, his unamused tone. But... the last time they'd spoken still reverberated in his head. Annaliese only wanted an alliance. Topher's loyalty and power. She and Nora. Nora, who was beyond someone in need of his protection or influence. Nora had the means to take care of herself and Annaliese. Once she had her pack, Topher wouldn't be a thought to either of them.

Topher felt pulled in so many directions. He'd just woken up, but he was exhausted. This world seemed to get heavier in new, creative ways with each passing night.

He didn't want to talk to Annaliese. Usually, he couldn't get enough of her. She'd been welcome to his space all last winter, and he'd enjoyed every conversation. Topher wanted to map out how her mind worked and listen to her voice constantly. But now he knew how one-sided the feeling was.

From her presence in his bed and the anxiety he smelled rolling off of her, Topher knew something was wrong, but he selfishly didn't want to put in the effort to ease Annaliese's tension. Not after she'd inferred he was only valuable for his vampire strengths.

He was so, so tired of being a vampire.

"Sorry. I guess I shouldn't have just assumed it was fine."

Topher sighed because he could hear more in Annaliese's voice now. She'd been crying. It wasn't just anxiety; she was truly upset. Was she in need of his vampire strength or just the comfort of his room? Why had she come to him? And how could he turn her away, no matter how weary he was? He slid a hand over the comforter and found hers. "What's wrong?"

"What do you mean?"

Well, he definitely didn't have the energy to pretend everything was fine. "What's going on, Annaliese? How can I help?"

She hesitated at his no-nonsense tone, then surprised Topher by rolling suddenly and tugging down the comforter so she could look at him. "You've been weird. You talk to me like you talk to Nora now."

Topher raised an eyebrow. If he talked to her like he did Nora, walls down and openly, she'd be charmed right now. "I don't know what you mean."

"I… with Nora, it's like a business deal. Like you're constantly watching yourself so you don't say something wrong. Like you're thinking about ten things at once. You seem worried you'll say something that will get back to Colbie, or Lana, or the supernaturals as a group. It feels… political when you talk to her."

Hadn't Annaliese made it clear she wanted the same type

of relationship? Topher rolled onto his back, rubbing at his eyes. He could go back to sleep so easily. It was still early.

But then Annaliese grabbed his wrist, stilling him. She was so warm. Her blood so near his mouth. "I thought you didn't want to be friends," Topher heard himself saying.

"When did I say that?"

"When you said you just wanted to make sure I was an ally."

"I didn't—"

Topher pulled out of Annaliese's grip. He sat up and twisted to look down at her. From the way she started, he knew he'd moved too fast. Like a vampire. He tried to calm himself, temper his motions, and smooth his expression. "I understand I'm a valuable person to have at your back and that you want to make sure I don't screw over Nora. I get that. I just can't make you any promises when I have my maker to consider. I'll do my best. I promise. You don't have to worry about me ruining things for you. Not if I can help it or find some way to warn you."

"Topher, are you okay?"

"No. I'm not okay. I haven't been okay in so long that I don't know what that would feel like. And I know you came here because you're upset, and I'm sorry I'm not making it any better; I just can't right now. If you want me to bite or charm you, I can help. Otherwise, I think you should go."

Annaliese pushed herself to sitting, brow furrowed. "Oh, no, you don't. Don't push me away. I was upset about Nora, but she and I have always worked things out. Tell me what's wrong."

Topher dropped his head into his hands, taking a breath. He hated it when the emotions bubbled to the surface like this. It made him feel out of control, and control was the most important thing with a human in his bed and his last feeding hours ago.

"Topher?"

"Sorry. I just don't even have a place to start, Annaliese. So much is fucked up."

A quiet fell. Topher counted Annaliese's breaths. The apartment was hushed outside. Colbie still sleeping. The TV quietly entertained everyone awake. Topher smelled Josh in the apartment. He heard Mouse scratching at something.

"Do you ever talk about him?"

That buzzing stillness that filled his mind when Dylan was brought up made Topher's stomach turn. "I should get to the club."

"It's a Sunday night. They don't need us yet. Lana probably doesn't think you're up. Do you want to talk about him or why you're being weird with me or is there something else? Come on, Topher. We're friends."

Topher let his hands fall, staring at his closed door. "Are we, though?"

Annaliese's eye roll was nearly audible. Her annoyance was unfair after their last conversation. He spoke before she could protest. "Look, I might sound like I'm talking to Nora, but the last time we talked, you talked to me like Lana does. Or Grace before her. Or Henry sometimes. Or Kallow when she gets me alone. Or so many other supernaturals and humans who wanted to make sure I was on their side. So no, it doesn't feel like we're friends. Just like it doesn't feel like I'm Lana's *darling*. Since my boyfriend was murdered before my eyes and I was changed into a vampire against my will, I've had very few genuine relationships. If you want to be one of them, my power isn't part of the equation. But you made sure I knew it was. And it was a good reminder."

Annaliese went quiet after that rant. Topher kept his eyes fixed on the door, refusing even to breathe. He wished he hadn't said anything. Why be so bothered by this? Of course, she'd wanted to ensure Nora had someone watching her back. He couldn't blame her for wanting access to his abilities. It wasn't like he wouldn't gladly use them to make sure nothing—

"That's valid. I'm sorry I said that."

"No, it's… I get it. I shouldn't have——"

"I don't like that tone. Topher, you're still human too. I'm sorry I treated you like just a vampire ally. I shouldn't have done that."

Annaliese was always so… present. Her dark eyes fixed on him, steady and unflinching. He loved her eyes. "Do you have anyone who treats you not like a vampire?" Annaliese asked.

"Well, there's Colbie, of course. Poppy. Ru. Josh is always refreshing." Topher shrugged. The list was short. That was his life now.

Annaliese scooted to rest against the wall. Topher turned to lean on the other, crossing his legs and leaving only an inch between their knees. "What about your parents? Or anyone else you knew as a human?" She asked the question cautiously, knowing there must be something wrong there. Topher and Colbie never mentioned their human lives.

And Topher was surprised to find himself wanting to talk about it. But still, he couldn't. Because Annaliese was Nora's best friend. Nora was still struggling with her old loyalties to Gabriel's pack. Gabriel had already tried to kill him twice. As always, the risks were right there. The fear of what happened to Dylan, to Colbie, to Julia… If his family was found and connected to him, what other horrors could befall the humans of his past?

"Why do you want to know?" he asked, deflecting.

"Because I do want to be your friend, only I know nothing about you. Where are you even from? I assumed here, but it's not that big of a city. I feel like we could have run into each other growing up."

Topher almost laughed. When Colbie had been looking for Nora to tell her she was an alpha, they'd been shocked to learn Annaliese lived right down the street from one of Topher's old teammates. They'd both been in the neighborhood for barbecues and team banquets and birthday parties.

"We probably came close a few times. I was born here. Were you?"

"Yeah. At NB Health."

"Same."

Annaliese grinned. "And you played soccer?"

Topher nodded.

"Club teams? I have friends who played club teams. They're my age, so the year below you, but maybe you know them."

Topher opened his mouth to answer but then all the friends he'd made through the soccer community came to mind. People who probably thought he'd dropped off the face of the Earth for how little they knew about him now. People who now played on new teams, attended college in new cities, and had jobs that took them far away.

People who might be home for the summer. People he still cared about deeply. People he had to keep separate from his new life.

"What about all this interests you, Annaliese? Why do you want to get involved with us, with the supernatural, when you have the choice? When you're coming in with your eyes wide open?" What drove her to risk herself to save him last winter? What did confidence like that feel like?

Annaliese pretended to pout. "This was finally my chance to ask you questions."

Topher crossed his arms, matching her feigned pout with a mock scowl. "You know more about me than I do you. Start talking."

"Fine. To prove I want to be friends, I'll tell you more about me." Topher braced. Getting to know Annaliese meant potentially liking her more than he already did. "I grew up more on the east side. My dad was a pharmacist, and my mom had a lot of health concerns. They fought a lot. I think now my mom was in pain so she kept picking those fights, but sometimes I hated her for it. My dad worked all the time and always took us for hikes or to the movies or anything to spend his free time together. One night, Mom said she was too tired. He wanted to eat at a new Indian place, and she told him to just pick it up. It was raining. There was an accident. He never came home."

Annaliese sounded mechanical as she talked. Careful. The waves of emotion contained, but barely. "It was... so hard. I was ten. My mom kind of shut down. I think she blamed herself. I didn't understand it. I didn't want to blame her, but she wasn't very good at comforting me either. The doctors put her on a new medication, and she got better physically, but our home was quiet for a while. Then, one day, she met Tim. I was twelve by then and angry at the world for taking my happy, energetic Dad." Annaliese sighed, picking at the hole in her jeans.

"Tim made my mom act like the world was suddenly the place Dad always made it out to be. They went out all the time. She started hiking. Like going on trips to backpack. She started smiling. She started calling me grumpy and apologizing for me in company. I didn't blame her when my dad died, but I got so mad she acted like the perfect match for my dad after he was gone. It was consuming. All the anger I felt for so long. My mom got pregnant, and then I was jealous, too. I decided if my mom didn't need me, I didn't need her. I hung out with Nora all the time. I went to the Den and was overwhelmed by the people there. But then Nora's dad died, and suddenly, we had that in common. No one understood what we were going through. We spent almost all our time together, hiding in my basement room. And she told me about the supernatural world, as much as she knew of it at least, and it felt like leaving my past behind. It felt like a new planet opened up for me. I know this is your reality, and you hate it, but it's my escape. It's fascinating what humans can do or become. Learning about all of you makes me excited. Thinking about changing the world with Lana's ideas makes me feel important. I like learning about all the layers of the world. I like being there for Nora. I know this is risky, but I believe Lana is right in that we can make the world better. All this would have intrigued my dad, and he would be proud of me for all I'm learning and getting out there." Annaliese shrugged. "That probably doesn't make a lot of sense to you."

And Topher laughed. It wasn't a real laugh, just a dry huff of air. But it was enough. Topher shut his face down immediately when Annaliese's went slack. Fuck. This was why he couldn't do this. He'd gotten too lost in the conversation, stopped focusing. It wasn't fair to her to—

"Stop. Whatever you're thinking, it's fine. Explain why you laughed."

"Annaliese…"

"I know. I know you didn't mean to charm me, and you think because it happens, we can't be friends. I'm saying it didn't bother me, and I want to keep trying."

"It doesn't bother you that I could charm you at any moment?"

"It bothers me that vampires can do that. Not that you can. Just talk. We're *friendshipping.*"

"That's not a word."

"I swear to god, if I just opened up like that to get nothing back, I'm going to push you out the window."

Topher lifted a hand, covering his mouth until his smile was gone. From the concentration on Annaliese's face, his eyes still had a touch of an effect, but her smile was pleased when she shook his charm.

"Alright. Fine. My turn. Our parents were pretty volatile people. They got pregnant with Colbie when they were young after knowing each other for a little over a month. They married and decided to make it work, but I think in the early days, having babies was the only way they knew to stay together. They had me right after Colbie, then, well." Topher caught himself. Still thinking of Nora and Gabriel, though it was easy to forget them in the quiet of his bedroom and the comfort of Annaliese. "Well, Colbie and I weren't the kids they wanted. Colbie was too loud, too brave. She was always getting herself hurt. Our mom was a perfectionist. Colbie never felt she was enough for her. Our dad was distant. He spent all his days working, avoiding home unless he and our mom were in a rare, good patch. When I was old enough for school, our mom was more than happy for me to leave the house. I couldn't sit still and she couldn't entertain me. But at school, I couldn't focus on the work. They told our parents to test me for hyperactivity and learning impairments, but Mom said she wasn't spending money on something so obvious and that I'd learn to deal with it eventually. And I just never settled down. I made some bad friends, then worse friends. By senior year, I spent so much time in the warehouses, partying and getting into trouble, that our parents canceled my soccer membership. They told me I couldn't play until I started behaving."

Topher sighed. "I met Dylan, and so much about myself suddenly made sense. It was like he grabbed all my floating, lost pieces and tethered me to the ground. I got sober. I wanted to leave New Brecken and all its disappointments. Then, he died. And here we are. I had a good childhood. My parents were successful. I just couldn't make use of the advantages I was given. I have always ruined everything I touch."

Annaliese considered his words, head tilted. "You're so calm now. So controlled. It's hard to imagine you like that. Harder to imagine that you ruined everything, especially since I know what happened to Dylan wasn't your fault."

"He wouldn't have been there if not for me."

"How is it your fault someone wanted to kill you?"

Topher ducked his head, instinctually hiding emotion, even the negative kind that wouldn't charm. He pressed his palms into his eyes. "I know! I know I never would have hurt him or Colbie or Julia if I could help it! But whatever I try, it's not enough. It's like I'm cursed. All I can do is keep people away."

"Or that's ridiculous, and you're making yourself miserable."

Topher frowned at her. "You really think you'll make it out of all this completely unscathed?"

"I'm good at looking out for myself. I don't trust easily. I'll ask Poppy more about warding myself since my friend says there are some ways for humans to do it. Plus, I'm going into this knowing exactly what I'm signing up for, including the risks of a friendship with you. Also, what happened to Julia?"

Topher's breath caught. He couldn't tell her.

"Topher."

He covered his face again. "You might tell Nora. There are so many things you might tell Nora. You're her best friend; if she rejoins her old pack, everything could be used against me. If she starts a pack and remembers how much she hated vampires, she could use it against me. I can't tell you everything. As much as I want to be your friend."

Annaliese considered that. "And you *do* want to be friends?"

Topher nodded.

"Alright. Then I'll work on Nora."

"Aren't you fighting?"

Annaliese pulled out her phone. "She's already texted to apologize. She's planning to see me at the club later."

Topher sighed, checking his watch. "I guess that's our cue to get up then."

CHAPTER 25

When Topher and Annaliese came out of Topher's room, Josh jerked awake on the couch. Poppy scrubbed the nap from her eyes on the armchair.

Topher went straight to Ru in the kitchen, giving her a hug. "How was Henry's, Rhuberry Muffin?"

Ru laughed. "That is not different from calling me Rhubarb, and you both use that one all the time."

"It *is* different. Answer the question."

"It was great!" Ru told him about her time at Henry's den as she pulled the no-longer-frozen pizzas from the oven. Josh burned his mouth on his first piece, and Annaliese sat at the island. She smiled her thanks as Ru magicked a plate with two slices on it her way. The vegan personal-size pizza sailed through the air toward Poppy. Annaliese's eyes followed the plate's progress, awe on her face.

"—and then Ari dropped the entire loaf! I barely caught it in time because I was talking with Daniel."

Topher smiled. Annaliese's eyes went blank, and Ru snapped her fingers, disrupting the effect of his charm without thought.

The entire room froze, all the stunned attention falling on

Ru, who was still chatting as she removed one of her charmed bracelets and handed it to Annaliese. She only paused in her story to say to Annaliese, "—The ward will probably wear off quickly around Topher, but if you bring it back to me, I'll refill it—And then, Henry came in and was *not* happy about the mess we made. He told me I couldn't use my magic or help them clean it. I was the only one not covered in flour, so he knew it wasn't my fault."

"Ru!" Poppy stood from the couch, shock rolling through her. "How did you do that?"

"Well, I was just really careful when we were measuring and stood out of the way when they started to argue."

"No!"

Topher and Josh were laughing. Annaliese stared at Topher, dimples and all, like she'd never seen anything like it. The new bracelet on her wrist glowed.

"How did you block Topher's charm?"

Ru blinked. Confused. "I just asked the magic. Casted like normal."

It was Ru's answer for most of her spell work. An answer Poppy couldn't fathom since she had to read the currents and find where the strength to cast would come from each time. This was the raw magic that raised the hair on Poppy's arms. Usually, Ru was too even-tempered to accidentally cast anything malicious, but what if she were angry? What if instead of infusing blessing into her charms, she was in a bad mood and infused a curse without fully understanding it? What if the spell she gave Annaliese was so potent that it drew from Ru's power until she had nothing left?

Poppy went to Annaliese and held her hand out. From the way Annaliese clearly didn't want to show her the bracelet, one would have thought it was entirely made of diamonds. Poppy ran her fingers over it. Nothing dark was infused into the black, shiny bead on the woven purple thread. It was filled with enough magic to be buzz under Poppy's fingertips, but Poppy couldn't trace it to Ru. Her sister had cast well, separating it from herself but packing the stone with power.

"You have to be careful, okay?" Poppy said to Ru, dropping Annaliese's wrist.

Ru nodded, relieved that she hadn't gotten in trouble and her magic had passed inspection.

"Thank you, Ru," Annaliese said pointedly like she couldn't believe getting in trouble would even be on the table. She cradled the bracelet to her chest.

Poppy pointed at the bead. "Like Ru said, when those get used, the magic runs out. The cast mostly blocks vampire charm, but the ward in it should distort the image if anyone tries to See you. Do you know how long it'll last?" she asked Ru.

"I usually refill them every morning, but I'm guessing around Topher and Lana it'll last a couple nights."

"You're probably right." Poppy leveled Annaliese a look. "Don't ever accept charms from anyone else without me or Ru looking at them first. If you don't question them, you'll put on a curse one day, and you better hope Ru is strong enough to break it."

Ru winked. "I'm strong enough."

"Why now?" Topher asked, drawing attention away from Annaliese's new jewelry. He sounded almost angry as he stared at Poppy. "Why haven't you given any charms? What about Oliver? Why didn't you give them to Julia?" His voice cracked on her name.

The atmosphere of the room immediately shifted. Suddenly, Poppy saw the different possibilities of the past. A past where Julia's charm grew hot as she was followed by dark magic, warning her enough to call for help. A past where Oliver's neck was protected from Lana's bite.

A past where Ru was exhausted from refilling the jewelry of everyone in danger around her. Where someone saw through the piece of magic and tracked her down. And Poppy forever not strong enough to make the bracelets. Not strong enough to protect her sister.

Poppy dropped her eyes. "I don't think I can, but I could try… I don't want Ru making too many, in case she gets discovered."

"We can work on making more together, Poppy. I'm sure I can hide who they come from."

Topher struggled with that, clearly resistant to getting mad at Ru for the past, but also unable to stop thinking about how things could have been. Colbie leaving her room broke the momentary tension. "What? Awake before me, Topher?"

Topher's smile was forced. His phone buzzed on the counter where Ru had left it this morning. Ru sent it his way with a wave of her hand, trying too hard to be nice and relax his furrowed brow. Topher quickly read the message. "Lana wants to meet with Kallow tonight. Zayn's coming to pick me up. You want to come, Popcorn?"

The nickname defused most of the tension from the previous conversation. Topher's attempt to show he wasn't mad. But his words added another layer. A meeting with the most open witch in the city. Poppy wanted to say no, the short, powerful word building on her tongue. But she glanced toward Ru, whose raw magic was enough to combat Topher's magic with a wave of her hand. Poppy was in over her head, trying to help her sister master that level of power. If Ru was going to make the humans charms, if she was going to leave Poppy's wards, Poppy had to make sure she was ready. "Okay."

"Want me to come?" Josh asked.

Topher shook his head. "Kallow said she was willing to meet Poppy, but its an invite only meeting. Colbie can't even come, but she has another errand. Will you make sure Annaliese gets to the club okay?"

Annaliese's eyes narrowed. She lifted a fist, shaking her new bracelet in Topher's face. "I can get there myself, thanks."

Topher's expression remained blank, but his eyes dropped

to the bead, and he remembered he could smile. He smirked, catching Annaliese's forearm. "Humor me. The club isn't entirely safe, and we don't know where Nora is."

And it wasn't Topher's charm that softened Annaliese's expression. She rolled her eyes. "Well, I'm not going to the club first."

"I'm sure Josh is up for a detour."

"You're as bad as Nora."

"I don't mind that. I like Nora."

Topher dropped Annaliese's arm, ignored his sister's surprise, and moved toward the door, pausing long enough to ask Poppy, "You ready?"

"No. But let's go."

Topher lifted an arm, tucking Poppy into his side when she approached. She was stunned to feel his solid cold and experience no butterflies. Poppy waved her goodbyes, eyes lingering on Josh and wishing he could come with her. He smiled, maybe seeing it in her face, and the door shut between them.

Topher hated meeting with Mother Kallow. He could never quite read her. It bothered him even more now as Poppy walked beside him into the witch's mansion. The wards were a cold wash that begrudgingly allowed him entry. Poppy winced at their tug. Her green eyes were wide as she took in the lavish space. The main room had maintained wood floors, eggshell-colored walls, and portraits everywhere. Crystals of various colors hung from the chandelier.

Kallow beckoned them deeper into the home, guiding them to the living area that was more like a showroom than a lived-in space. It was conspicuously devoid of witchcraft. Lana perched herself delicately on a high-backed chair as if she didn't want to leave an imprint on the pastel blue cushion.

Kallow didn't sit. She went to the fireplace and rested an elbow on the mantel, watching Zayn and Topher take their positions standing behind Lana's chair. Poppy sat on the couch, unsure about her every movement. Kallow's focus narrowed on her. "You're the witch then. I didn't expect one of Tiff's."

Poppy started. "You know my mom?"

Kallow rolled her eyes. "Of course. Jennings, Rosenfield, and I were the only ones to come forward to represent the witches at the time of the law makings."

"And what side did she fall on?"

Kallow lifted a surprised brow. "You don't know?"

"My mother didn't have a very open parenting approach."

"She was against the laws. She foresaw demons and darkness, she claimed. She thought the laws would make it worse. She only came to the meetings to warn us against pursuing them. She's been quiet lately. What is she doing now?"

Poppy squirmed. "She dismantled our coven. I don't know."

Topher was surprised by Poppy's honesty. She watched Kallow intently as the words landed. *"Dismantled your coven!* Why would she do that? And now, of all times? We're being hunted!"

"We're all being hunted," Lana said. She was annoyed. She hadn't counted on having to share so much of Kallow's attention. "It appears Jennings was correct in professing darkness over our city. What have the leaders been doing about it?"

Kallow shrugged. "Gabriel is in charge of hunting the unclaimed lowers. Solas is trying to find the demons. Patter is looking for the connection between the groups. They come to meetings with body counts and theories."

"And what do you think?"

"I think we're losing the humans' support. I'm already exposed and set on keeping them happy. I'll explore other options if Solas, Patter, and Gabriel can't do that. Tell me why I should consider aligning with you."

Topher and Zayn shared a quick look. Sure, Lana had gotten Henry on her side, but he was open-minded and considered an outsider in their city. Lana's only other followers were unestablished, young supernaturals. If she could sway Kallow to her side, that would give Lana the credibility she so badly craved. Likely, this would be the first step to getting her seat back among the city leaders or creating a new group of leaders entirely. She could rise above Grace's other seconds while they scrambled for power on Fourth Street and ownership of Happenstance. Lana claimed she was above that battle and content with Alpha's Den, but Topher could taste the lies in the air whenever she broached that topic.

Lana wanted this. She straightened, her southern upbringing exposing itself in her crossed ankles and perfect posture. She smiled, and Poppy's expression twisted with wariness, cringing away from the vampire.

"As you know, I have the strongest of the vampires in my pocket. I have the alliance of a witch," she gestured vaguely toward Poppy, "Who is so far happy with her compensation and position. I have Henry's support, the largest pack in the city, no matter what anyone says about his level of establishment here. And I have the daughter of Luis Morales. How valuable of an ally will Nora be, Poppy?"

Poppy was startled to be brought back into the conversation so quickly. She cleared her throat, fiddling with her thumb ring. "I've never felt a well of power like hers. Once she makes her pack, she will be the strongest werewolf in the city."

Kallow's brow quirked. "You've tasted her power?"

Poppy blushed. "We believe in working together," she said by way of answer.

When Kallow got nothing out of Poppy on the subject, she turned back to Lana. "*If* she makes her pack at all. Gabriel is certain this is just Morales's teenage rebellion come late."

"Gabriel *would* diminish her to that to save face," Topher said.

Lana nodded. "I've spoken with Nora. She misses her old pack, but she's only brushing the surface of her strength. She won't submit. And so, I have the next generation on my side. I have the future. You must decide whether you align with tired traditions or the new world. There is so much magic in potential, isn't there?"

Kallow strode over the plushy white rug to the bar cart against the opposite wall. "You know, that's exactly how the Big Three talked about outing ourselves and creating the new laws. I'm beginning to think Jennings was smart to be wary. I long for the old days. I long for my daughters to go back into hiding, to never know the fear we've suffered. The loss."

Lana's shoulders drew together. "And what good has longing for the past ever done anyone?"

"True." Kallow turned back to them, an amber liquid in her hand. "So, what would an alliance require?"

"Nothing for now. Poppy has warded my new club well. She's on hand if I need magic. What I will need is a seat at the next meeting of leaders. You have the most political sway in the city. If the legality of my club is ever put into question, you'll be prepared to argue in my favor. And, as my darlings and I get closer than anyone else in the city to solving the mystery of the drainings, you'll be there when the time comes to pursue the attacker. You and your coven."

"Oh," Kallow spoke dryly. "Is that all?"

"Not quite." Lana stood. She approached Kallow too quickly. The liquid in Kallow's glass sloshed as she stepped back, but Lana followed her, eyes narrowed, face as serious as Topher had ever seen it. "I want Beth stripped of her place in your coven. She failed to protect my darlings and my club. She aided Solas and Patter when they unjustly captured me, my maker, and the last of my darlings. She is responsible for Grace's death and the death of my lowers. I want her to pay."

Kallow's expression darkened. "That's quite an accusation."

Lana tipped her chin up. "What Tiff Jennings did to her

coven is proof you can do as I ask. One day, and one day soon, you will want me on your side. That is my price."

"That is a steep price."

"And a fair one." Lana's smile was sharp, her red lips pressed flat. "Beth is on the wrong path. You won't want her name tied to your own for long, not if you truly wish to win office."

Lana considered those adequate parting words. She turned to leave, Kallow glaring at her back, flushed in a red hue. Poppy was slow to stand, looking between Kallow and Lana, surprised at the turn the meeting had taken. Zayn followed Lana, but Topher waited for Poppy to find her voice.

"Mother Kallow, if I were to have questions about cast—"

"Did you not just hear what your vampire demanded of me?" Kallow asked, cutting Poppy off. "You may not remember the bond of the coven, nor do you know the fierce love of motherhood, but you should understand no true witch would pay that price. You think we are still allies in this after Lana's demand?"

Poppy tipped up her chin. "I know as well as anyone family can make the wrong choice. That love shouldn't tear you and drag you down with them. I have questions that have nothing to do with La—"

"Get out. You are no longer welcome in my wards."

Kallow strode away, slamming the heavy wooden door behind her. Poppy seemed to deflate, coming around the couch to Topher's side. He sighed. "I hate to agree with Lana, but Kallow will regret this."

Poppy nodded slowly, chewing on her thumbnail.

"What are you thinking?" Topher asked.

"About Beth. What if she's the witch we saw with Gabriel? If it wasn't her, how many witches were working with the vampire leaders and him? Who did aligning with Lana pit me against? They're all stronger than me."

"When did you see a witch with Gabriel? And these are

people you would have been against, either way, I hope. *And you aren't weak, Poppy.*"

Poppy nodded, but Topher didn't love the expression on her. "I need to find my mother. I have too many questions." She glanced to the left as they stepped outside, lowering her voice. "And I think I have a way to do it."

Lana and Zayn were waiting in the car, talking. They didn't seem to notice Topher had stopped just outside the doors with Poppy. The two of them wouldn't have much time.

Poppy quickly explained Gus. How he'd attached himself to her, how he'd followed Topher that night and found Julia. How he'd helped her fight Julia off and how she'd used him to follow Matt and Adriana.

Topher's eyes were wide, his skin paler than usual when she finished. He tried for lightness, "So that's where the remote keeps going."

It was too forced for Poppy to laugh. "I think I can make him find my mom."

Topher nodded, eyeing Poppy. "Why haven't you yet?"

"I'm not sure how to force him to do things." Poppy glanced toward Gus, who was glaring at her, arms crossed. What she meant was she wasn't sure how she felt about it.

"We should be going to *join* your mother," Gus said, "not trying to get Kallow to answer questions. Not working with vampires. If I find your mother, I'll tell her who you're working with instead of her."

"What's he saying?" Topher asked.

Poppy swallowed and explained.

"But you can make him go?" he asked.

"Yes. I'm just… scared. Asserting my control after our bond is already so deep. I don't want it to go deeper, but I don't know how to make him go to her and not tell her what we're doing. If he warns her, she can ward herself against me or hide. Or she'll find me. Or Ru. He might not even really go find her."

Topher nodded, accepting her excuses. "Where is he?"

"There." Poppy pointed to the right.

Before Poppy could brace herself, she was encompassed in a flare of Topher's charm. He turned his eyes to the area she'd indicated, freeing her to take a breath as the weight of his magnetism shifted, and her wards could relax again.

"Go find Tiff Jennings and report her location to Poppy. Nothing else. Tell Tiff nothing. Indicate nothing about our plans to her. Do everything you can to avoid alerting Tiff to your presence. No notes. No signs you were there."

Gus stiffened under the weight of the charm. For a moment, Poppy was certain it wasn't going to work. How could it? Vampire charm was a power meant to entrap humans and living creatures to make it so a vampire could feed easily. It barely worked on other vampires, and Poppy knew it didn't work on the drainers.

But... Topher was strong. He'd charmed Poppy. He'd charmed Nora. And after fighting hard enough for his color to flare near solid, Gus nodded. Poppy gasped as Gus vanished.

"Did it work?" Topher asked in his normal voice, the force of his charm diffusing from the air. He wasn't even winded.

"I think so. I guess we'll have to wait to find out. He's gone. He's never left like that without me telling him to go before."

"Well, then we wait." Topher grabbed Poppy's hand and moved to the car, ignoring Lana's annoyance that they were late now.

Poppy's heart race with the possibilities. She still hated the idea of taking free will, but Topher had done it. Finding Tiff could mean the answer to so many questions. It could mean solving so many mysteries.

It felt worth it when Poppy hadn't made the command, but also far too easy.

CHAPTER 26

Nora approached cautiously, eyes on Annaliese as she sat at the table outside the brewery. They stayed close to the Alpha's Den in case Raven called them in early, but since this was a Sunday night, Raven, Janelle, and the humans were all working the first shift. With rumors spreading that the Alpha's Den had vampires employed, this draw wouldn't bring people in until full dark. Annaliese and Nora weren't on the schedule for another half hour and Jay had texted to ask them to meet in the spare time.

Jay appeared more comfortable this time around. After checking out the Alpha's Den, they had a better idea what to expect from this supernatural friend group. They had a friend with them. Annaliese and Josh were talking as if it were just a standard hang, not a meeting to talk about supernaturals, but the tension shifted as Nora took her place across from them. Annaliese had a question in her eyes. She wanted to know where Nora had been. If Nora had gone to meet with Gabriel. If Nora was still going down the path that Annaliese thought was right for her.

Nora kept her expression neutral. She knew she wouldn't be returning to Gabriel. What she didn't know was how to put her thoughts into words. How to shift her entire being into someone who didn't want to be in her father's pack. How to claim it out loud after spending her life staunchly in line with Gabriel. What did that girl sound like? What did she want if not that? As she'd walked here, Nora had started picturing herself as a pack leader. Even in her most recent imaginings, the pack had been a carbon copy of her father's, now Gabriel's, but still so similar to how Nora had grown up. With one significant change. No murdering to earn their place.

This led to Nora wondering, after her conversation with Gabriel, what else would she dare to change? Could she simply do away with everything that made her uncomfortable? Gabriel promised she would understand all of it when she became a wolf, but she felt the same even now. Did that mean she could do away with the mating system? With the idea of claiming a beta? With having full authority as an alpha? With keeping secrets?

Could she date whoever she wanted, even while leading a pack? Could there be room for a vampire in her life if she so chose?

"Is this another vampire?" Jay's friend asked before Nora could find her voice to greet them.

Jay's smile faltered. "No, this is Nora. A werewolf."

The friend leaned forward. He had blue eyes. Striking blue eyes. Just like Colbie's. It made the world shift a bit to see them. Nora glanced at Annaliese, who only shrugged at the boy's intensity. "I thought werewolves were supposed to hate vampires. What do you know about them?" he asked.

Nora glanced at Josh. He knew more than she did. Copying Annaliese, Josh shrugged. "Chance didn't like my take on vampires in general."

"What do you mean?" Nora asked, looking between them all.

Chance's tan cheeks flushed. He started to fidget before

shifting to sit on his restless fingers. "I'm just surprised you're all so accepting. I mean, they're *vampires.*"

Nora sighed. "You sound like me a few months ago."

"What changed?" Chance waited like Nora's answer was of the highest importance. Something about him continued to nag at Nora. The ice in his eyes and the way he sat stiffly in his seat as if he didn't want to take up any more space than necessary. It made her think it *was* vital that she get this answer right.

"I saw more of the supernatural world and learned about myself. There are good and bad vampires, werewolves, and witches."

"Can a vampire be good?"

"Yes." Nora was sure of that, at least.

"Can a vampire be changed against their will?"

"Um, not legally."

"You know, Chance, I'm starting to think you're talking about someone specific," Josh said. Nods in agreement all around.

Chance started and dropped his eyes, picking up his water. His hand trembled. Annaliese took pity on him, turning to Jay. "You never said how the two of you know each other."

Jay's immediate blush spoke volumes. They slid a glance at Chance and answered when he stayed quiet. "Through soccer. We were on the same club team. A friend of his had a dead aunt cheering on the sidelines. When he kept seeing me look that direction, for whatever reason, I told him what I was seeing. He said hi to the aunt, and we've been friends since. He called me a few weeks ago asking what I knew about vampires."

"And you asked about vampires specifically because..." Josh waited.

Nora realized they were all tensed. All waiting for this human's answer because there was something about him. He was timid, shy, and uncomfortable, but beneath that, Nora caught a hint of anger burning—an unhealthy fascination.

And because everyone here loved the West siblings and Zayn, they were ready to go to bat against that anger.

"What do you all really know about the murders? The demons you talked about earlier?" Chance posed the question like it was his first blow against the city's vampires.

They shared a weighted look. As far as the majority of New Brecken knew, there was a serial killer on the loose, and all the groups were working together to search for the culprit. For now, people were advised to avoid going out alone at night.

Nora didn't feel that the serial killer story was so far from the truth. Whoever created these drainers and let them loose on the city had to be the equivalent.

"What do *you* know about them?" Annaliese asked.

Chance's knee was bouncing. He studied her for a long moment, debating how much to tell. If it was only a tired theory about how vampires were responsible, Nora was going to be disappointed.

When had she started thinking like that?

"So, you're a werewolf?" Chance asked, his attention flipping to Nora. It was like being caught in headlights, the force of his blue eyes.

Nora nodded.

"You must have hunted vampires."

Josh choked on his beer. Annaliese snorted. "Unsuccessfully," she muttered, dodging the kick Nora aimed at her under the table.

Chance deflated a bit with that answer. "If you know how to hunt them, I'm trying to find my sis—"

"They're done already?" Annaliese asked, interrupting. Her attention up the street.

Nora turned. Topher, Zayn, Poppy, and Lana were headed toward the Alpha's Den. Seeing Topher, Nora couldn't help thinking not only did Chance have eyes like Colbie's. He looked *just* like Topher. It was an impossible jump until the two were this close. It was Topher's mannerisms that Chance's posture made Nora think of. Chance had lighter hair and was darker from time out in the sun. He possessed fullness to his cheeks and build. Maybe these differences wouldn't exist if Topher were human. If Topher had seen the sun in the last year or eaten anything besides blood.

Nora realized who Chance was. She itched to call Colbie and ask what to do, but Topher was approaching too quickly for Nora to think anything through. She stayed frozen.

Chance didn't check what had caught Annaliese's attention, so he didn't see how Topher grew impossibly paler, his eyes stuck on the back of Chance's head, his nostrils flaring as he confirmed Chance's identity. Chance didn't see Topher immediately look to Lana, fear evident on his features for only a breath before he cleared his expression, leaned into Lana's ear, and said something that made her face light up. She stepped readily into his side when Topher snaked an arm around her waist. Topher glanced back as he swept Lana down the nearest alley, communicating something to Zayn in his silent panic. Zayn's face clouded, eyes focusing on Chance as he changed course and approached.

Topher didn't want Lana to know about Chance. After what had happened with Colbie, Nora more than understood why. The West siblings had kept Chance a secret for this long, and now here he was, two doors down the street from what would soon be the hub for supernatural progressives.

Zayn sent a quick message on his phone before hurrying into the brewery patio. Poppy was confused but kept pace. She spotted Chance and understanding cleared her features, neither were as shocked by Chance's existence as Nora felt.

"Poppy, I didn't know you were coming by!" Jay said.

Josh made room for Zayn on the bench, Nora shifting to do the same for Poppy. Zayn's dark eyes darted up and down the street. Shoulders tense. Nora had only seen Zayn like this when Oliver was around, the protective side of his personality in full force. Protective of Chance for the sake of the West siblings.

"Yeah. Just thought I'd stop by before I went to the club." The air smelled faintly of earth and heightened the scent of Josh. Nora realized Poppy was casting, drawing from Josh's strength. She was being careful, too. Chance was oblivious to the complete shift around the table as almost everyone figured out who he was to their friends.

Zayn offered his hand and introduced himself to Jay and Chance.

Jay's eyes widened behind their green-framed glasses. "You're Oliver's boyfriend? The vampire?"

Chance came to attention, fixing Zayn in a cold, wary stare. That one reminded Nora far too much of Colbie's face at her angriest. "You're a vampire?"

Goosebumps erupted down Chance's arms. Nora smelled the fearful spike in adrenaline, though his chin was raised and eyes hard, trying to mask the terror. He went still in his attempt to hide his emotions. Like Topher would. The family resemblances grew more and more uncanny.

Zayn gave a curt nod.

"Who's your maker?"

Zayn tilted his head, his expression open. Charm buzzed right under his smile. Would he make Chance leave to assure Topher his brother was safe? Would Nora be okay with the charm if it kept Colbie's brother from danger? "What do you know about makers?" Zayn asked.

Chance straightened, and Nora almost gasped at how this posture shifted him from being Topher's brother to Colbie's. It was a feigned confidence but still rung of her. He glanced at Jay. This was why Chance was here. Why he was interested in vampires. He was searching for Topher and Colbie.

"I know plenty. I've seen the registrations. All of you are under the Big Three, and then their lowers."

Annaliese frowned. "I thought those are only open to classified people."

Chance's chin went up again, a refusal to explain. "Who's

your maker? Are you under Solas? Patter? Or were you one of Grace's? Or one of their seconds?"

Zayn settled back, draping an arm behind Josh. Casual in all appearances. "You do understand why we chose not to advertise that information, right?"

Chance rolled his eyes, but he was still afraid. His knee was bouncing again. "Roll up your sleeve. I know you all advertise. New Brecken gangs have always loved their stupid tattoos."

Zayn's mouth quirked, but he stayed quiet. Annaliese met Nora's eyes and mouthed *what the fuck?*

Nora shrugged. This was for Zayn to handle. Topher trusted him to do it while he distracted Lana.

"Fine, don't tell me. But I know you are all close. I know about the new club, and I know you can tell me where my sister is."

"Your sister?" Jay asked. They appeared hurt that Chance hadn't told them his real reasons for looking into the supernatural.

"She was attacked. Changed against her will. I'm going to find her and make sure she gets justice."

Zayn's relaxed posture dropped. He sat forward too quickly, and Chance sucked in a breath. "And how do you know that?"

"Her room was a wreck. There was blood everywhere, and she was just *gone*. Now, she's suddenly on the registration, claimed by some maker named Lana."

"And you didn't report this? Or tell your parents to?"

Chance rolled his eyes. "They think my sister chose this. But she didn't. She was attacked, and I know whose fault it was."

Zayn raised an eyebrow. Nora held her breath, waiting for Chance to level the accusation. Maybe it was more than just protecting his little brother that made Topher stay away. Maybe he couldn't face him.

Words sounding rehearsed, Chance said, "My brother. He

was always getting into trouble. He was registered first, a year before my sister and right after she was attacked. He must have gotten in too deep and pulled her down with him. He would constantly go to her for help, and now he's gotten them both caught up in this bullshit forever. I want her to know she still has people who care. A family she can count on. She can come home, and we'll make it work." Chance glanced at Poppy. "Maybe we can even find her a cure."

"But not your brother?" Zayn asked, tone cooling.

His brother who had just flirted with his maker to keep her away. His brother, who had done everything Chance accused him of but hated himself far more than Chance ever could. His brother, who had always been kind to Nora, even while he was tied to a chair in her pack's basement.

Nora realized then how much she'd come to like Topher West. She hated how involved she'd been with everything that had happened to him at Gabriel's behest. She opened her mouth, a defense building in her lungs, but a hand on her shoulder stilled her.

Even though Nora hadn't heard her approach and there was no smell to announce her presence, Nora immediately knew it was Colbie. The vampire stared at her youngest brother. He hadn't noticed her presence yet.

"Topher made his bed. I want nothing to do with him after what he did to Colbie," Chance said.

Annaliese sucked in a breath, gaze flying to Colbie. That finally directed Chance's attention to the sister standing behind him. Colbie crossed her arms, the weight of her hand gone and leaving a numbness in its place on Nora's shoulder.

"That's too bad you feel that way, Chancy. You know Topher and I have always been a package deal."

Chance gaped and scrambled to stand, staring at Colbie as if she'd just risen from the dead. "Colbie…"

Colbie stepped back when he moved toward her, and Nora forced herself to keep to her seat instead of getting between them to act as a barrier that Colbie no doubt didn't need or want.

"You… you're okay? We thought you were dead! For so long. Why didn't you call?"

Colbie took another step back. Nora gripped the bench to keep seated, but when Chance moved toward his sister again, Nora couldn't help it. She was suddenly between them, a hand out but not touching Chance, just stilling him.

Chance looked down at Nora's hand, then at Colbie over Nora's shoulder. Nora's focus was rooted on him. Whatever he saw from Colbie wasn't very encouraging.

"Chance." Colbie sighed. Nora felt the breath on her shoulder. "I can't come home. I don't want to. This is my life now, but it is dangerous for humans. We didn't call because we didn't want you to get caught up in all this. It isn't safe."

Nora ignored how Annaliese stiffened in the corner of her eye.

Crossing his arms, Chance shook his head, but his eyes were glassy. He was fighting tears. "You have to come home, Colbie. You've missed everything. My graduation. My last soccer tournament. My—"

"Please, Chance. We know you got into your dream school. That you were signed up for summer classes there. I don't know why you didn't go, but it's better for everyone if you do."

Nora heard the whisper of footsteps, and Chance's expression paled with shock. As was her way, Colbie left without a goodbye. Probably without a backward glance. Nora knew how badly that could cut and flared with sympathy for the boy before her. But then Zayn said, "You should check on her, Nora."

That was all the encouragement Nora needed. Without a word, she hurried after Colbie toward the Alpha's Den. Tonight, Oliver was standing at the door, studiously checking IDs. He smiled at Colbie while he let her pass, but it was subdued. He'd heard from Zayn already.

"You going to talk to her?" he asked Nora.

"I'll try," she said and ducked inside to trail Colbie down the hall and to the back patio where they last spoke. There was a human couple making out against the wall. Colbie charmed them into going inside without thought and sat heavily on the steps.

Nora hesitated a beat before settling down next to her. There were no words. Nothing that felt remotely sufficient. Nora forced out the first thing to come to mind. "I didn't know you had a brother."

Colbie crossed her arms on top of her knees and rested her chin on them. "Really? I could have sworn you'd met Topher before."

"You have *two* brothers?" Nora forced shock into her voice.

Colbie snorted. Nora's heart raced as one corner of her mouth twitched, a very near smile. But it died quickly. "Speaking of family members we haven't talked to recently, how's Gabe doing?" Colbie raised an eyebrow, hurt poorly concealed in her expression. "I hate smelling him on you."

Nora stiffened, remembering Colbie's words weeks ago. *You reeked like him, you know that, Nora? So you're going to listen to me because you broke my heart and tried to murder me. Because you slept with someone else while I was locked away and still trying to think of how to forgive you for lying to me and hurting my brother. Because even after that, Topher wasn't mad at you, so I thought maybe I could come around. I imagined how to convince you we could still be together. And what were you doing?*

All that hurt. All the mistakes Nora made, just under the surface. Colbie probably thought Nora had done it again. She probably hated Nora as much as ever. Why had Zayn told Nora to follow? Why did she keep forcing herself on Colbie? She kept hurting both of them, over and over, like a scab she couldn't leave alone or a bruise she needed to press.

And she wanted to defend herself. For all of it. The inexcusable and the innocent. Like today. She hadn't rejoined the pack. She'd basically challenged Gabriel if he didn't leave her alone. But telling Colbie would be too little too late.

"Do you want me to go?" Nora asked.

Colbie didn't say anything, which was a hopeful enough answer for Nora to keep pressing. "Do you want to talk about Chance?"

Colbie turned her head, resting her cheek on her wrists and giving Nora a flat look.

So that was a no.

"Do you want to talk about Topher?"

Now, an eyebrow quirk. Colbie was still here; she hadn't left, so she wanted to talk about *something*. Was it possible she did want Nora to press the bruise? To try to explain? Was that why she brought up Gabriel?

Nora's voice dropped to a whisper. A hesitant, unsure, unalpha-like whisper. "Can I tell you about meeting with Matt?"

"I'm both painfully curious and terrified to know."

Nora's laugh was flushed with relief. She couldn't meet Colbie's eyes while talking about her old pack, so she leaned back, resting her elbows on the top step and tipping her head to take in the growing moon. It would be full tomorrow night. Half of her dreaded another lonely run. Half would always crave the full moon's power.

"Well, maybe stop me when you don't want to hear any more?"

Colbie's bun bobbed with her short nod. Nora took a deep breath. Where to start? "Matt texted me today, asking if we could talk." Nora paused. Colbie didn't react, and Nora felt free to keep going. "We went to the park near the Den. I don't know what I was expecting, but Gabriel showed up, and they both just—" Nora drew in a sharp breath, the pain of it all striking again. "I don't understand how they can talk to me like that. How I never saw it before. Is it the alpha telling me I can't be treated like that? Is that why I notice it now?"

"Maybe you did everything you could, and when they still treated you like shit, you realized you couldn't win. It started hurting more because you couldn't do anything about it."

Nora waited for the defensive skin prickling to rise like it did when Annaliese ventured to talk about her old pack. It didn't come. Nora debated her next words. Colbie was still listening; maybe she would hear this too. "I didn't do everything. I didn't give them everything."

Another eyebrow raised. Nora closed her eyes. She couldn't bear to see skepticism cross Colbie's face. "That night. I didn't have sex with Gabriel. We fooled around for a bit, and I slept in his room, but I got too upset being in my parents' old bed. And I couldn't stop thinking about you. I didn't do anything more with him. He promised we'd have time after the change and that it would be easier when I was a wolf."

"Nora—" But whatever Colbie was going to say, whatever look might have been on her face, it vanished when the door burst open, and Poppy appeared, expression wild. "Have either of you seen Topher?"

Colbie stood, seeing the panic in Poppy's green eyes, but she used Nora's shoulder to get up. Her touch lingered. Nora was hopeless but to stand with her, close by Colbie's side. It would take a bulldozer to get her away after that conversation and the hope that bloomed from Colbie's touch.

"He's not bartending?" Colbie asked.

"No, Zayn had to get behind the bar. Lana hasn't seen Topher for a bit either."

Colbie frowned. "He's probably making sure Chance gets home okay. Why do you need him?"

Poppy bit her lip. She checked her phone, then stepped fully outside and closed the door behind her, eyes focused on a distant point to the right. "We decided to look for my mom to ask about her involvement with the drainers. I found her, but I think she's in trouble. I have to go to her *now*."

"You don't think there's time to wait for Topher?" Nora asked.

Poppy shook her head. She bit her lip.

Colbie studied her roommate for a beat before she nodded. "Let's go then. He doesn't need to see her anyway. Where'd you park?"

"Really?" Poppy hesitated, glancing back at the club like she'd rather find someone else to ask for help.

Colbie read that just as clearly and rolled her eyes. "You've been gushing about how strong Nora is. I'm not entirely hopeless. If you think we have time, we can wait. Or we can go. Right now."

It only took Poppy a breath to consider that before she nodded, and they cut through the alley to get to her car. There wasn't a moment of hesitation for Nora over whether she would come along. Colbie, whether she meant to or not, hadn't questioned Nora's loyalty. She'd had faith that Nora would stay by her side. Nora wouldn't do anything to break that faith again.

CHAPTER 27

Seeing their younger brother wasn't what Topher had expected. It wasn't like going to their quiet childhood home in the dead of night. It wasn't just a sudden influx of thoughts and memories that robbed him of breath.

It was a whirlwind of broken promises, jealousies, and new painful threats. *Lana* had nearly seen Chance. His brother was so similar to how Topher had looked when he was changed. People used to ask if they were twins, but now Topher felt decades older than his brother.

Since Topher had last seen Chance, he'd gone through his senior year. Played goalie in the state championship and won. Given a speech as valedictorian. He'd been accepted into the east coast school he'd always dreamed of. Gotten a summer internship over there. Their mom constantly posted Chances achievements and Topher kept diligent track on a fake account. But, lately, the updates about Chance had tapered off. Ever since he'd decided to stay in New Brecken this summer instead of starting the internship. Ever since he'd began searching for Colbie.

And now he was right there and, according to Zayn, blamed Topher for everything. Justly. For all their differences, at heart, Chance and Topher were too similar. Topher fought the urge to go up and tell Chance he was right. He'd been right all along. Now, Chance needed to move on and live the promising life set up for him. If he could, he should take Colbie, too.

But that wasn't possible. And when Chance threw up his hands in frustration at whatever Josh was saying, Topher knew his brother was at the end of his leash. He'd be leaving soon, though Jay's hand on his arm stilled him briefly.

Annaliese shook her head, checked her watch, and came to the bar. They'd made eye contact when Topher first sat down. He kept up a light charm to keep the other humans from looking his way, but the bead on Annaliese's wrist ensured she'd known he was there. Topher liked that too much.

Shaking her head, she sat and accepted the beer Topher slid her way. "He isn't like you and Colbie."

"Much to our parent's pleasure."

Annaliese frowned down at the pale liquid in her glass. "Do you think this is good on any level? Are you at all happy that he's shown back up?"

"You say that like you don't think it is."

"Well, he's kind of an asshole."

That made Topher laugh a bit. He could do that in front of her now. "He thinks this is all your fault. That he can swoop in and do something for Colbie. He wants to find a cure for vampirism for her and didn't want to hear it when I said if she wanted a cure, she had more resources than he does. I told him should try contacting her without deciding what was best for her."

Topher raised an eyebrow. Knowing the people Chance had been surrounded by his entire life, it was hard to imagine anyone talking to his brother like that. But of course, Annaliese would. Fondness crept over Topher. "But, he seems well?"

"Yeah. He seemed good. An asshole, but good."

"Wasn't too long ago you were calling me the asshole."

"But good."

Topher didn't know how to respond to that. Movement across the patio pulled their attention, watching as Chance got up from the table. Jay was trying to stop him. Josh looked almost angry. Chance had put his foot in it. He shook off Jay's arm and left, face set in a scowl that slipped as soon as he was out of sight.

Chance was devastated. He'd seen and lost Colbie in moments. He probably hadn't gotten any of the answers he sought out from Annaliese, Josh, Poppy, or Zayn. He'd probably had his hopes up for this meeting and was going home empty-handed.

"I'm just going to make sure he gets home okay," Topher told Annaliese. "You be careful at work."

Annoyance and sympathy in equal measure flooded Annaliese's soft eyes. "Just, don't talk to him, okay? What he thinks is wrong, and I know you think the same at your worst. You don't need to validate that negativity."

Chance had ridden his bike to Twenty-Fifth Street. The sight of it flooded Topher with human memories. They had received the same present for Christmas three years ago. The green mountain bikes were an upgrade from their childhood bikes. Topher had been annoyed he'd had to wait a year longer than Chance for this version of freedom.

How often had his bike taken him to a party he shouldn't have attended? How many times had he ridden it to Dylan's? How many soccer practices had Chance and him raced to on their matching bikes, their energy young and wild and reckless? Everything about them so similar, just one step off.

They had plans to try their bikes on one of the trails in the national park. They were going to get better at swimming and try a triathlon. Always there was an undertone of competition, but they'd both handled it better when it came to physical matchups. Soccer had been the one thing that brought them closer, but they'd had to play on different teams. Different friends. Different games for their parents to watch.

Topher felt keenly how much everything had changed as he followed his biking brother easily on foot. If he'd been able to do this during their childhood, he would have smirked, pointed, laughed as Chance struggled to keep up. Now, it was another reminder of what Topher was. It called attention to the distance between them.

It was hard to regret a stolen night with Dylan, but how different would things be if Topher had stuck around more? What if he'd seen past his emotions and explained how their parents devotion to Chance had been what drove the wedge between them, instead of Chance himself. Chance had listened to their parents' dismissal and dislike of his siblings. He'd heard only their side about Topher's skipping class and drug use and trouble. Chance had done all he could to keep their parents happy with him, and Topher and Colbie in return grew as distant to him as they had their parents. Chance never had an opportunity to know them. Topher had realized all this in the past year now that true distance had been achieved. How different would things be now if he'd seen it earlier?

But… if he hadn't felt so hopeless about their relationship, what if he'd gone to Chance's room the night he turned Colbie? What if he'd doomed both of his siblings?

It had to be better that they didn't talk. It had to be, or the pain of losing everyone would rise again to rob Topher of breath and will.

Topher spotted the swerving car before Chance did. Head down, Chance focused on pedaling, working through his feelings in the physical manner that all the West siblings did. Swearing, Topher put on a burst of silent speed, gaining on his brother, and putting himself closer, just in case. The last thing he wanted was for Chance to see him, but the car was going too fast, approaching the same intersection as Chance without any hint of slowing down.

Chance stopped at the stop sign. The car finally noticed the sign on their corner of the four way and screeched to a halt. Topher stepped into the shadows of a cluster of bushes and let out his breath in relief.

It was short-lived. The driver's side window rolled down, and a man stuck his head out. "Hey! If someone was in town looking for a vampire bite, where would they go?"

It was the wrong night to ask Chance about vampires. He shifted forward, standing with the frame between his legs rather than perching on his seat while stopped. "It's not worth it," Chance said.

The man's head went inside for a moment. Long enough for Chance to get his feet back on the pedals and start crossing. The man jerked his car forward, breaking again suddenly. The movement was enough to startle Chance and nearly unseat him. Roaring laughter poured from the open windows. Chance stopped in front of the car, turning to glare.

"Keeping going," Topher muttered, too quietly to urge his brother on. But he didn't like the mix of smells coming from the car. Didn't like the mean, too-loud laughter spurred from Chance's fear and subsequent anger.

Chance did not keep going. He smacked the hood of the car. "Oh, fuck off!"

Silence fell in the car. Topher cringed with every snap of the gearshift going into park. The door opened, and the driver got out. "Did you just touch my car?"

"You could have killed me! Clearly, you do need a vampire fix; maybe it'll help with your desperately macho personality disorder."

And there was the Colbie influence. Chance started biking, attempting to dismiss the man. But now, the passenger's side door opened. Topher sighed. It was a Sunday night. The murders had led to the city being quiet for weeks. Of course, Chance's luck brought him to this situation.

The second man rounded the car and reached to catch Chance's handlebars.

"Hey!" Every head twisted in Topher's direction as he stepped out of the shadows. Chance nearly lost his seat on his bike as he turned, but Topher didn't look at him yet. He narrowed his eyes at the driver. "Hear you're looking for a bite?"

"You a vampire?" the driver asked, suspicious, but with a thrill of excitement pulsing in his blood.

Topher bared his teeth, fangs slipping out. The man's eyes widened. Chance made a noise. The driver stepped forward eagerly, but it wasn't in the submission of someone wanting to be bit. This man was spoiling for a fight. And he wanted to prove himself against a vampire.

How boring.

With the entire car's attention, Topher let his fangs slip back in. He reached for the ever-present charm. "Get back in your fucking seats."

The men scrambled to do his bidding. Entirely under his charm, the submission was there now. Topher jerked his chin at the driver. "Apologize."

"Listen, man," the man hung half out of his window to talk to Chance, refusing to leave his seat. "I'm sorry about that. It wasn't cool."

Topher didn't wait for Chance to think of a response. "Reverse and pull the car off to the side of the road. Don't move until you're sober and can drive without hurting anyone."

They did as he instructed. Topher finally looked to Chance. His face was pale, eyes wide. For now, there was only shock, but in moments, Topher knew he would shift to anger. Topher waited for Chance to decide what to do. Leave Topher without a word. Yell. Hurl the accusations he had already spewed all night in Topher's face.

Topher tried to brace for it, but since he had been turned,

it was like every nerve was exposed. There was no more escaping. He had to face it all, feel it all, acknowledge it all.

He hadn't had to feel the force of Chance's hurts for a long time. Every time Topher didn't show when Chance asked him to, every time Topher acted out under the influence of one substance or another, every time Topher mocked Chance for being a nerd, a goalie, a year younger… all those petty words that masked what he really felt. Topher hadn't dealt with anything as a human. Not sober. Not without having Dylan to run to afterward. Topher reached into his back pocket, unable to face his brother fully. He lit a cigarette, distracting himself while Chance searched for words. Topher knew he could leave instead of going through this, but the night had already proven unsafe. He would see Chance home if it killed him.

The car parked, the men inside falling silent as if anticipating another order from Topher. A long moment of quiet passed until Chance's bike squealed. He turned in Topher's direction and went onto the sidewalk. He spoke, still straddling the bike, ready to take off at a moment's notice.

Topher's hand shook on his cigarette. "Hey." He'd promised himself he wouldn't speak first, but the word slipped out when the quiet became oppressive.

"Tell me what happened. I deserve to know that much."

Topher almost dropped the cigarette. He'd told Colbie, brokenly, that Dylan died, and it led to his changing when it first happened, but he'd never had to tell the whole story. Poppy and the rest had seen it. Part of Topher had been relieved he'd never had to explain what happened that night. The words were too hard to push past the tightness in his throat even now. He cleared it and pulled another drag. Tried to organize his thoughts. By the time the vaguest of explanations was there, one he thought he might be able to voice, Chance's face had shifted into the guarded one Topher hated. The one that said no matter what Topher came up with, Chance knew better than to believe it. He thought Topher was coming up with a lie. It was the face Topher had associated with his addictions and relationships.

Chance shook his head. "Whatever, Topher. I'm done. Keep spewing your excuses to Colbie, and she'll keep choosing you over us. Have a nice life together."

Chance started to turn away, and Topher went still. This was what he wanted, wasn't it? Chance would be safe. He'd live his whole life separate from Topher. Maybe he'd even leave town, escape the drainers and all things supernatural.

But Chance would lose Colbie. Colbie would lose any hope of a relationship with Chance. That wasn't fair to either of his siblings. Suddenly, Topher felt crushed by the weight of all he'd lost. He didn't want to lose anymore, not when there was something he could do. And there was something, wasn't there? There were witches and werewolves and charms infused with wards and a vampiric strength that *had* to be capable of doing some good.

There was Colbie's confidence in her choices. Annaliese's steady, fearless gaze. Poppy's soft glow. His world wasn't all dark, and maybe he could make it lighter. There was a possibility he could repair something of what had happened in the past. He couldn't save Dylan. He might not save Julia. Could he keep both of his siblings?

"I can show you," Topher said, the words wrenched from the rawness in his core.

Chance stopped, his back to Topher. He considered long enough for Topher's heart to drop. Finally, he asked, "What do you mean?"

"I can't... talk about it. But there's a way you can see what happened. It's, it's not pretty. But if you really want to know, I can show you."

Chance studied Topher for too long before finally giving a curt nod. "Fine. Show me." Chance braced himself like Topher was going to charm the knowledge into him.

Topher shook his head. "You'll have to come to our apartment. A witch has to show you, and my friend Ru is there."

"And she'll show me?"

"Yes. If you really want to know."

Another too long beat. Chance always thought things through. Topher and Colbie inherited all the impulse their parents had to offer. Finally, in an unexpectedly soft voice, Chance said, "I want to know."

Topher beckoning for Chance to follow. He felt rushed now, in a hurry to do this before he or Chance changed their mind. Chance started to get off his bike, but Topher shook his head. "No, you'll need to ride to keep up."

Chance raised an eyebrow. Topher almost let himself smile over the familiar, competitive gleam that entered Chance's eyes. He didn't, though. The thought of charming his brother made his stomach roll.

Topher took off. Chance swore and got on his bike, pedaling furiously to catch up. Topher didn't go as fast as he could, mindful of Chance's lack of night vision and the other traffic on the road. He took bike paths when he could and slowed whenever cars were nearby.

It took them fifteen minutes to get to the apartment. Topher realized he'd gone too fast when Chance stopped, panting hard and glaring at him. Once he caught his breath, his words were not what Topher expected. "I'm just waiting for you to tell me you won."

It was a jarring reminder of who Topher had once been. "It's not like you knew where I lived to get here first."

Chance tipped his head back, taking in the brick, sturdy structure of the apartment. The keypad on the front door that didn't work, but Colbie deemed a fancy deterrent. Lights were strung up in rooms, a blue glow from Poppy's window high above. Flowers and green herbs overflowing her fire escape. The overhead light in the living room was on, too. Good. Ru was still awake.

"It's nice. Doesn't seem like a spooky vampire lair."

"Doesn't it?" Topher waited for Chance to lock up his bike before leading him inside and up the stairs.

"Wait here a second," Topher said, ducking into the wards and entering the apartment. "Rhubarb?"

"Yes?" She sang the word, sweeping out of Poppy's room with a book and a greenish face mask on.

"Um, I'm bringing a guest in. Can you let the wards know?"

Ru's eyes widened. "Once I take this off!"

She ran to the bathroom, and there was the sound of furious scrubbing. A curse as she dropped her towel. She came out with dripping eyelashes and wet sleeves. After a moment of concentration, she nodded to Topher, and he opened the door to let Chance inside.

Chance did so slowly, looking around with evident curiosity. He took in Colbie's books stacked on the coffee table, the reality show Ru had on, the vials of some potion on the counter, and a startled Ru in the middle of it all, water droplet clinging to her chin.

Topher went to her, putting an arm around her shoulders. Her expression shifted to concern when she felt the tension radiating off him. "Ru, this is my brother, Chance."

Ru's eyes widened even further, mouth dropping into an 'o' shape.

"Chance, this is my good friend Ru." Topher turned to her, hating to ask this. She'd seen the memory the first time. She'd cried when she apologized for watching it. It had been traumatic and awful for her and everyone else to stumble upon the memory. "Ru, I have a favor I need to ask, and I'm really sorry to do it."

Topher briefly explained the situation and what he needed of her. She was shaking her head before he got a chance to finish. "No, Topher. I'll just tell him. It's too awful to watch."

Chance's expression was verging on stony. "I think I need to see this for myself."

"Why? Don't you believe us?" Ru asked, genuinely confused.

Topher sighed. "I've lied to my family a lot. He won't believe anything I tell him or that you tell him, thinking it came from me. He doesn't want to hear excuses. He just wants to know what happened to Colbie."

Ru's eyes narrowed. "Topher wouldn't lie about this. If you're his brother, you should believe him."

Topher shook his head. Whatever Poppy's experience in their coven, Ru's had been the opposite. They spoke of family ties like night and day, though Poppy would do anything for her little sister. Ru thought this was the norm between siblings. While it might be like that between Topher and Colbie, it wasn't always so easy between family members. Chance's expression confirmed that. "If you don't want to show me, I'll just go."

Ru heard the finality in that. She looked to Topher. "You sure you want us watching this?"

"Of course I don't want you to, but it's our only option if Chance wants to know what happened."

"I want to know," Chance said, and that was the thing about him. He always did want to know. No one chased answers as doggedly as Chance West. Topher didn't want this quest for knowledge to lead Chance somewhere like Fourth Street. This was the worst and best option.

"I'll wait in here," Topher said. His voice shook and he cleared it, reaching for his cigarettes again.

Ru's nod was hesitant. She led Chance to Topher's room.

Topher waited at the window, smoking. Mouse came to weave between his ankles. Topher took comfort in stroking his soft fur as he heard Ru go to his closet and retrieve the sweatshirt. She explained that they were going to watch the memory the fabric held. They had to hold hands, and Chance needed to open his mind to see the truth. The flare of the candle being lit. The quiet chanting, then… silence. An occasional sucked in breath. A gasp. Increased heart rates. Topher tried hard not to relieve the memory they were watching but he couldn't help it. Horror robbed him of breath, the grief striking yet again.

What would Chance think? Would he understand that Topher hadn't chosen this, even with all the bad choices he made that led to that moment? Would he see what Topher had lost when he lost Dylan? Would he realize that was where Topher had been all those nights, hiding the truth from their conservative-leaning parents in the same way Colbie had? Neither of them bothered to come out. They never gave their parents a chance to react, both feeling it wasn't worth the effort. Their relationships weren't deep enough. But Chance… they could have been more open with him. That was one of Topher's biggest regrets. Just because their parents had adored Chance, it didn't make their family two units. But it had been in his mind—Topher and Colbie against their parents and Chance.

Now, that would all come to a head. Chance would leave Topher's bedroom with all the information. Topher didn't know what to expect from him.

What he didn't anticipate was having barely enough time to process Chance's stricken expression before he was in Topher's space and drawing him into a hug.

CHAPTER 28

"Topher still not answering?" Nora asked as they drove toward Fourth Street.

No one was happy that Gus was leading them in this direction. They passed Patty's, then the street where the drainer apartment was, and kept going, eventually turning right so they were parallel to the clubs and driving down Fifth Street. Poppy could hear the bass from the combined noise of Happenstance, Blank Space, and Blue Blood. Nora kept cocking her head, likely hearing far more than the hammering music.

Colbie sighed, dropping her phone into the cup holder. "He must have left his phone somewhere."

Poppy drummed her fingers on the steering wheel. They were all tense, knowing how easily it could be something worse. How quickly Topher had disappeared last winter, not once, but twice. But Topher was eating now. He stayed away from Gabriel and Fourth Street. It wasn't uncommon for him to leave his phone places. Ru had used it more this week than he had.

And no one wanted him this close to Fourth now. Maybe it was better that they couldn't get ahold of him.

Nora looked toward the clubs. "Who runs Happenstance now?"

"Last I heard, Grace's other seconds," Colbie said. "They weren't getting along, but they were keeping it going. Someone is probably in the leadership position by now."

"Why would your mom stay so close to the clubs?" Nora asked.

Poppy's smile held little humor. The question came from the werewolf who didn't know she was Poppy's neighbor their entire childhoods. "She likes to hide in plain sight. If she thinks the vampires are the biggest threat, she'll stay where she can monitor them and passively use their protection. No one would think to find her here." Poppy should have. It made too much sense for Tiff Jennings.

Colbie twisted in her seat toward Poppy. "What did your grandpa say to expect?"

Poppy coughed. It was startling for Colbie to refer to Gus in this way. The relationship was rarely acknowledged, but of course, Colbie would slice to the center of it all. "Not much. But he's worried. It's weird to see him worried."

Right now, Gus was a light gray smudge in the night ahead of them, leading Poppy as quickly as she could drive through the streets. Sometimes, he'd vanish and appear at the next corner, waving her on.

It was frustrating having no idea what to expect. All they knew was that Tiff Jennings was in danger, but Gus wouldn't say more. His urgency had convinced Poppy to do this without Topher, but by the Mother, how she wished he were here. Or Josh. Hopefully, Nora's strength wouldn't fail them in whatever they came up against. Poppy's mind skipped over all the possibilities. Had her mother's demons turned on her? Was all the dark magic infecting her? Could her mother be the one making the drainers? What if she'd been captured by the vampires and that was why she was so close to Fourth? Were they about to come up against Solas and Patter?

The only way to get answers was to keep going. Gus finally stopped in front of a single story, quaint little house. The shutters were drawn over the windows, and there was only one light on that they could see. Aside from the distance pulse of music, their car doors closing was the only sound on the block. The grass and any other plants surrounding the home were dried up and lifeless despite the rain they'd had. Poppy winced, staring down at the carnage. Had her mother used plant life to cast? How many times had Poppy been punished for exploiting that aid?

"Hard to imagine the type of people who would want to keep living here after the vampires set up," Nora said, glancing down the block of homes.

Colbie jerked her chin toward Fourth Street. "I'm going to assume they're all getting blissed, or the vampires own these houses now."

Nora's face darkened at that. No matter how much time she spent around Oliver or the vampires, feeding continued to make the werewolf uncomfortable. Though, Poppy agreed the blissed humans at the main clubs weren't how vampire feedings should go. Too much life was drained. Was given. Poppy didn't know the long-term effects of that, but Lana's assurances weren't enough to completely rid Poppy of her worries, either.

They walked up the sidewalk. Poppy's first sign that something was truly wrong was the ease with which she passed the warding. She reached back and took Colbie's hand to pull her friend through, but even that was a simple request to the magic. The spell wasn't strong enough for Nora to notice as she walked up to the front unhindered.

Huddled up at the door, Poppy felt Nora and Colbie's eyes on her, waiting for Poppy's next move. Colbie stood closer to Nora than she usually did. The ice continued to thaw between them.

Poppy glanced back at Gus, hovering outside the wards.

His shape shimmered, buzzing with energy. "Should we knock?" she asked him.

Her real question: Was Tiff able to answer the door?

Gus flickered in and out of view, not bothering to answer. Poppy realized how dumb the question was. If he couldn't get through Tiff's wards, he wouldn't know how dire the situation was. He was only going off what he felt from the magic around the home. Like Poppy, he was concerned by how weak it was but knew little else. He hadn't provided details because he didn't have any.

Poppy had even more questions now. How had he found Tiff at all? Was Topher's charm that strong, or Tiff's wards that weak?

"That's still kind of creepy," Colbie said, following Poppy's line of sight and seeing nothing.

Poppy raised an eyebrow. "You just learned I'm being haunted. When did you expect it not to be creepy?"

Colbie shrugged. "I've gotten good at rolling with the punches lately."

Poppy glanced at the lack of space between the vampire and werewolf. "That's true enough," she muttered, raising a fist to knock.

Now that they were within the wards, they could hear movement in the house. Tiff had probably felt their approach. "Mother?" Poppy called.

A quick inhale on the other side of the door. Lock after lock flipped, and then, finally, the door was cracked open. Tiff's wide green eyes met Poppy's first, but then she caught sight of Colbie and the glare on Colbie's face. Poppy abruptly realized it was a mistake to bring the vampire along. Tiff gasped and tried to close the door, but Nora quickly caught it, and Tiff's strength couldn't begin to fight the alpha's.

With a scoff, Tiff allowed Nora to open the door fully and stepped back. Poppy's stomach dropped when her mother came fully into view. Tiff was nearly as gray and pale as Julia had been. Her shirt hung off her loosely, collar bones prominent where the baggy neckline exposed them. Tiff's hair hung oily and lank around her face. She wasn't wearing makeup. The only adornments on her were her customary charms.

All those admonishments from childhood came back to Poppy in a rush. Tiff screaming at her for bringing dirt into the house. Telling her to go shower and attempt to make herself presentable, though they rarely went further than the fenced yard. The emphasis on image that Tiff Jennings had put on herself and her daughters. Enough to leave no question of their coven's refinement, power, and beauty on the few occasions they were seen.

Tiff had lost it all, but she acted regal as a queen when she straightened, chin tipping with pride. "Penelope, what strange company you keep these days," she said, slow gaze sweeping up Colbie in her distressed jeans and cropped T-shirt, Nora's scuffed white sneakers, and then catching sight of Gus hovering outside the wards.

"All an improvement. Unlike your current situation." Poppy realized how perfectly she was employing Tiff's haughty tone and swallowed a wince.

At least it had an effect. Tiff's expression flattened. "What do you want, Penelope?"

"We thought you were in trouble."

It was the wrong thing to say. Tiff rolled her eyes, her magic weakly attempting to close the door again.

"Well," Colbie said, holding it still with only her pointer finger, "we weren't wrong. But we also want answers."

The vampire's glare still hadn't slipped. Colbie was Topher's advocate in everything. Seeing Tiff had to set off every protective instinct. Colbie knew Tiff had killed Dylan and left Topher to die. She knew Tiff's actions had led to Topher's change. Had led to her own change. Poppy's mother and her demons were the catalyst for all of this.

The tension between them sparked, both women fierce,

stubborn, and immovable. But Tiff stood alone while Colbie had Nora right there and knew Poppy would back her, too. Tiff broke the stare off first, falling into a coughing fit. Once she started, she didn't seem able to stop. She stumbled under the force of her hacking, and Poppy stepped forward without thought, grabbing her mother's arm to steady her.

When Tiff lowered her hand, there was black spattered on her palm. Tiff quickly wiped it off on her dirty pants, pretending she hadn't seen it. The tang of rotted magic clung to her skin.

Tiff shook off Poppy's grip and she was relieved to step away, but the smell clung to the air. They watched Tiff stumble to the recliner, sitting heavily as she caught her breath.

"You need help," Nora stated. She sounded more certain of herself with every day that passed. "And we have questions about the demons. Let's work together."

Tiff raised an eyebrow at Nora. "The Morales girl. Talk of town. How did I get so lucky to be graced by your presence? I'm sure you *do* have questions."

Nora and Colbie traded a look. Colbie jerked her head in a quick shake. When Tiff fell quiet again, they cautiously took seats around her, the threat of Tiff's magic or cutting words dulled by her apparent weakness. Colbie perched on the empty fireplace hearth, and Nora sat beside her after only a second of hesitation. Poppy took up her position between her friends and mother on the cluttered coffee table. It held mugs with dregs on the bottoms. Poppy glanced inside but read only death and darkness with her minimal knowledge of tea reading. She swallowed, taking in the candles of hard, dripped wax. Scraps of paper with frantic writing and burned edges. Charms. Bones and crystals and strings knotted. Cinnamon sticks and sage and unevenly tied bundles of herbs. From the feel of the air hovering over the clutter, these items were likely the last of Tiff's wards.

All crutches, but not a potion in sight. Figured.

"What's going on?" Poppy asked her mother, eyeing the black smears on her pants.

Tiff's smirk was forced nonchalance. There was black still clinging to her guns. "Didn't Mommy always tell you to stay away from dark magic?"

"You're corrupted?" Poppy asked, going cold. Had her mother turned fully to sorcery?

Tiff snorted. "Toeing the line. I'm refusing it, but it's fighting me." Tiff's scrutiny was chilling and familiar. When Poppy sensed she might not be coming up short for the first time, she wasn't sure what to do with the sensation it stirred in her chest. "I do need help, Penelope. You can't imagine what I see our city falling to." Tiff gestured toward the teacups scattered. One lay broken against the far wall as if Tiff had hurled it when she didn't like what she saw within.

"So tell me," Poppy said.

Tiff leaned back, satisfied. "For a price, of course."

"No."

"I need protection. I need to get my strength up. Take me into your wards, and once I'm safe, I'll tell you everything you want to know."

Poppy squinted at Tiff, not trusting a word.

"Vetoed," Colbie said. "You aren't coming anywhere near my brother."

"Why would we do that?" Nora asked, crossing her arms. She was walled off from the creeping, seeking tendrils of Tiff's magic. To Poppy, it appeared Nora didn't even notice Tiff's failing attempts to draw from her power.

"Because I can tell you what happened to your father. I can tell you how he died."

Poppy didn't expect this to have the effect it did. Nora's interest was far too peaked. Her eyes widened; hands clenched into fists. "Why would I believe your version?"

"What would I have to gain by lying?"

"What do you have to lose by just telling me?"

"Time. Precious, precious time."

Colbie stood, breaking Nora's focus on Tiff. "This is ridiculous. She's not going to talk, and she's not coming to our apartment."

Tiff reached out, grabbing Poppy's hand. Poppy stared. Tiff had never reached for her like this. "Penelope, please. My sweet girl, you'd leave your mother here to die?"

Colbie rolled her eyes and stomped outside, finished with the farce. After a beat, Nora followed, though she waited at the door, looking back to see what Poppy would decide.

Poppy withdrew her hand. "You brought this on yourself, Mom." The words came out shaking.

Tiff jumped on Poppy's obvious faltering. Poppy didn't want to leave her defenseless, and Tiff saw it. She probably smelled how Poppy's childhood desire to please her mother was warring with Colbie's displeasure and her need to keep Topher happy. "Penelope. I *will* die here alone. Like so many witches around our city. Killed to make those monsters. I need help stopping the sorcerer. I'm the best chance we have with my demons. I just need more time, time *you* can give me. Is that so much to ask?"

Poppy stood frozen. They needed answers. Topher would understand if it meant getting help saving Julia. Poppy *could* help her mother. Tiff must see how strong she'd gotten, how the potions and plants might be the answer. Tiff was asking *Poppy* for help. Maybe Poppy could stay here. Lay some wards around this place and—

"Only you know where Ru is, Penelope. She's strong enough to help me. Her power could replenish my own, and her wards would be secure enough to keep me safe. Nowhere else in the city would be as protected as a place under *her* magic. I know that's how you've protected yourself. You can take me to her. Ru would be happy to help me. It's cruel of you to keep us apart. She's my baby."

Every fissure that had started to soften toward her mother

calcified. Poppy imagined herself turning to stone inside. Tiff only wanted to use Ru. Maybe Poppy could handle Tiff using *her*, but she would never drag Ru into this.

"You abandoned her the same as all of us. Whatever is happening to you, Mother, you brought it on yourself. I hope it was worth it."

It was later than Poppy realized by the time they made it home. Gus was an angry shadow floating in Poppy's peripheral vision, but she refused to acknowledge him or explain what had happened. Tiff was too stubborn. Poppy should have known better than to hope for her help. Gus should have known it wouldn't work. He had no right to be surprised by Poppy's choice to leave Tiff alone with the consequences of her actions.

Outside the apartment building, Oliver and Zayn sat on the stoop. Zayn's arm was slung around Oliver's shoulders, and he was talking in Oliver's ear. Whatever he said made Oliver laugh, turning under Zayn's arm to smile at him.

What they had was so simple it took Poppy's breath away at times. They'd needed someone, found each other, and made everything work after that.

What would it mean to have a constant person beside you? A reliable source of love and support? Someone to face the world with? Josh's face came to mind. Poppy still didn't know how to feel about her body's new reaction to him. Josh could be simple, constant, and reliable. If Poppy wanted what Oliver and Zayn had, Josh was her best option. But, maybe simple wasn't for her. Or perhaps Zayn and Oliver just made it seem that easy. Maybe they got lucky, and Poppy didn't have that kind of fortune. If she did, wouldn't she and Josh be together now? Or maybe Oliver and Zayn were two fearless individuals who found the right person to give their whole selves to.

Maybe Poppy's problem was that she couldn't imagine being so brave.

The couple stood when Poppy parked the car. Zayn's eyebrows rose to see Nora and Colbie together as they got out, but he didn't say anything before holding out a phone. Colbie took it with a frown. "Topher left that at the club. We were bringing it upstairs, but we got distracted," Zayn said.

Oliver smiled and touched the scars on his neck before reaching for his boyfriend's hand.

"Thanks." Colbie took the phone. "Let's go up. Team meeting."

"Team meeting like text the whole group?" Oliver asked.

Colbie shook her head. "Like friends and family."

"Then we should call Josh and Annaliese," Oliver said, opening the door for everyone.

"Yes. Fine."

"Okay, good. I already told them to come over once they finished up at Alpha's Den. Thought we might need a soccer game after tonight. They're already on their way." Oliver smiled happily at the way Colbie shook her head at him, but her disproval was feigned. The last effects from seeing Tiff easing from her features.

Though, the tension came right back when they entered the wards. "What the hell?"

Zayn and Nora shared a glance as Colbie went to open the door. They must smell something. Poppy's wards were fine, so it wasn't an unwelcome presence. Still, she wasn't expecting to see a very gloomy Ru on the recliner while the two West brothers sat stiffly on the couch beside each other. Ru wore the countenance of someone who had done something wrong, especially when Colbie stomped inside, distinctly displeased.

"What's going on here?" Colbie asked.

Topher stood, lifting his hands to calm Colbie's approach. "We're talking it out. It's fine."

"It's *not* fine."

"It is. Ru showed him the sweatshirt."

"You showed him?" Colbie was shocked. Poppy blinked, realizing what that meant. Topher had explained himself. He'd made an effort to keep someone from thinking the worst of him. When had that progress happened?

"You two shouldn't have to be apart because of me. I've been explaining to Chance all the risks—" So he did it for Colbie. That made more sense.

"Did you tell him about Julia?" Colbie asked, crossing her arms as if she'd made a point.

"He did," Chance said softly, expression bleak.

Nora stepped forward. "What happened to Julia?"

Of all their friends, Nora was the last person Poppy would choose to tell. The apartment building on Seventh Street was incriminating. Poppy held her breath as Colbie, first silently checked with Topher, then at his reluctant nod, turned to Nora. She was the only one with a chance of explaining the captive drainers.

When Colbie finished, Nora looked slightly sick. Also speechless. Ru was cringing. She must have heard Topher tell Chance about Julia's fate, but Colbie was blunt and painted the situation with harsh honesty.

While Nora recovered, Colbie faced Chance. "If you want back into our lives, and I do mean *our* lives as in you have to get along with T, that is the risk. Not just death by all the bad supernaturals we come up against. *That's* what could happen to you."

Chance bristled. "I know, Colbie. Topher told me. You know I'm not stupid. I want to think about it, but Topher insisted I stay long enough to talk to you, then he'll make sure I get home. Ru can remove all the scents from here, so I'm not linked to you if I don't want to be. He's trying to convince me to leave town. I just… need to think about it. In the meantime, he said he would answer my calls. Can you promise the same?"

Colbie and Topher shared a long look. To Poppy, Topher's

expression was too guarded to pull anything from it, but no one knew him as well as his sister. She relented with a quick dip of her chin, right before Annaliese and Josh's noisy arrival broke the moment.

"Oh, you're still here?" Annaliese asked Chance unhappily as she went straight to the couch to sit next to Topher. Nora moved to perch on the cushioned arm next to her friend.

Chance just nodded while Colbie walked to stand in front of the TV, the center of attention in the middle of the living room. Poppy felt Josh at her back. She leaned back into his chest as Zayn and Oliver took the stools at the island. A sense of rightness settled over the apartment with everyone present.

"So, we talked to Tiff Jennings tonight," Colbie started, too casual for what that meant to everyone in the room.

Topher's eyes widened and flew to Poppy. She nodded grimly, ignoring how Josh stiffened behind her. She'd promised to tell him if she went looking. Guilt bubbled in her chest, but Poppy couldn't deal with all that right now. "She isn't doing well. She claims she has answers for us but—"

"Will only give them to us in exchange for protection," Colbie finished tightly. "She didn't tell us anything useful, and I don't think she knows anything about the drainers. We need to find answers elsewhere."

"What do you mean she isn't doing well?" Ru asked.

Poppy hesitated. It was too hard giving Ru these painful truths.

Colbie never had a problem delivering information. "The dark magic she's been using to summon demons has really fucked her over. Her wards were shit, and she's terrified of whatever has been killing witches. But none of that excuses how big of an asshole she was to Poppy and how she told Poppy to bring her here, to *you*, so she can use your magic and hide behind the strength you have to lick her wounds. I believe her exact word was you would *replenish* her, and I don't like the sound of that or how she talked as if Poppy were useless. We left her there after that."

Ru's brow furrowed. Then she did something that melted everything in Poppy's chest like butter. "Are you okay, P?" she asked. More concerned for Poppy than Tiff.

"I'm fine, just worried about her," Poppy said, unable to meet Colbie's eyes. "She doesn't have much time, but maybe she has *some* answers."

"Answers that will help Julia?" Topher asked.

"I don't know about that. But she knows more about demons than anyone else we could talk to. If they're using demons to make the drainers, Mom could tell."

"Then, the question is whether or not to let Tiff into the apartment. Or Alpha's Den would be safe, too, right?" Oliver asked. He was trying to juggle all the emotions in the room, attempting to keep peace.

Colbie scowled. "It's not a question. She murdered Dylan! She left Topher to die. She isn't staying here, and I don't want her in the club. I know she's Poppy and Ru's mom, but I don't trust her or her demons or her poltergeist that won't leave Poppy alone. Nothing good will come of giving her anything she wants."

An awkward quiet fell. No one but Poppy, Ru, or Topher could say much after that. All eyes were on them. Poppy didn't want to make a decision. It wasn't as if she carried fond memories of her childhood, but Ru's face was drawn, her focus on her clasped hands. Poppy glanced to Topher. He was looking at Ru, too.

Topher spoke. "She can come here. I'll just stay with Lana for a few days. Until Tiff is better."

He was usually so controlled. So perfect at hiding his emotions so as not to charm anyone. This time, his voice cracked, and he fought valiantly not to show his upset.

"Topher, we literally just watched her murder your boyfriend," Ru said, gesturing between herself and Chance. "I don't want her coming here. Maybe Poppy and I can go over there and enforce her wards when the sun is up."

Topher blinked. Ru undoubtably just melted his insides like she had Poppy's. Poppy moved to her sister, sliding onto the armchair with her. They barely fit, but Ru was a cuddler, and the tension in her shoulders relaxed with Poppy near.

"I'll go with you and make sure nothing happens," Josh said, voice stilted. Poppy finally looked at him, trying to convey gratitude. She was unsure what to think of his wooden expression.

"You don't owe her anything, Ru," Colbie said. "Remember that before you decide anything, especially before you give her too much."

Ru nodded. "I know, Colbie. But she *is* my mom. She's someone in need of help. It's not like I could live with myself if I sat back and let her wards fall."

Colbie looked between Poppy and Ru for a moment, the fight slipping out of her. She saw their decision and accepted it before turning to Topher, eyes skipping over Chance. "You okay?"

"Not great, but I think that's the right choice. And if worse comes to worse, this is their home, too. If they want to offer their mom a safe haven here, they can."

Colbie's jaw clenched, but after a tense pause, she relented. "Fine, but never without enough warning for you to get out of here."

Topher did his almost-smirk. His expressions stayed hidden with Chance, Oliver, and Annaliese in the room. Poppy hated getting this muted version of him during such a meaningful conversation. "That works for me," Topher said, the argument settled.

She heard the stool creak behind her. Oliver spoke up. "How about a game?"

"Yes, please," Topher agreed eagerly. He stood and, seeming without thought, held out a hand for Annaliese. She'd been tucked into the couch close to him, exhausted after the second long night in a row, but she took the offered hand readily.

"Want to play?" Topher asked Chance. "Then we can take you home."

"Play what?" As the words left Chance's mouth, a soccer ball came sailing at him from Colbie's direction.

She'd thrown it hard, but Chance caught it to his chest easily, a slow smile turning up the corners of his mouth. His grin was such a perfect combination of Colbie and Topher's. A smirk with too much twist that was all Colbie, but the dimple tucked into his right cheek was Topher.

Poppy rarely experienced the hands of Fate, the lines of Fortune that crossed the veil, but she saw the room brightened then. Like everything clicked into place. The third West sibling had been missing, the space where he should have been an open wound between Topher and Colbie. Even this hint that the void was closing made the air around them lighter. It was *right*.

"Let's go!" Ru said, struggling out of the couch and pulling Poppy with her. Her smile was a touch pained, a lot hopeful. Awareness of the five sisters missing between them seeped into the moment. Ru was suffering in their absence. Poppy swallowed a sigh as she let Ru pull her toward the door.

Was this Fate telling Poppy where her focus should be?

CHAPTER 29

Colbie ran full out to tackle Chance within the goal. Just like she would have over a year ago. His oof fell into peals of laughter while everyone else observed with mild concern at how fast she'd been running. But Chance was sturdy, and Colbie would never hurt him.

"I don't think I've ever been able to see you smile like that," Annaliese said, stopping in front of Topher.

He almost wiped away the grin, then realized she wasn't charmed. The bracelet she wore was glowing but already starting to fade. The bead couldn't hold much magic. Topher lifted Annaliese's wrist, amazed at how tiny her arm was in his hand. She was never small in his head. Never seemed small when she walked into a room, yet he easily touched his thumb and pinky when he circled her wrist. Her skin dark and smooth. Barely any hair. His good mood allowed him to take in all the little details. The scar at the base of her palm. He brushed it with his thumb. "What happened here?"

Annaliese bent to examine where he indicated rather than freeing her wrist from his loose grip. "I don't even see anything," she said.

Topher smirked, and the bracelet flashed again, weaker, but it allowed them this conversation at least. He'd have to ask Ru to make more. Maybe he'd keep them on hand to give out. It was one of the most hopeful thoughts he'd had in a while. "It's a scar."

"Oh," Annaliese trailed off a bit, tipping her head back up at him, eyes captivated. Topher glanced at the glowing bead and stilled under a wash of shock.

All those moments when he caught Annaliese watching him. All the times her gaze had gone a bit dreamy when their eyes met. Every act she took to make sure he was okay, even risking herself at the Den to rescue him… Topher had chalked all that up to his charm. Just his vampire allure drawing yet another victim in.

But if the bracelet was working, the interest was all Annaliese.

Julia's face flashed in Topher's mind. He dropped Annaliese's wrist. Well, gently lowered it while letting his fingertips linger.

The game was starting back up. Topher needed to think about this. Was it a betrayal to Julia? Aside from their messy breakup, she deserved his focus now. And he needed to think about Dylan's memory. Dylan had known precisely what Julia was to Topher. He hadn't been jealous of her. But Annaliese wasn't Julia. The way she studied at Topher was nothing like Julia's interest. It felt… deeper. Not like Dylan, but just as expansive. What would Dylan feel even about this line of thought? It hurt to even consider.

Topher needed to decide if pursuing anything was worth the risk of more pain. He knew he wasn't ready for anything serious, but the touch was so good. Being in Annaliese's presence was so good.

She didn't ask for him to go down this thought spiral. There was interest, and then there were relationships.

Annaliese was thoughtful and brave and understanding, but would anyone be okay with how much Topher missed Dylan? With how often his mind was on someone else?

Why was he even considering this when the pain was so raw?

Topher signed and turned away, knowing the answer. Because it was Annaliese and she was special. Catching the ball in his chest and sending it to Zayn across the pitch, Topher tried to focus back on the game. Annaliese chased after the ball, fearless and sure on a pitch full of supernaturals.

Because she was Annaliese. In the sea of Lana, and too much power, demons and monsters, stubborn siblings and delicate friendships, feeding off humans and clinging to humanity, Annaliese was the reliable lighthouse beam above the churning waves. If anyone could handle this life Topher was thrust into, maybe it was her. The quiet of dusk in his room with Annaliese warming the bed beside him— could that be Topher's new peace? A slow one, a tentative building to see what else was between them. Maybe he didn't have to be alone in the dark.

It was far too tempting an idea.

Topher tried to swallow the hope. It was habit at this point to shut that emotion off. It didn't seem fair to anyone. Not to Annaliese, not to Julia, not to their friends, and not to Dylan. But Topher was surprised to find he could hold the idea of it, of them, at all. And that made it something to consider.

Everyone was exhausted. They'd played out the majority of the tensions that had been building over the last few days in a matter of hours. Poppy and Topher went to drop off Chance, Poppy glancing worriedly at the time as Topher's blinks lengthened. Nora and Annaliese had dropped Ru and Colbie off on their way home. Nora hoped she hadn't imagined the way Colbie hesitated at the door before going inside. Their eyes met for long enough that Nora thought about it the rest of the drive.

"Full moon tomorrow night," Annaliese said, tossing her keys onto the small table by the door as they entered their apartment. "Any progress with the pack building?"

Nora kicked off her muddy sneakers and fought the urge to fall onto the couch, instead perching herself and her dirty clothes on the stool in the kitchen. "Janelle decided I wasn't the right fit after Matt and Adriana showed up at the club and I embarrassed myself. We're back to square one."

Annaliese frowned, disappointment passing her features. "Want to talk about it?"

"Not really." Now that the onslaught of emotion had subsided from seeing Gabriel, the hurt spurred by Janelle's decision was overwhelming.

"And things with Colbie? Did you decide to focus on that instead?" Annaliese asked as if that had been an option all along.

"Things with Colbie are… warmer than they were, but I don't want to assume that means they're going anywhere."

"Warm is good," Annaliese said, sounding distracted. She was slowly unlacing her shoes, thinking.

Nora didn't want to discuss her nonexistent pack or jinx the fragile situation with Colbie. She switched the subject to the mystery that had been gnawing at her. "I want to ask your advice on something. Something that might make things cold again with Colbie."

"Oh?"

"Tiff Jennings said she was there when my dad died. She could help me figure out if Topher or Gabriel was lying about who killed him."

Annaliese nodded slowly. "That's been bothering me too. Why would either of them lie when it doesn't change where we are?"

"Doesn't it? If my dad was in favor of the laws, if he didn't want to keep killing vampires, that proves Gabriel was in the wrong. That I wasn't betraying my dad by not joining his old pack."

"Do you want Gabriel to have been in the wrong?" Annaliese asked carefully, their recent fight still fresh between them.

Nora hesitated for a second. "I want the truth. But I don't think I could submit to Gabriel. The wolf in me wouldn't allow it. When I saw him yesterday, there was nothing there. I realized how much I was forcing submission before. I just wanted to growl at him."

Annaliese laughed at that. She was proud of Nora but trying not to show it after their last argument. "That seems like a good thing. You deserve to know what happened to your dad; I just don't know if Tiff Jennings is the person you should ask. Especially running off as little sleep as we currently are. Maybe you should think on it?"

"That's fair," Nora admitted. It wasn't a no. Annaliese didn't shut down the idea. Did that mean her friend thought it held some merit?

When Nora woke, the sun was high in the sky. Annaliese snored in the room over. A few more weeks working at the club and Annaliese would probably end up with the same sleep schedule as the vampires.

Nora's body buzzed with energy gifted by the full moon fast approaching. Not even the events and games of last night had taken the edge off for long. She dressed and stomped into her muddy shoes, deciding to go for a run. The apartment felt too small, her thoughts too expansive.

But her plans were thwarted as soon as she stepped outside and caught a scent. Nora could probably slip away before having to confront the person, but... she met with Matt and gave him a chance. Didn't she owe that to the rest of her former pack?

Nora braced herself and turned, spotting Heather down the block, sitting on a bench with two coffees. The distance was purposeful, as most of Heather's actions were. She was giving Nora space and an opportunity to avoid the talk. That was a good enough show of respect and boundaries that Nora approached with less trepidation. Heather watched her, a sad smile on her lips. She offered Nora one of the drinks and, when Nora took it, rested her empty hand on the growing bump of her stomach.

Nora's heart squeezed. She'd been genuinely excited to meet this new pack member. Yet another person Gabriel had stripped from her. Or that she'd taken from herself in refusing to follow him. Or Topher had… the blame was so hard to cast even now.

Heather was examining Nora as if looking for bruises. She used to do this when she'd babysit Nora. Always worried Nora might have gotten hurt under her charge. They were ten years apart in age, but those nights of Heather playing silly games, the makeup parties, and brownies always made Nora feel close to her.

Heather would make a good mom. She was good at everything she attempted. Nora mourned the opportunity to watch this version of Heather come to life.

"Hi, Nora," Heather said. "You look good."

"You sound surprised."

"Well, I've heard it's hard out there for wolves without packs." Nora couldn't read Heather's tone.

"It's easier for alphas. At least, I think. It's not easy, but… I'm not at risk of going full wolf or anything."

"I'm glad. We've been worried about you."

"Have you?" And the bitterness crept into Nora's words. They'd blocked her. Hadn't reached out. Heather could have found her this whole time. She just hadn't. Until now. "Not worried enough to check."

Heather stiffened. "I checked Nora. I used to walk by that burger place. I liked to keep an eye on you. I thought you were doing better. Figuring things out. Then we hear you aligned with that vampire?"

It was a leading question. Heather waited like she expected Nora to start defending herself. Instead, Nora shrugged and took a sip of the too-sweet coffee. Heather drank some light, floral-scented tea. With Heather's notorious sweet tooth, she'd probably gotten Nora the drink she would have if she weren't pregnant.

There was a metaphor about the pack in there. One that would make Colbie scowl. But Nora enjoyed the drink anyway. This might be her last piece of Heather.

"Were you there when my dad died?"

Heather coughed on her tea, the question catching her off guard. When she could breathe normally, she answered. "No. I was with you. Don't you remember?"

"I don't remember much of that night. Or the ones after. I don't even really remember Gabriel telling me what happened. He said Reelings did it?"

Heather faced Nora fully. "You sound like you don't believe it."

"Do you?"

"Nora. You *know* Gabriel wouldn't lie about that. No matter what you think he did, he's not cruel. He believes in this city and our duty to protect it. He believes in your father's legacy and in you. He wouldn't do that to you. I wouldn't be growing this baby if I believed anything different."

The real problem was that Nora couldn't imagine Gabriel lying. It didn't change her feelings about what he'd done to her, but this was too important. Yet she couldn't imagine Topher lying either. It was enough to make her mind feel like splitting.

"What did you want to talk to me about?" Nora asked.

Heather's mouth quirked. "I heard Matty got to talk to you. I was jealous. If Gabriel is letting us speak, then I wanted my turn."

Nora had to drop her eyes. She'd missed that ring of love in a packmate's voice, but the bond was missing. There wasn't that inherent connection. That magic thread between them. In its place was resentment. Distrust. Betrayal. "I've been right here this whole time. I've been calling and hoping at least someone would show up. Separate from pack politics, my family abandoned me after one night and one decision."

"Gabriel says it wasn't just one night, Nora. He said—"

"Fine. Do you want to know what happened? What my big crime was? Remember Topher? Chris? His sister. I… like her. I liked her then and was seeing her, and I like her still." The confession came out in a rush, Nora's head going light with the relief of it. "I would follow her to the end of the world. She's a vampire and a girl and progressive and beautiful and fierce and… she makes everything better and brighter. I was blinded by her back then, but I can't regret those choices. I don't regret her or the world she showed me was possible. The world Gabriel hid from me. Then, he tried to make me kill her. She was in the basement that night and I've never been more…" Nora shook her head, still unable to describe the horror of that moment. "Of course I haven't come back."

Heather was silent. Nora was trembling, relief tumbling to fear.

Annaliese was there while Nora discovered these crucial parts of herself. Nora had never come out to someone. The thought of more rejection from Heather, rejection for more than pack issues, but of this core, beautiful part of Nora… it was devastating. She didn't want this newly lit spark dimmed by anything, but Nora longed to be known by this woman she'd always admired and adored.

But no one in her pack talked about this stuff. Mating with the opposite sex was a given. What if Heather didn't approve?

What if Heather didn't want to know her? What if she purposefully tried to snuff the spark? Did Nora know and love herself well enough to protect it? Why had she risked—

Heather's arms came around Nora: home and the familiar. "I'm so sorry, Nora. I didn't understand. Of course, you couldn't be around Gabriel. I saw the way he looked at you. I thought you welcomed it… but you're so young. What he wanted from you was so, so much. You must not have felt like you had a choice. I'm sorry I didn't realize. I never even thought to question your relationship with him."

Nora needed to hear those words. She needed the touch of her pack. Some form of acceptance. Nora dissolved. The tears were uncontrollable. Heather hugged her through the onslaught, a stand-in for the family that was gone.

Eventually, Nora calmed enough to back out of Heather's hold.

"I'm really happy you told me that, Nora." A twinkle in Heather's eye. "But I have to say, a vampire? Really?"

Nora laughed and wiped her cheeks. "If you saw her, you'd understand."

Heather sighed and sat back on the bench, hand resting on her stomach again. "I can't say I'm happy with Gabriel's choices. He's been even cagier since you made your change. I think only Matt knows everything he's up to. Maybe not even. Packs aren't supposed to hide things like that. Not that I'm suddenly doubting if Gabe lied about your dad. I'm just saying, I don't think you were completely wrong to leave."

"And you? Are you happy to stay?"

"It's my home. I didn't think it was possible to leave." Heather examined Nora, assessing. "But I feel the draw to you. I can't believe how immune to it I was before."

Nora fought a triumphant smirk. Heather's pregnancy was the greatest testament to Gabriel's success and power. If Nora was strong enough to make *her* doubt…

"I'm not going to tell you to leave. That's too big a choice.

But you know where to find me if you ever need me, Heather."

Heather laughed. "I never imagined the day I would go to little Nora Mora for anything. But you're not that girl anymore, are you?"

"No. I'm not."

CHAPTER 30

She and Heather talked longer than Nora could have anticipated. When the older wolf left, Nora's stomach rumbled with hunger. She decided to stop by the deli where she used to grab sandwiches during her breaks at her old job. Nora ducked her head as she passed in front of the burger place, wincing to remember how she'd abruptly quit over text but also knowing she was far from the first person to do so in that industry.

Still, because of her luck, another server recognized her. The door clanged open, and Maddie called out her name. Nora stopped, forcing a smile. Her cheeks were stiff from crying, but her mood far lighter after talking with Heather. "Hey! What's up?"

"I was just wondering if you've heard from Ricky?"

"Ricky?"

"Yeah. He quit when he heard you did—made it sound like he was going to follow you to your new job. We haven't heard from him since. You haven't seen him?"

"Um, no. Sorry."

"Oh, well, if you do, let him know he left his jacket when he left. It looks nice, so we're holding it for him."

"Yeah, okay. I'll keep an eye out for him."

Maddie stood, shifting from foot to foot. There was a sheen of sweat on her forehead, and her hair was escaping her braid. She was clearly in the middle of a rush, but there was more she had to say. "Will you try calling him? He won't pick up, and he just, he seemed really off when he realized you quit. Left in a panic but wouldn't explain it."

"I mean, we weren't that close. There must have been something else happening, but I can try."

Maddie nodded, relief easing her pinched brows. She stepped back and into the half-open door. "You work at that new club on Twenty-Fifth?"

Nora nodded, surprised Maddie knew.

"Well, maybe we'll come by. Grab those drinks we never went to while you worked here."

"Yeah, I'd like that."

Maddie's smile was pleased. There was a glimmer in her eyes as they dipped quickly up and down Nora's body. Was she…"I'll see you later then, Nora." Maddie winked and vanished back into the chaos of the lunch rush.

How had Nora missed the flirting? Or was that the first time? Did they actually miss her here? What else had gone unnoticed amid Nora's grief? She must not have been as sullen and moody as she thought she'd acted.

Although, this news about Ricky was unexpected. Nora made it to the deli, placed her order at the window, and as she stood off to the side waiting, she called him.

He answered on the first ring. "Nora?"

"Hey, Ricky. Sorry, I never got back to—"

"That's okay! Can we talk? In person? Soon? Please?"

Maddie was right. He did sound panicked. Strange for someone she didn't know well. Nora glanced at the time. If she wanted to talk to Tiff Jennings, she'd need to go soon. "Um, I'm a little bus—"

"Please, Nora. This is… well, I don't know what it is. But,

for some reason, I think you're the only one who can help?" He ended on an uptick, making the statement a question. He sounded as confused as Nora. "I was trying not to bother you too much, but I'm glad you called."

"Alright. I'll make some time."

"Now? Please. I'm sorry to do this but…"

Nora debated. Ru and Poppy were probably warding Tiff now. They would understand Nora's need to ask questions, but if she went later the wards might try to keep her out and then—

"Please, Nora."

"Okay. I'm coming."

Without really thinking beyond the address Ricky sent her, Nora picked up her sandwich and turned to leave, abruptly halting when she nearly collided with Janelle. "Nora. I need to talk to you."

"Damn, I'm popular today. Get in line." Nora's tone could have been kinder, but Janelle's rejection still stung.

"Of course you are. It's a full moon tonight." Janelle didn't say it, but the *idiot* was implied in her tone.

Nora cocked her head. "So…?"

"I had some questions about what you expect from tonight and the club."

"Oh, not Henry?"

"Not Henry."

"Can we walk and talk then? I have somewhere to be."

Ricky didn't live too far away. Janelle agreed, and they started in the direction of his building. Nora didn't have much to say to the alphaless wolf. She had nothing to prove, no real ties to Janelle aside from the Alpha's Den. Janelle had chosen Henry. She should be with his pack, preparing to run together for the first time. Nora had her walls up and didn't love this reminder that she was back to the beginning of her search. Hopefully, by this time next month, she'd be closer to having members. Lana was already getting impatient, and they'd only been open for two nights.

At least Nora had more time to learn how to be an alpha now. Henry could explain it to her in the weeks to come. It was surprising how open she was to another meeting with him. Something had shifted in her. This new purpose, the letting go of her old pack, left Nora ready to move forward. She was excited by the possibilities.

And maybe she would even ask Henry about his connection to her mom. If anyone could help Nora get her back or squash the hope that it was even an option, it would be him.

They reached Ricky's building. Nora realized she and Janelle walked the whole way in silence. Companionable silence, but still. "Sorry, I was lost in thought. What did you want to ask me?"

"Are you getting back together with the vampire girl?"

Nora blinked. Out of everything, she hadn't been expecting that. "I don't know; it's up to her."

"But you want to?"

Nora nodded. The fact was terrifying, but very true. In a passive, comforting way, her thoughts always seemed half on Colbie. Wondering how she was sleeping. If she dreamed. If she dreamed of Nora.

"That's not normal."

Nora scowled. "Oh, thanks for telling me. I hadn't realized. Was that what you wanted to talk about? Is that why you chose Henry?"

"No, I didn't mean it like that. I just meant... Henry is normal."

"Thanks for clarifying yet again why you picked him over me. I can't blame you. I tried to hate him, but I couldn't. But if he's claiming you tonight, you should probably be with—"

"Nora!"

Ricky was waiting on the steps leading into his building. He stood, rushing toward her. And it all made sense. That smell

Ricky had that always drew her in. The way he'd focused on Nora. The desperation on the phone and his attempts to hang out.

Nora gasped. "Ricky! You're a werewolf?"

He let out a hysterical-sounding laugh. His voice was several octaves too high. "I'm a *what?*"

"Oh, this isn't good," Janelle muttered.

The alpha inside Nora rose. It entered her voice as she said, "We should go inside. We have a lot to discuss."

Ricky relaxed and nodded, the command instantly soothing his panic. Nora and Janelle shared a look before following him into the building.

Ricky paced his bare studio, holding his hair in fists as he shook his head. Janelle stood by his door, watching him intently as though he might shift any second and wreak havoc in the space. Hours had passed. First, working through Ricky's denial of what was happening. Nora had to make the shift to convince him werewolves were real after he started questioning even that. Janelle and Nora had taken turns explaining their upbringing within werewolf packs, and Ricky had described his own packless childhood. Now, he seemed to be processing and silently panicking. Nora could feel that his wolf was still buried. It wanted out, but it would wait until the moon called.

Henry's voice in Nora's ear was far calmer than the situation warranted. "And he didn't know?"

"No. He says his parents… well, they don't sound like they'd be open to including werewolves in their household."

Ricky had laughed off and on for about thirty minutes after Nora had explained what she was and what she thought was happening. When Nora asked if he had any family members who habitually disappeared during full moons, he explained, "My mom told me if I came to New Brecken for school, I was inviting the devil in. UNB was the only place that offered me a scholarship, and it *called* to me."

His father was a pastor. His brother on the path to follow in his footsteps. Ricky hadn't spoken to any of them since moving to New Brecken.

He was as starved for a pack and a family as Nora was, yet he hadn't known fully what the ache in his chest meant, only that it was slightly easier to breathe when he worked with Nora and it nearly consumed him when she vanished.

"This doesn't happen often, Nora," Henry was saying, "but it does happen. Be gentle. It sounds like he found you now because it will be his first shift."

"Should I bring him to you?"

Henry paused. "Do you need to?"

Ricky had stopped pacing, staring out the window at the slowly darkening sky. They had so little time. All of Nora's other plans were put on hold. This was more important than talking with Tiff. More important than napping or meeting up for coffee or answering Annaliese's phone call.

Nora had so much to explain. She could even give Ricky a choice if he didn't like the sound of her involvement with the club. Nora opened her mouth to answer but didn't know what to say to Henry. She didn't want to bring Ricky to him. Her alpha side wanted to do this and was already protective of Ricky. Henry spoke first, "Nora, bring him if you have time. If you need to. But I have to go."

"Okay."

Henry hung up shortly after, and it was just the three of them again.

"Ricky, I think you'll make your first change tonight."

Ricky whimpered, the animal sound the only indication he'd heard her. Also, a sign the wolf was right there.

"What do you feel?" Janelle asked him.

He shook his head. "Whatever this is, it wants Nora." He turned to Nora fully, his pupils blown wide with the alarm he barely contained. "I've thought about you since you started working with me. When you left, it was like this *huge* panic. I stopped sleeping and had this constant anxiety. And I felt so betrayed. I couldn't talk myself out of feeling that way when we barely knew each other. I just couldn't believe you'd vanish without telling me."

"Ricky. I'm so sorry. I—" Nora cut off when Ricky yelped, doubling over and gasping. Nora's eyes flew to the window. The sun was setting at an alarming speed. Where had the time gone?

Ricky clutched his head again, crouching by the window, under the touch of the sun's rays. "Nora… help. Please. I don't care what you have to do."

Nora glanced at Janelle. Checking with another wolf wasn't something an alpha would do, but she couldn't just do this. He didn't know what he was asking. This bond… it was supposed to be for life.

"Do it," Janelle said. She sounded sure. Far more confident than Nora.

"Nora. Please."

Nora could barely think over the sound of Ricky's begging. The alpha was right there. It *wanted* him. And that felt wrong. Like what Gabriel must have felt he had over Nora. "I can't just claim him. What if he regrets it? Maybe you should get Henry. I don't think we should move him. He doesn't know me or who I am as a wolf. I'm sure he'd rather be—"

"His instincts led him to you, Nora. His wolf chose you. Explain everything after."

Nora swallowed and looked down at Ricky. He was watching, hands flexed on the ground, fingers curled as if ready for claws. There wasn't time. If she was going to do this, the alpha told her she had to do it now. "Fine. But you should leave. I don't want to accidentally claim you too."

A loaded pause. Janelle pushed off the door and

approached, but Nora was entirely focused on Ricky. "So don't do it by accident. Claim me."

Nora whirled to face her. Janelle tipped her chin up.

"What do you mean? You prefer Henry. You said—"

"I changed my mind! People do that. I thought I wanted to join Henry, but his followers, the people who chose him, they're all so peaceful. They're closer to humans than wolves, even in the change. It isn't bad, but it isn't what I expected."

"It's not like I don't want peace!"

"No. You want power. The power to make your own peace, not to negotiate and compromise. Deny it. Try."

And *that* was the one thing that Nora had always wanted. She'd wanted power enough to think she could live her life as Gabriel's mate. Once she'd become alpha and everyone told her she'd gotten the power without him, the cost made it too much to think about. But now, with Janelle looking at her like that…. Damn. It was how she'd dreamed of people looking up to her, listening to her, seeing her as her father's daughter. But she wasn't that different from Henry, was she? She also admired him.

"Henry has power."

"Henry does. He has a big, adoring pack. He listens to them, but they never disagree with anything he does because he'll only accept you if you agree ahead of time. He walked me through everything he expected, down to the room assignment. Sure, they'll get involved in city drama, but I want to live in a pack, not a dorm room. Even when you didn't impress me initially, I couldn't stay away. It's why I'm still working under that god-awful vampire. It's why I missed you last night when you didn't show. It's why I'm here instead of waiting for Henry to claim me under the full moon. I want you to be my alpha. Ricky does, too."

"I don't—"

Ricky shuddered. A keening started in his throat. Suddenly, Nora remembered how Gabriel had made her wait.

That torture of the first shift. Nora was out of time. "Alright. Okay."

She shook out her hands and searched her gut, remembering Henry's advice on how to accept a pack. After one last steadying breath, Nora stepped up to Ricky. Janelle stripped and made the change. She began to pace and let out a whimper of her own. Janelle was searching for a connection like Ricky. Like Nora. She'd been good at hiding the longing as a human, but now Nora sensed Janelle in the hollow space left after Topher broke the connection with her old pack.

Nora straightened. Her mind snaked out, hooking into Janelle's searching thread of longing. Janelle barked— happily? The connection took hold. Locked into place. Flooded Nora's nerves with soothing rightness. Even in human form, Nora knew exactly where Janelle was. She knew Janelle's racing heart, her desire to run.

Ricky stared at Janelle as a wolf, eyes wide, body trembling. The human afraid, the wolf eager.

"Are you ready, Ricky?" Nora carried the alpha in her voice. It rang deeper, more potent. Like when her mother hit her with the serious tone that brokered no argument. But also something else. Something magic.

Ricky's features relaxed. "Yes."

"Don't change yet."

He nodded, body stilling. Command wrapping around him. It was easy after that. To leave the apartment. To get in Ricky's car and speed toward the Park, Janelle following.

Nora called Colbie as she drove, unsure if the vampire was awake but not wanting to stay away for a night without explanation. She left a voicemail, her voice giddy. A bit embarrassing, but not the most humiliating message she'd left Colbie. Before Nora had time to doubt whether Colbie would even want the update, the forest came into view. Nora's heart thrilled at the sight of it. A knowing settled over her. She was doing the right thing. There was freedom in letting go of the vestiges of hope to rejoin her old pack. Freedom in moving forward. Fully into this life, this power. Making the people who mattered most proud. Colbie. Annaliese. Maybe even her father. And Nora was proud of herself.

It felt *so* good.

At the edge of the trees, Ricky exited the car, riveted on Nora. The moon was just breaking. Nora took up the bottom of her shirt, pulling it over her head. Ricky did the same. She smelled his adrenaline, his sweet wolf scent.

He smelled like her memories of home. Janelle, too, as she reached them, panting from her run but unable to stop moving, tail whipping and nose busy. Nora faced Ricky. She didn't even have to voice a command. The bond took hold, her mind finding where his was untethered.

She said the words anyway. "Alright, Ricky. Time to change."

And change he did, in time with Nora's shift. Furiously, painlessly, the wolf ripped through him. Ricky let out a surprised yelp, but he was on four paws, and he could feel Nora like Nora felt him. She knew he felt Janelle through her connection, too. With only the slightest urging, Nora led them into the trees at a full sprint. She'd never been stronger. Happier.

They howled to the moon, and Nora could have sworn its pulsing rays of magic light answered. A caress that went straight to Nora's core and filled her with assurance. Euphoria followed.

Josh was anxious. Ru beyond frustrated—verge of tears and kicking rocks frustrated. Poppy checked the progress of the setting sun and made a decision.

"Ru, you should go home. This isn't working, and whatever Mom's so afraid of, you shouldn't be here when it comes. I'll keep trying."

Ru swallowed. She was fighting the tears hard. "Why isn't it working?"

Attempting to cast into their mother's wards had only led to the magic taking hold, then sucking and sucking from their power with no end in sight. Ru had barely been able to separate them from it. That was at noon while Tiff slept quietly inside.

They'd gone home, forced to rest and eat. After quick naps and gathering what plants Poppy had left after warding the Alpha's Den, they'd come back. This time, Tiff was awake and waiting on the front porch. She'd put some effort into her appearance, but Ru had still gasped in horror at the sight of her. Ru sat next to Tiff while Poppy started planting, Josh standing watch between them as stony as she'd ever seen him.

He hated Tiff Jennings. It was a strange emotion to see on him.

Poppy tried not to pay her family any attention as she infused the wards into the plants and started placing them along the wards. She was digging a hole for the sixth one when Ru groaned. Poppy followed her sister's gaze over her shoulder. The first of her poor plants had already withered and crumbled. Poppy sat back on her heels and shared a long look with Ru. That's when Tiff started begging, telling Ru how powerful she was, how great. She was Tiff's pride and joy. Of all her children, Tiff hadn't wanted to leave Ru the most. Only Ru could keep her safe now.

Ru stood, face hard. "You shouldn't talk like that. You shouldn't act like Poppy isn't right there, doing her best to save you."

"Poppy can't save me. She doesn't have the strength. But *you—*"

"Go inside, Mother. We'll keep trying, but I don't want to listen to this."

Ru left Tiff stunned on the porch. She crouched next to Poppy, coaxing more strength into the plant.

Now, they were surrounded by brown leaves and withered stems, shoulders slumped with exhaustion. Poppy didn't know what else to do but stand guard and hope her personal wards were strong enough to protect her while she tried to keep Tiff safe. She had an arsenal of potions and Josh right there.

It didn't feel nearly sufficient.

"Poppy, I don't want to leave you."

"I know. I know you don't. But if the demons are searching for witches, they may not feel me or Mom with how weak she is. They *will* feel you, though."

It wasn't entirely true. Ru's wards were a stronghold, growing more flawless by the day. Even so, Poppy intuited danger and wanted Ru far away. The night was building around her, dark with suspense. It might have been the full moon and Josh's energy cascading under it. It might have been Tiff's fear where she hid inside, but there was something in the air. Something that made Poppy's hair stand on end and whispered in her ear that Ru needed to leave.

"Why don't you go home and tell Colbie and Topher what's happening? Maybe one of them will come help me. You've used too much magic today, Ru. You're exhausted." She really was. Guilt swept in when Poppy realized it took her until now to notice. She'd been too focused on planting and the gentle urging of her own magic. She hadn't noticed how much Ru was still pouring into the wards or the plants. Pouring into the void that was their mother.

After a long moment, Ru conceded. "Okay. Fine. But you have to understand one of these days, I'm going to be done with taking the backseat. I'm getting older and stronger. I'm almost in control of my magic. When that happens, you have to stop treating me with kid gloves."

Poppy gave her a sad smile, pulling Ru into a hug. "Make me," she said in her ear with a singsong voice reminiscent of childhood taunting.

Ru laughed and stepped away. "Take care of her," she told Josh.

He gave Ru a mock salute and let the change rip through him, ruining all his clothes but startling a laugh out of her.

Just as Ru was getting to the car, the door of the house banged open. Tiff must have been sleeping again. Her hair was wild, and eyes swollen. "You're leaving?!" Tiff screeched. Gus stood beside Ru, shaking his head, but barely there after Ru had spent the day banishing his presence. "Baby, you can't leave me! I *need* you!"

Ru glared at her, already halfway in the car. "But I don't need you."

Tiff stumbled down the path. Josh growled as she passed him.

"You can't leave me, Ru. You can't leave me to die."

"Then let Poppy help you."

"Poppy?!" Tiff's voice pitched higher. Josh's ears tucked back, and Tiff let out a shocked titter of laughter. "Poppy is useless!"

"Mom…" Poppy barely listened to her, only tracking her progress to the edge of her weakened wards. The warning went unheeded.

"You leave me with Penelope, and I'm *dead*."

Ru's expression flattened. "Because of Poppy, I'm not dead. Listen to her, Mom. That's the best advice I can give you."

Ru shut herself in and started the car as Tiff's laughter dissolved into sobs. Poppy was forced to step forward and bodily block her mother to keep her from leaving the wards. Tiff muttered a tracking spell, bidding the magic to cling to Ru, and when Ru's wards blocked it, tried to track the car.

"Mom, stop! What are you going to do, follow her?"

"If it means surviving this, then yes!" Tiff was winded from attempting to cast.

Poppy searched for patience. "We can work this out. We

just need to get you to focus on life. On vitality and the magic that comes from—"

Tiff laughed a cruel sound that had haunted Poppy's childhood. She pushed out of Poppy's hold. "What do you know about magic? What have you ever known about magic?"

"Enough to trap you! Enough to keep myself and Ru safe!"

"That's all Ru's power! You're using her as much as you think I plan to! You. Are. So. *Weak.* My greatest embarrassment. Of course you're the only one here now!" Tiff spread her arms, ignoring Josh's cautionary growl. "My pathetic middle child. Always searching for someone to take care of her. Trying to make friends with the power around her. You didn't understand it then, and you don't understand it now. What do you think, working together and love will be enough to survive this? Do you think this is one of those TV shows kids watch? That holding hands and singing will keep the boogieman away? GROW UP!" Black spittle flew from Tiff's lips. Poppy stepped back as Tiff advanced. Josh moved, planting himself between them with a snarl.

The shadows lengthened, and the streetlights flickered on. There was a scuffling sound down the road, but Poppy couldn't take her focus from Tiff to check what it was.

Faint howls sounded, getting closer. Hopefully, it was Josh's pack. Not Gabriel's.

Tiff wasn't finished. "You're supposed to be a witch! A witch wouldn't cower behind a werewolf. We are the strongest supernaturals in the city! Our magic, my magic, is strong enough to read the future and change it! And yet you come along. You can barely read the leaves. Barely light a spark between your fingers. You should have died, not Jane, with all her promise and fire. Not Natalie with her quiet, deadly storms. When I broke the coven, I barely noticed the sacrifice of a connection with you. If you want to help me, bring your sisters. If you want to help me, let the beasts get *you* instead!"

Poppy thought maybe she was crying, but mostly, she was

numb as she followed her mother's pointing finger to the darkness surrounding them.

The music striking in the clubs was like a pulsing heartbeat in the night. In the shadows, claws edged outward. Strings of drool glistened. Josh kept up a constant snapping, growl. Poppy swallowed, glancing back at her mother.

"You should go, little flower," Tiff said, mockingly gentle. "You're too fragile for this darkness. I will survive another night."

Josh nudged Poppy away from the shadows, but Ru had taken the car. Poppy swallowed hard. She was trapped. Her mother's wards may hold for her for the night. But they wouldn't protect them all.

Poppy tentatively called for her magic, and the shadowy figures hissed excitedly. She couldn't even tell yet if they were demons or drainers. A car suddenly rounded the corner, headlights making whatever they were shrink back.

Poppy didn't dare look away, but she relaxed. It must be Colbie. Coming for her. Ru had sent her in this direction. But… Josh's growling didn't let up. When the car door opened, he let out a harsh sound that had Poppy whirling, heart high in her throat.

It wasn't Colbie. It wasn't anyone Poppy knew, yet the energy she tasted rolling off him, the power, was far too familiar. She'd felt it off Lana. Topher. Zayn. Colbie. The glimpses she'd had of Grace.

Her mother confirmed the suspicion, the impossible thought rising in Poppy's mind.

"Reelings," Tiff said. "I see you've come to taunt me."

CHAPTER 31

"Christopher."

"Lana."

Topher heard Colbie leave the apartment. He shifted in bed, rolling so Lana's voice was more distant from his phone on his pillow.

"Someone is at the apartment."

That got Topher to sit up. "Poppy? She said she'd be trying to—"

"Not Poppy. We need to get there now."

Topher didn't need to hear more. In seconds, he'd thrown on a hoodie and sneakers and left the apartment. Topher ran. Faster than he'd crossed the city since Ru was attacked last winter. It took him minutes, but when he and Lana drew up to the apartment building simultaneously, it was not the chaos Topher had expected.

It was quiet. Still.

The front door open.

Inside empty.

A distant scream.

"Fuck," Lana breathed the word.

Topher couldn't summon a reaction. Dazed and too, too

hopeful, he stepped up the decrypted steps and entered the building. The doors on the first floor were ajar, and rooms abandoned. Nothing living or otherwise waiting within.

The hope was dying.

The next floor, open doors. Nothing.

The third floor. Open doors. He almost couldn't bear to go to Julia's, checking every apartment but hers. It seemed like a waste of time to bother, but when he finally peered inside her door, he gasped.

She was there, huddled on the ground, arms crossed tight over her stomach where she knelt. Topher blinked, unable to believe that, for once, the hope had somewhere to go rather than sink into painful disappointment. She'd *stayed*. "Jules?"

Her head snapped up. Topher could have sworn there was recognition in her eyes—just a brief flare.

But then Lana came up the stairs behind him. "Raven said someone tried to get into the club, too, but the wards held. She didn't see who it was. Poppy is quite g—" Lana halted, seeing that Julia remained. Topher couldn't tell which of them were more shocked.

"I want out," Julia whispered. "But… I don't want to kill. He told me I had to kill. Do you have that drink? I need more." She gestured feebly toward the pot still on the stove.

Topher got out his phone, hitting Poppy's contact as he spoke to Julia. "Who? Who came here?"

"I don't know. He… he was so familiar. He told me I don't remember him, but he said he…" Julia choked off. "He said not to describe him. To describe someone else."

Lana and Topher stiffened, exchanging a look as Topher's phone rang and rang without an answer in his ear.

"What do you mean?" Lana stepped fully into the room, making Julia cringe back, hugging herself tighter as if it would hold her and her monstrous urges in place.

Julia's eyes went to Topher, and his stomach did sink then. There wasn't any of the Julia he used to know in those dark clouds. "His voice tasted sweet like yours. But… too strong. So strong."

Lana barked a laugh. "Stronger than Topher? Impossible."

"*If you would like to leave a message*—" Topher hung up his phone.

"What else can you tell us?" he asked.

"I don't remember. He told me to forget, so I did."

"Can I try and make you remember?"

Another distant scream in the night outside. Julia dropped her head, clutching her ears. "I smell them. I need them. I'm so, so hungry."

"Julia, can I try?"

She stared up at him from her position on the floor. Eyes clouding further. She was hungry. So desperately hungry that Topher could see it consuming her, smothering what little control she possessed.

What was Julia? How much of this restraint was Poppy's potion or Julia's humanity or—

"He wanted me to tell you something," Julia whispered finally. "I remember that now. He said to tell Christopher West if he wants real power, he'll stop following—"

"Lana? Toph?"

Everyone in the apartment stiffened at Zayn's call at the base of the stairs. Then, "Oliver, no, stay in the car."

Topher sense of time snapped. It slowed. It sped. It condensed into the knowledge that Oliver was right outside.

Lana spun, calling down to Zayn. Julia met Topher's eyes for only the barest of glances. Long enough for him to shake his head. Long enough for her not to heed his silent warning. Long enough to see the last of what had made Julia, his best friend in middle school, his girlfriend in high school, his comfort post-Dylan, disappear completely.

As if muffled, Topher heard Oliver responding. Human life drenched the cadence of his voice. He was so vibrant and irresistible.

Julia was finished resisting.

She lunged and tried to sidestep Topher, but he was faster. The lack of sustenance for weeks had left Julia weak. Scrawny and breakable under Topher's hands in a way that cracked his chest. She was weaker, yes, but the desperation wasn't something he'd prepared for either. She nearly slipped the hold he had on her biceps. He had to pull her back into the room, diving for her waist, twisting and struggling until he had her pinned on the ground beneath him.

Panic roared as loudly in Topher's ears as Julia began shrieking, "DO YOU WANT ME TO DIE?!"

Topher cringed from the question. Julia lifted herself between the wrists Topher kept pinned to the ground. Her spittle flew. It smelled unspeakably horrid.

Topher stared into her wild eyes. Distantly heard Oliver and Zayn arguing and a shout as something came up on them, but he was too busy with this.

"No," Topher's protest was lost to Julia's teeth-gritted screaming. She kicked her feet, intermittently trying to buck Topher off. When it didn't work, she slammed her head back into the carpet with as much force as she could summon. Someone was sobbing. When Topher couldn't catch his breath to talk again, he realized it was him.

She was going to hurt herself. She was going to get loose and hurt someone else. Julia wouldn't have wanted any of this. Topher began summoning that damned charm. The charm that had worked only one miracle, but that had been enough to save Colbie when he freed Nora. Maybe it could be used for good. He hadn't been trying hard enough.

Julia paused, sucking in a breath, eyes pitch black as if she'd knocked the darkness loose. Topher looked deep into those eyes and pulled out a mock, hideous smile. It was so wrong, but smiling always helped the charm slip under the other person's defenses. "Julia, forget whatever charm that man put on you. Remember being human."

Julia stilled. "Stop," she gasped the word, wincing.

Topher knew her pain; it exploded behind his eyes. "Julia, remember! Come back, you can fight this!"

Julia thrashed again. Topher could barely hold her and his charm. "Please! Please, make it stop!"

"Julia, come back to me!" They struggled against each other. Topher could feel the charm that had made her forget. A wall keeping his own laced words from taking hold. It was foreign, nothing like Julia's essence. It didn't have a motivation for Topher to cling to as he tried to vanquish its hold on her. Someone had messed with her mind. Had made her forget. That had to mean it could be reversed. Hope powered Topher's next burst of charm.

"JULIA!"

…And he knew immediately he had pushed too far. Julia gasped, the pain let off, and she slumped into the floor beneath him. Julia stared blankly, eyes no longer focused. He could tell somehow, even with everything gone black. The rest of the building had fallen quiet.

Topher let out a whimper, unable to accept what he was seeing but *knowing* what had happened. It had been so long since Lana made him push far enough to break someone's mind. He remembered Mary. The way she'd stilled. The way Grace had eventually stepped forward to snap her neck like it was nothing.

First, he made himself let go of her wrists. He got off her, crawling up the length of her body to kneel by her head. He gently turned her cheek in his direction. "Julia?"

She sighed, a wordless answer to the charm that had intentionally slipped into Topher's voice.

"Oh, darling." Topher whirled on his knees to find Lana in the doorway, shaking her head at him with sympathy. His maker wore all red. The dress was splattered with blackened blood. "She's gone."

Gone. Like the first of the drainers that Topher had

broken. If Topher and Lana left right now, Julia would waste to nothing. Just lying here, empty. Gone.

"She was going to be a lawyer or a doctor or both." That was what Julia always said. Since they were twelve, and someone asked what she wanted to be when she grew up. Then Topher started shrugging in response to that question, no career feeling right, and people frowned like the two didn't fit together. They frowned harder when he and Julia started dating.

Everyone knew being with Topher would bring Julia down. They worried for her dreams when Topher sank deeper and deeper into trouble.

Now, Julia would be among the missing and murdered. Lana wouldn't leave her here to rot. To starve to nothing and decompose. Topher knew once he stood, Lana would finish what he'd started. She would drop Julia's body off at the station like the other drainers. The police would do their best to identify her, the humans would further distrust the supernaturals, things would grow more yet more fragile, but with everyone benefiting from the alliances, they still wouldn't break.

That was Julia's legacy. This was how low Topher could bring someone.

"Darling, why don't you head home?"

Topher stroked Julia's cheek. She almost seemed to respond to the touch. Topher's voice held nothing—just flat words. "You said you'd protect and hide Colbie if I did what you said. You said you'd keep Julia hidden and safe if I did what you said."

"I didn't do this, Christopher. None of this is my fault."

"But what did you do to stop it? Any of it? Why should I keep following you when—"

"Stop talking like this." There was charm in Lana's voice.

Topher sighed at her attempt. He thought she'd realized

how useless her power was against him. "When it never bene-
fits me?"

"We *are* doing good with the Alpha's Den. We got close
with the witch to helping Julia. Maybe we couldn't save her, but
there are others. This isn't over, and you know we need each
other to see it through."

"I don't know that I need you. You think you need *me*,
though." Why anyone would need Topher was beyond him.

"I do need you, Topher. I also know who you need. There
is always more to lose. Humans that we now have to protect
because you allowed them in."

Topher's scoff was a half-hearted noise. "You want to mess
with Oliver and lose Zayn? Or Annaliese and lose Nora?"

"I don't want to *mess* with any humans. I'm just saying I
know where they are. I know this city quite well now, and I saw
someone very interesting last night before you pulled me away.
Someone who smelled as delicious as you tasted when I turned
you."

The weight of Lana's threats was so familiar he barely
noticed it settling. "Fuck you."

Dazed and trembling, Topher stood. He looked down at
Julia one last time. He wished he could at least see her eyes.
They were such a beautiful color. He could feel his own hunger
pushing at his control from using so much energy on Julia, but
Oliver's scent was no longer in the air. Lana was still talking,
trying her charm, but it was easy to ignore her and slip out the
door. It was a relief to realize he didn't need to feed. The deal
with Lana was off, and they had yet to articulate a new one to
keep Chance safe. Even Lana wasn't cruel enough to do
anything on a night like this. Not when she'd be too busy
disposing of Julia's body. Topher stumbled but forced himself
to keep going.

Did he want to feed?

He knew he didn't deserve it.

Topher ran home, silently promising himself he didn't need

to leave his bed for the next week. Or ever if he could last long enough.

Poppy was in disbelief, eyes darting between her mother and the man approaching. Movement behind Reelings made her still. Colbie snuck through the shadows across the road from him, awed as she followed Reelings's progress. Colbie had come, but she was alone.

And the lead vampire of New Brecken had already enthralled her. Without using a single word or even knowing he was being followed.

Tiff, still cruel, still horrible, laughed at Poppy's shock. She casually gestured toward Reelings. "This was what I wanted to tell the Morales girl."

Reelings hissed at the name, and Tiff's brow rose. Instantly, Poppy knew her mother was playing her cards. Working to protect herself. Whatever had happened, Reelings still hated Morales. Tiff was implying a connection to Nora intentionally. Colbie's eyes narrowed.

"You're supposed to be dead," Poppy got out, feeling ridiculous. People didn't say that. Not in real life. Only in dramatic television.

Reelings smirked. His charm brushed against Poppy's wards, the power dancing along his southern accent. "I am supposed to be, aren't I? I convinced most people of it. Unfortunately, no matter how strong a vampire is, they can't charm a wolf. Morales had to be taken care of, and Tiff had to keep her side of the deal." He addressed Poppy's mother. "I need my demons."

Tiff glared, but Poppy saw some triumph in her mother's gaze. It wasn't something most people would pick out, but Poppy had occasionally seen it directed at her sisters when they accomplished great magic. She had been searching her entire life for that gleam to be directed toward her.

"What do you mean? What demons?" Tiff asked innocently.

He glared. "You were supposed to vote against the laws. To stay out of my way."

Tiff laughed. "I haven't seen you since that night. Is that not out of your way?"

Josh was trying to subtly nudge Poppy backward, away from the vampire and witch standoff. But Poppy knew her mother wouldn't be able to hold her own. She glanced at Colbie, who stood listening so intently she didn't feel Poppy's stare.

Poppy knew what Colbie wanted to hear. "How are you alive?" Poppy asked. Josh growled softly as she drew Reelings's attention again.

Reelings seemed pleased by the question. "When I became aware my seconds were planning to betray me by siding with the werewolves, something had to be done. I refuse to work alongside humans. They have no right to hinder our power. It's against the natural order. We are so far sup— Never mind, I can see you don't want to hear about that." He chuckled, like the disgust on Poppy's face portrayed a harmless, adolescent opinion.

"Whatever my reasonings, I wanted nothing to do with the laws. I thought Grace, Patter, and Solas were with me. They should have followed me without question, but instead, they wanted to be contained. Within the new laws, the damned checks and balances, they were going to act as if the wolves could keep the vampires in line. My seconds asked the alpha to kill me, since my power over them hindered them from doing so. They thought the alpha was strong enough to end the conflict. Just like that. But his followers were as loyal as my own. I'll skip past the gory details, but in the end, with some help, I won't take full credit, I was able to kill the werewolf. But I couldn't stay, not when I didn't know who I could trust. I charmed my seconds so well that they all were convinced I had died, then I left this damned city to plot my revenge." His smile then was self-deprecating, like he was embarrassed to be caught monologuing like a villain.

"And you knew about all this?" Poppy asked her mother.

Tiff shrugged, though she seemed put out. She had planned to use this information to get Nora's help.

"Why are you back?" Poppy asked, nearly afraid of the answer. What revenge could a person like him come up with?

Reelings smiled again. "Now that, I can't say."

Poppy swallowed her next question. *What happens next?* She again checked the darkness surrounding them, hoping to see Topher's familiar form. Nora's bulky wolf. Henry's pack at ready.

But no. It was Poppy, Tiff, Josh, Colbie, Reelings, and a swarm of demons creeping out of the shadows so gradually Poppy hadn't known they were surrounded. These were not Tiff's to control. Horror, cold and sudden, washed over Poppy. She swallowed, looking back at Tiff—a girl looking toward her mom for guidance. But Tiff focused on Reelings, eyes cold and calculating. Poppy was nowhere in her thoughts.

Guilt flared. This wasn't worth the risk. Tiff wasn't worth bringing Poppy's friends into this. Poppy reached for Josh. She couldn't ward him directly, but she began to cast her wards out to create whatever barrier she could around them.

But Colbie was still there. Standing alone just behind the ring of demons. They were more interested in the witches' life energies than her vampire essence. It seemed a miracle she'd gone unnoticed this long. Poppy tried to convey with her eyes that Colbie should leave, but of course, they weren't so lucky.

"You should come with me, Jennings," Reelings said to Tiff. "This pathetic ward won't last. Holding it will leave you weaker in the long run."

Tiff barked a laugh. "Once I learned about the vanishing witches, I knew it was only a matter of time."

"Well, you really should have kept to our deal. Should have

stayed out of my way. Tell me, Jennings, how many of your daughters have died at this point?"

Tiff's hands balled into fists. In the quiet that fell between them, Poppy noticed the clubs were going at full volume. There was laughter only a couple blocks away. A car drove down the parallel street with its bass so loud the windows rattled on Tiff's small home.

Yet all was still between them.

When he realized Tiff had nothing to say, Reelings again regarded Poppy. A demon tested her wards, scratching at it from a few feet away. Josh was tense but hadn't noticed how close one was to them. The demon couldn't get through, and Reelings raised an eyebrow as if impressed.

And that was when he spun to acknowledge Colbie.

Colbie blinked, but she didn't appear scared. Colbie was far too brave for that. Instead, she sized up Reelings just as he did to her. "I've heard of you," Reelings said. "You're the other West vampire. They talk all about your brother and those ice-blue eyes. They say you aren't nearly as powerful."

Colbie's lips quirked. "They also say you're dead." She shrugged a narrow shoulder. "I don't put much stock in what they say, do you?"

He laughed. "They *also* say you live with a witch." Reelings tilted his head to Poppy, the silent question. *This one?*

"What, are *they* stalking me?" Colbie asked, voice light.

Reelings smirked, pivoting back to Poppy. "They also say witches and vampires don't make good friends. You shouldn't mix life and death. That only makes monsters, little witch. I hope this lesson was worth your memories. I hear you discovered how my creations were being kept by your vampires. What kind of friends keep a secret that big? That dangerous? Who knows how many died tonight when they got loose."

Josh stiffened. Poppy let go of his fur. Reelings dug the knife in further. "No one can trust a vampire. We only know how to use. How to drain. How to take our power. You shouldn't have become friends with the West siblings. It will cost you your life."

Reelings faced Colbie. His charm filled the air. "Take out your phone," Reelings commanded.

Colbie's eyes narrowed with concentration. For a beat, Poppy was sure she'd shake off the charm. Vampires couldn't just go around charming each other. But then, Poppy remembered a maker could charm their lower and then their lower's lower with even more ease. Reelings was too many steps up the ladder. In seconds, Colbie's eyes unfocused, and her voice lost all the animation that made her speech so distinct. "I don't have it on me."

Reelings sighed. "Well, when you get it, or any phone, you'll text me the address where you live with the witch. Every moment you're awake, you'll text me to keep tabs on her."

Poppy's heart raced as Reelings moved far too quickly to stand in front of Colbie. He handed her a business card. Colbie barely glanced at it before she moved to put it in her pocket. "Ah, ah, ah." Reelings stopped her. "I want you to memorize the number first. Wouldn't want someone to take the card from you before you have a chance to put it in your phone."

Colbie was too charmed to hesitate. She studied the card, lips moving quickly as she repeated the numbers to herself. Eventually, she lifted her eyes and nodded. Poppy's heart dropped.

"It was easy, just so you know," Reelings said to Poppy over his shoulder. "Usually, there is more resistance. This vampire didn't have a problem letting in my charm, even if it meant risking you. I told you. You can't trust us."

He grabbed Colbie's arm, pulling her close to whisper more into Colbie's ear. The pit of dread in Poppy's stomach grew. She had no way of knowing how he was charming her just then. How cleverly he could make Colbie lie or follow Poppy or if his bidding would lead to Colbie exposing Ru.

Poppy held her breath, terrified of the next words out of Colbie's mouth, but again, Colbie only nodded. Then he spoke to the demons. "As soon as her wards fall, take the witch."

Tiff sucked in a breath, but Reelings was already gone, running down the street almost too fast for the eye to follow. He might even be faster than Topher.

Colbie blinked and stumbled forward. "Poppyseed?" When she reached Poppy, she halted, frowning in confusion when she hit Poppy's wards. They stopped her, the same as the demons.

Colbie sighed. "That's fair. Keep them up, but we need to go. Now." She eyed the demons warily, but they were entirely under Reelings's control. Each of them stared at Tiff, who was terrified as her situation dawned on her fully.

Poppy couldn't move. She couldn't trust Colbie right now. She couldn't risk Josh. She didn't know how to help her mom when not even Ru's magic had been strong enough.

"Didn't I tell you to leave, Penelope?" Tiff's voice was still full of venom but fear, too. Maybe it was *all* backed by fear. Tiff went inside, slamming the door behind her. They heard as she fell into a fit of coughing as soon as she was out of sight.

"Josh!" They jumped at the shout down the street. Werewolves arrived in a growling surge, and the demons didn't try to hold their ground against them. Suddenly, Poppy could breathe. Henry's arrival felt like there was suddenly a sane adult around to tell them what to do. Josh left Poppy's wards as Henry shifted back to wolf. They must have some way of communicating because Henry's hackles raised, and he turned in the direction Reelings had vanished. For a second, Poppy thought they might follow him, but of course, the vampire lacked a scent that could be tracked.

"Josh is going with them," Colbie said softly. "We should leave, too."

The demons were gone, but only for now. "My mom won't last." An obvious statement.

Colbie's jaw tightened, making it difficult for her to speak gently. "I can't really make myself care. Poppy, she's cruel. She's awful. She's a murderer and has hurt you so much. We can try dealing with this again tomorrow. Being out in the full moon with drainers and demons running around is too risky."

Another cold wash of fear. Poppy stepped back. "Are you just doing what he said? Trying to make me leave so you can get to a phone?"

Colbie scoffed. "Are you just trying to stay here so he knows where both of you are? I'm saying there isn't anything we can do and nothing that she wants you to do! We need to regroup, find Topher, and figure all this out!"

"But… she could die."

"Will she last the night?"

"I don't know."

"Can you do anything tonight?"

"We could fight off the demons. With Henry and Josh's help…"

But Colbie was right. The wolves were leaving. "The pack already had their battle tonight with the drainers. We can't ask more of them. Do you think the two of us could fight off the demons? Do you really want to try?"

And Colbie was asking almost as if she were considering staying here if Poppy wanted to. But what if she was just thinking about when Poppy's wards failed, and Colbie could contact Reelings?

"Come on, Poppy. Please. We have to go. You have to trust me when I say this is the only option."

Poppy stared at Colbie for so long that they heard the hissing arrival of the demons again. She glanced back at the house. It held the air of abandonment.

There was a choice to be made here, and Poppy didn't know what Colbie was charmed to do. She didn't know what Reelings had whispered in her ear. Swallowing, Poppy attempted to listen to her gut. "Fine. We'll go home. But you keep your hands up at all times. If you try to get to a phone, I'll have to use my magic on you."

"I—"

"Shut up. I'm scared and can't trust you right now. We need to get to Topher."

Colbie nodded, more compliant than she'd ever been with Poppy. She lifted her hands, making her shirt rise and Poppy's heart stop. Colbie's phone was in the front pocket of her cargo pants. With a snap, Poppy sent it sailing into her hand.

"Must have forgotten that was there," Colbie said dryly.

Poppy shook her head. That had been too close. Clutching Colbie's phone and maintaining her wards, Poppy called a taxi. They didn't share another word until they reached the apartment.

CHAPTER 32

L ana sent out a group message as they returned to the car. Nora didn't bother to read it, not with her body still buzzing with adrenaline and her soul finally tethered by a pack. But Janelle did and made a noise of surprise.

"She decided to only open the upstairs Sunday through Wednesday. Only do the speakeasy on Weekends and Thursdays."

"I guess that makes sense," Nora said. "I was supposed to be there tonight. Oops." She pulled at her shirt. That run had been so natural, so easy, that clothing didn't feel right. She was acutely aware of each thread brushing against her skin.

Nora had more than just that message from Lana populating her phone. The other one mattered far more to her. It was from early in the night.

Vampire Colbie: I know you're out doing full moon wolf things (BIG congrats), but if you get back before I go to sleep, I'd like to see you.

The moon was still overhead, but they'd filled themselves on her power and finished early. The questions were prickling too intensely at Ricky for them to keep up their peaceful loping and eager howls. The forest had been quiet. It was rare not to hear other packs in the trees on a full moon. Not even Nora's mother had shown herself, but that had stung less than usual with a pack at Nora's side.

Two wolves. A tiny, young pack. But it had made all the difference.

"I need to run by Colbie's place," Nora said as she got behind the wheel. Anticipation was a pleasant twist in her belly. It seemed impossible that this night could keep getting better.

"Colbie?" Ricky asked. He was so much calmer than Nora had ever seen him. Solid in their pack bond and his newfound understanding.

Nora could sense Ricky's curiosity and the waves of relief still rolling under his surface. Janelle was faintly amused. "Nora's girlfriend," she said.

Ricky raised an eyebrow. "Damn. Maddie is going to be so disappointed."

He picked up Nora's water bottle from the cupholder, taking a big drink without asking. Already falling into pack habits. Nora smiled.

"She's a vampire," Janelle told him as he was mid-swallow, leading to a coughing fit so bad that Nora had to drive and thump Ricky's back at the same time while Janelle laughed.

"Don't worry," Janelle said over his ragged breaths, "She's still super hot."

"Watch it," Nora pointed at Janelle through the rearview, and her packmate started laughing all over again.

They fell quiet when they reached the apartment building.

"What is that?" Ricky asked.

"That's Poppy's ward, the first one. They get stronger as you enter the apartment, but I'll call Colbie and see if Poppy will let you both in. It's better to be invited."

Ricky was still confused, so Janelle leaned between the seats to explain wards while Nora called Colbie. And immediately deflated when Poppy answered instead. "Nora?"

"Hi. Is Colbie there?"

A pause. "Yeah."

"Well, she asked me to come up."

"So, come up."

"Can you ask her if she needs to see me alone?"

"I don't think now is a good time for Annaliese to come over," Poppy's voice was tight. The hair along Nora's arms rose. Something wasn't right.

"I'm not with Annaliese. I accepted two pack members tonight."

"Oh!" The surprise in Poppy's voice made it sound like this wasn't something Poppy had expected Nora to get around to. Nora bristled. "Let me ask her."

Muffled conversation. Then, the wards eased for Janelle and Ricky. Nora hung up and started the trek upstairs. As soon as she entered the apartment, a growl ripped from Nora's throat, quickly echoed by Ricky and Janelle. One of Poppy's vine plants was set at Colbie's feet, wrapping around her from ankle to shoulder and surrounding her with a blue glow. Nora stalked forward, intent on ripping Colbie free.

"I'm fine, Nora. Don't. She just thinks I'm charmed."

"So?" It was a full moon, the wolf was present, the alpha unleashed, and Nora didn't like seeing Colbie contained. Janelle and Ricky waited by the door, standing with tense attention. Nora lifted a hand, claws growing, but Colbie shook her head. With one bound hand and limited movement, she patted the couch cushion beside her. Nora sat immediately, snaking an arm protectively behind Colbie.

Colbie grinned, and that was all that calmed Nora's rage. "What's going on?"

Those blue eyes went to Poppy first. The witch stood behind the armchair, arms crossed tight, and face pinched. "Popcorn, I have to tell her. Can you at least free an arm?"

Poppy's expression eased just a bit. "Don't let her touch a phone, okay, Nora?"

"Um, sure?" Colbie could do whatever she wanted as far as

Nora was concerned, but if the promise freed at least a bit of her without conflict, Nora would give it.

Poppy rolled her eyes like she knew this but still snapped. The vines loosened enough for Colbie to wiggle an arm free. She reached for Nora, putting a palm on the knee Nora hadn't realized she was bouncing. "Poppy was at Tiff's tonight. Her wards are still failing, but Poppy couldn't fix them. I went to join her as soon as I woke up, but someone else got there first."

Colbie's fingers tightened. Then, she told Nora about Reelings. About Nora's dad. This version of the story was a strange mix of the two she'd heard before. And it was the true version, Colbie wouldn't lie. Blood roared in Nora's ears; the wolf begged to be freed. She stared at Colbie's hand on her knee and tried to make sense of it.

Her father had been betrayed. By someone in her old pack. Who could have benefited more than Gabriel from Morales's death? Who still hated the laws and bemoaned what they had done to the city?

Only Colbie's grip kept Nora in place. "Do you think he was lying?" Nora asked her.

"I don't, no. I think he was… bragging," Colbie winced at the words. Nora moved, clutching Colbie's hand as bile rose in her throat. "He's alive, and your dad isn't. I have difficulty believing that wasn't by Reelings's design."

Nora traced the bones of Colbie's hand, the knobs of her knuckles, the soft skin, centering herself as her emotions warred. She couldn't describe the feeling taking precedence. This story was true. She knew it. She hated it. But there was also something almost like relief in the knowing.

Like closure. Direction. This sense that her questions were answered and she was finally, finally free to think forward. To let go of any loyalty to Gabriel, to direct all the built rage and grief. Nora had made the right choice, creating her pack. Topher *had* freed her with his charm rather than ruin her.

And even bound for unknown reasons, Colbie had wanted

to tell Nora this first. She had known Nora needed this. Needed a direction to move in. It was a relief that Colbie moved the same way. And she wasn't smug. Not proving a point. Even though she hated Gabriel and likely Reelings from the way she'd said his name, Colbie kept her version of the story centered around Nora's father.

"Thank you," Nora whispered, too quiet for even her pack-mates to hear.

Colbie leaned forward until her forehead was resting on Nora's temple. "Are you okay?"

"I don't know. I want to go rip out Reelings's throat. Or Gabriel's. I feel like I should be crying, but…" She also wanted to kiss Colbie. Kiss her with gratitude, with relief, as an assurance, as a promise. That urge felt wrong given the topic at hand and how Colbie was tied up.

Colbie tipped her chin forward to kiss Nora's cheek, an instant reprieve from the longing, and then she sat back. "Do you want to tell them the rest, Pop Rocks?"

Poppy began to nod but stopped, glancing toward the door. "Annaliese is coming up."

No one had time to remark before Annaliese knocked briefly and opened the door. Nora's friend took in the scene, raising an eyebrow when she saw how Colbie was bound. "No one is answering their phone," Annaliese said. "I got worried, but now I see I just didn't know about Nora and Colbie's secret exhibitionist tendencies."

Janelle laughed. Ricky coughed. Poppy rolled her eyes and came around the armchair, sitting down heavily. Nora knew there was more bad news when Annaliese's joke did nothing to ease the tension. She pulled Colbie closer with the arm on the back of the couch. Then, Poppy explained how the night passed, finally getting to the reason Colbie was currently bound and not allowed to touch cellphones.

She was finishing with how they'd left Tiff behind, guilt choking her voice, when the front door opened again.

Poppy jumped up. "Topher! Finally! Why weren't you answering your phone? We needed you! Colbie's been charmed and—"

Topher was impeccably expressionless, voice flat as he asked Colbie, "Are you charmed?"

"No," Colbie's response was quick and sure.

"Reelings probably told her to say that!" Poppy insisted.

Topher moved slowly. There was a lifeless gray tinge to his skin like he used to get last winter when he didn't eat. His face was still a blank mask, yet Nora could feel the slight shift in his attention when Poppy said Reelings's name. "What do you mean?"

And so, they had to sit through another quick summary of the night. Topper nodded slowly. He was fiddling with his box of cigarettes. "He made the drainers?"

"Well, yeah, but Colbie is the priority right now. Do something! Charm her to forget the other commands."

Topher's wince was slight. He shook his head quickly, trying to hide it, but Colbie sat forward in a rustle of leaves. "Topher, what's wrong?"

He shook his head again, ignoring the question. "Colbie isn't charmed. She can't be charmed by anyone but me."

Then he moved to go to his room like that settled the matter. Poppy opened her mouth to protest, but Colbie's voice cut through the room. "Poppy! Get these fucking plants *off* me. Topher, tell me what happened!"

When Poppy froze, too surprised by the tone to do anything at first. Nora gave in to her need to free Colbie and yanked the plants off. Magic burned at her fingers, but the sting didn't last long. Still, it was enough to make Janelle and Ricky let out twin snarls. Colbie squeezed Nora's knee in thanks as she stood, vaulting over the back of the couch to go to her brother. She grabbed his chin, forcing him to make eye contact. "Tell me. What happened?"

That's when Nora noticed Topher was shaking. He reeked

of cigarette smoke. His clothes were rumpled, torn, or pulled loose in places as if he'd been fighting.

Again, the front door opened, this time with a bang that made everyone jump. Ricky let out a growl, but Nora's look cut the sound short. Zayn ran in, immediately going to Topher. He pulled Topher into a tight, tight hug.

And Topher's control collapsed. Colbie was now nearly shrieking in her demands to know what happened. Topher was sobbing tearlessly into Zayn's shirt, shaking his head in denial.

Oliver followed Zayn into the apartment, as drawn and solemn as Nora had ever seen him. "Julia's dead," he said brokenly, quieting Colbie's shouting. "It's all my fault."

Topher couldn't fight sleep much longer after that. He didn't say another word and appeared relieved when the first gentle rays of the sun pulled him under. It was nearly instant, his succumbing. Topher swayed and would have collapsed if Zayn hadn't been there to easily maneuver him to bed. Now, everyone else sat around the couches, trying to discuss the night's events before Colbie and Zayn followed Topher into slumber.

Colbie pulled one of Nora's arms around herself, snuggling as tight into Nora's side as she could. She kept touching the skin under her eyes like tears might fall. Her voice was choked every time she spoke. Mostly to say how unfair this all was and to give small moments of memory to the room as if they all needed to know why it was sad Julia was gone.

Poppy knew. She really, really knew. She was supposed to help. She was supposed to have time to think through a more potent potion and save Julia. Poppy had let Julia and Topher down in the worst way possible. After Dylan, after everything he'd been through. The Topher clinging to Zayn in heaving sobs was not a boy that Poppy knew. What if this was what broke him?

And right when the biggest threat to the city had finally made himself known. They needed Topher more than ever.

It felt selfish as soon as the thought crossed Poppy's mind, but she was realizing how important it was that Topher possessed his abilities. He solved almost all their problems before they happened.

Like Colbie, who told them what Reelings had tried to charm her to do eventually. "He wanted me to give Topher a message. It was creepy as fuck, and I'm not repeating it now. Reelings must have known that Topher would go to the apartments. He sent someone to open the doors as a distraction."

Oliver sniffed. Lana had told him that Julia had been mostly tame before he showed up. No amount of reasoning from Zayn or Colbie convinced him that Julia wouldn't have held long enough to prevent what happened when Julia smelled him. Whatever did happen. Lana hadn't shared the details with them.

"I just don't get how Topher is the only one who can charm you," Annaliese said.

Colbie shrugged. "I asked him to ensure it. A while ago. He didn't want to place a permanent command on me, and the ones we tried that would have made it so he couldn't charm me either didn't stick. His magic wouldn't cripple itself, if that makes sense. So, eventually, we found out that if I let him in, let all my defenses down, and if he charmed me in a way that his instincts felt benefitted *him* the most, we could do it. Lana's tried charming me a few times since, and I pretend it works, but Topher's has held strong this whole time."

"Don't even think about it," Nora grumbled to Annaliese in response to her thoughtful expression. However much things had changed between all of them, Nora still didn't want Annaliese charmed on any level by anyone. That much was clear.

Colbie patted Nora's arm. "I doubt Annaliese could let her defenses down like I did. I really had to give myself to the charm, and I only could because I've known Topher my whole life. I trusted him with all my mind to put whatever control over it he needed. I just can't imagine many other people being able to do that."

Oliver made an oof sound, drawing everyone's attention. Zayn had slumped to the side where the couple sat against the wall. Oliver struggled under his weight. Colbie yawned. "You two can take my bedroom. I'll sleep with Topher. He shouldn't be alone right now."

They were beyond surprise, so no one reacted when Colbie gave Nora a kiss on the cheek before rising off the couch. She turned, bending to Nora's eye level. "Be careful today, okay?"

Nora nodded. The expression on her face wasn't one she gave anyone else. Soft, open, willing. Nora was usually quiet, suspicious, and stubborn. Even at the peak of her and Colbie's relationship, Nora had held back, keeping up walls and secrets and her heart.

This time, even Poppy could tell she was trying desperately to prove she was all in. Colbie sighed, stroking a finger down Nora's cheek. It was harder to tell if she was similarly invested.

Poppy hoped the revival of Colbie and Nora's relationship wasn't a distraction that would harm them in the days to come. Yet another selfish worry, but no one seemed to be taking this new threat as seriously as she was. Did they not realize how simply Reelings could gain control of the vampires in addition to the drainers? What were they going to do?

Someone reached over to pull Poppy's thumb away from her mouth. She hadn't even noticed her sister was awake, but Ru's eyes were wide with concern now. "I heard most of it. What do we do?"

Poppy was the older sister. She should have the answers. She wanted so badly to keep Ru from harm, but there was nothing to say. Topher's door shut behind Colbie. Nora and Ricky helped Oliver get Zayn into Colbie's bed. Poppy saw Oliver climb under the covers and position Zayn's arms around him, rolling to bury his face in Zayn's chest before Nora closed the door.

Nora looked at her new packmates. A fierce joy was brimming in her eyes. Evident pride in what she had accomplished. "That was a big first night," she said apologetically to the two of them.

Janelle shrugged, but the casual movement was spoiled by the excitement in her eyes. Ricky shook his head, still processing.

"What are we going to do?" Annaliese repeated the question that pressed in from all around.

What was Nora going to do now that she knew her father's killer? What was Poppy going to do to keep Ru safe? What were they going to do about Tiff Jennings? Topher's grief? The drainers?

Josh's silence?

Nora's eyes shifted from Annaliese to her new packmates to the door separating her from Colbie. When she met Poppy's gaze again, a decision had settled. "Tiff is the only person in immediate danger, right? She won't last another night?"

"Right," Poppy whispered the word.

"If you want, I'll go with you to check on her. I think we should take her to Alpha's Den, if for no other reason than to keep Reelings from accessing her magic."

Relief was sharp in the back of Poppy's mouth. She couldn't believe someone was still willing to help Tiff after all this. Poppy couldn't believe *she* wanted to after everything Tiff had said. But Ru snuggled in close. Poppy would do it for her.

"You think this is the right call?" Janelle asked, peering at Nora.

Nora, shockingly, didn't fidget under her inspection. She was as calm as ever. Like an alpha. In charge, thoughtful. Poppy relaxed in Nora's presence. Even Ru let out a breath, sinking back into the couch.

"I do. I think it's best for everyone as long as we keep

Topher away from her. I would like to ask Tiff questions if I can, but mostly, I want to keep the witches out of Reelings's hands. We have to stop him from making any more drainers."

Annaliese's eyes were bright with emotion. "You're right."

"Why not?" Janelle said. "She's too weak to be a threat, and the drainers sleep during the day." She paused, glancing at Poppy, "They do sleep during the day, right?"

It was decided. Poppy was more than happy to keep moving, all of them loading into Annaliese's car. Annaliese grabbed the keys from Nora and told them with lingering annoyance about her chatty rideshare driver this morning. She kept eyeing Ricky and Janelle, trying to figure out how well-matched they were for Nora and what this pack might become. Poppy knew this because she was trying to figure out the same things. She had no knowledge about building packs. All she knew was that Nora moved in her strength with a newfound confidence.

They made it to Tiff's house. Without leaving the car, Poppy saw the trip had been a wasted effort. The front door hung open only on the top hinge. The windows shattered. Poppy stayed in the car while Annaliese, Ricky, Janelle, and Nora searched the building.

Gus, who had been quiet all night, appeared in the seat next to her. He voiced the bleak thoughts in Poppy's head. "You should have gotten here sooner."

They returned to the apartment, quiet heavy in the car. Poppy's dark mood lifted only when she saw Josh waiting outside. His hands were stacked on his knees, chin resting on top as he watched them park and leave the car. Poppy's lips were getting ready to offer a small smile, but Annaliese's question halted their progress. "What's wrong, Josh?"

Poppy came up short. She hadn't even noticed the tension in his shoulders. The frown tugging at his lips wasn't a very

Josh-like expression. Poppy had seen it before, but she wasn't expecting it now. She'd been searching for comfort, she realized. Without hesitation, she'd seen him and thought he was here for her. Because her mother was taken, and they had no idea where or how to find her.

Josh stood, brushing off his jeans. He had to clear his throat twice to talk. Poppy stepped forward, reaching to take his arm.

He dodged her hand. A sharp pain broke in Poppy's chest.

"What happened last night was entirely preventable," Josh said. His voice was scratchy. "Did you know about the drainers?" he asked Nora.

The alpha shook her head.

Josh nodded, reaching back to rub at his neck. His agitation wasn't aimed directly at the situation. It was inward. Josh was guilt-ridden and upset but didn't want Poppy's comfort. He'd stepped away. She didn't know what to do with that.

"I shouldn't have— I shouldn't have kept the secret. Are you fine with all the secrets?"

Nora shrugged. "I'm still trying to figure things out. No, I'm not okay with secrets, but mostly the ones that Gabriel kept. Knowing Topher, I can understand his instinct to hide Julia."

Josh's jaw clenched. He really wasn't himself. "We didn't think it through. It happened so fast, but we shouldn't have hidden them. If I'd told Henry, if he'd known about the risk of them being set free, we would have been ready for so many of them to potentially attack. We've never seen drainers move like that. They'd been starved, and they were desperate, and they fought. Hard. We could have been watching that block along with the club. We could have found Reelings before he let them all out."

Josh's brown eyes had never been so steely before. He turned to Poppy again. She shrank under his scrutiny. "I gave you another chance. You were supposed to have my back. Yes,

I'm accountable for keeping the secret, but I got swept up in being around you again. Henry doesn't blame me, but he doesn't want me around you. We kept more of Topher's secrets, and now Daniel and Quinn are hurt, and the city is in danger. Henry will be in contact with Lana, but we're easing back with the alliance. We won't be protecting the Alpha's Den. It's clear the influence you have on me is harmful for the pack. We can't trust you." He looked to Nora again. "I truly hope you have this handled. Best of luck."

When Poppy reached once more for his arm, asking him to wait, he shrugged her off and kept going. They hadn't even noticed the car idling against the curb until Josh climbed in and slammed the door behind him.

"Well, shit," Janelle muttered.

CHAPTER 33

Tiff's personal wards fell at four that evening. Ru had been searching for her in a candle flame when the location suddenly became clear.

"We should try to wake Colbie up at least," Poppy said. Her voice had been flat all day, swallowing so much feeling she couldn't even let out an inflection. Nora knew the sensation well.

Yet, when the witch looked toward the door where the vampires slept, reluctance pulled at her features, breaking the careful mask she'd held all day as they searched, napped, ate, and waited for nightfall—waited for the other shoe to drop.

Annaliese was the most comfortable with Topher's room. It didn't bother Nora like it used to when Annaliese nodded and walked in like she owned the place. Moments later, Colbie stumbled out. Her bun had fallen to the side, and she'd lost a sock.

She was beautiful.

Colbie went directly to Nora and let her body fall over the back of the couch, nearly kicking Ricky as she crashed into Nora's space.

Nora touched Colbie's curls, her cold cheek. She had the

urge to squish Colbie's face between her palms just to make sure she was here and substantial. Nora couldn't believe her luck. She couldn't believe she'd made it to this moment. Pack members nearby. Annaliese nearby. Colbie on top of her. Nora could die a happy woman right this instant.

Well, aside from the secrets and threats of the city that loomed. Colbie looked up at Nora, blinking the sleep from her eyes. It was early for her to be awake. "Tiff?"

"Her wards fell." Poppy didn't turn from the stove. "She was in a circle, captive. We couldn't see anyone else in the room but a warded figure. Probably the sorcerer. They're going to use her to make a new unclaimed." The spoon clanked too hard against the metal pot as Poppy stirred. Potion sloshed over the side.

Colbie's eyebrows bunched. "Unclaimed, Pop Rocks? Thought we were calling them drainers now."

Poppy stiffened. "Well, they're Reelings's, aren't they?"

Nora sensed more than the city's threats looming. Something was breaking here, cracking down the middle. For the life of her, Nora couldn't decide if anyone was at fault or if there was anything she could do to help the situation.

But she wrapped an arm around Colbie's waist, remembering the sight of her tied up in Poppy's vines. At least Nora knew who she would support in this. Now that she had a new pack and her life was entirely under Nora's control, picking Colbie was effortless. Nora only wished it had been so easy last winter. She wished Gabriel hadn't taken those weeks from them. She wished she had never hurt the girl who could compact herself so well to fit in Nora's lap like this. Colbie's face pressed into Nora's neck. She smelled like Nora and fresh laundry. It was enough to give Nora the urge to lift her, carry her somewhere private. Somewhere they could forget everything making the air so hard to breathe.

"What do you want to do, Soda Pop?" Colbie asked. If

Nora hadn't been holding her so close, she would have missed the way Colbie's body didn't match her relaxed tone.

Poppy still hadn't given Colbie her phone back.

Poppy set down her wooden spoon carefully. She slid the pot off the burner. It smelled like worms. Slowly, she turned but kept her gaze fixed on the counter as she spoke. "I think we have to stop Reelings."

"I agree," Colbie said. She was being careful.

"I think I don't trust you to come with." There was a tense pause. Ricky sucked in a breath. "I don't trust Topher's charm against his. Reelings could be as strong as Topher is. They're both just vampires. There's no reason to think Topher could beat the original maker in the city. Especially not after what happened last night."

Colbie shifted very calmly to wrap her arm around Nora's neck. It was a possessive hold. Nora's core heated inappropriately for the context. "So, who are you taking? Ru? Josh?"

Poppy winced at Josh's name. At the idea of taking Ru. "I'm going to go. If Nora wants to, she can too. Reelings killed her dad."

"You think I don't remember that? You think this is only personal for you and Nora? You think—"

"I think you want my mom dead. I think my mom is terrified of what's happening in the city. My mom only wanted to keep my coven safe, and maybe she thought power was the only way to do that, but I can show her I have power, too! That I'm not useless."

Colbie stood now, going to the counter across from Poppy and slapping her palms flat on the stone. She was vibrantly awake. "Your mother destroyed your coven! She makes you feel like you have to prove yourself when we've only ever believed in and loved you!"

"You don't! Topher never did, and you always have to have your way!"

"I'm stubborn. I speak my mind. I love you as much as

Topher does! Which is a fuck ton. Poppy, please. Remember how we all felt for Nora. Remember how hard it was watching her be less than she could be when her family made her small."

"This isn't like that! Even if it was, if Gabriel's life was currently in danger, would you really be telling her to sit back and let it happen?"

"Poppy. I don't want to lose you. Topher and I lost everything. What we got out of it was you, Oliver, and Zayn. You're our family. We're yours. If you have to do this, don't go without us."

"Maybe I don't want to lose you either. That's what Reelings's charm would do. It would take you from me." Poppy's voice cracked.

"Topher *is* stronger than Reelings," Ru said, breaking into the argument.

Poppy rolled her eyes. "You can't know that."

Ru lifted her chin. "I do. I've sensed things, and after watching the sweatshirt again, I have a theory. I think Topher would agree with it."

"Ru! Now is not the time to test theories," Poppy said, exasperated. "It's not the time to argue. We have until nightfall to get to Mom, and I need you to stay here."

"What? You trust the vampires enough to watch me but not to have your back in this? Poppy, don't be ridiculous."

Poppy took in a deep breath. "Ru, I promise, one day, you'll be strong enough and old enough and in control enough to be a true part of all our problems. Today is not that day. I don't want to imagine what they would do with your power." She speared her sister with a look. "Whatever happens, don't tell Colbie where you Saw Mom."

Ru warred with this; face set in a stony glare. She glanced at Colbie. The fight drained out of the vampire as their eyes met. Colbie's lips twisting in a wry, insincere smile. "It's alright, Rhubarb. Listen to Poppy."

At those words, Ru scoffed and got up from her seat. She

slammed the door to her and Poppy's room behind her. Poppy addressed Nora, "Are you ready? Do you want to come?"

They had to go. Had to protect the city. This was what Nora had always wanted. But…

Colbie rolled her eyes at Nora's concern. She came close again and bent to give Nora a tight hug. Nora stayed absolutely still as Colbie reached between her back and the couch, slipped the phone from Nora's back pocket, and shoved it into the couch cushions. All out of Poppy's sight.

"I'll be there," Colbie whispered.

"5983," Nora murmured her passcode back.

Colbie pressed a kiss to Nora's cheek. It stung a bit that they weren't really kissing again yet, but maybe that was just disappointment. They would work their way back to true kisses. It would be worth the wait. Colbie reluctantly let go and flopped onto the couch. She crossed her arms as she watched Nora, Janelle, Ricky, and Poppy gather their things. Nora was the last to leave the apartment. She paused at the open door, glancing back at Colbie.

Colbie let the cheerful mask slip. She showed Nora the real worry brimming inside. The fear deep in her blue eyes. "Please be careful, Nora."

"You, too." There was so much more Nora wanted to say, but she'd never been good at summoning the right words. She could only hope they'd have time for Nora to figure them out later.

She closed the door between them. Poppy was already down the hall, so she didn't hear Colbie begin speaking into the phone. "Josh, it's Colbie. What happened last night?"

They drove in silence. It felt weird to be *driving* toward conflict. Nora needed to be running. To be drawing from the moon in wolf form and basking in the sensation of a pack moving together.

Instead, Poppy gripped the wheel at ten and two and muttered to herself as she followed traffic laws and GPS instructions. Ru's Sight had shown her a warehouse but searching through images online had provided an address.

"How long do we have until Reelings wakes up?" Janelle asked. She was abuzz with thrilled, adrenaline-induced energy. This was the excitement she'd wanted from an alpha, from being in a pack.

Ricky was anxious beside her, getting his cues from Nora and Janelle. "Are you sure I should even come along? I don't even know how to turn wolf on my own."

Poppy fielded the first question. "We probably have another hour and a half until Topher wakes up. I'm going to guess Reelings is about the same."

Nora answered the second. "I know this is a lot, Ricky, but I promise your wolf will answer when you call it. I feel it right there. But if you don't want to——"

"I want to come. I'm just nervous."

"What's the plan, then?" Janelle asked. "It's not like Reelings is the only one running this situation. What about the sorcerer?"

"I'm going to deal with the sorcerer," Poppy said. "They shouldn't be able to do much to you. Even dark magic has less effect on wolves. Just watch for them manipulating the environment around you. You all will be busy dealing with whoever else is on guard because I doubt it's just the sorcerer. But Reelings and the demons were the biggest threat. Without them awake, I think we can get in and save my mom. We just have to be quick."

Poppy's voice wobbled, but she had her chin lifted stubbornly. Her eyes kept darting to the rearview, checking the empty space between Janelle and Ricky.

"I don't like this," Nora finally said. It felt good to voice her thoughts. To embody the authority to do so. "What if we go by

Henry's first? You can apologize and explain who Julia was and say that's why you didn't—"

"No. You heard Josh. That wasn't the first time I'd let the pack down. They won't want to work with us anymore."

"So we wait for Lana or Za—"

"No vampires! Every vampire in this city came from Reelings! He controls them all enough to fuck with their memories even years later."

"But maybe not Topher. We should wait for Topher."

"By the time Topher wakes up, it might be too late. Are you in this or not?"

"I am. I just think we're rushing and have time to think of our options. What if we call another witch? Jay knows one. They might be able to help us."

Poppy slowed the car. After throwing it into park, she twisted to fully face Nora. "We're out of time. It's just us, but you're the strongest werewolf in the city. Magic slides off you, and wolves all turn in your direction. Your power wants an outlet. Stop doubting. Stop holding back. We're enough."

"Who are you trying to convince?"

Poppy opened her door, leaving the car without answering. Nora hesitated. She'd only just gotten her pack; was this worth risking them?

"The drainers have to be stopped," Janelle said.

Ricky nodded. "I love New Brecken. If we can help the city, we should."

Nora couldn't argue with that. They moved as one, following Poppy inside. Another damned warehouse loomed over them. Nora stumbled. Poppy stared at the building with an expression that mirrored the turmoil Nora was experiencing. It was the same warehouse. Hunter's warehouse.

"The humans are in on it?" Poppy asked as if Nora knew any more about this than she did.

"Maybe everyone against the laws is in on it. The gangs hated the vampires being able to bliss humans legally."

"Idiots." Poppy shook off her surprise and stomped to the metal doors. She pulled out a small vial, popped off the cork, and splashed the contents at the symbol above the frame. With a hiss, the wards ease off. Nora hadn't even noticed them until the magic was lessened.

Poppy put her hands on the double door handles. "They know we're here now. Last chance to leave."

"I'm afraid it's too late for that," said a voice behind them.

The hair on Nora's neck rose, a growl building in her throat. They'd been too distracted by memories of last winter to look around. To smell the air, checking for people downwind. The mistake, Nora's first as a true alpha, allowed Gabriel to sneak up on them. Matt was on his right. Lupe at his other side. Adriana. Paul. Tio Marcus. Patrick. Luis. All of them except Heather.

The change threatened to rip through Nora, but Gabriel shook his head. "You have to know you're far too outnumbered. Let's just try talk, Nora. I know you can be reasonable. I know we can work through this."

Nora swallowed down the change. There were so many things she wanted to say. All she got out was, "No lies?"

Gabriel smirked. "I've never lied to you. But we can refrain from holding out certain details."

Matt's eyes were wide with warning and pleading. Even Adriana looked uncertain. No one wanted this fight. No one but the alpha in Nora and the same force emanating from Gabriel. His words said wait; his alpha said *blood*. They were like opposing magnets, making it hard for Nora to stay close. She wanted to flip him, make him submit to her powerful pull.

While Nora and Gabriel stared at each other, Poppy seized the moment and opened a door, slipping inside. Gabriel didn't even watch her go, his entire focus on Nora, Janelle, and Ricky. "So you did it. You started your pack. Where did you scrounge these kids up from?"

Janelle was probably Gabriel's age, if not older. Nora

cocked her head, feigning innocence and remembering Henry's words from days ago. "Oh, they found me. Apparently, I draw them in. It wasn't all that hard."

Unlike Gabriel. He'd never brought in a new pack member, only had her father's people to build his pack from, and, if her memory of her aunt could be believed, he hadn't kept them all.

The words had the desired effect. Gabriel's expression darkened. Matt stepped forward hastily. "Nora, why are you here?"

"Why are *you* here? Are you working with *Reelings*?"

There was shuffling. Uncomfortable glances thrown Gabriel's way. Nora could taste Gabriel's will in their silence. He'd used his alpha to order them not to talk.

It took Nora a moment to realize the emotion rising in the back of her throat was rage. She'd always swallowed it where Gabriel was concerned, but this was still her family. He'd put them in this position and taken their voices. She turned to Gabriel and couldn't stop the alpha from slipping into her voice. "Explain yourself. For once in your goddamn life, tell me what's going on!"

CHAPTER 34

Poppy slid inside the darkened warehouse. Her wards were coiled so tight around her that not even the sound of her footsteps escaped the magic. Poppy still held her breath as if it would help her go undetected. She braced herself for the worst as she went deeper inside the aisles of empty shelves.

It was too dark. Unnaturally so. The windows high above were covered with tarps, only a rectangle of sunlight peeking through the edge of each one. There was an office room to the right, and the lights were on, but no one was inside that Poppy could see. Even with these lights, the shadows were far too thick. Poppy kept going. This deep into the building, something was stacked in rows. She crept closer to a pallet but stepped back quickly when she thought she recognized the white bags inside.

Drugs. Guns in that one. A car around the next bend jacked up and in the process of being worked on. Everything here was so illicitly human. Nothing like the world of magic and life energy and blood that Poppy inhabited. The musty smell in the air made it seem like she'd stepped into the past. There was a pile of empty beer cans overflowing from the trash.

"We shouldn't go further," Gus muttered. Poppy started, clapping a hand over her mouth. She'd forgotten easing the wards would allow him in, too. "You're in over your head." Gus stared into the shadows as if he saw more than Poppy.

Poppy ignored him. She continued down the rows. There was a new scent in the air, and she pulled her wards even closer in response. She'd been counting on Nora at least being close enough to draw from when she had this confrontation, but she'd have to rely on the potions in her bag. On the strength of her wards. On Ru's raw magic infused in Poppy's charms.

Squaring her shoulders, Poppy stepped into the thickest sweep of shadows. Looking back, she couldn't see the light of the windows or the office anymore. Darkness swirled around her. Shivering, Poppy tried to ignore the sweet rot and cloying sulfur. Her wards blocked most of it, but she could feel how they were being tested, pulling at her strength.

The dark magic wanted her life energy. Poppy's steps slowed as she whispered encouragements to her wards, willing them to hold. To remain strong and not flee into the darkness. Her magic had always been a feeble beast; it complied with her bidding now, but Poppy didn't know how long it would hold.

Between one step and the next, Poppy left the rows of illegal substances and entered a bright, open space. The overhead light shined, but a wall of shadow remained at Poppy's back. Reelings sat on a table against the wall, feet kicking in the air in a far too juvenile manner. Gus lingered in the shadows. He settled in their midst far too comfortably.

Tiff Jennings stood hunched in a summoning circle, trapped and drained. She rolled her eyes when Poppy appeared but couldn't muster further reaction, not even when Reelings picked up the gun beside him and pointed it at Tiff's head.

Between Poppy and them was another witch. She stood and dusted off her hands, a finished summoning circle at her feet. The shadows reached for her. Not a witch. A sorcerer.

"Hi, you must be Poppy. I'm Beth. If you'd be so kind as to step into the circle I have ready for you, we won't have to shoot the Mother." Beth pointed to the third circle on the ground, furthest from Tiff's.

"She isn't a Mother. She doesn't have a coven," Poppy said, unable to stop herself from making the correction.

Reelings made a show of releasing the gun's safety. "It's been a long time since I've had to handle one of these. I would move quickly if I were you, Penelope. Don't want my finger to slip."

"How are you even awake?" The magic at play was unlike anything Poppy had seen or imagined. Her curious mind wanted to escape the pounding fear. It wanted to focus on the puzzle that was the shadows and Reelings's consciousness and the dark shade of the circles drawn onto the floor. There was one ready for her. How had they known Poppy would come?

"Poppy. The circle."

Poppy blinked, surfacing from the questions in her head. She looked at Beth. "You burned the Maker. You killed all of Lana's vampires."

"Yes. She and her lowers were the biggest threat." Beth shrugged, unfeeling and unconcerned by the reminder of the blood on her hands. "As often as Tiff saw the demons destroying the city, I saw Christopher West's influence. Too bad he's so hard to pin down."

"Not for long," Reelings said. "He's received all the messages. He knows this is a fight between us."

Beth frowned, unconvinced. Reelings laughed, pointing at Poppy. She stepped back when she found herself staring down the barrel of his gun. The shadows nipped at her heels, cold where her wards momentarily faltered with her fear. "We have his friend! His sister is on her way. I will call for his girlfriend, and it will be easy after that."

"Julia is dead." Poppy cringed. Why couldn't she keep her mouth shut?

Reelings's lips tightened. "Shame. She could have been so useful. Once I told her to remember again."

He sighed, pointed his weapon back to Tiff, and pulled the trigger. Tiff screamed, but it took a few breaths for them all to see the bullet missed her.

"Shame," Reelings repeated. "Into the circle now, Penelope. I'll be aiming next time." He turned to Beth as Poppy took a step in that direction, the sound of the gun echoing in her head, making her want to shriek in terror, even knowing it hadn't hit anyone. Her adrenaline wouldn't subside.

Spell work like the circle she approached was only meant for death. Poppy's magic down to her charms flinched from it.

"We'll need some more motivation," Reelings told Beth. "Just to be sure. Send a wolf to grab one of his human friends or something. We don't have anyone to change yet. We'll use whoever they find."

She heard a sigh behind her and then experienced the stretch as Gus left. Abandoned her. She hadn't even known he could do that without her telling him to go.

Beth nodded, pulling out her phone and sending a text. It was like Poppy wasn't even in the room anymore, yet when her progress slowed, the gun came back up. She didn't want to get in the circle. She could feel how it would numb her magic. How she'd have to let down her wards to get inside. How helpless she'd be. How alone. Not even Gus, bound to her by blood, had stayed behind to watch Poppy.

She thought about the vials in her bag. She wasn't useless, but the timing would be everything. The element of surprise was all she had left. Making herself appear as small as possible, something Poppy had learned well when trying to avoid Tiff's anger after each failed spell, Poppy walked the rest of the way into the circle.

Just as she did, her bag was ripped from her shoulder and tossed carelessly to the side by Beth. The sorcerer's smile was dark and evil. Looking at her, one could barely tell she was using dark magic. How many witches had she made suffer the price? How many lives had she taken to use forbidden spells without consequence?

How many spells would she be able to wring from Poppy and her mother before they too died?

Beth smirked and turned her phone, showing the vampire her screen. Reelings laughed suddenly, far too gleeful for the darkness surrounding them. "Oh good."

"What is it?" Poppy asked.

"Christopher West will be joining us tonight. His sister has a good memory. She just texted to let us know she's on her way and has delivered my message."

Reelings was right about one thing. It was stupid to trust a vampire.

Topher could get used to this. Waking to Annaliese's smell so close, her body right there, curled against his side.

It was almost enough to make a dent in the hollow space that was his… heart? Core? Soul?

Almost.

"You awake?" Annaliese asked.

Topher rolled, pushing his face into the pillows. His head still pulsed with pain from the amount of charm he'd used last night. He was slightly amazed at himself. It wasn't pride, but he really couldn't believe he hadn't sucked every ounce of blood from Annalise's body upon waking.

Zayn had barely kept Topher from attacking Oliver the last time he'd been this hungry, and Mary had been dead. He held still as Annaliese sat up. "He's awake," she called.

Topher's door was pushed open. Oliver entered, Zayn a step behind him. Ru followed.

Had they just been waiting for him to wake up? "Where's Colbie? And Poppy?"

The beat of quiet following the question was answer

enough. Topher thought himself currently beyond emotion, but dread crawled up his throat as thick as bile.

Then Annaliese took his hand. "Topher, you know Reelings is targeting you, right?"

"Yeah." He'd put it together. Whoever had turned Julia had the charm to alter her mind beyond Topher's reach. He still didn't understand how. But he'd tried to leave a message with her. The message that Colbie had delivered last night.

Topher had woken just enough when she got into bed with him. He heard her whisper, "He wants the city, Topher. He thinks he has all the vampires. He wants to make sure he has you, too. He said to come to him tomorrow night or what happened to Julia would only be the start. He said to be ready to cooperate, and the city can belong to you both."

"Why does he think I want this place?" Topher had asked, his hatred of New Brecken saturating the question.

He'd fallen back to sleep to the sound of Colbie's humorless laugh. To her hugging him tight and whispering it would be okay. It wasn't okay now, but one day it would be.

"What are you going to do?" Zayn asked now.

All Topher wanted to do was sink into this bed and never face the world that he kept breaking, and that kept breaking him. He found himself staring at Annaliese. If there were another option worth getting out of bed for, she would be the one to think of it.

Annaliese raised her eyebrow at him. "We find Reelings. We stop him from doing this again."

Oliver made a noise of dissent. "Topher's mourning. Everyone always asks him to do so much. Topher, what do you want to do?"

What did it even feel like to want? Topher thought of Dylan. It took a moment to find his voice. "I can't let Colbie deal with this alone."

Oliver came fully into the room, sitting at the foot of Topher's bed. Topher held his breath. "You don't have to do anything, Topher. I heard Poppy decide to leave. I heard Nora decide to leave. I heard Colbie decide to leave. They made these choices. *You* make yours."

But Topher just looked back at Annaliese, swallowing hard.

"You're afraid to even wonder what you want now," she told him, and it was true. "I see it, but it only makes sense when your charm wraps around me. You aren't so different from Nora; only you hide from the power—the potential. You wanted to run with Dylan when you saw how capable you were in Hunter's world. You wanted to hide in the Maker when you saw how the humans reacted to you. You let Lana and Grace charm you. Why does the power scare you, Topher?"

He swallowed. No one had flat-out asked him that. "I'm afraid of the pain."

"Why does it hurt?" Ru inquired like she knew the answer.

"Because it's Dylan." When his charm came, it was Dylan's voice in his ear, his smell in Topher's nose. His arms holding Topher snuggly inside his own body when his mind pushed to escape. "Because I want revenge as much as Dylan does. I'm scared he'll leave when I get it. I'm scared it'll use all of his essence up. I don't deserve his power."

Annaliese blinked. That had not been the answer she expected. Oliver spoke, awed, "I always feel slightly in love with you when you smile. When you charm me. It made me feel so guilty, but that's just what you two felt, wasn't it? It's blinding. Irresistible."

Topher shrugged, and Annaliese caught his chin between her fingers. He didn't particularly want to meet her eyes during this conversation, but Topher did anyway. "He *wants* to be used. Why else would the charm leave you so easily? We all want you to be fearless. Reelings can't get away with this."

"If I use my power, if I show it, I can never hide again." His life would flip in one moment, in one show of force. He wouldn't be Lana's darling.

He'd be all on his own. Who could be near him with that

target on his back? But what choice did he have? Oliver's stormy expression suggested there was still one left, but how could Topher live with himself if he hid from this?

He would always be there for Colbie.

"If you do this, you have to be at full strength. You can't keep holding back. And we have to hit hard," Annaliese said. She was so confident that it made the air easier to breathe.

But then, she held out her wrist. "Ru said her charm can keep away the worst of the bliss. You need to be strong, and we need to go now."

Topher stared at the offered limb. When he took her hand, he was uncomfortably reminded of how small she was. How fragile. When he met her eyes, he remembered how silly that was to think. "You sure? With Julia, it…"

"She was already addicted to you. She wanted your love and probably was willing to believe what she felt under your bliss and charm was just that. I don't trust so easily. But I trust you to do this. I have an idea, but we don't have time to hash it out."

Topher didn't want to cut Annalise's wrist and drink so impersonally. He sat up slowly. He felt like a different man than the one who had woken up last night. That one had still thought hiding problems would keep them safe. That thought hoping for more time could be the same as making it. He had listened to people who preached caution.

Tonight, he was listening to someone who summoned fire.

Annaliese didn't flinch as he pushed her braids behind her shoulder. Her breath shook as he leaned in. Her hand twisted in his, clutching at his wrist. He smoothed his thumb over her soft skin. Her body went soft, pliant. Maybe she was more trusting than she thought.

"You sure?" Topher asked the question into her neck. There were goosebumps lining her skin. Her pulse raced under his lips. It wasn't soured by adrenaline. It was warmed with the heat of attraction. It smelled so, so good. His mouth watered.

Topher wished they were alone. He tried to smother the part of himself reacting. He hadn't felt this level of rising heat in so long.

"I'm sure, Topher," Annaliese said, voice husky.

Topher licked her skin, enjoying the first salty-sweet taste, anticipating what lay underneath. He knew he was losing his head when he teased them both for a moment, teeth skimming her skin, letting her hypnotic heartbeat race.

He bit down gently, breaking skin with his razor-sharp fangs so quickly that Annaliese didn't feel the pain before his saliva flooded her. He had to catch her as her body slumped and a moan left her lips.

Ru's charm burned power under his hand, but it wasn't holding up to the force of his bliss, just keeping the worst of it at bay.

Topher didn't drink long. It was hard to pull back even after he'd healed the puncture in Annaliese's neck. When he did, she blinked at him, dazed. She lifted a hand, running a thumb along his bottom lip. "Oh," she said. Breathless.

Everyone had cleared the room, perhaps knowing this was far more than a feeding. It didn't need witnesses.

Topher couldn't stop his slight smile. The real one was still far away, but Annaliese was so different from anyone he knew. She didn't remind him of grief. She was a distraction every time it threatened to strike. "Tell me what else to do," he said.

Annaliese didn't pull from his arms as she gathered her thoughts. Then, holding him as tight as he held her, she told him what she had planned. What she believed he could do for them all.

"I don't want to use my charm," he whispered.

"You'll be great, Topher."

CHAPTER 35

Nora felt like she couldn't quite catch up to the situation. It felt unbelievably foolish and arrogant to think she, her tiny pack, and Poppy could stroll into this situation and save Tiff Jennings before the vampires woke. A witch who didn't even want to be saved by Poppy. Yet, what else were they supposed to do? And where was this power that Poppy continually promised Nora?

It didn't take long for Gabriel, Matt, and everyone who had once been Nora's family to surround her and her new pack. Half of them were in wolf form. It still haunted that she couldn't feel them. The connection was just in reach, on the tip of her tongue, but nothing would bring it forth.

"You have three options here, Nora," Gabriel said. "Leave now, without the witch, and stay out of this business. Fight us to get to the witch. If you manage to do so, your prize will be facing the most powerful vampire in the city, a sorcerer, and who knows what kind of monster he has in there."

Gabriel paused, searching her face, disgruntled when he couldn't read Nora's reaction. How much had their knowledge of each other stemmed from a half-formed pack bond?

"You said three options."

Gabriel pivoted, sweeping an arm to the door. "You can come inside. We'll answer all those questions you have. Maybe you can't be one of us, but you could work with us."

Distrust flared from Janelle. Reluctance from Ricky. The poor guy hadn't even fully believed in supernaturals two days ago. Nora turned to them. She spoke in a low voice even though her old pack no doubt heard. "I don't think I can just stay out of this."

"I don't think I can fight that well," Ricky said.

"I don't think we should go inside, but it's our best option," Janelle agreed.

Gratitude surged. Their bond held uncertainty about the situation, but not about following this through. No doubts about Nora herself.

She was turning to tell Gabriel they would go inside when she caught movement out of the corner of her eye. Wolves started growling but made room for Colbie to enter the huddle. Nora couldn't quite believe she'd come. Even with her confidence in Topher's charm, it was such a risk.

When Colbie was a few steps away, she tossed Nora her phone and smirked. It was such a familiar twist of Colbie's lips that Nora pulled in a steadying breath. "You okay?" Colbie asked.

"Fine. T?" Nora was still hesitant to let Gabriel know the depth of her relationships with the vampires, though the scowl that darkened his face said he knew exactly who she was referring to.

"Was just waking up when I left. Shall we?" Colbie linked arms with Janelle, already so comfortable with a girl she barely knew. It allowed Nora to stick close to Ricky's side as they entered the warehouse and the thick shadows filling it. Nora focused on the white of Colbie's sweatshirt, a soft beacon in the darkness.

Why would someone wear white to this? Colbie never wore white. What a strange choice. Fondness swelled in Nora's chest.

Colbie made every situation lighter, easier to face. Even if unintentionally. Nora would do everything to get her vampire out of this safely.

Gabriel's pack swarmed, guiding them through the shadows, and suddenly, they crossed the wall, blinking at the sudden light.

A gasp. Poppy stared at Colbie as she stepped out of the darkness. Colbie let go of Janelle's arm and continued forward while Nora and her small pack hung back, Gabriel's pack blocking them from Reelings. Nora stared at the man. Her father's murderer. The blight on her city. She hated, hated, that Colbie approached him alone.

Colbie stopped in front of Reelings, not bothering to return his smile. "Your brother?" he asked.

Colbie made a show of checking her watch. "He'll come."

"Why didn't he come with you? I told you to bring him."

"Unfortunately for you, I'm not strong enough to haul his sleeping body across the city, and also, charm commands don't work over text."

Reelings flicked a wrist, batting away Colbie's words. "Go stand by Beth," he said, charm infused in the command.

Colbie went. She stood directly across the lit space from Nora, her face more blank than Nora had ever seen it. The first swirl of doubt turned Nora's stomach. Colbie *looked* charmed.

Poppy stared at her roommate with hopeless betrayal. Her expression going even more bleak as she looked at Nora, her tiny pack surrounded by Gabriel's. Poppy couldn't leave the circle painted at her feet. Her bag had been left on the desk behind her. This was… not good. Not good at all. Nora tried to plan. The first thing she needed to do was run for the bag of potions and get it to Poppy. Then—

"Here she comes," Beth said. "With everyone here, Topher won't be far behind."

Hair rising, disbelief blanking her mind at the approaching

scent, Nora watched the next figures step out of the shadows. Some vampire lower, possessed a charm-blanked expression and a tight grip on *Annaliese's* arm.

Nora's world narrowed painfully. Gabriel and Matt weren't surprised. They had anticipated this. Another betrayal, nearly as deep as working with her father's murderer. They knew Annaliese was coming. Had they given her name? A snarl ripped from Nora's core. She nearly shifted, but Matt and Gabriel lunged and had a hold of Nora before she was able to recover her shock.

"There she is. My next little monster. You ready to begin the ceremony, Beth?"

Topher followed Annaliese's scent, the dread and anxiety and doubt, doubt, doubt heavy from his head to his heels. Each step a chore that promised the next wouldn't be any easier.

He hated this. He hated this city. This life he'd been born into. Turned into. This fear he always carried. This hole in his chest that wouldn't stop aching. He hated that this fell to him.

Topher was so tired.

He took another step and slowed, tipping back his head to take in the warehouse. Wolves circled—Gabriel's pack. None had noticed him in the shadows. Topher had told Henry what was happening. He'd asked Henry to stay away, and Henry had quickly agreed. He didn't want much to do with Topher right now, that was clear. Topher couldn't say he blamed him.

He was trying. He really was. He didn't want to be weighed by self-pity. He didn't want to be ungrateful for what Dylan had given him. He wanted to be strong like Annaliese, sure like Colbie, able to learn and grow like Nora, loving like Poppy. He knew these pathetic thoughts of reluctance weren't for others to hear, but they rattled around in his head, striking with enough force that he sunk even deeper into them with his failure to resist.

And he couldn't even blame himself too much for the defeatism when Annaliese's trail led directly to Hunter's warehouse.

This place used to be like Fourth Street. People used to avoid this section of the river, knowing of the parties happening in the abandoned, looming structures. And the parties were well stocked by Hunter's products. Dylan's father had been very quiet lately. What did it mean that he was back in the thick of supernatural matters?

Topher reached into his pocket. His key ring hadn't changed much after he was turned vampire. He carried it mostly out of habit. A key to home, though his parents had probably changed the locks. Julia's spare car key. Half of a BBF heart keychain that Dylan had shyly and jokingly given him back before they'd kissed. Back when they thought it might be friendship. Back when they were both denying it was more and afraid of how large the feeling might become once acknowledged.

And lastly, a key to Hunter's warehouse. A copy of Dylan's they had made so Topher could meet Dylan in the quiet hours of the morning when no one was around. With ever heavier steps, Topher retraced the path he'd taken often. He went to the side door, hidden enough by overgrown vegetation off the river that not even a wolf stood guard. Topher unlocked it, pushed it open, and paused to observe the swirling shadows. They spilled into the night and lapped at his ankles but went no further. They were oddly welcoming. Their brush a beckoning. Topher lifted a hand, and the shadows rose to intertwine with his fingers. Cool and gentle, he could barely feel the slithering kiss on his skin. If he were still human with dulled nerve endings, he probably wouldn't have sensed it. Maybe he only imagined feeling it now.

Topher couldn't say why, but he made a shushing sound before he stepped inside and shut the door behind him. He felt the shadows answer to his intent. All sound became muffled, so Topher didn't even hear the door latch. The swirling darkness separated, breaking into an path. It was a strange enough distraction that Topher thought of nothing but the darkness as he followed, but reality hit grotesquely as he reached the brink of the shadows and beheld the scene he would somehow have to fix. His heart beat low and steady. It didn't react to nerves like it used to, but Topher could hear it in his ears.

The scene was daunting. Doubt made him hesitate. Dread made breathing difficult.

Dylan. Topher could do this with Dylan. He did it every day.

Nora struggled against the hold of her former family. Gabriel shouted with the alpha in his voice, holding her back with the help of Matt and two others. Annaliese watched. She was trembling as Reelings stepped forward, grabbed her wrist, and led her to stand in the last circle painted onto the floor, between Poppy's and Tiff's.

Poppy looked defeated. Her eyes kept going to Colbie, betrayal deep. But Colbie waited behind Tiff, eyes on the shadows. She was the first to notice Topher, and her smile turned less forced. She nodded, just slightly. It was the same nod of encouragement she'd given Topher before games, right as he stepped onto the pitch. The same nod she'd given him when he came out to her. When he was struggling to ride a bike and she was letting go of his handlebars. That nod had been helping Topher enter scary situations his entire life.

He left the shadows. Annaliese let out a relieved breath. Nora froze. Beth's eyes widened—she'd always been wary of him. Poppy groaned. Reelings smiled.

"Look who it is," Tiff Jennings broke the silence, eyeing Topher. They hadn't faced each other except the one time. When she killed Dylan.

Topher was not expecting the rage. He rarely fell to anger. Colbie said once he hadn't been made with that setting. But it struck now. Hard. Hard enough that one look at Tiff Jennings held enough charm to quiet her after a single whimper.

Reelings's smile grew, aware of Topher's power in the air. Topher fought the urge to do worse than shut Tiff's mouth. There was no reason why she should be here while Dylan wasn't. No reason to believe a universe that allowed this had any good in it.

Except maybe Colbie, watching him close where she stood behind Tiff. She wouldn't let the witch get away with anything else. Her presence was steadying enough that Topher drew in a breath.

He directed his anger elsewhere, looking at Gabriel and his tight grip on Nora's arm. "I didn't expect to see you here. Was that you working for the vampire last winter, then? Ordered to take me out?"

Gabriel bristled. "No. I saw you as a threat to the city. You are still. The greatest threat."

Reelings snorted. "That's yet to be seen, wolf. Don't insult me so. I made Topher just like every other vampire in the city. His charm may be strong, but it comes from my own." The maker turned to address Topher directly for the first time. "I've been going back and forth on what to do with you. Gabriel's actions were all his own, but I can't say I didn't appreciate the intent. Yet, when I returned to New Brecken, I told him to step back. You made good use of your time while he left you alone. A new club. A den of my creations. Thus far, you haven't broken the charm I placed on them. I was waiting to see if you could crack it."

"That wasn't a charm. That was something worse," Topher said. When he'd realized Julia was blocked from her memories, he saw it wasn't a wall of charm but a void of her essence. If Reelings had charmed her, it was during the change. It had more to do with that dark magic than Reelings's strength.

Topher was counting on that theory. The thought of calling up his charm purposefully made his stomach turn, but he had to believe he was stronger than Reelings. He had to salvage this.

This was a horror movie. A perfect storm of all things fucked up. Colbie under Reelings's control. Nora restrained by her former alpha and best friend. Annaliese helpless in a witch's circle. Topher standing off to Reelings, doing his best to ignore Tiff. Tiff silent and watchful and powerless. Poppy felt the same within her cage.

Reelings and Beth and Gabriel meant to show force tonight. They were going to use Tiff to change Annaliese. That was the intent in the circles. Poppy could sense it. Only, she couldn't figure out *why*. This was too far for Gabriel to go to assert dominance over Nora. Lana's name hadn't even been mentioned. This wasn't targeting Poppy, not with her lack of magic. Tiff was too far gone to be a real threat. Poppy didn't get it. Not until Topher walked in. Reelings's eyes had lit up. Beth had tensed. Gabriel shifted his focus.

This was all about Topher.

He stood alone; all attention centered on him. Even the shadows seemed to reach for him. Beth stared at them, her lips moving as she wove magic and fought for control. She kept glancing at Tiff and Poppy with hunger as the dark magic pulled at her life force. She wouldn't last much longer unless she sacrificed someone else.

Nora's eyes darted from Annaliese to Colbie and back to Reelings and Topher. Janelle and Ricky behind her, also held in place by members of Gabriel's pack. Poppy and Annaliese were within reaching distance if the circles would have allowed it. Colbie behind Tiff. Poppy felt so alone, so young. Everyone else looked it too. Any confidence gifted from starting the Alpha's Den and Lana's talk of the future had wilted.

And Topher stood rooted in place, even more apart from them all. He hadn't entered the lit area from the same direction, catching everyone off guard. Poppy couldn't read anything in his expression. There had been a flash of emotion when Tiff first spoke—something dark and vast and chilling—but nothing except collected calm since. There was no way for Poppy to know what he was thinking. What he made of his charmed sister. Of Annaliese's capture. Of Reelings's appearance in New Brecken.

Poppy had never thought Topher arrogant before, but he'd strolled in here like he was untouchable. He'd put himself in Reelings's hands, as simple as that, with no one else to help him. He'd put not just himself at risk, but all of them. The power Reelings would have with a charm to put Topher at his beck and call… Poppy's hands fisted with anger. Freaking *vampires.*

Reelings was right. They couldn't be trusted. Poppy wished for Josh. What she wouldn't give to have Henry standing in Topher's place right now. To have that pack supporting her instead of her roommates.

"But," Reelings was talking with subtle enough charm that Poppy's bracelet warmed. Topher probably didn't even know it was being worked on him. "I have decided I don't want you as an enemy, so I will explain. I'm confident I can persuade you to see my side. After all, I convinced Gabriel."

Nora stiffened. Gabriel's betrayal was cutting deeper and deeper with each confirmation. It was plain to see on Nora's face. Was he truly behind Morales's death? Did it go that far?

"It is impressive how you convinced a whole pack to follow you," Topher said, voice steady and clear. "Or was it just Gabriel? A teenager at the time and the only available wolf with alpha potential?"

It was a quiet blow, but Poppy saw how it landed among the wolves that backed Gabriel. The grips on Nora, Janelle, and Ricky's arms were loosening. Nora heard Topher's underlying suggestion. She was looking at her old packmates differently now. It was the calculating look she'd given Janelle before bonding.

A flare of something softer than hope grew in Poppy's chest, but she quashed it. Once charm became involved, it wouldn't matter that Topher made the wolves doubt their leader. Between Reelings's charm and Gabriel's alphaship, they were far, far too outnumbered.

"They see now that we had to do what we did," Reelings said, speaking for Gabriel in a way that made his pack even more wary. "Your sister was there last night, so you know some of it. You know my lowers don't know I charmed them into forgetting I was alive. At the time, I didn't have the numbers to convince them I was in the right. I was struggling against Morales and his pack. The alliance between them meant he was monitoring my charm. He was very good at sniffing it out. The thing about lacing a great charm is it happens when everyone is least aware. So, he needed dealt with. Which meant the numbers had to be on my side. Yes, I spoke to young Gabriel, but he knew that the laws would be a curse on the city the same as I did."

Gabriel's face was stone. He was pretending he couldn't feel Nora's glare.

"While we have very different ideas on why the laws shouldn't be passed, we were aligned in our efforts to stop them. He ensured Morales was positioned just right on the way to the meeting, rounding a certain corner all alone. Then, it was only a matter of charming my lowers and striking deals with the witches who bore witness. If Morales hadn't been followed more closely than we'd intended, I may have been killed by his wife and packmates. I barely made it out, but I knew with him gone, I was free to return when ready and reclaim my city."

Topher wore a slight frown, looking back at Gabriel. "And if he controls the city? What then? You would allow vampires to rule?"

Gabriel glared, refusing to answer. Topher rolled his eyes. Whatever Gabriel's plans in the long run, he knew better than to announce them.

"While the laws may have brought Gabriel to my side, our opinions on the natural order has kept us in agreement. Wolves were not meant to be the pets of humans, running around and upholding their laws. Vampires were not meant to live in easy luxury but to fight for our standing and be rewarded for our strength. If New Brecken wants a supernatural city, we will give them one. They asked for this when they acknowledged us, but monsters of the night aren't meant to live under human thumbs."

Topher shifted, crossing his arms. He appeared to be listening intently, his eyes no longer flicking to Nora, Annaliese, or Colbie. Poppy couldn't help but notice he hadn't looked her way. "So, you want to rule the city. That's your big plan?"

"Of course. New Brecken is a jewel. My lowers will submit to me again, and I will own Fourth. My power will spread south. Not even former leaders like Hunter will contend with me. I know this all appeals to you, Christopher. You must have had big plans to rise in the city, getting mixed up with a man like him while you were human. When I told him I planned to align with you and rule the city myself, things between us grew difficult. He had some unpleasant opinions about you, but I dealt with him. My first kindness to get you to my side."

Topher's head tilted, emotion in his eyes, but nothing Poppy could define. Her anger at his presence here began to ease. Topher had to hate all of this. "You killed him?"

"Not technically." Reelings's smile was chilling.

Poppy's hair rose. Reelings kept monologuing, talking with flourishes and arrogance that rang of old-school vampire villains. He was hard to take seriously the longer he spoke. But the light way he said that… suddenly Poppy was fully aware of the dark glint in Reelings's eyes. The lifeless pull of his lips into a smile. The hunger when he looked at Topher. This *wasn't* a horror movie. This was happening, and Topher was the only thing in Reelings's way.

"Right," Topher said. "And Henry's pack?"

"Well, we landed quite the blow last night. He didn't come here for a war. He'll leave for his next city, his next forest. Wherever the conflict seems easy and solvable. His pack has only reached the size it is because he doesn't challenge them. They are a group used to swimming with the current. This isn't their city."

Topher nodded, like that made sense. His eyes found Beth. "I just can't figure out your place in all this. Why murder them all?"

Beth shrugged. She didn't meet his gaze, still watching her shadows. "You were supposed to be there. At the time, Gabriel and I still thought getting rid of you would be the easiest way for Reelings to regain his power."

"They've seen the error in their ways now," Reelings said dismissively.

"Have they?" Topher asked. "They haven't apologized." He was playing the game, testing Reelings's strength.

Reelings looked at Beth and then Gabriel, a feigned disappointed father figure. "You need to make friends with the vampires at this point, my friends. Christopher deserves an apology."

Beth glared. "This is about being equals. I'm not in this to take orders. You'd be nowhere without me. You'd have none of these monsters."

And the dissent was noted by Topher. He relaxed the slightest amount. "Listen, Reelings, you've given me a lot to think about, but I will need some time. Time that doesn't involve you hanging my friends or sister over my head."

"Well, that's the thing. I need a decision. Now that I've shown my face, I'm all out of time. The friends and sister are here very deliberately."

"And if I don't want to follow you?"

"It's easy. You make the right choice anyway and give into my charm. You don't resist, then, whatever you do, it won't be your fault and they won't be hurt."

"You don't seem very confident in your abilities against me. Shouldn't you be able to charm me to believe that anyway?

Reelings winked. "It's more fun to win without having to cheat. These are the cards I'm playing. Your best next move is compliance, and I suggest you let me know your decision quickly." He turned away from Topher. "Bethany, dear, begin changing the human."

Some spells, when practiced enough times, answer to a witch's bidding without the witch making any indication. Beth barely moved, but the dark magic flared.

They were all out of time.

CHAPTER 36

"Shall I explain the process?" Reelings asked over Tiff and Poppy's gasps. The witches fell to their knees within their circles. "Beth will call the magic. She's using some of Penelope and Tiff's strength, but mostly, she draws from Gabriel. That's very important. It means he has some control, and also, the creatures won't respond to charm like a wolf won't. No charm but my own, as a vampire lower would. These are hybrid creatures. You can see now how it's affecting the human."

Sure enough, Annaliese slumped forward, grimacing within her circle. Gabriel's arm was loosening around Nora. It was draining him. Weakening him.

Nora knew about channeling her magic through Poppy now. She could almost see the path Gabriel's energy was taking. Well, it was more of a smell. An intangible sixth sense. Most of Gabriel's power was lost to the shadows, but the rest went through Beth to Annaliese. An idea struck and Nora didn't hesitate. She sent her own power that way, pushing Gabriel's toward the insatiable shadows. It was far too easy to do; a press of will and her essence moved. His couldn't compete.

If Annaliese had to suffer this, it wouldn't be Gabriel's power she imbibed.

With the shadows now consuming his strength, Gabriel's grip on Nora's arm slackened enough that she knew she could shake him. Even Matt's grip had loosened with shock. He didn't approve of this. His eyes were fixed on Annaliese, filled with horror.

"Now, I charm her into submitting to me and only me. Well, myself and hunger. That's all that will be left. After my commands, the rest is similar to changing a vampire, except the shadows play a role. This is where the balance is difficult, as we tend to strike with too much night and not leave enough life. Ideally, the creature should be able to move in daylight, sustaining themselves off the lives of humans. That's the goal, and that's why we need the life energy in this process, too. Full life energy."

Reelings looked at Beth. She considered, concentrating, then shook her head. "We'll have to kill the young one. We need more life. Tiff is nearly finished."

Beth turned her attention to Poppy. They had to act *now*.

And act they did. Nora ripped out of Gabriel and Matt's holds. Her goal was Poppy's bag. Combat magic with magic. But she'd underestimated the reaction time of her old pack. Adriana's lunged, blocking Nora's path, snarling and ferocious. It was enough to bring Nora up short. Adriana was all blood-lust and animal, shrinking the part of Nora that hadn't actually thought her old pack, the family that raised her, would ever hurt her.

"You truly approve of this?" Nora asked. Without her intending, the alpha was in her voice. Ricky and Janelle straightened. "You want Gabriel to have this power over you?"

And there was a hesitation, even in Adriana. Gabriel's power was draining, cast uselessly into the shadows. The bonds of her old pack were opening like Janelle and Ricky had been before Nora grabbed the threads. Gabriel was losing his hold. His humanity spilled into the darkness.

Bolstered, Nora looked at Matt. "You know this is wrong. Reelings killed my dad. Gabriel helped him do it."

Nora opened herself, a mental hand in offering to the weakening cohesion of her old pack. Matt's eyes widened as he sensed the choice Nora presented. Gabriel howled. The change ripped through him. Strengthened in wolf form, Gabriel walled himself off from Beth and her shadows. He fought desperately to pull in the threads of his members and keep Nora from them.

Nora changed right with him. It was harder to keep focus as a wolf, to not shove too much toward Annaliese, to keep the bonds open for her old pack, to keep her current pack calm, and also prepare herself for Gabriel's strike. But Nora could do it. On some level, she knew she'd been born to carry this much. Nora faced Gabriel and *knew* no one had been exaggerating when they spoke of her strength. She believed them all for the first time. The widening in Gabriel's eyes as he faced her, Nora so much larger and faster and commanding, said he was realizing all this too.

As a force to be reckoned with, to be respected, Nora challenged her former alpha.

Between one second and the next, Reelings had breached Annaliese's circle. Topher ran at it full force and rebounded off the wall.

But he felt it tremble. He felt the shadows within it pause, like a questioning. With Tiff and Poppy's strength, Beth was in control, but she didn't speak the language. She didn't fully understand this darkness she summoned.

Topher felt like he always had.

"The only charm you will listen to will be my own," Reelings told Annaliese, standing over her. "Be still."

The charm was thick enough that Topher had to shake it off. Colbie wavered in her movements, too, stepping toward Annaliese. Topher met her eyes and looked at Tiff. Colbie knew where she needed to be. Wincing, she stepped back into position, both of them glancing toward Poppy on the ground.

Annaliese's bracelet pulsed. Ru's magic at work, holding, but not for long. Annaliese's skin glistened with a fevered sweat. Her movements were not quite right when she rolled, avoiding the bite Reelings aimed for her neck. She smelled sick, even through the wall of magic. She smelled like death.

The rage was back.

The surprise of Annaliese's dodge brought Reelings up short as he crouched. He turned to stare at her. Topher took advantage of the hesitation and hit the wall hard with both fists. "Open to me!" he shouted, charm lacing the words. The magic let him slip inside. Topher was on Reelings in the next instant.

Breathing heavily, Annaliese crawled as far away from the two of them as the magic allowed. She huddled against the wall. She was slowing, even her heart.

A tackle, dodged punches, fingernails raking sharp as claws. Topher eventually allowed Reelings to get on top of him. Their eyes met. Reelings was ageless, depthless, unspeakably powerful, and hungry. His eyes were a mix of colors that dared Topher to think of a description. That intriguing hue drew Topher in and filled his mind. A question and hidden answer. A lulling magic. A caress that promised relief if he just let it in…

"Christopher West." Reelings's charm was crushing. "I'm tired of the games. You will bite this human. Turn her. Make her my strongest monster yet."

Everyone paused, even Nora where she had Gabriel pinned under her bulk. Colbie stood watching, waiting. Some wolf let out a wine. Poppy dropped her head into her shaking hands, hopeless.

Topher grabbed onto the charm, that nameless color and sensation—he *pulled*. Reelings followed. Succumbed. "And you will fuck right off," Topher said.

No one expected the result. No matter their level of faith, they hadn't believed without a doubt that Topher was stronger than Reelings. Not Nora, who had once suffered from his most potent act of charm. Not Gabriel, who had been able to capture him and tortured him for answers and thought him weak. Not Poppy, whom Topher had to be careful not to charm despite her protections.

No one knew what Topher was fully capable of. He had purposefully kept himself weak. He had refused to drink until full, refused to dig deep, shied from the pain that was feeling Dylan brush close.

The shadows flared, danced. They felt Topher's calling. Dylan's scent perfumed the air. Head swimming with grief and fear, Topher forced himself to hold the charm. Everyone here depended on him.

The magic answered.

Reelings especially did not expect what Topher could do. He thought he was simply dealing with a vampire, not a monster more dangerous than his own creations, made in similar ceremony and circumstance. But Reelings didn't have time to process the shock before his mind blanked with charm. He'd only been able to fight it long enough for his eyes to widen, then compliance took hold.

Reelings stood, left the circle, left the warehouse. He fucked right off.

Shock replaced all aggression in the room as Reelings vanished into the shadows. But Annaliese was still dying. The darkness wanted her, and only a burst of light would solve it. Poppy knew this, but she couldn't speak or act.

Colbie knew this, and she could.

Poppy's roommate barely hesitated. The circles were falling, only meant to last as long as it took to change Annaliese. It allowed Colbie to step over the line of Tiff's circle. No one else was paying attention to the lower vampire in their midst. No one else bore witness as Colbie snapped Tiff Jennings's neck.

Annaliese gasped, life rushing back. Her cheeks flushed, her heart raced, the circles fell, and the spell failed without Reelings to complete it.

Topher let out a strangled noise. He opened his arms, and Annaliese threw herself into them. Poppy felt the magic break completely as Beth sprinted into her rapidly receding shadows and followed Reelings into the night. Tiff's death saving Beth from the toll of dark magic as well as Annaliese.

Nora, snarling, allowed Gabriel to stand. He'd been cowed by her. What did that mean for wolves? Had she challenged him and won? Poppy didn't know enough about pack dynamics to fully understand what happened next, but when he followed his allies from the warehouse, tail low, not all of his wolves followed him. The rest took position around Nora, sniffing and nuzzling, not bothering to watch him go. Colbie walked between them all to kneel in front of Nora, ignoring protective growls and checking in Nora's eyes whether the girl inside the wolf was okay.

Nora licked Colbie's face, and the ensuing bark of laughter broke the tense silence.

And Poppy knew, out of everyone in this room, she was the only one who cared that her mother's body was growing cold on the warehouse floor. The loneliness was the worst part.

CHAPTER 37

Topher let go of Annaliese and turned to Poppy. But she was gone. It was a heartbreaking sight. A dead body in the circle on one side. Emptiness in the other. Maybe Topher had saved Annaliese and stopped Reelings for now, but they hadn't won.

As the danger passed, Topher's emotions rolled darker and darker. There would be no hiding his charm now—no hiding in Lana's shadow. Gabriel or Beth or anyone else here would spread the story of what happened. Topher, who should just be one more lower in this city of vampires, had proven himself the strongest. It didn't matter that he hadn't made the Big Three. Solas, Patter, and even the city's lowers would challenge Topher or submit to his rule. That was the vampire way. Exactly what he'd been avoiding with desperation this entire time.

There was no way of knowing what the next days would bring, but he'd need Colbie's smiles, Annaliese's support, Poppy's life-giving trust, and even Nora's newfound strength. He'd need that whisper of Dylan inside him that was wrapped so tightly around everything that made Topher powerful.

Topher stood and offered Annaliese a hand. When she

reached to accept, the bracelet around her wrist fell away, the charm having burned too hot. They looked down at it, broken on the ground between them. It took Topher longer than usual to arrange his features, mostly because he detested having to put this wall between himself and Annaliese. Once he was sure all the charm was swallowed, he met her eyes.

"What happens now?" she asked. This was as far as her plan went. Ru had felt the test of the wards. Annaliese had answered Jay's phone call; her friend panicked about Gus's message that Reelings was after Topher and looking for one of his human friends. Jay had gone to their witch friend for safety, but Annaliese had acted quickly to ensure she was the one taken. Not Jay. Not Oliver. Not Chance. Annaliese left the apartment unprotected, and Topher had followed far enough away to see her get taken and not intervene. She'd put every-thing on the line because she'd believed Topher could save her.

"Now we find out who our real friends are."

"Should you leave New Brecken?"

Topher sighed, glancing toward Colbie and Nora. "I would be followed. New Brecken is the center for the supernatural. For any vampire that wants to rule here, they would know I could come back and ruin things at any time. They'd want to find me to take care of any potential threat. I won't be able to escape." His life was written out before him—a life of power struggles and mistrust.

"I'm sorry," Annaliese whispered. "I couldn't think of anything else to do."

Back in Topher's bedroom, she'd asked Ru to recharge her bracelet and made Zayn promise to stay with the young witch and Oliver. Zayn was also in charge of lying to Lana so she'd stay away. Then, Annaliese had asked Topher to use his charm, reveal his power, and do what it took to save her once she allowed herself to be captured.

Annaliese had known what her plan asked of him. Topher

hadn't wanted to pay the price of revealing himself, but hiding would have cost far more. He'd agreed.

"There wasn't anything else I could have done and still lived with myself. I'm sorry I didn't act fast enough. I'm sorry you sti—"

"Topher, you saved me. You did *exactly* what I asked you to do. I'm fine right now because of you."

She was saying Topher hadn't let her down. That she was okay. This realization was slow to dawn and brought a strange sense of warmth. That, along with Colbie jumping on him from behind and squeezing his neck as she gushed about her cool little brother, was enough to break Topher's control of his features. Relief was just so sweet.

He smiled. Then, tensed, which quieted Colbie, which brought on Nora's attention, now in human form but ruined clothing. They all followed Topher's eyes to Annaliese.

She blinked. "What?"

Colbie gasped, jumping for Topher's back. "Annaliese, touch your toes."

Annaliese screwed up her face in response. "You are so fucking weird, Colbie."

Colbie was grinning. Topher was slow to match it. He didn't want to think what else this strange circle and the spell it had carried had done to Annaliese, but at least one effect proved to be positive.

Happily, Colbie declared, "And you are so not charmed."

At the end of the night, Nora couldn't complain about how things turned out. The bad was heavy and present, but the good... it gave Nora hope for what could come.

They'd tried to go home to Colbie and Topher's apartment, only to find two bags waiting for them on the steps and a note asking them all to stay out. Colbie had deflated, looking ready to cry. Topher had taken her hand, picked up the bags, and turned away. They all wouldn't have fit in the apartment anyway, so they went to the Alpha's Den and found an outraged Lana.

"I don't want to believe the stories I've been hearing about you, darling," she said to Topher, holding up her phone. The last word came out through gritted teeth. It was the most flustered Nora had ever seen Lana.

Topher shrugged. "I don't care what you want. I'm done pretending to be your darling, and I told you that."

Lana narrowed her eyes. Annaliese stepped forward like the vampire was hers to take on.

"We may have lost Julia, but you're still mine. I know about Annaliese. I know about your brother. I know—"

"Then forget them. Or I'll make you."

Lana's jaw worked. She gestured at the club behind them. "This place is mine."

"And Nora's. You made sure her name was on everything. Made sure she knew there was a place for her pack."

Nora stepped forward. This part was still far from believable. "And here's the pack. We're going to need those rooms." Behind her stood Janelle and Ricky. Then Lupe, Luis, Patrick, Chase, and Heather. They were uncertain of this proximity to vampires, but above that, Nora felt the rightness of this new balance. The relief they felt at the reunion. At being in Morales's pack once more.

Zayn came up behind Lana, smile in place, Oliver tucked into his side. He and Topher shared a look, and just like that, Lana recalculated. She was an intelligent woman for all her faults. She knew when she was outnumbered. She knew when to back down, at least for the moment.

"So, we're taking on Reelings then?" she asked. "Is that your brilliant plan?"

"We're taking on anyone who wants to ruin your precious city," Topher said, but he was agreeing.

Lana nodded. "I can be happy with that. But this place is still mine, even if you aren't."

Topher and her stood for a tense moment, staring each other down. Whatever passed between them, Lana was the one to lower her eyes. Topher stood aside, sweeping out an arm in invitation so Nora, Annaliese, and the pack could enter ahead of him.

Everyone relaxed when they felt the wards welcome them, but it was painfully obvious Poppy was missing. Topher remained at the door, and Colbie paused there. A wordless conversation passed. He really did say a lot with his expressions when he wasn't focused on swallowing his charm. Nora read enough to know what Colbie would say when she turned.

"Go," Nora said first. "We'll wait here. Just… be safe?" She didn't want to order Colbie around. She didn't want to push against boundaries yet. She wanted to keep that impossible love-struck expression on Colbie's face for as long as possible.

Nora could tell her pack would need time to get used to this side of Nora. At least the new members. Or old, depending on how one looked at it. Colbie flounced to Nora, took her face between her palms, and planted a solid kiss on her lips.

The world stopped spinning. Nora had forgotten all the forms of bliss Colbie's kiss could bring. She forgot how it felt when her body was fully relaxed. When her heart raced in the most profound pleasure. She'd forgotten what her core was capable of feeling. That heat. That longing.

God. She didn't want Colbie to leave even more now.

When Colbie leaned back, it was gratifying to see she was similarly dazed. Nora put their foreheads together, close enough to whisper fearlessly, "Really. Be careful."

"I will. I doubt anyone will be wanting to mess with Topher after tonight."

"We didn't see any drainers or demons, but they're still out there."

Colbie patted her side, where she carried Poppy's forgotten messenger bag. "We'll be fine." Unlike Annaliese, Colbie seemed mildly entertained by the protectiveness. She didn't seem ready to run away. Nora kissed her one last time and watched Colbie leave, heart content with the pack around her and Colbie glancing back.

A year ago, Nora would never have thought herself capable of making such good choices.

But a year ago, Nora would have been equally as sad as to know Matt was still stuck. Gabriel had gone to lick his wounds, and now they knew who he worked for. Now they knew the rest of Nora's old pack was on his side and willing to fight for the control of supernaturals over the city. Over the humans.

No matter what, the bad was still there. Heavy and present.

Poppy felt them at the door for the second time. She heard the knocking and debated blocking the sound. Gus stared at her. Ru stared at her. All of them were deep in their grief, though it seemed they each mourned a different Tiff Jennings. Poppy mourned a chance to prove herself to the woman who raised her. Gus mourned what he thought Tiff was capable of accomplishing. Ru mourned her mother—a complicated mother, but for her, a loving one nonetheless.

"Please, give them a chance," Ru whispered because although Poppy had explained what Colbie had done, her brain also worked in a complex way.

"Don't open that door, Penelope," Gus said.

Ru gaped, and Poppy realized she'd never told her sister she'd acknowledged him. There were too many things to juggle.

She didn't meet their eyes, staring down at her phone. She'd texted Josh in a moment of weakness. Immediately, she'd sent an apology and told him not to respond. He *was* responding, though, and the dots gave Poppy enough hope to resist opening the door for the persistent vampires on the other side.

Josh: Poppy. Quinn died last night. Those drainers escaped and attacked everyone and it took our whole pack to subdue them. Quinn is dead because of a secret we kept. Henry isn't happy and I have so many regrets. Maybe that's enough for you to understand why I don't want to talk anymore. I'm sorry about your mom. I'm sorry this won't work. I can see things from both sides, but Quinn is dead and I have to put the rest of my pack first

Poppy gaped at the message like she was staring at wreckage. *I can see things from both sides, but Quinn is dead.* But Tiff Jennings was dead. But Julia was dead. But Dylan was dead. But this city, this world, was tearing apart every decision they'd made. Poppy had been angry Topher hadn't told her about the apartment, but she'd forgiven him.

If that spell had kept going, Annaliese would have died. Poppy could have died. Likely, even if Colbie hadn't done what she'd done, Tiff would have died from her dark magic.

Maybe there were too many sides. Maybe Poppy wasn't capable of thinking through all this. "Ru. Why should I let them in?"

"Because they love you."

"Colbie killed Mom."

"Mom was dying," Ru's voice cracked. "Colbie saved Annaliese. She saved you. I understand magic enough to know that's the truth. The truth isn't always easy, but love can be."

Poppy stared at Ru. "How do you know that?"

Ru was crying again. "Because all I know is this is my home." She pointed at the door. "They're my home. I don't think Mom and her coven ever were."

That was true for Poppy too, even if it wasn't easy. Poppy got up and opened the door. It was Topher there first, wrapping her in a hug so quickly Poppy didn't even get a chance to look at him. He put his cheek on top of her head and squeezed until it was hard for Poppy to breathe.

It was perfect.

"I'm so sorry about your mom, Pop. I don't know what else we could have done." So that was why he hadn't been able to look at her in the warehouse. He and Colbie had understood the sacrifice that had to happen. Poppy couldn't tell if it was better or worse that they'd thought the murder through.

Colbie's arms snaked around, joining the hug. "I'm sorry, too. I'll go if you want, but I had to say I'm sorry that it came to that."

Tiff Jennings had been a horrible mother. As a witch, she'd brought even more dark magic into the city. She may not have deserved to die, and it was probably messed up that Poppy was hugging the person who killed her, but sometimes, if Poppy decided things could be simple, maybe they could be.

She hugged her roommates back. She sobbed in their embrace for a long time, but vampires didn't get tired. They held her steady through her tears, bringing Ru in as soon as she approached.

Eventually, Poppy cried herself out for the moment. "No more secrets."

"No more secrets," they promised in unison.

"I'm going to find my sisters." Poppy was tired of standing alone. Ru's arms tightened around her.

"We'll help in any way we can," Topher promised.

"And Beth needs to be stopped. She's barely controlling the shadows as is."

"If anyone can find the light to stop her, it's you," Colbie said it like a promise, and Poppy believed her.

"You can't be serious," Gus said, stunned.

Poppy turned to him. "I wish you'd go away." She hadn't slept, hadn't relaxed in months.

Topher offered Poppy his hand. Somehow, he seemed to be looking directly at Gus. "He might be able to find your sisters like he did Tiff."

"Not with their wards."

"Then maybe try saying that again."

Poppy stared at Topher's hand and felt his charm like a buzzing in the air. She remembered how the shadows reached for him. Poppy took the hand Topher offered carefully, like it was a live wire. She felt then how much Topher held back. She felt Dylan's power and the connection to the shadows. Like Gus, but pliant, willing.

Poppy had never drawn on a vampire, but it didn't feel like death. It felt like a wolf under a full moon. The life that broke through the night. It tasted like sparks and fizzed in her blood. The room darkened as the shadows felt Poppy work them, as the veil paused and looked at her in confusion.

Poppy glanced at Topher and understood the gift he was offering. This was power. This was knowing. This was trust. He smiled at her encouragingly, and Colbie nodded, feeling *something* in the air.

It was so shockingly pleasant that Poppy laughed as she turned to Gus. "Why don't you fuck right off."

This time, when Gus vanished, Poppy knew it would be until she summoned him back. Why she ever would was a mystery, but knowing she had the power was unlike anything she'd ever experienced.

"You have to be the strongest conduit there is," Ru said, stunned.

Poppy had never had a name for her magic, for her weakness. But when Ru called her that, she didn't feel weak at all.

Colbie rubbed her hands together. "I don't think this city is even remotely ready for us."

Topher sighed. Poppy hugged him again. It was freeing to let go of the hurt and distrust. This was what she wanted, maybe even where Fate was directing her if the sense of rightness in her core was to be trusted. "I know it's not the city you want, Topher, but you are New Brecken's."

"And New Brecken is all yours," Colbie added.

The four of them standing in a tight huddle felt like all the family Poppy had ever been missing. This new challenge was everything she'd been waiting for. The goal to find her sisters a brand-new beginning. One that Poppy controlled.

She hated to leave regrets in her wake as she forged forward, Josh's face so sweet and his presence so lovely, but magic had a cost. Tiff Jennings had taught Poppy that, and Poppy had always headed her mother's lessons, then warped them to suit her own needs. Poppy wouldn't be the witch she was today if she hadn't.

ACKNOWLEDGMENTS

I enjoy so much writing the first book in a series—the second and third not as much. This book and the one I published before it were both sequels, and making this a very long writing year for me. So thank you to every person who listened to me complain, every person who read my already published books and gave me feedback, and every person who voiced an encouragement when I wondered why I was doing this at all.

Thank you to everyone who asked for a sequel, you made this book happen for both of us.

ABOUT THE AUTHOR

Kelly Cole graduated from the University of Wyoming where she studied English and Creative Writing. She is working on a self-publishing career and enjoying every step along the way. Kelly is most active on Instagram and enjoys sharing her latest and favorite reads. She lives in Wyoming with her two crested geckos and her dog, Maya. She spends most of her time writing and playing seemingly endless hours of fetch (not with the geckos).